T0117250

THE BLOOD
AND THE
HEARTLAND

THE BLOOD AND THE HEARTLAND

An Exploration into the Bonds of Love
and the Unfathomable Power of Denial

BUCKAROO LENNOX

ARCHWAY
PUBLISHING

Copyright © 2018 Buckaroo Lennox.

All rights reserved. No part of this book may be used or reproduced by any means, graphic, electronic, or mechanical, including photocopying, recording, taping or by any information storage retrieval system without the written permission of the author except in the case of brief quotations embodied in critical articles and reviews.

This is a work of fiction. All of the characters, names, incidents, organizations, and dialogue in this novel are either the products of the author's imagination or are used fictitiously.

Archway Publishing books may be ordered through booksellers or by contacting:

Archway Publishing
1663 Liberty Drive
Bloomington, IN 47403
www.archwaypublishing.com
1 (888) 242-5904

Because of the dynamic nature of the Internet, any web addresses or links contained in this book may have changed since publication and may no longer be valid. The views expressed in this work are solely those of the author and do not necessarily reflect the views of the publisher, and the publisher hereby disclaims any responsibility for them.

Any people depicted in stock imagery provided by Getty Images are models, and such images are being used for illustrative purposes only. Certain stock imagery © Getty Images.

ISBN: 978-1-4808-6824-3 (sc)
ISBN: 978-1-4808-6823-6 (e)

Library of Congress Control Number: 2018958125

Print information available on the last page.

Archway Publishing rev. date: 10/23/2018

Inspired by my daughters Alexcia and Sadie.
Sorry for all the cussing.

INTRODUCTION

Please open your heart, but protect it. We will be going somewhere you may not be prepared for. But I had to. It helps to make sense of these things.

In doing so, I full heartedly learned that nothing worth anything is ever really lost. Sometimes it just waits on the other side of the universe for you. And sometimes it's in South Dakota.

ACT I

CHAPTER 1

NOWHERELAND

Leif Wainwright was an asshole. As assholes went, he didn't notice the beautiful weather or the picturesque views around him while driving his SUV through the quaint California wine country town of Petaluma. Instead, his world was full of other assholes in cars who all pretty much had it out for him. Because he hadn't given much credence to his intuition for a while, he ignored the soft voice that told him not to worry about others' schemes that ran contrary to his. It was that same voice that begged him to appreciate the redwoods and oaks and the surrounding hues of green that formed quilted patches of vineyards, farmland, and dairies that stretched all the way to the Pacific. Mathematically speaking, he knew his contempt for the world around him didn't add up, but it was all he had. So he jetted forward, aligning what he could to his will and running over the rest.

Eying the road like a hawk, Leif weaved through the saturation of hybrids that slowed on the incline that led into the town of Cotati. He was running late to pick up Sarah, his fourteen-year-old daughter. She would be waiting for him at her high school, which was fifteen minutes away in Santa Rosa.

Leif always felt that his time was more important than than the time of the drivers he needed to pass. Still, he'd pace each one for a moment to offer his disapproval by looking at them while shaking his head before moving on. Leif was considering the epidemic of fast lane abuse when a lightbulb went off in his head. *I'm going to create a fast-lane awareness page on Facebook.* He thought about how he could include pictures of obvious offenders. Maybe he could get Sarah to take pictures or- better yet- videos of him flipping off slow cars in the fast lane.

Leif found himself boxed in by a minivan to his front and an environmentally friendly "flatulence-powered" Prius covered in self-righteous bumper stickers to his right. And both drivers were driving the exact same speed. Although the fault of the disruption in his desired cruising speed laid on the car in front of him, he turned to look at the driver of "Bumper Sticker Salvation" to his side.

"Go ahead and save the world fuckstick! Start by getting in the hippy lane!"

Declarations of assumed superiority often tore through Lief's exaggerated lip movements, helping ease the discomfort of his commute. Or so he thought.

His cell phone rang through the car's audio system, prompting him to hit the "hands free" receive-call button on the steering wheel, with his hand. It was Sarah.

"Are you coming?"

"I'm on my way! I'll be there to get you in six minutes if I can get around this slow moving- *argh…* Assfacehole!"

"Ok"

Sarah used one extra syllable by adding the *o* to her usual *k* response.

"Meet me at dirt corner."

Leif then caught the eye of the driver in front of him and gestured for her to move.

Off the cluttered freeway and into the far more congested surface roads, Leif reached his rendezvous at the school lawn corner where all of the grass was missing. The light at the intersection adjacent to dirt corner turned yellow and, although he had plenty of time to cross it, he stopped instead of punching the gas pedal, much to the dismay of the cars behind him. He needed to scan the crowd of purple and blue haired students, hoping to locate his slouched dishwater blond haired daughter before the light turned green again.

Sarah spotted Leif and ran to the car just as the light turned green. "Get in. Quick!"

He moved an inch or two forward while Sarah boarded the car in order to show the cars behind him that he respected their time.

With Sarah in the car, Leif started in with his usual complaints.

"I can't keep doing this. Why? Tell me: why am I the one that has to drive out here everyday? I'm the one that moved out here to appease your mom."

Sarah had learned to tune him out long before then, knowing that any response would only make matters worse.

"I think we ought to get you in a school closer to our house. I mean-"

Leif's phone rang through the car speakers again. He did not recognize the number, meaning it was a client.

"Shhh! Stop your yapping. It's work."

Sarah smiled and, in a flash, Leif transformed into a calm, cool, and collected businessman with perfect posture. It was if he had not been ruffled one bit before accepting the call.

"This is Leif."

"Good afternoon Leif, This is George from Grand Cabinetry."

"Well, hello George. How goes it there?"

"I'm doing well I suppose. Hey look, just calling to let you know we've had a chance to look over your proposal and we'd like to talk about it more."

While listening to George concede to the sale, Leif drove past a Honda Element driven by a fifty-something white guy wearing a puffy blue thing that resembled a life vest. Leif correctly guessed the man was wearing slip-on Crocs that matched his flotation device. Leif wondered what seemed unusual on that particular car while he waved half of a peace sign at it. Sarah snickered, causing her father to stop his hardened gaze at the other driver just long enough to share a smile with his child. *Only one bumper sticker?* he thought. *Coexist? Really? That's all?* Without missing a beat, he rejoined the conversation that was going on outside of his head.

"That's great, George. I'm free to meet Tuesday morning and Thursday afternoon, if either of those will work for you."

"How about Thursday at 2?"

Leif all but secured the sale with a routine, sincere sounding confirmation.

"Perfect! See you then. Have a good day."

He looked in his rear-view mirror at the Element in the distance.

"Coexist? Coexist? Really? *Pff!* Hug a suicide bomber. See how that works out for you."

Leif again shook his head.

As usual, cars were backed up all the way from the dysfunctional red light at the end of their offramp in Cotati. Leif disregarded the line of cars and pulled into the left shoulder to drive around them. The maneuver teetered between legal and illegal because, closer to the light the shoulder turned into a new, empty lane. That was the exact sort of gray area you would find Leif taking advantage of in most areas of his life. Having adjusted his speed to make the turn, he hit the intersection just as the light turned green, sped through it, and then flew across four lanes to make a quick right turn.

Cotati was a strange little town that was a remnant of a more drug-induced era. It was the smallest incorporated town in all of Sonoma County, but it had a rich musical history dating all the way back to the 1960's. Fifty years later, one could still smell the pungent pot smoke in the air from the summer of love. The city council members did their best to preserve things the way they were. That was apparent by all of the weeds, missing sidewalks, and overall lack of aesthetic awareness, even by a burned-out hippie's standards. But, it was the roadways that made the least sense to Leif. He griped to Sarah, who wasn't paying any attention to him.

"I'm pretty sure they skipped any traffic study when they re-did these roads."

"Huh?"

"I think they just winged it. Fucking retards."

Leif had a hard-fast opinion about the way all things were and he tended to disagree with most ways. Fortunately for the outside world, most of his ranting was limited to when he drove. Somewhere between point A and point B, Leif complained about the operational flaws with any given system around him. There was always an "ass-faced idiot" or a "fucking retard" who was at fault for not doing things in the most efficient way possible. Every perceived mistake was grounds for fighting words, but in his fits he only fought himself, completely unaware that he was a self-righteous hypocrite. It was sad and too hard for anyone else to watch for long.

Among some of the easier things for Leif to complain about were different types of drivers. To him, older drivers were a hazard to keep a close eye on. The more gray and white hair or the more hunched over, the further he distanced himself from them. Every time he'd read in the news that another "geriatric," as he referred to them, had plowed into a crowd of people, he'd blow up. But Leif was an equal opportunity critic so he profiled all drivers. Generalizing the driving habits of people from around the world sometimes broke down to generalizing another's ethnicity. Leif's favorite ethnicity of drivers included black Americans. He felt most of them drove like him, unless they were old. Leif least liked the way the majority of Puerto Rico, Puerto Ricans drove, but he could tell the difference between them and the American Puerto Ricans. He was fine with them. He attributed the difference to his belief that most of the American Puerto Rican's were from New York.

Regardless of how baseless and ignorant most of his beliefs about other cultures and races were, Leif justified them all, maintaining that he accepted different cultures better than most people did. Xenophobia and racism, to Leif meant, that people had different ways of doing things, according to their cultural and national upbringing. He felt most people just wanted to be acknowledged for their differences and not lumped into the sum of every other bad driver on the road.

Leif neared the end of his short drive across Cotati as he drove past a weathered barn centered in a field of sheep. And then he drove into his dirt driveway. He sang an exaggerated operatic style song as they exited the car.

"We are hoooome, Get out of the fucking car. We are hoooome. Let's pet the mangey cat and go inside our hoooome."

Sarah did not react to her father's strangeness because it was not strange to her, it was her upbringing.

Their home was a modest rental that was built in the 40's. Outside of the lime-green and lemon-yellow tiled bathroom, the home had been renovated at during the turn of the millennium. They kept it tidy and it was the perfect sized home for the two of them. Leif's favorite feature of the home was the wrap around bench and deck around two massive old growth redwoods in his backyard. They were the tallest two trees in Cotati. On the rare occasion that someone in town needed directions to his home, he'd just point them to his tree's that towered above the other hundred redwoods in the area.

Sarah's favorite part of their home was the large 10'x7' window in the living room. That day, just as every other, she took a seat on the beat up, tan covered couch in front of the large window to start her homework.

"How much homework do you have today?"

"A lot"

"A lot? What's that?"

"A lot"

"Would you say that you had a plethora of homework?"

"I just have a lot."

"Would you say you have a thousand homework."

"Yup, I have a thousand homework."

"Hey, what's that?"

"What's what?"

Sarah looked around all of the items in her vicinity to see what her father was referring to.

"That- That yellow book."

"Ohhh, it's something I have to read and then do a project-report kind of thing about it. It's called Flatland."

"No way! That's so strange. Seriously, I was just looking around online at books about parallel dimensions last night and this one came to the top of the list."

"Cool"

"Yeah, so let me know if you need help with that one. I'm probably going to read it soon anyways. I saw that it was about a world where all of the people were shapes and stuff."

"Yeah, it has different places in it too."

Lief changed the conversation.

"Are you hungry?"

"Uhhh, no."

The days when Sarah said more than one or two word answers to questions were long gone. She was a quiet kid who smiled only on the rare occasion. Leif had always hoped she'd be more interested in doing more than just putting her head down into her books. He wanted her to go out to do something, anything, especially socialize. Leif often thought back to what he was doing at her age in order to determine if her behavior was abnormal, and it was. It broke his heart to no end. As a routine, he would ask himself what he had done wrong in raising her. He was aware that his inability to deal with traffic, his constant yelling, and a few other things didn't help her, but he knew that her shyness towards everything was beyond that. He'd often wonder if it was his bitter divorce with her mother before she was two that caused her social inwardness, but he'd soon dismiss that possibility when Leif remembered how common divorce was, even among the families of her more adjusted peers. Even he was raised in two homes with a lot of bickering and he knew many other people that had similar circumstances. They all seemed to enjoy life more than Sarah. Although he could never quite figure out what was underneath all of her trouble, he knew they had a special relationship and he loved her more than the world. He was confident that she felt similar.

In the usual fashion of the after work day transition, Leif sat in front of his computer at his desk, catching up with the digital realm. He spent a significant amount of his social existence there, conversing with digital people, who sometimes commented on whether or not they felt that his latest digital thoughts were digitally clever or not. Although Leif had a hard time resisting posts of his political opinions, he refrained due to the inevitable lack of praise that would follow. Leif had a lot of disdain for various political entities following the previous election cycle, when he became convinced that there had been voter tampering in Pennsylvania. Since that point, he kept his news browsing and commenting to movies, music, and sports. Even his doctors advised him to avoid exposure to the news, explaining that, with the severity of his anxiety disorder, any accelerants could cause a heart attack.

Above all other benefits that the web provided, dating websites were the most useful to him. Cyber dating, leading to real dating, was his second biggest priority behind raising his daughter. Leif's looks helped get things done in that arena, because he was a handsome dishwater blonde, green eyed, six foot tall, ex-model, who kept himself in good shape. He averaged a couple of real dates a week, but that required a lot of online marketing and follow up. After all, he was a salesman by profession. He kew that twenty calls equalled one close in sales and it was the same with dating. Those numbers led him to his two dates per week, which meant he had to contact forty new people per week. That was a job in itself. As a seasoned salesperson, Leif had hypothesized that the easiest way to get a sale was to "not fuck it up." According to his theory, there were a handful of ways to secure the sale, but there were a million ways to fuck it up. When he applied that principle to dating, less said was best.

Browsing the thumbnail pictures of possible matches, one attractive brunette caught his eye and prompted him to enlarge her picture.

"Hmm. Yes, I'd do you. You are most definitely doable."

Sarah yelled from the next room.

"Daaaaad"

"Whaaat?"

"Will you type my report for me? It's due tomorrow?"

Leif thought it would be funny to give her a hard time by pretending not to hear her.

"Whaaat?"

She knew that trick all too well, so she ran into his room with her handwritten assignment.

"It's not that long. I'd have to use your computer anyway to print it."

"Whaaat?"

"You heard me Dad."

"What? You know I don't listen to you. Alright, but only if you play basketball with me."

It was Sarah's turn to play stupid.

"Whaat?"

"That's the deal kiddo. One game of Horse for one typed report."

"Ok"

He swiped the report out of her hands.

"What the hell? I can't read this. Read it to me and I'll type."

She sat on the bed behind him and read her report aloud as he fumbled through the proper punctuation and spelling.

A quick game of Horse ensued as promised. Sarah made every shot except one, never giving up the lead to her father. Leif managed to accumulate all of the letters and was on the brink of elimination. He was trying to avoid the game ending "E". Leif called upon everything he had been taught about basketball over the years, which wasn't much. He aligned his elbow with the direction he wanted the ball to go, visualized it going in, used a little lift and a slight flip of his wrist, and then flung the basketball toward the hoop with the gracefulness of a ballet dancer, with wooden legs. He missed.

"That's Horse, Dad."

"Fuck! That damn money shot of yours. Good job, I guess."

She had beat him fair and square. Leif believed that it was important to never just let her win. He made her earn every victory on her own best efforts. He knew that was better for her and her self-esteem in the long run.

Later that evening they sat down for fish tacos that Leif prepared for dinner. He loved to cook and had found a couple things that they both could tolerate. Fish tacos were one of them. He drowned his tacos with his coveted, homemade, half mango, and half habanero hot sauce that he called Habanango. Sarah took hers straight as usual, having somehow retained her bland, unadventurous toddler-like palate.

"Alright Kiddo, when we're through here, I'm going to run out to meet a friend for coffee, K?"

"K"

"You gots to shower and don't stay up too late doing your homework, mmm-k?"

"K"

"Good. And brush your teeth."

"K"

He grabbed his keys and his wallet, but he kept at her in an effort to get her to say more than just "K".

"…and then brush your teeth again"

"K"

"…and pick up your room"

"K"

He walked through the doorway, continuing to tell her what to do while on the way out.

"Sarah stay"

"K"

"Stay"

"K"

"That's a good girl."

She smirked as he closed the door.

―― ――

Leif pulled into his favorite parking spot nearest the front door of his favorite Starbucks. On average he spent an hour a day at that coffee shop writing screenplays as a hobby after work. It was a distant dream of his to one day make a movie. Because he spent so much time there, all of the workers had gotten to know him to a small degree. Leif also conducted the majority of his first dates there. It was a comfortable environment for him to break the ice with someone new. The barista at the register asked him if the well dressed woman, waiting at a table across the way was another one of his dates. It appeared so. He took a deep, somewhat sad, breath. *Here we go again.*

The next morning was another manic dash for Sarah's school. With excess speeds of 85mph, his car's suspension couldn't keep up with the dips in the road and the car came close to launching into the air a couple of times. His driving was reminiscent of a car chase straight out of the 70's tv show The Streets of San Francisco. In a ride that would cause the toughest kid on the block to soil his jeans, Sarah was accustomed to her father's driving and sat calm, looking out the window at the early morning birds, wondering what it feel like to be one. As Leif squeezed in front of the car to his right, trying to pass a beater in the fast lane, his phone rang again.

"Hello, this is Leif."

A white and nasally sounding man spoke on the other end.

"Good morning Leif, this is Frank Zimmer, from Triple A Paving. Hey, so we were scheduled to meet today at 10."

Leif clenched his fists in frustration knowing, without a doubt, what was about to happen. He mimicked punching the steering wheel before responding in pleasant manner.

"Yeah…"

Mr. Zimmer continued to cancel his appointment in the same exact way everybody else canceled after they either went with another company or were experiencing cold feet.

"Yeah, I'm sorry, but I'm going to have to reschedule. I had another appointment previously scheduled before the young lady with your company scheduled to have you out. Yeah, I didn't have my calendar in front of me. Sorry about that."

Leif passed a Prius that was abusing the fast lane, flipped off the driver, straightened his posture, and then continued his conversation with Mr. Zimmer.

"I see Frank. Well, that happens and it's no problem. I'm free Tuesday and Thursday afternoon to come back out if one of those times will work for you."

Mr. Zimmer fumbled his speech a bit.

"Ok, Hmm. Well, ahh…"

Leif knew his only chance in salvaging his appointment was to remain dead silent, no matter how awkward the silence became. To talk first was to concede according to Sales 101. The awkward silence pursued and remained so long that Leif thought the call had dropped.

"Frank, you still there?"

Mr. Zimmer was still there and may have been aware of Leif's trap, because he won the battle by not responding first.

"Yeah, sorry. It's just that I'm not really sure what you guys are about besides, you know, marketing and stuff. You know…Well, we're going to be pretty booked for a while so I'm sorry. We did just hire one of those search engine optimization companies to help us market. How bout this, let me call you guys back in a month or two and lets see how things look then?"

Leif was experienced in getting around the exact objection that Mr. Zimmer had laid out. All Leif had to do was throw him an elevator pitch, followed by a "No Brainer Proposal" that Mr. Zimmer could not refuse. As Leif prepared to recite his textbook rebuttal, he paused to look out his window at a murmuration of Starlings flying in unison like an elaborately choreographed dance. *Just like fishes*, he thought. His racing blood pressure slowed as did the speed of his car. Like a weighed down man who had been treading water for days on end, who at last gives in to the deep blue sea, Leif sank into his seat. He was holding a heavy fifteen years worth of stress and insanity from selling himself short in the form of varying products and services. Leif reached that dreaded place that he feared would feel like a tortuous death, but strange as it was, he felt a peace bloom from within, reassuring him that it was ok to let his former notions go.

The Prius that he had flipped off just moments before, passed him on his right, returning the one finger salute. Outside of a deep breath, Leif had no reaction.

"Hello, Leif, you still there?"

"Yeah, sorry. Sure Frank, that sounds good. We'll talk to you then. Have a good day."

Leif ended the call, knowing they would never speak again. He lost the sale because, for the first time, he knew he never wanted the sale or any other sale for that matter. In his heart, he knew he was no longer a salesman. He had some thinking to do.

Later that day, Sarah sat crouched on the living room couch with her face in her massive geometry book. The room was dim with only a crack of natural light coming through the curtains that covered the oversized living room window. Through the crack, Leif saw Esther the cat, their grey tabby with white boots, scratching the spooky oak tree in the front yard. Sarah scrunched forward even further to punch numbers into her calculator, before scribbling more numbers into her note book.

"Sarah. Open up some windows. You need some more light in here."

"Do you mean open the curtains?"

Leif had been delegating orders while passing behind her with load of laundry in his arms. He dropped several articles of clothing when she quipped back at him. Because Leif always found it too time consuming to locate the laundry basket, he spent twice as much time finishing the laundry, considering everything that he dropped without the basket.

Laundry free, Leif walked in front of Sarah and paused, looking at her with a blank face. Monotone and emotionless he laid down the law, in his own dead pan, but loving way.

"It closes the pie hole or else it gets the hose again."

Sarah smiled, appreciating his odd humor in referencing the psychologically disturbing Silence of the Lambs. Then Leif's face lit up with surprise when he remembered something huge that he needed to share with her.

"Oh my fucking gosh, I can't believe I forgot to tell you!"

Mimicking her father with wide eyes, she returned a bit of the sarcasm that was, all to often, dished out by him.

"What?"

"Do you remember how I told you how you may have a sister in one of those Dakota states?"

"Uh, yeah."

"Ok, Well, I ordered a test to determine absolutely whether she is or not. Isn't that cool?"

"Sure. Can I do my homework now?"

A knock came at the front door.

"Who could that be?"

Leif opened the door to a man in a full body Bigfoot suit who was holding an antique looking suitcase in one hand and a drum cymbal in the other.

"Oh geez. Did she kick you out again Chewy?"

"What? Oh, you mean the suit case? Funny, no. Dude, you got to check this out."

Outside of Sarah, Bigfoot was one of the only people that Leif had contact with on a regular basis. He was a drummer that would often play music with Leif. The two sometimes referred to themselves as a band and, on the occasion, would gig together under the name Gas Station Rose.

Bigfoot was not named Bigfoot because he had big feet. He had little feet, but he did dress in a Bigfoot suit, everyday. Because of his fascination with fur, along with a few other oddities of his, many questioned his mental stability. Lief wasn't concerned about what other people thought about Bigfoot though. As far as he was concerned, all musicians were eccentric in one way or another. Bigfoot's eccentricities were more obvious than most, but Leif was used to them and seldom took notice. However, Bigfoot opening luggage in the middle of the living room, did seem a little odd to Leif.

Bigfoot pulled out drum pedals, cymbals, a cymbal stand, and all other sorts of drummer paraphernalia. He then took the case, latched it back up, stood it upright, attached the kick pedal to the bottom, and then thumped the case with the pedal, rendering it, no longer just a case, but a drum as well. Bigfoot pulled his stool up to what had become an assembled drum kit. Leif's jaw dropped.

"No way!"

Bigfoot tapped out an amazing drum solo while Leif had minor spiritual experience. For an uncertain amount of time, Leif zenned out in a state of wonderment, observing a new frontier in his musical landscape.

"Wait a minute, I'll be right back."

Leif ran out of the room, and returned, lugging in his Fender '65 Twin Reverb amplifier and his Taylor T5 electric guitar.

The two jumped right into their rehearsed songs, with Leif strumming chord progressions to Bigfoot's beats. They played their songs without making any mistakes. Even their synced hard stops were flawless. Sarah tapped her foot, although she tried to appear disinterested.

"Dude. Ahh, this is, um… awesome?"

Leif spoke with all the lackluster he muster, trying hard to not just spout out the millions of ideas running through his head. Trying to appear calm, Leif asked one question, slowing his speech as much as he could.

"Do you think I could retrofit some old luggage with a battery powered PA system?"

"Yeah, I bet you could. Wait- If you did that, we could busk anywhere."

"Yup. Something great just happened. This changes things man."

With the knowledge that the universe had expanded before their eyes, the two resumed jamming and played for the next hour straight. Sarah took her homework into her bedroom.

Leif was less abrasive the following morning when he drove Sarah to school. His softer side peaked its head out of its hole long enough see there was no shadow, because that day he was on a mission to build himself a luggage PA system and he was going to start the second Sarah got out of the car.

"Kiddo, have a good day. Remember that you are going to your mom's after school."

She acknowledged and shlepped her shredded, manufactured in China, back pack full of oversized honors text books out of the car towards another day of social awkwardness. Knowing all to well the discomfort his daughter was experiencing, Leif's heart sank as he watched her walk away. It didn't take long for his thoughts to redirect to his quest though, sending him to the closest cluster of thrift stores to find the perfect piece of vintage luggage.

— ~ —

The musty smell of old clothes paired with an effervescent bouquet of mothballs overpowered the best attempts of the tropical breeze plug-in scents throughout the first thrift shop Leif visited. After circling the store twice and then asking a non-english speaking clerk for help, he decided that the store had no luggage for sale. It was on to the Goodwill store around the corner.

Lief once heard that the owners of secondhand stores rolled in the dough, which to Leif, was counter-intuitive and, therefore, notable. As far as an owner of a thrift shop doing well, Leif's opinion was, *more power to em'*. He loved that capitalism still existed in the U.S., and that it allowed someone to be creative enough to make a business model out of the concept that one man's garbage is another man's treasure.

Although Leif was an impatient opinionated self-important grouch, he had a few near-redeeming qualities. One of which was his frequent visits into the imagination, or moreover, the wonderful things he brought back. On that occasion, while Leif was driving in between stores, he amused himself with a made up scenario that played out like a part of a movie. It involved a day that the owner of a thrift store drove his luxury car to the store, forgetting to take his modest banged up sedan that he had always used in order to hide his prosperity from his destitute workers who had been demanding higher wages for months. He had always explained that he'd pay them more if he could, before pacifying them with stories of his own financial hardships. But on that day, he exposed his wealth, causing a thrift store uprising. Large green glass ashtrays from the 70's, off white vases from the 80's, and stacks of VHS exercise tapes from all of the decades that they were never used, were hurled at their pudgy balding boss on his way through the front door. It was the thought of him diving for cover behind the clothing rack of that month's featured pastel knit sweaters and cardigans that made Leif laugh out loud at the story going on in his mind, while failing to drive when the light turned green at the intersection. He must have looked crazy to the angry drivers that drove around him. Embarrassed at his faux pas, Leif scolded himself for thinking that thrift store mutinies were a laughing matter.

Back to the hunt, he rummaged the next Goodwill without finding any luggage. Convinced the thrift stores wouldn't net him any results, he left the strip of thrift stores and headed for the more upscale thrift stores called antique shops. There were a handful of them ten miles south in downtown Petaluma. He knew if he found a case there it would cost more, but he needed himself a good piece of vintage luggage and he wasn't going to stop until he found one.

Although he was on a mission, he remembered that he had a "real job" too. That day, he had only one set appointment with a building contractor. Leif knew that the call center person who scheduled the appointment had been setting less than solid appointments in order to meet quota that month. It was nearing the end of the month and Leif had a quota to meet as well. Making his musical apparatus to street perform wasn't going to pay the bills, but it made him happy.

Leif racked his brain for ways to get rid of his appointment without canceling it. Canceling would get him fired quicker than he would have liked. A light came on when Lief remembered that half of his appointments canceled when he'd call to confirm them. All he had to do was call the person he was scheduled to meet so the prospect would weasel out of their meeting. Leif got ahold of the contractor who claimed that he knew nothing about the appointment. The phone call saved Leif a forty-five minute drive to Napa for what would have been a no-show anyway. The day was going well for him.

　—　—

Leif's luck continued and his shopping strategy paid off because the next, higher quality, antique/ consignment store he went into was a goldmine. He found five suitable vintage cases, but one of them stood out. It was an elegant chestnut brown, faux alligator skin, 1940's Samsonite suitcase that was in incredible condition. It was the one, but uncertain thoughts remained. He wasn't sure if it was big enough to retrofit with a battery powered PA system. He would need them to lower the price as well. The tag read $75, but Leif had more like $50 in mind. He approached the checkout kiosk, smiling at the fifty-something, chubby woman behind the counter.

"Hi, there."

"Hello. Well that's a beautiful case."

"Yes, yes it is. It's actually exactly what I'm looking for, but a little outside my budget. I wanted to ask you what kind of flexibility you have on your pricing."

"Let me take a look at it."

Leif set the exquisite case on the counter and she checked the tag to determine who the consigner was.

"Because all of the items are on consignment, sometimes we can contact the owner to see if they'll lower the price. Some are more flexible than others. Unfortunately, this one doesn't budge."

Leif's head sunk.

"Darn"

"I'm so sorry."

"It's ok, it was worth looking into."

She paused, tilted her head, before handing the luggage back to Leif to put back on the floor. Her next words need not have followed because her body language had already given away the farm.

"You know? Let's see. What did you have in mind?"

"All I got is fifty. Could you do that?"

"Alright, yeah, sure. Let's just do this quick in case he comes in here."

Leif opened his wallet and pulled out three-hundred and fifty in cash and gave her fifty of it. She took the money with a scowl, a scowl Leif was accustomed to. He thanked her, walked out to the street, and placed the beginning of his passion project into the back of his car with care.

"Luggage- check! PA system next"

Galaxy of Stereo, a DJ equipment store, was just a block up from antique store. He was close enough to take a gander at what kind of options were available for battery powered PA systems there. He approached them with trepidation because they had suckered him into paying too much for a vocal processor there a year prior. That time he was going to stay on guard from the swindlers from within while doing a PA price check.

Inside, speakers pumped shitty techno while multicolored lights whirled nauseating patterns onto every tacky surface in the store. Leif saw many personal amplification systems, including some that were battery powered, but all of them were much too big to fit into his luggage. It was going to be tricky to find one that was small enough, but powerful enough to play over Bigfoot's drums. The fact that he even found a battery powered system was encouraging for him though.

Leif went online and checked the price of the PA he was looking at, one that could possibly work. As he suspected, it was marked up by one-hundred dollars. He could make his purchase online, but he wanted it that day. As Leif contemplated a purchase, the sleazy sales person approached him with an air of arrogance, chest puffed out, and belly sucked in while he finger combed his greasy hair. He spoke to Leif without looking at him on his approach.

"My friend, you need help with that?"

Leif looked at him straight-faced, paused, and then walked out of the store without a response.

Leif again drove through the rolling green fields of Petaluma along the Old Redwood Highway. On that drive, he enjoyed all the landscape had to offer. He knew how fortunate he was to live in such a beautiful part of the world, and he recognized that, after all of his many travels around the world, he would have a tough time finding a better place to raise his daughter. All too often, he overlooked those things in between sales calls. That drive was different because he wasn't just spinning his wheels in the gravel going nowhere. He was moving towards a dream.

Banana's at Large, a Santa Rosa music shop, was Leif's next stop. Leif had bought a large PA system there years before and they took good care of him. He brought his luggage into the store, turning a few heads as he walked to the amplifier section. The store was stocked full with everything from guitars to kazoos. In no time, Leif found a compact battery powered PA system that was powerful enough to play over drums. He took it and placed it into the suitcase to see if it fit. His actions drew the attention of one of the sales people who ran over to stop a possible theft in progress.

"Excuse me, can I help you with that?"

It occurred to Leif that his actions must have seemed odd.

"Oh, yeah, sorry. I needed to see if this would fit in here. I'm looking for a battery powered amp, PA rather, that I can retrofit into this piece of luggage. I'm going to use it for busking with my drummer. He made a really cool drum kit out of luggage, using the case as a kick drum."

For a moment, the sales clerk looked down in contemplation about what Leif was describing, then looked back up smiling.

"No shit? Wow! That's cool man. This one here is powerful enough, and check this out, the battery is internal so all you have to do is plug it in to recharge it. It's actually kinda perfect for that."

"Yeah, totally. I just need to see if it fits."

The amp and the suitcase were starting to look like a match made in heaven, but upon further evaluation, it didn't quite fit. It was about an inch to thick, and didn't allow the case to close shut.

"Aw, shoot. This sucks, it's too big. Hmm…"

The salesman knew there would be no other viable solution so he did some quick thinking to help Leif see his project through.

"How about this, you gotta do some adjustments to the case right?"

"Yeah, I need to make the speaker hole and attach the two somehow."

"Why don't you buy the system and see if it fits after you, you know, build it or whatever. Then you could use it for measurements as you go. If it doesn't fit just bring it back. We got like a two week return period."

The sales guy was right. It was the one.

"Yeah! Yup- you're right. I'll take it."

On the way to the register to ring it up, Leif saw a compact wireless mic system. It cost more than the amp, but he didn't flinch and grabbed it too. After the case, he knew his next step would be to work out a mobile microphone set up. As synchronicity had it, both the mic and the PA system had the same brand name, Samson and the suitcase was a Samsonite. All three were a match made in heaven.

"I'll call him Sam. PA system check."

—◦ ◦—

Sarah's school was just getting out when Leif drove by on his way home. Knowing he wasn't getting her that day, he felt a sting that was more or less a reminder of a larger pain that had persisted for over twelve years, after her mother Brena and him had divorced. Since then, he no longer saw Sarah everyday. Even though he was heartless in most regards, Sarah was the apple of his eye and he missed her when she was gone.

Leif's heart just wasn't big enough for many others. With the exception of Leif's mother, Ms. Wainwright, who lived a couple hours away in Sacramento, he didn't speak with the rest of his family much. They fell apart just as soon as he and his nine siblings could launch. They all lived hundreds to thousands of miles apart for a reason. It would be virtually impossible to keep in touch with all of them anyway. This was ideal for Leif; He had a great excuse to decline invites to family functions.

The thought of family exhausted him. He refocused his attention on the task at hand. He had to figure out how to get the PA system fixed to the case and not only make it functional, but aesthetically pleasing as well.

—◦ ◦—

Leif pulled into the parking lot of the local hardware store. Whatever he needed he'd be able to get there, but he still had no idea what he needed or even where to begin with his design. Leif opened his mind to the aether and let its creative juices, all sparkling with silver magic, fill the vacuous space between his ears. Leif pulled out a note pad and a pen to dictate the process. He guessed the measurements and sketched out the case, as if it were open. Then he recited the usual magical incantation to himself, *How the fuck do I get this to work?*

Then it hit him. If he laid the case flat, with the top opened, pointing upward at a forty-five degree angle, the raised side could serve as the speaker face. All he had to do then was cut a rectangle the size of the system into it, put a thick wooden frame on the outside that would be covered with speaker cloth, and then build a reinforced cabinet and wooden base on the inside to harness the PA system. The plan was perfect, because the inch and a half speaker frame on the outside gave him the room needed to fit the overlapping system in the case. Also, the sound would be directed to the listeners at an ever so perfect angle from the ground.

With the design drawn up, Leif got what he needed in the hardware store, then made one more stop at a fabric store for a burlap material to use as speaker cloth. He took the materials into his garage, then put it all together with the patience of a saint, his power tools, adrenaline, imagination, and pure passion. He finished his project late that night and then slept like a baby.

The next morning he called his furry friend.

"Bigfoot! It's done! I made my PA system! When can we test our luggage together?"

Bigfoot was at his drum kit. Ba-dop-ba—clang, the crash cymbal rang out.

"Fuck yeah! Tonight my brother. Downtown Petaluma. I know the perfect park with a gazebo-like stage where we can busk. Are you free?"

"Yup, I know the one you're talking about. It begins tonight then."

They set a time and began what they both believed to be the next big chapter of music for them and although he didn't tell Bigfoot, Leif was cooking up something much bigger. Leif's idea was vague, speculative, and contingent on many things falling into place, but his new musical opportunity was integral in making it happen. Whether Leif's larger plan came to fruition or not, he felt that something big was on the horizon, taking shape into something beautiful. New life was rising from the smoldering ashes of the unremarkable dead end that had become his existence.

⁓ ⁓

The sun was setting over the turn of the century victorian neighborhood when Leif arrived at the Petaluma park wearing tight bright red skinny jeans, a white t-shirt, and a tan camel hair thrift store blazer that was two sizes too small. He was twenty minutes early. He couldn't wait to get the show started and was hoping Bigfoot showed up earlier than planned as well. That was not the case. A couple of parents sat on benches supervising their children who played on the park gymnasium. A group of hipsters in their early twenties huddled to one edge of the park, smoking pot or something stronger. Leif could have been mistaken for a musical hobo, sitting there with his suitcase and guitar.

Bigfoot pulled up in his old banged-up, rusted white truck. They waved to each other across the park before meeting on stage. They introduced their luggage for the first time.

"Bigfoot's luggage, meet Sam."

"You named your luggage?"

"Yeah, it's a Samsonite case and a Sampson amp and mic, I had to."

"Yeah, you're right. I'm going to name mine Gonzo then. You know, like-"

"The drummer from the Muppets. Nice."

Both of them unloaded their suitcases center stage of the gazebo enclosure in the middle of the park. No one paid much attention while they set up. Leif laid his luggage at the opening of the gazebo, which was the front of the stage. He hinged the speaker side open to the forty-five degree angle, pulled out a two-foot wooden dowel, and propped it up between both ends of the opening to keep the case open. Bigfoot walked around to see what was inside.

"Whatcha got under the hood there? Whoa! That's amazing man. I dig the woodwork. What? You have your vocal processor in there? That is too cool!"

"Thanks man. Do you smell the rich mahogany? Really, I used mahogany."

"Ha! Stupid. Wait, where are you going to plug in?"

"What, my guitar? Right here."

"No, the power chord?"

"Oh shit! Naw, just kidding, it's battery powered."

"No way!"

Both were set up and had the full attention of everyone in the park.

"We're Gas Station Rose and we're going to play some songs for you."

A couple kids clapped, everyone else at the park just turned their heads and stared with blank faces like cows chewing cud, watching a car drive by.

Leif and Bigfoot started in with their flagship song, "Deepest of Love". Someone had once described the song as the love child of an Elvis Presley, Jim Morrison, and Kurt Cobain ménage à trots due to its hound-dog bluesy rhythm, its sultry baritone verse, and the chunky distortion on the guitar during the screaming chorus. It was not typical busking material.

> "Why would he, Why would she, Plain to see
> The deepest of Love
> Locked in gaze, Spark to blaze, Saw the same
> Deepest of Love
> See a truth, Know a truth, It's your love
> You put it there
> The Deepest of Looo-ove
> The Deepest of Looo-ove
> The Deepest of Looo-oo-ooovvve
> Now as one, Just above, Forged into

The Deepest of Looo-ove
The Deepest of Looo-ove
The Deepest of Looo-oo-ooovvve"

By the end of the song, the parents had dropped their cud, leaving their mouths agape while their children all had tilted their heads in curiosity. The hipsters that were at the other end of the park had migrated over to the foot of the stage, clapping like they had paid tickets to a rock show. The obvious alpha rebel of the pack had led them over as she gave the band props.

"It's the luggage band! Wohoooooo! Yeah! Luggage, that's the shit right there."

Leif corrected her.

"We are Gas Station Rose, but yes we are currently playing with luggage as you correctly observed."

Dreams began to take form in their set of songs with Leif and Sam covering vocals and guitar while Bigfoot and Gonzo provided tasty beats. Synced more with each song their act passed Leif's litmus test of how feasible his much grander plans were, although they would remain close to his chest until something else unfolded, if ever it did.

As they rolled further into their set, Leif thought of how much the gift of music meant to him. He remembered how painful it used to be to play in front of others, knowing full well how painful it was for them too. Through much perseverance, Leif overcame that phase of being an aspiring, but awkward entertainer, until he observed people enjoying his music. At a point in his gradual progression of improvement with the art of live performing, people had even begun to dance to the songs he wrote and sang. Leif believed that to be the biggest compliment a live musician could ever receive. He gave them his heart and they gave him their's in return. It was love until the music stopped.

Immersed in his thoughts, Leif forgot what he was playing and wrapped the song up with a heavy strum of whatever chord he was using. Bigfoot did his best to compensate for Leif's mistake, by looking as natural as possible while ending his shuffle.

Before their last song, with the families long gone, the coyest of the hipsters walked up and placed a five dollar bill in Leif's guitar case at the front of the stage. He had been bumming cigarettes from his friends during the entire set, so it very well may well have been the last cent to his name. Leif's heart swelled a little at the kind gesture. The band's gracious fan complimented them.

"You guys are pretty rad. You should play at the cafe I work at. Um, I book all of the shows. Here's my card."

He handed the card to Leif. It was handmade and contained his pertinent info along with a sketch of a guitar and microphone.

"Thank you. We'd love to play at your cafe."

The two wrapped up their set with another original called "Love on the Holodeck", a sci-fi love song about "spiritual awaking and fucking", as Leif liked to put it. They got a last round of applause and then packed their gear. Leif started a timer on his phone to see how fast they could get it all broken down and re-packed.

When Bigfoot snapped shut the last latch on his case, Leif stopped the timer.

"Four minutes and thirty-two seconds!"

"What?"

"I thought it would be useful to know how quickly we can split in the event law enforcement shows up."

"Oh yeah, good thinking. Do you really think we'd get busted though?"

"Not if we're fast enough."

"Truth. So, what are you plans for the rest of the evening?"

"I'm meeting a lady for coffee right up the street."

"Cool. Another web date?"

Leif's response was flat.

"Yup"

"You don't seem very excited. How's all of that going for you?"

"I'm really kind of tired of it, but I'm not sure what else to do. I do have a strange feeling that a good change is on the horizon though. Until then, I'll just keep meeting them and hope to meet someone I really connect with, but I'm really, really tired of looking."

"I'd call that a gold plated problem. Well, dude this was awesome. Let's talk tomorrow about where we're going to play next. Good luck tonight."

CHAPTER 2

THE OUTSKIRTS OF NOWHERELAND

Oxytocin levels ran high between the two new lovers as Leif looked deep into her eyes. Although no words left his lips, Leif asked her where she had been during his perilous years, the decades of endless searching for the one that could save him. Reversing his gaze from her soul, he pulled back to observe her piercing emerald green eyes, although they tried to hide behind the long bangs of her blonde hair. He marveled at the plumpness of her perfect lips and her titillating breasts. He ran his hand along her creamy skin that curved into dips inside the edge of her protruding hips. Leif knew her intimately, although there were nothing but blank spots around how he knew her. He tried to retrace the steps that led her to his bed, but he couldn't get beyond the perimeter of the moment. Leif looked back through her eyes and into her mind for clues. There where no images of the past, just future moments where they walked together along a path, sharing a singular conscious. It was not until that moment that Leif understood the depths of his former loneliness.

Both laid naked in bed, embraced body and soul, until she stood up, smiled, and turned towards his bedroom door.

"I have to go now."

"Wait. What? I don't understand, you're just going to leave? Wait,

wait, I know this sucks, but how do I- Ok, I'll just say it, what's your name again?"

"Silly man. I'm K. Why, does it matter? Let me just say, you lit me up, you can call me whatever suites you."

"K, y- yes, yes, yes. Sorry, I don't know how it slipped my mind? I just don't- Wait, don't go. At least let me walk you out."

She hadn't even put on any clothes and was walking towards the door to leave when a loud buzz filled the room and she vanished in front of his eyes, before she even reached the door. But she was only gone for a second and reappeared when the length of the intrusive buzz ceased. She came and went in flashes, each to the interval of the obnoxious sound all along making her way towards the door. Leif didn't understand what was happening, because what was happening was impossible. Nonetheless, the pleasure he received from the sight of the naked goddess in front of him helped him tolerate the sound which brought on the sensation of an ice pick to the brain. His pain grew with her distance as she walked through the bedroom door and into the hallway. It wasn't until she began to turn out of his line of sight at the end of his hallway, that Leif realized that the sound was coming from his alarm clock. With a calming expression on her face that promised the answers to the mysteries of the universe, Kay looked at him one last time as he lunged for the snooze button. He smacked the top of the clock and the sound was gone, but so was she. Lief kicked off his bed covers to run after her. The motion catapulted a tube of K-Y Jelly into door frame. When Leif attempted to jump out of bed, his foot snagged on the bed sheet, causing him to fall towards the floor. Little did Leif know, one of his hands was covered in the lubricant, so when he tried to break his fall, his hand slipped across the hardwood and Leif's face smacked the floor. Looking up, baffled and panicked, he tried to calculate what had happened. Logic explained he was dreaming, but Leif fought the rational in order to preserve her. In the end it didn't matter. Either way she was gone.

It was time for Leif to assume his mundane life, which included waking up Sarah for school. He slithered back into bed and called Sarah's cell phone.

"Get up!"

"Wha-What? I'm up. I'm up already."

No matter how alert she tried to sound, he knew that it was his call that woke her. He also knew she would go back to sleep just as soon as the call ended. He set his timer for seven minutes and laid his head back on his pillow. He imagined K's face, trying to bring her back, but his rude awakening that included a sore face made her return impossible.

Noticing a slight itch, Leif scratched his chest, finding little relief. The discomfort of his itch became insatiable. He first thought it may have been an insect bite. He then noticed the itch extended onto his arms, both legs, his back, and even his feet. He found himself scratching his entire body.

"Definitely, not a insect bite. What the fuck?"

Leif got back out of bed to investigate the situation further. His reflection from the mirrored closet door revealed that his entire body was covered in blotchy red hives.

"Great!"

He had no idea what could have caused the disturbing bumps all over his body. It had been years since he had an allergic reaction to anything, and never to that magnitude. Leif freaked out and called his local VA hospital, but the recording reminded him that they wouldn't be taking calls for a couple hours. That set Leif's anxiety to full throttle.

Everything he needed to do that day flashed through his mind. Getting the kid to school, attending an early work appointment in the town of Sonoma, and then going to another appointment up north in Cloverdale constituted a full day for him so trying to squeeze in an emergency room visit somewhere in there was not feasible. There was nothing he could do about the first appointment because he didn't have his client's number. Also, he was scheduled to meet him for breakfast before Leif could reach anyone at the office. His professionalism wouldn't allow him to leave someone hanging. It became clear that he needed to take the kid to school and then make his first appointment, spots or not.

He threw on the business casual ensemble that he laid out the night before. It consisted of a crisp collared shirt without a tie and a pair of dark pressed slacks with a tan belt to match his brown oxford shoes. Leif never wore a tie. He learned the hard way that, in the wine country yuppie turned yippie business climate, a tie was synonymous with capitalist salesperson, and therefor a mark for death. He'd joke that business owners had traded in their protest signs for "No Soliciting" signs to keep the capitalists away from their thriving capitalistic businesses.

Before he left the house, Leif did a once over in the mirror. He felt that he was missing something, but he couldn't put his finger on it. He needed something to match his contempt for the day. It turned out to be a perfect day for a red, white, and blue tie that was sure to offend the California Communist Culture.

"Sarah. Let's go!"

Sarah was delivered to school on time, as always, and Leif made great time to the breakfast spot. Upon entering the waiting area, a young hostess greeted him, but he did not respond, instead he scanned the restaurant for anyone who looked like a contractor who may have been waiting for someone. No one sat alone that day and all the customers looked well beyond a reasonable retirement age. A hunched over elderly man, carrying a large brown weathered briefcase entered the restaurant after winning the tug-of-war match he had with the hydraulic resistance of the thick glass, metal framed front door. Although Leif could have helped with the door, he instead took notice that the man's case resembled his own vintage suitcase, wondering if they could have been part of the same set.

Leif was wound up tight, even more than usual, after completing his first two tasks of the day. His itching was getting worse to boot. For whatever reason, Leif had always found comfort in the unusual act of talking to himself out loud whenever he was stressed, which meant he had many solo conversations. Without a care, or worse, the ability to care, he started one such conversation.

"Where-The-Fuck? You fucking, fuckjob? Anytime now."

The hostess, who was no more than four feet from Leif, was appalled at what she assumed was an insult directed at her, but he caught his mistake.

"Sorry, not you. I'm waiting on someone."

She shrugged off his vulgarity and greeted the old man, who let her know that he was there to meet with a gentleman. The hostess smirked as Leif cringed, hoping his client hadn't heard him. Leif then took a dreaded turn to introduce himself.

"Good morning. I'm Leif. You must be Mr. Schmidt."

"Oh please, call me Larry. Good morning to you too, young man. It's a pleasure to meet you."

Either Mr. Schmidt hadn't heard Leif, or he let him off the hook because his tone was more cordial than a man who had just been called a fucking fuckjob.

"Larry, nice to meet you as well. Shall we?"

The amused hostess escorted them to a table.

"Please excuse my appearance. I'm having some sort of allergic reaction and didn't have time to reschedule."

"Oh no, I hope you're ok."

Leif assured him that he'd be able to make it through the appointment before getting to the hospital.

The two sat and traded the usual, shallow chit-chat while ordering their food. Just after the waitress came and took the order, Leif inquired into the nature of Mr. Schmidt's contracting practices, while plugging a few marketing benefits of his own company along the way. The food arrived and the two slowed the business conversation to a few words between bites.

"I'm very familiar with what your company has to offer. Actually, I came here to meet with someone from your office, uh, I dunno, maybe a year ago."

Leif took a closer look at Mr. Schmidt and realized that the two had already met for breakfast to discuss doing business, no more than six months prior.

"Yeah, that's right. That was me that you met with."

Mr. Schmidt, embarrassed, looked down at the table and took a few more quick bites, before replying with a mouthful.

"Are you sure? I thought the gentleman I met with was Keith or Rief or something like that."

"Close. They do both rhyme with Leif. I remember clearly now. We met, let's see, six months ago and I told you all about what we had to offer you. You wanted to think about it before getting back to me. You said you weren't sure, but you were considering retiring."

Leif was eager for a response, because their meeting should have amounted to a signed contract, considering the nature of their previous discussion. Mr. Schmidt's eating pace sped up even faster.

"You know, that does ring a bell now. Now that you mention it."

Leif paused, hoping for something more than Mr. Schmidt's acknowledgment that they had met. Mr. Schmidt did not respond, but continued to shovel his last few bites of food in his mouth.

"So, you know about the company and what we can do for you. Nothing has changed on my end, except for a some huge benefits that we have added, mind you, while keeping the pricing the same. I'm guessing you had enough time to think about it before letting us schedule you in for another breakfast meeting. I can only assume, by us meeting, that you're ready to do business."

Mr. Schmidt put down his fork and fumbled about with his napkin before speaking.

"Yeah, you know… I'm still not sure if I'm going to retire."

Leif was furious, but resisted raising his voice or letting his heightened emotional state surface through his body language, but he wasn't letting him off the hook either. That was the second free meal Schmidt was getting while wasting more of Leif's misplaced time. *Restraint of tongue*, Leif thought, then attempted just that.

"Mr. Schmidt, if you already knew what we had to offer, and your position hasn't changed, why would you have me come out here to buy you breakfast and, uh, talk business again?"

Mr. Schmidt was a taken aback at Leif's directness.

"Ah Kieth, I mean ah, Leif, is it? Give me a week to think about it."

Leif had enough of the on the fence act, threw all professionalism out the window, stood up, and pointed to the hives on his face.

"You see all of this? You need to think about it? Think about this, I need to be in a hospital and not here telling you the same thing I told you six months ago."

Leif scribbled his signature on the check that had been dropped off moments before.

"Have a good day Schmidty or Shitty, or whatever you call yourself."

The veterans clinic opened the same time Leif left his unnecessary appointment. When he called and described his condition, they urged him to get in as soon as he could. On his way to the hospital, he speed dialed the office and let them know that he wasn't going to be able to meet with any later appointments because of his medical emergency. He also requested that they never let Schmidt talk them into another free meal.

After ruling out all of the usual causes for red bumps all over one's body, Leif's doctor determined that the condition was a result of too much stress. Leif was having an allergic reaction to his heightened discontent with life, and the extent of the reaction was grave. He was told that once hives cover a certain percentage of the body, that steroids were needed to fix the spread before they couldn't be treated. That meant death.

He was instructed not to do any activities that would cause him to break into a sweat, sex included. On top of that, he was informed that the steroids were going to be turning everything he ate into sugar, which would cause him to gain weight. He felt as if his dating life was slaughtered. He was fine with taking a break, although he would have never made the decision without a life or death scenario. Making light of the situation, Leif joked with the doctor.

"Well, at least the steroids will increase my batting average, right?"

"No"

The doctor did not share his sense of humor, nor any other detectable form of humor for that matter.

Before leaving the hospital, his doctor gave him a parting shot by suggesting that, in addition to Leif's hives, his stress may have also given him an ulcer. He was encouraged to get that checked at some point during the following week

The heaviness of the prognoses prompted Leif to pause a for a few moments before he drove himself into an inevitable fit in the thick of traffic on the 101. As he sat in his car, he ruminated in his lifestyle's wake up call. He looked at the dash, and then along the contour of the passenger armrest, then turned to look at the rear seats and remembered the time that they were folded flat to fit all his music gear in the car for a road trip to a gig in Salt Lake City. At the beginning of that trip, he had named his silver CRV the Tin Can. Back then, it wasn't just a hate filled death trap that drove straight lines between routine sales calls. Back then, it was a call for unknown, but certain adventure.

Then he considered the timing of it all. First, he admitted he no longer had the psychological fortitude to continue in his sales career, but he didn't know the next move. The next day, he found himself physically barred from his occupation. His initial admission may have been all he needed, because that act alone tipped the first domino into the next to start an elaborate chain reaction contraption machine, the sort that always ended with a bang. But, before the finale, it was time to go home and watch the Lord of the Rings, all three of them.

***

The sun was setting as Leif walked into his home and began sorting through the mail. He set his laptop bag on a kitchen stool at his raised dining room table, then opened a bill from his life insurance company. His cell phone rang and he thought it strange that the numbers 0000 were listed as the caller.

"This is Leif"

A matter of fact sounding female greeted Leif in voice that was on the deeper end for a woman.

"Hello, this is the Santa Rosa police department. We are trying to locate the address of Sarah Wainwright."

Baffled at the nature of the call, Leif responded with caution.

"I am her father. She lives with me, well half-time. She's with her mother today. Why? What's going on?"

The officer paused- much too long before responding.

"Sir, uh, you're going to have to talk to her mother about that."

Leif ran through all the possibilities of what the officer could have meant to that point. He had, at least, figured out that it was good in no way. A scenario surfaced and a cold sweat swelled from all of his pores, stinging his hives. He replayed what was said and the blood sank from his head, turning him pale as a ghost.

The call could have meant only one thing, but something blocked his mind from arriving at the logical conclusion that fit. His thoughts leaned towards the worst possible thought a parent could ever have. The stark reality was pulsing in his mind and trying to force its way into his heart where every beat and surge of blood within forced it away.

He could not think of what else to say to the officer in his state of shock, so empty words followed.

"Ok, I'll call her mother. Thank you."

Leif was full of adrenaline, but still he struggled to stand while scrambling through the contacts in his phone, trying to call Brena. He found her number and called. Her phone rang and rang and rang, then went to voice mail. He called Sarah's phone next, and again, no answer. He called her mother back and left a voicemail that time.

"Hi Brena, I ahh, I got a very alarming call…"

He could not finish his sentence without choking up.

"The pol- the police called about Sarah. Please call me."

Leif knew that no matter how the outcome of the situation surfaced, life would never be the same for him again. He began walking in circles and fixating on his phone. His mind teetered on a pinnacle that dipped him into the reasonable and known world then leaned into a another completely unknown and far away place, a place where the story had not yet been written. Wave after wave of panic crested above him then receded, leaving him on an unfamiliar shore. *She hasn't seen her birthday presents yet, how does life support work,* and *how quickly can I get to Thailand,* were just a few strange thoughts among the many that ran through his slipping reality. He then asked himself if it was time to start drinking again, but quickly reached the conclusion that there would be no way to escape the pain that could follow, even if he got wasted.

Then another, more useful thought came to mind, urging him to call upon what he referred to as the creative force of the universe. It was the same great unknown resource that saved Leif from an alcoholic death seven years prior. He pointed his thoughts upward to the stars, but spoke them aloud just in case it helped transmit his message.

"In the past you have helped me through some very uncertain situations. Right now I have not yet learned my daughter's fate, but I'm about to. Will you please let me live in a set of circumstances that include her continuing in the same plane of existence as mine? I know I'm not supposed to ask for specifics, but this is possible, and if she does not continue in this world then neither will I, because I can't live without her. I do hope this is in line with your will."

Leif prayed with an unshaken belief in the entity that had once burst the fabric of existence into the ever stretching reaches of eternity, knowing that if it could accomplish such a feat, that it was also powerful enough to bend space and time in Leif's favor, if only that once.

Next, Leif pulled his laptop out of his work case to go online to post an s.o.s. message on Facebook to help reenforce his plea for help. He believed that the more people focusing on a desired result, the greater the chances would be for that result to manifest. The message read «Friends, I just got an uncertain call from the Santa Rosa police regarding my daughter. While I am trying to figure out what happened, I'd like to ask for your good thoughts and prayers for a positive outcome. It won't matter if you believe in this sort of thing or not, because it won't hurt either way to try. Thank you!"

He stepped away from the table and took a step out the front door to feel the cool air on his sweaty face. He looked up and sighed, then walked back into the house. The unthinkable thought that his heart had been denying, returned and rushed straight for his faltering heart, that time with the force of a tidal wave. He again spoke aloud.

"My daughter is dead."

The blood that was left in Leif's head flooded every chamber of his heart, causing him to loose the last of his strength. In slow motion, the world swirled around him like a tornado. His legs buckled and he fell forward, smacking his head on the kitchen table on the way to the ground. He laid motionless while a pool of blood gathered around him.

ACT II

CHAPTER 3

THE HEARTLAND

Vectors of violet and pure white light appeared above Lief. It was so bright that he had trouble opening his eyes. Outside of the light, the first thing he noticed was that he was laying flat on a padded surface. He raised his hand to shield his eyes from the brightness. The flesh around his blurry fingers glowed yellow and orange due to the overexposure of light passing through them. He strained to focus on his arm, first seeing a white plastic bracelet, then a red tube taped to his forearm, and then he noticed that his hives where gone. Unrecognizable echoing sounds began to take the shape of human voices. Soon, he made out a woman's voice.

"He's waking up. Lief, Lief. Can you hear me?"

The space around Lief came into focus. He was in a hospital room. The woman speaking to him was Sarah's mother, Brena. His friend Kelly was there too. The two being there together confused him further because they hadn't known each other.

"Brena? Kelly? What are you two doing here? And why am I here? Where am I?"

Lief's words were strained while he continued to squint his eyes. He figured out that he was on a gurney because of the cold steel rails on the sides of the bed. Brena began to fill him in on the details.

"Lief, you're in Santa Rosa Memorial Hospital. You took a hard fall and they've stitched you up. It looks like you are going to be ok."

"Huh? Ok, how did you two arrive here? I didn't think you knew each other."

Kelly's explained her part.

"Dude. I found you laying on your floor when I came by to return your movies. I thought you were dead, just looking at all of the blood around you. It's actually just a really weird coincidence that the ambulance took you to the same hospital as Sarah-"

"Sarah! What happened? Is she ok?"

He rushed to sit up and felt a tug across his chest and upper arms where several electrical wires had been attached. His quick upward movements caused a head rush that made him nauseous. Lief put his hand to his forehead and felt a row of stitches where he had smacked his head on the table.

"Mother fucker. That hurts- bad!"

Brena explained what had happened as concise as she could.

"She's going to be ok. She hurt herself, but she'll be ok."

If her eyes had not welled up, when she explained that Sarah was alright, Lief may have found some comfort in her words. Also, Lief knew better than to associate "hurt herself" and "ok" with each other.

Kelly interjected.

"Hey guys, you have some big things to attend to here. I just wanted to make sure you were fine, and seeing as you're up, I'm going to give you some space to work things out. Ok? Call me if you need anything, alright? Oh, and your movies are on the tv stand, that Cat-Woman movie sucked ass."

Lief thanked her, but was quick to turn the conversation back to Brena.

"Hurt herself?"

Brena did not speak out loud, but mouthed the words "cut herself" while running a finger across her wrist. Her not speaking the words, told Lief that his daughter was close.

"Where is she? Can I see her? Are they letting anyone in? Why would she-"

"Slow down, we're still trying to figure out what happened. Just try to stay calm, she's here and that's the best we can ask for, for now. Let me check on something. I'll be right back."

Lief could hear Brena speaking with a woman across the hallway, but could not make out what they were saying. A voluptuous thirty-something, blonde nurse entered the room. Her name tag read "Beth M.» In a spaced out, almost robot like manner, Beth addressed Lief.

"How are you feeling Mr. Wainwright?"

He had to wonder if she was joking with her sedated sounding, Napoleon Dynamite-like voice.

"Alright, I guess. I'd really like to see my daughter. Am I allowed in there?"

Beth inspected his heart monitor on the other end of the wires, making sure Lief was stable before attempting to remove his blood transfusion tube and EKG wires.

"I think that should be fine. Let me get these off of you."

Nurse Beth removed his transfusion tube and then popped off the wires connected to round white sticky pads on his chest. That was the easy part. Next, she prepared to remove the adhesive pads.

"This is going to hurt a little. I find it hurts less if I pull quickly, do you mind?"

"Go for it."

Lief winced, but persevered.

"You did great. Let's see if you can stand."

She lowered the rail between them and braced his arm as he slid off the gurney. He planted his feet on the ground. Lief was weak at first, but wasn't going to let that get in the way of seeing his daughter. Lief looked across the hallway to Sarah's room and took his first steps with Beth's help. It wasn't long before he regained enough of his strength to walk without her assistance. Looking through the doorway, he saw his little girl. His heart sank seeing her laying on an observation table with her wrists bandaged, but the tears that followed were a result of both joy and pain.

Sarah looked up at her shirtless, pale, and stitched up father standing in the doorway.

"How ya doing kiddo?"

Tears began to gush over her cheeks as if she was releasing years of pain. Lief spoke to her directly from his heart.

"Sarah, I want you to know that the feelings you have right now are so important and very valid. I know you're in pain and you are going to get the help you need to feel better. I love you so much."

Sarah wiped tears from her face with the back of her hand before responding.

"I love you too."

Lief's heart melted because it had been years since he had heard those words from anyone, especially Sarah, at a time when they could have no greater impact. His daughter was there, alive, and things were already calming down after the ominous phone call.

He was correct in thinking that the phone call he received earlier would change his life forever. His prayers were answered though. He knew that the time he had with his daughter was the most significant thing he would ever have the opportunity to experience. Each moment forward with Sarah was going to be cherished like never before. He was more grateful than he had ever been. He sat as comfortable as he had ever sat, smiling bigger than he ever had, albeit, on the inside. He rejoiced in his ability to have new thoughts, thoughts that weren't based in fear.

His moment appreciating the grace of the universe was interrupted when Beth the nurse came back in to summon Lief.

"I'm sorry... Wait, I was sorry about something, but I don't remember what. I came to the room, and now I'm here. I'm supposed to tell you something. Hmm... Oh yeah, the doctor needs to see you now."

Lief let Sarah know that he would be back to her as soon as he could, before crossing the hallway back to his own hospital room. Brena returned and popped her head into Lief's room.

"I'll keep her company. Let them fix you up now. Your daughter is going to be needing a lot from you soon. Just let me know when you're free. We should talk about some things."

He agreed.

Lief was diagnosed with a concussion. As a symptom of the

concussion, Lief was easily distracted from the doctor's overview and instructions. He observed a hunched over elderly man being escorted down the hallway by a woman that Lief could not see because she was standing on the old man's opposite side. Something about her movements and presence called out to Lief. He tilted his head trying to get a peak of the woman's face. Lief could see that she was slender and blond, but due to his vantage point he still could not see her face. It wasn't until she walked in front of his room that her could see her face. Revealed in full, the sight of her triggered a deja vu, one in which Lief had been with her, frozen in time while he tried to understand her beauty. He thought it strange that he couldn't recall where he had seen or met her before. Then the two made eye contact. Their eyes carried the same sadness, but seemed to also share a similar reassurance. *Do I know you?* She offered him a small, but authentic smile.

The doctor noticed Lief wasn't paying attention to the important recovery details.

"Mr. Wainwright, you got all that?"

"Oh, a-ha, yeah"

The doctor cautioned Lief in a tone one would use to address a child.

"Alright, now you're free to go. Ok?"

"Yeah, alright. Thank you."

"You're very welcome. Remember if you are having a constant headache with confusion, you know, like having a hard time paying attention or having a hard time remembering common things, if you have dizziness, any vomiting, you know throwing up, get back into the emergency room immediately. Ok?"

Lief was expecting the doctor to hand him a lollipop on his way out of the room. He made his way into the waiting room, where he found a tweed, cushioned fabric, and probably germ ridden, chair.

A short while later, Brena found Lief sitting in the waiting area. Sarah was speaking with a psychologist at the time so Brena, at last, had the chance to share more of what she had learned about the sequence of events that led to Sarah being in the emergency room. She explained that Sarah had been communicating online with a boy in Florida before she cut her wrists. When the boy learned of her intentions, he called 911, who in turn informed Sonoma county emergency services. That was when emergency services tried to track down her location. It was during that process that Lief received the devastating call from the Santa Rosa Police Department.

Some things started to make sense to Lief, while other details remained a mystery, such as why she did it. Lief asked Brena what she thought. She was as in the dark as he was. It was obvious that Brena was uncomfortable delving into that aspect of the situation in front of Lief. She had always kept her emotions locked up and it seemed some of that closed off disposition was passed on to Sarah. Brena said she wanted to see if the doctor was still talking to Sarah. Lief understood, because he avoided exposing much of what he was feeling in front of her as well. As soon as she left the room Lief lost control of his emotions and broke down. Looking down to conceal his tears, Lief heard someone sit down in the waiting area. He looked up, thinking Brena had returned, but to his surprise it was the mysterious woman he saw in the hallway. Lief was quick to look back down, but he couldn't stop thinking about how he knew her, if he did. Lief then heard her speak.

Are you ok?

He was caught more than a little off guard and found it hard to formulate a response.

"Oh, ahh, thanks for asking. Yeah."

She looked perplexed.

"Excuse me, were you just talking to me?"

Lief was confused.

Didn't she just ask me if I was ok?

Lief then heard her speak again.

I thought to ask him if he was ok, I didn't say it out loud did I? Did he hear it? Wait, can you hear my thoughts?

Lief's thoughts replied.

Uhhh, I think so, maybe… I'm going to start talking out loud now so that I don't think I'm crazy.

Lief hesitated, then addressed her out loud.

"Sorry, I guess I'm talking to myself out loud again. Anyways, what brings you to this lovely establishment this evening?"

"Oh, don't worry, I do the same- Talk to myself. I'm here with my father. He had a fall. We think he broke some ribs."

"Oh no. Sorry to hear that."

Lief didn't like small talk and avoided it at all costs, but the confusing conversation going on inside his head was interfering with his social skills. *Telepathy? Am I imagining this? This is nuts.* In case she could hear his thoughts he tried to limit them, but that was improbable. She was wrestling with her mind just as much, then stammered out her own hollow words.

"What about you? Are you here by yourself?"

Lief wanted to answer, but doing so would trigger the feelings he was doing his best to conceal. She took a second to observe Lief. She saw the tear induced reddish tint in whites of his eyes and read his demeanor to be that of a drowning man who had just been saved. She didn't need to see the tears gathering in the corners of his eyes to know that he had gone through something horrendous. Her kind inquisition filled Lief's mind with a calming assurance that all would be well. She saw a peace gather in him before he answered.

"No, no, my daughter is being seeing too."

"Oh no! What happened? Sorry if I'm being too nosey."

"It's fine, no, you're not being too nosey, I'm just- I had a head injury, and I think I'm a little foggy. It's kind of strange, but my daughter and I had separate injuries in different places and then, strangely, we both just- coincidentally? Ah... ended up here. I'm still trying to grasp what happened."

He spoke as if he was also trying to explain it all to himself, because it all seemed a little too far-fetched. He thought about it too long and began to cry again. He looked down in embarrassment while he held his hand over his eyes.

She gasped, feeling his pain, before her eyes also welled up with tears. As a reflex response, her empathy caused her to place her hand on his to comfort him. It was then that he was convinced that he knew her.

"Thank you. Sorry, I'm having a hard time right now."

Her following smile was consoling.

Lief sucked up his tears, readjusted his posture, and pulled himself together, into a manner he perceived to be more composed. He explained that Sarah's mother, labeled with a very pronounced «ex», was also there, talking with the doctors.

"My heart goes out to you. I work with teenagers as a high school teacher, an art teacher to be exact. You know, so many are, well, it's just such a tough age."

Lief agreed and then told her that Sarah was in an art program at her school. She lit up with enthusiasm learning that Lief's daughter shared the same passion as her. Then she introduced herself.

"My name is Kay."

The moment he heard her name his head snapped up and a cocktail of adrenaline and serotonin surged through his veins.

"What? Wait. Your name is Kay?"

"Yes? Well, or Mrs. Jellings depending who you ask."

"Have we met before?"

"I don't think so."

Although Kay was justified speaking her answer, her thoughts provided a different answer.

Yes, I do think we've met, but that was just a wonderful dream.

Lief found himself in the strangest of places. He had just experienced the biggest near tragedy of his life, leaving his feelings, or existence for that matter, without a strong footing. Moments later the carpet was pulled out from underneath his weakened stance by a woman that he had fallen in love with in a dream that same morning and, on top of that, she was speaking to him with her mind. His reality was a mess, alternating between vivid and overwhelming, then disassociated and trace. When his strong feelings surfaced he'd replay the terror following the uncertainty about Sarah, which made him feel guilty and selfish for accepting the comfort of a beautiful woman. Then in the next moment, his judgement faded, leaving him blank and numb. In those moments, he experienced the true meaning of the phrase "ignorance is bliss». Part of him wanted to float away, but each time he started to drift, her words threw a grappling hook into his heart.

Brena returned to the waiting room and interrupted Kay and Lief's conversation.

"The doctor wants to speak to the both of us now."

Lief stood up and excused himself.

"Kay, it was nice talking to you. My name is Lief, by the way. I hope your father's ok."

She thanked him, but was sad to see him leave before they established a way to keep in touch. Lief knew he had to go and had considered getting her number, but he decided it would have been inappropriate. He nodded goodbye, walked out of the room and down the long hallway, and then he turned the corner and disappeared from Kay's life.

Brena and Lief spoke with the doctors, who suggested that a 5150 hold may be the best course of action for Sarah until they found a more tailored treatment plan for her. Brena explained that there had been an administrative error in her medical coverage that caused it to lapse, which was news to Lief.

"Fucking Obamacare!"

She shook her head, clenching her jaw in frustration, before explaining that anything beyond an emergency room visit was out of pocket. The psychologist suggested a less expensive alternative plan.

"Are either one of you available to stay near her for a good couple of days while she has some follow up appointments? And when I say stay with her, I mean 24/7."

Lief jumped at the opportunity.

"I'm currently excused from work for the next week, maybe longer. I can be with her every second till I go back."

Brena was onboard with the plan, and so it was. The next appointments were scheduled, beginning with the first taking place bright and early the following morning.

Within an hour, Sarah and Lief were home in their kooky little town of Cotati. Lief brought out stacks of blankets so they could sleep on the living room couches in front of the tv that night. He asked Sarah to pick a movie so that she wouldn't think it too strange that he wanted them to sleep in the living room. Lief wasn't letting her out of his sight. Sarah put in the first season of *The Sarah Conner Chronicles*, the made for cable tv *Terminator* series, and then got situated on her couch.

There was a flickering light coming from the flatscreen that told a story of robots chasing down humans and then the other way around. Lief felt like he was approaching the best sleep he may ever have. He was in the most quaint house he ever had the privilege to live, laying on the most comfortable couch he had ever felt, across from his safe and snug teenage little girl.

CHAPTER 4

ELEVEN ELEVEN

Effulgent rays of sunshine beamed through the living room window onto Sarah's face causing her to squint before she buried her face under her blanket. Lief began to stir as well. He yawned, then picked up his cell phone to look at the time. It was 11:11.

"Sarah, check it out. It's 11:11. We slept in."

"So what. You don't have to take me to school today."

"Yeah I know. We were up pretty late. Did I ever tell you the significance of 11:11?"

"Yesss. New beginnings or perfection or something like that."

"Yup, all of that. How do you feel today?"

"Tired"

Sarah grumbled and put a pillow over her head to signal she'd like to be left alone.

From the couch Lief could see the large blood stain he left on the carpet near the dining table.

"There goes my deposit."

Looking up and around the dining area, Lief noticed that everything seemed sharper and more enhanced than they were in the days before. The house was always clean, at least by any bachelor's standards, but that day it glistened.

The next good fortune the day brought was in the form of his commission check arriving in the mail the second he went outside to look for it. That never happened. The rest of the day was succinct as well. Everything bounced his way, quite literally in one instance when he was disposing a saturated teabag that he had just pulled from his mug. He ran toward the garbage to throw it away, but the bag slipped from his hand, sure to fall on the floor. Somehow it defied gravity and floated past the rim of the garbage, and fell inside without a single drop reaching the ground.

"Wow! Look at those skills!"

Sarah wasn't as impressed.

The biggest improvement that the new day brought was his understanding of the happiness he felt every time he'd look at his daughter. He knew that she was going through a tough time, but still he couldn't help but think of how grateful he was for the chance they had to go through her troubles together.

Lief had his own obstacles to deal with, but during those days, pessimism was not one of them. He was a born again optimist. He recalled his past studies of metaphysical theories, including the law of attraction and any other explanations of harnessed manifestations. Years before, during a sales training retreat in Phoenix, he heard a motivational speaker say "The thing you think about the most is what you move towards." That made perfect sense to him. He had lived long enough to wrangle many of his biggest wishes. Sarah was too young and had not had the opportunity to experience any consistencies in magic at that point in her life. Lief wanted to teach her some of those concepts to give her reason for some sense of hope. Hope was first and foremost.

Sarah and Lief went to several counseling, medical, and psychological appointments in the following weeks. Lief saw immediate improvements in her outlook, but anytime he inquired into why she hurt herself, she backed away so he was careful not to press her too much. He left that mystery in the hands of her teenage psychology specialists.

Lief was in love with his new take on life. His leave from work was extended to three weeks. He found space for a a small amount of his earlier, more purposeful life to return. This meant music and dating were again on the schedule. Lief also planned for Sarah and him to go on a four day cruise down to Mexico. They were scheduled to sail exactly two weeks after the incident.

Sarah was ecstatic at the news of the cruise. As far as activities and vacations went, Sarah loved going on cruises more than anything else. To be specific, it was the teen club aboard the ship that she loved more than anything. Lief always gave Sarah run of the ship and even let her keep her own hours which she chose to spend with her compadres in the teen club. Together they'd play video games, visit the twenty-four hour pizza and ice cream bar, and many other social events tailored for her age. It was the only place she ever felt comfortable socializing. She felt a degree of anonymity because there was no permanence to any of it. She'd leave the ship with a clean slate because she'd never see any of them again, so any perceived bad thoughts of her were inconsequential. Seeing her socialize on the boat was Lief's favorite part of the cruise, but he hoped that she would one day be comfortable making friends at home. It baffled him that his beautiful, smart, and kind hearted daughter wasn't more social with her classmates. He wished she could see that there was no real risk involved. Regardless of the transient nature of her cruise friends, any social contact was exactly what she needed.

For Lief, the cruise was to be a lasting memory of his kid that was growing up too fast. He started to take more mental pictures and a few actual pictures of certain experiences the two had together, knowing that those types of experiences may be the last. He had started to adopt the reality of that years before. On one occasion, he took a selfie of them holding hands while they skated around the ice-rink near their home. He suspected he'd never again get the chance to capture such a cherished moment because she was getting to the age where holding hands would no longer be cool. He was right, because the next time they went skating together, she saw some of her classmates skating in the rink and stayed as far away from her father as possible.

The most memorable and picture worthy cruise experience was when they snorkeled with giant sea turtles in the Caribbean while visiting Barbados. Lief was fifteen feet from Sarah who was treading water, looking downward into the turquoise sea for turtles when a turtle peaked its head out of the water a foot from Sarah's face. Her eyes lit up as the turtle looked at her with curiosity. The contour of the turtle's beak made it appear to be smiling, just as Sarah was. Lief didn't have a camera with him in the water, but the moment was not only forever preserved in his memory, but it would be in her's as well. She'd be able to think of the time she swam in the tropics, face to face with sea turtle. She'd also remember that she was there with her father when it happened. Lief went as far as to exaggerate that thought to the point that he imagined she might think of the experience at his funeral. That line of sentimental and self obsessive thinking would bring him to tears when he considered how close he was to losing her.

In the remaining days before the cruise, Lief took Sarah to several more counseling appointments, they played video games, watched lots of movies, and hung out in the local coffee shops. On top of the extra activities he was able to do with his daughter, Lief found plenty of time to go out busking with Bigfoot.

Lief and Bigfoot bounced between playing nearby coffee shops in Santa Rosa and Petaluma. Each time they played, their set got tighter and tighter. Many people stopped and showed their appreciation by tipping well. One time, they were even left a twenty.

Most of their songs were in the vein of alternative folk rock. Often they'd cover bands like Radiohead and the Pixies, then they'd rotate into originals, but were always adding new material to see what people responded to best.

Lief was impressed by how much they were entertaining others. He wasn't concerned about the money. He gave most of it to Bigfoot, who didn't make much money elsewhere. Also, with Lief's grander thoughts of what the two could do with the show, it would be better if Bigfoot had a prudent reserve in his savings account. Wrapping up a busking set in the affluent tourist town of Healdsburg, Lief knew they had mastered their performance when he saw how much money had been deposited in the guitar case. He also knew that his unspoken aspiration became a legitimate reality and that it was time to reveal it to Bigfoot. Just before Bigfoot picked up his case to leave, Lief stopped him.

"Hey, today was good. We played well. Well, you played well."

"Thanks, yeah we did, didn't we?"

"Yeah, you actually seem different today. I can't place it, you just seem spritely."

"Oh yeah, It's the fur spray I'm using."

"Fur spray?"

"Yeah, for my suits. I got some specialized shiny spray for fur that I spray all over them after I do the laundry. It makes me shine."

"Them? Meaning you have more than one of those?"

"Yeah. What did you think, I wear the same one everyday? That wouldn't be very hygienic."

"I guess not. Anyway, I've been thinking."

"Yeah... What's up?"

"I've been thinking about something for a while now- About what we may be able to do with the show."

"Really, what's that?"

"Ok, this is kind of big, but I'm starting to think it's possible. What if..."

"Yeah?"

"What if we took the show on the road. You know, like do a small tour of, maybe, the western U.S. We could busk in certain areas, like big cities like, I dunno, maybe Portland & Seattle. Maybe even Denver, maybe some National parks along the way. And here's the thing that I think would especially be amazing- We film the whole thing and make a documentary about it."

Lief explained that he thought it was a good time for both of them to pull it off. He built his argument by adding that he had a pass that gave him free access to National Parks for camping because he was considered a disabled vet for his PTSD and a traumatic brain injury. He also had several friends that they could stay with in many of the big cities. On top of that, he had a trick he used to stay at Marriott Hotels at a discounted rate. Lief further explained that he had just filed for disability insurance at his doctor's recommendation, which would extend his time away from work.

Bigfoot's excitement at the idea was obvious as Lief rolled out the details of his plan. It all made sense. It did, in fact, turn out to be the perfect time for Bigfoot as well, though it would be contingent on him getting the time off of work, which he was sure he could do. As synchronicity would have it, the recording studio he worked at was going to be taking a week long break. Bigfoot promised to give him an absolute affirmative after double checking with his boss.

Lief knew Bigfoot would be onboard before he ever told him about his big plans. Bigfoot would have said yes for the road trip alone. Filming their adventure was icing on the cake.

Although Lief was honest about many reasons that he wanted to do the trip, he kept the most important motive close to his chest. It involved Lief having a good reason to visit someone. Touring with a band with an incidental stop in her town would have made a visit seem casual enough that she'd have less reason to decline meeting with Lief.

On the way out of the park, they promised to talk more about the big idea later. Lief checked his cell phone for any possible missed calls. While looking down at his phone, he felt a tap on his shoulder. Before he had a chance to see who it was, a familiar woman's voice spoke.

"I liked listening to your music."

Lief spun around and saw that it was Kay.

"Whoa! It's you!"

"What a nice coincidence that we bumped into each other."

"Yes it is. I had a feeling we'd bump into each other again. Maybe, it's not a coincidence?"

"Hmm, you're probably right."

They chatted about safe, superficial things that were just a step above the weather. There were so many better things to discuss, like all that had transpired since their fortuitous meeting at the hospital. It seemed small talk was all they could afford though, because both of them believed that there was too much at stake in the way of continued contact to be bold and disclose their attraction to one another with fears of rejection.

The only thing discussed of any real importance was the fact that their injured family members were on a path to recovery.

Lief had a funny way of knowing a person's character with a great deal of precision, often within moments of seeing them. Sometimes, just seeing a picture was enough to assess the frame work of one's personality with accuracy. He had dismissed the notion of his ability for years until he heard about the face readers hired by corporations to get a feel for a people before doing business with them. He then saw it as more of a science that anyone as sensitive as him could hone. To say the least, he benefited from his character recognition abilities when it came to sales. Using those same recognition skills, he would soon reap the rewards from understanding how wonderful Kay was. Along with knowing how great she was all around, Lief had a good hunch that Kay had several things in common with him. He had a guessed that, like him, she was not a drinker, that she was a traveler, that she had great taste in music, and that she had a wicked sense of humor.

Continuing their conversation, the pool of available small talk ran dry. Lief had to think of something quick so he could stay in contact with Kay once they went their separate ways. A small voice spoke to Lief from the lonely recesses of his mind, *Don't be chicken shit! Ask for her number.* Just then, a swift chilling wind swayed the palm trees and caused a rustling in the sturdy old growth redwoods surrounding the park. The gust also blew Kay's long bangs in front of her eyes. As she brushed them back with her fingers, Lief observed Kay's movements in slow motion, like in a makeup commercial which always follows with the model saying something in french. His intuition always told him that a woman was attracted to a man if she touched her hair in front of him. He knew in this instance that Kay touching her hair was so she could see, but the association still triggered an assumed interest in his subconscious. Kay shivered and wrapped her arms around her shoulders. For a moment, they stopped talking and just stood there smiling at each other. The silence was awkward at first, then a calming levity overran the strangeness. Again, the voice urged Lief to get her phone number.

As he opened his mouth to speak, she beat him to the punch and ended the silence first.

"Maybe we could exchange numbers, in case we want to meet up again. Wait- What are you up to now? It's a little chilly out here. I was going to grab a cup of coffee. Wanna join m-"

Lief was quick to respond before she finished her sentence.

"Yeah. Totally. How do you feel about the Flying Goat around the corner here? It has my favorite coffee in the world."

"Yes! That's where I was going. I love that place. Do you need a hand with anything?"

Kay carried Lief's guitar to his car while he carried the rest of his gear.

"It's a really beautiful guitar."

"Thank you! It had been my dream guitar for seven years until I justified dropping the money on it last year."

Shallow conversation resumed.

"I couldn't have picked nicer weather to play in today."

She did not respond, instead she looked into his eyes, then beyond, and deep into his mind where she transmitted the thought, *You are safe with me.*

Lief lowered his guard. He felt like he could hug her right then and she would reciprocate.

They sat at a small table halfway tucked into a bay window and sipped their coffee. It was an artsy, minimalist cafe that had checkered black and white tiles on the floor, exotic wood tables, a stainless steel coffee bar, and matching yellow coffee producing apparatuses. Not one more word of small talk was spoken. Kay confirmed that she also was not a drinker, and had been sober for two years. She explained that she lived a half-hour south of Lief in San Francisco, which threw a slight wrench in logistics were they to meet again. It was a good thing they both loved to travel. They agreed they had several other paramount things in common, including liking kooky movies with nice colors, a dislike for shitty pop music, and, at the top of the list, they both possessed a deep appreciation for dry humor. As Kay had assumed, Lief admitted that he carried a pain around relationships in the form of abandonment and intimacy issues, but as luck would have it, she was an understanding, patient, and nurturing person. That thought warmed his heart.

After coffee, Lief walked Kay to her car. Both were in amazing spirits having had the opportunity to become aquatinted. They promised to call each other soon afterwards. They locked eyes one last time before saying goodbye. As they leaned in for a hug, Lief shifted at the last moment, risking a kiss on her cheek. He could feel her excitement. She pulled him back against her and returned a proper, passionate kiss on the lips. It was one for the ages. With each synced and slight movement the kiss grew deeper as did their embrace. Lief's mind released a resounding exclamation.

Mrs. Kay Jellings, You are so fucking amazing!

Her mind stirred giddy in the romanticism of his thought/words. Her mind responded.

Mr. Wainwright, I think you're pretty cool too.

——— ～

Due to prior engagements it appeared that Lief and Kay would be unable to meet with each other before he left on the cruise with Sarah. Thanks to the miracles of technology they were able to speak to each other on their computers digitally, face to digital face. It was no different than sitting down for coffee, outside of the fact that they couldn't touch each other. On their first computer conversation they talked for an unbelievable six hours. Never since high school had Lief spent as much time talking to a romantic interest. They talked about everything from their perverted peculiarities to a few of their virtues. Without conflict, they navigated through the tough stuff like politics, religion, and sex, including a little show and tell. They remained compatible after revealing all the stuff they'd never discuss with anyone, including the usual deal-breakers. If it weren't for Lief falling asleep right in front of Kay mid-sentence, they'd have spoken into and through the sunrise. She later admitted that it was one of the most peaceful things that she had ever witnessed.

—— ——

Two days remained before his cruise to Mexico. Although Lief looked forward the trip, he regretted the timing due to his blossoming relationship with Kay, but he knew she'd be there for him when he returned. He also had no confusion about what the cruise was about. It was for Sarah and she couldn't wait. He came to realize that everything was as it should be after he gave it some more thought.

All of the good things going on in Lief's life following the heartbreaking call from the police, began to make him a little suspicious. He gave credence to the many metaphysical philosophies that would characterize the good experiences as being in the flow. Lief had been in the flow several times before in his life, however, he could't remember ever witnessing as much synchronicity. He would tell himself to accept the good. To Lief, that was much easier said than done. The status quo of his life was turbulent to say the least, making smooth sailing a cautionary event. Either way, Lief was going to do his best to establish a new precedence by rewiring his mind to believe that life was supposed to be better. He even came up with another clever motto worthy of bumper sticker lore. It would read "Happiness is not a Selfish Venture".

As it turned out, Kay could not wait to see Lief until after his trip, so she made some adjustments with her schedule, hoping she could see him that evening although it would to be in her neck of the woods. Lief jumped at the opportunity and cleared his schedule for the night as well. Although they only agreed on having dinner, Lief brought his toothbrush, just in case.

They made plans to have dinner at a trendy mediterranean restaurant in the gentrified Mission district of the city which was once a haven for homeless alcoholics, drug addicts, and many other sorts who were in deep pursuit of hitting rock bottom. Lief was so excited about meeting that he overlooked his healthy fear of driving in the city. Nine times out of ten while driving there, he had an anxiety attack, or worse, a car accident due to the crazy driving conditions up and down the steep hills laden with trolley cars, mass transit busses, and careless eco-friendly bicyclists.

The good kept rolling for Lief and his drive to the city was no exception because he witnessed a miracle on the way to meet Kay. He drove through twenty-five green lights and then found an open parking spot in front of the restaurant. He sat for a moment to consider how he made it across the Golden Gate Bridge and through the city without ever having to stop his car for anything, not one wayward pedestrian, stop sign, red light, trolly car, ambulance, or earthquake for that matter. Nothing stood between him and Kay that evening. He had more reason to suspect that life was but a dream.

The long line to the hostess podium was backed up out the door and past the end of the building. It looked like Lief's luck had just run out. As he made his way along the sidewalk to the back of the line, a woman in black, sitting inside at a table, caught his eye. He stopped, to do a double take because she looked just like Kay, but the heavy glare on the window made it impossible for him to positively identify her. Then the woman waived to him, but he wasn't sure if it was him that she was waiving to, so he pointed to himself and asked,

"Who, me?"

There was no way a person in the dining area could hear him through the glass, and to the people in line, he appeared to be talking to himself. He chuckled and walked to the back of the line.

He wasn't in line for long when he thought he heard someone call his name.

"Lief. Lief, over here you big dummy. I guess you didn't see me waive to you from the table?"

"Ohhh, that was you. Whew, for a moment there I felt like an idiot. I guess I don't need to stand in line."

"No, I got us, a table?"

"Great! Let's eat"

He no longer felt like an idiot, he was one.

Their table was a quaint two-top next to a Spanish styled tiled fountain. As the natural light faded with the sunset, the candlelight at the table grew warmer and was just luminous enough to light their vicinity without exposing much more of the dining area. They were in their own private solar system experiencing a planetary alignment. Kay reached across the table and smoothed the top of Lief's hand with her fingers. He smiled because he knew that he was in the exact perfect place, at the exact perfect time, with the exact perfect person, about to eat perfect Spanish tortilla, gluten free croquettes, and green olives stuffed with anchovies.

— ‿ ‿

Dinner rested well in their bellies while they took a stroll through a nearby victorian neighborhood on their way to Delores Park. Lief studied the ornate designs and amazing craftsmanship of the homes that were well over a hundred years old. His eyes followed the balustrade balconies, to the colorful trims around arched bay windows, their curved transom doorways behind columned portico, and all the way up to the bracketed cornice under the low angled rooftops. The relaxed pace they were walking gave him ample time to review his thoughts. *When and where did I learn about victorian design? Should I hold her hand? I'm glad these homes survived the earthquakes. I wonder when I'm going to have sex with her.* Kay's thoughts responded, *Not tonight,* but she did grab his hand.

When they reached the park, they took a seat on a bench and enjoyed the cool, thick San Francisco evening climate. They were at the top of a tall hill and were able to see the grid of the city streets, lit with yellow street lights that faded to orange and flickered the further they were away.

"So what's with the toothbrush?"

"What?"

"Your toothbrush, it's sticking out of your pocket."

"Oh yeah, so it is. That is my toothbrush. I brush my teeth with it. After most meals, sometimes, well you know, it's a hygiene thing."

"I had already planned on inviting you to stay the night, on the couch."

"Really? I would like that. Good thing I got my toothbrush."

— ⁓

During Lief's debut visit to Kay's apartment, they laid on her bed in her messy room and kissed, but true to her word, they did not have sex. When the passion cooled down Lief sat up with puffy hair and looked at Kay laying on her bed. Their minds were connected, but their thoughts said nothing. After a while, Kay sat up and let Lief know that she had a few things to tend to on the computer for work before she went to bed. She showed Lief to her living room couch and gave him some blankets.

"I'll be right back. I forgot I have to return a few emails. I have a feeling I'll forget to do it later. So, I'll be right back.'

Lief studied the decor and state of her living room. It was disheveled and cluttered with art projects covering all of her surface space. Pictures were plastered on the walls without any rhyme or reason and there was a pile of clothes in the corner. The furniture appeared to be second hand and was just as mismatched as everything else in her apartment. Lief had forgotten that she was an art teacher. Once he remembered he was able to make sense of the disaster.

Situated on the couch for his slumber, Lief felt an eerie presence in the room. He called out for Kay who had been away longer than he expected.

"Kay, you haven't gone to bed already have you?"

She didn't respond so he figured she was in the restroom, but the eerie presence remained. A cliche saying from the movies came to his mind, *These walls have eyes.*

Lief caught a slight movement in his peripheral vision. It was Kay who had crept to the end of the hallway and peaked around the corner into the living room, exposing only a portion of her face. Lief did not say anything because he was dumbfounded at the quirkiness of the magnificent woman who was taking hold of his heart. She looked at him with an unsettling Boo Radley persona. Kay's mind had heard Lief's cheesy movie phrase and responded.

"These walls do have eyes."

Then she receded back behind the corner. Lief's heart skipped a beat because it had no way to comprehend his ever increasing appreciation for her. He couldn't keep up with her splendor.

Kay came back from around the corner to give Lief a goodnight kiss. He was nestled into the couch and was as content as content could be.

"My work here is done."

"For now"

            —   —

The following evening, the last night before the cruise, Kay rearranged her schedule again so that she could spend the night at Lief's home. Earlier that day, something even more significant transpired when Kay met Sarah for the first time. They liked each other right off the bat, but Lief already knew that they would. Sarah and Kay had spoken about art and Sarah's art program at her high school. The rest was history. Lief was amazed that Sarah opened up with Kay as much as she did.

Later that evening, Kay shared her observations of Sarah.

"She's such a beautiful girl. I'm really sorry she's going through such a hard time."

"Yeah, the doctors all agree that she needs to socialize with her peers more right now. That's why this cruise, with the teen club and all, is the perfect thing for her right now."

"I don't want to intrude or be, you know, nosey, but do you have any idea what caused her to go so far? Is it because of her… well her ar-"

"It's just that she was in a lot of pain as far as I can tell. She hasn't spoken to me much about it. She has a really hard time communicating with other kids, I dunno, low self esteem stuff. There might have been some feelings hurt over a boy too."

Lief took a deep breath to sigh. Kay's eyes turned red as if she was going to start crying.

"Sweetheart, I can only imagine what you're going through with her. I wish I could help."

She gave him a consoling hug then rested her cheek on his neck.

That evening, Kay and Lief had dinner at a Vietnamese restaurant in Cotati. Sarah stayed behind because she preferred her chicken tenders at the house. When they got home, Lief checked in with Sarah to make sure she wasn't feeling cast aside because of Kay. Sarah was fine with everything.

Kay and Lief prepared for bed separately, taking turns in the bathroom, grooming as one would when sharing a bed with another for the first time. The thought of laying next to each other all night caused butterflies to flurry in both them.

They settled in under the freshly washed sheets and cover, cuddling while pretending to be interested in the movie, Love Actually, that played loudly on the flatscreen fixed to the wall in the room. Within an irresistible proximity of each other, the movie was lost in the background while "love actually" occurred in real time. For one fraction of a second, their experience was the newest biblical union on the planet, and behold, it was good.

CHAPTER 5

SEALAND

Persevering the traffic in the Bay Area, Lief and Sarah at last hit open road when they merged onto the southbound I-5. Their cruise ship was in L.A., a seven-hour drive for most law abiding citizens. Lief normally made it in just under six hours by setting the cruise control to 82 mph while Sarah kept an eye out for the California Highway Patrol. They saved time by limiting restroom breaks only to fuel stops.

Sarah was no stranger to long road trips. When she was much younger, her and Lief lived in Reno for two years, while her mother lived four hours away in Sonoma County. The split custody arrangement created an eight-hour back and forth commute for her twice a month. Sarah had learned to nod off as soon as she got in the car. Lief had no doubt that she would grow up to be a traveler just like him and he often boasted that they had already traveled to ten countries together.

Lief and Sarah arrived in Los Angeles. In order to avoid the ridiculous parking fees, Lief arranged to park at his grandmother's home in Bellflower, a rundown city in the greater Los Angeles area. It was close to the port though. Bellflower and, the much more well known, Compton sat next to each other. They were, for all intents and purposes, the same town and any differences in appearance and socio-economic climate were indiscernible. Simply put, she lived in gangland. Because of the rough neighborhood it was a gamble to park there. Lief shrugged off concern because he had good car insurance.

Lief referred to his grandmother as Bellflower Grandma for obvious reasons. Bellflower Grandma offered to drive them to the ship from her home which was generous for her because she rarely drove more than a couple of miles from her home after turning seventy.

Just as Lief recognized that several regular events with young Sarah would prove to be last experiences as she grew up, he was aware that each visit with his grandmother may be a last one as well. He treated each visit as such, making sure to give his entire attention to what she had to tell him. He loved her beyond measure and had spent a lot of time with her in his early years when he also lived in Los Angeles.

Bellflower Grandma and Lief had a special relationship. They spoke often exchanged playful banter full of inside jokes. Lief would often concoct stories just to see how far he could take them before she'd call his bluff and laugh. They spent about a half-hour chatting with Bellflower Grandma before she drove them to the ship. The ship was so big that they could see it from a mile away. Sarah could no longer hide her excitement about the trip which was evident by how quick she ran for the growing embarkation line when they arrived. Lief's grandma gestured for a hug. As she approached with her arms spread wide, Lief could see that she had something in her hand that she was trying to conceal. Lief intuitively knew it was money. She then handed him two twenty-dollar bills.

"Get yourselves something in Mexico from me."

Lief hated to accept it, knowing she didn't have much money on her fixed income, but he also knew that resistance was futile.

"Aww, thank you grandma. I'll see you in four days".

He ran after Sarah.

After boarding the ship, meaning waiting in several long lines of security checkpoints, they found their room. Lief had a surprise for Sarah waiting for her in the room, or to be more accurate, underneath the room. He had booked an oceanside cabin above the teen club, the closest room to it. She'd be able to take four steps to the stairway in front of the door, go down one floor to the promenade deck, and arrive at her favorite place on the planet. Lief was an expert travel arranger. He found as much pleasure in making arrangements as he did traveling. He sometimes wondered if he may have been a travel agent in a past life.

They settled into the cabin, then made their way to the formal dining room for dinner. For some unknown reason, Lief didn't walk to the stairs as he usually would have. Instead, he walked the other direction to the elevator. While the two of them waited in front of its door for their lift, Lief experienced a sense of a deja vu. Upon careful review, it was no deja vu at all, it was a memory, and not a good one. It occurred to Lief that they were standing in front of the exact elevator that they used fourteen years prior on their first cruise when Brena, Lief, and Sarah were still a family. Lief was holding, the then six-months old baby Sarah and they had become squished into the front of the elevator by four large passengers that were also aboard. Food inclusive cruises attract obese to the buffet like moths to the flame.

When the already full elevator had stopped on a floor to pick up more obese people the passengers squashed together to make room. In the shuffle, Sarah's arm had become wedged between the door and its frame. As it opened it pulled her arm into the small space between the thick metal frame and the door. It took Lief a moment to notice what was happening to his baby girl's tiny arm. She started to scream when the powerful hydraulic door system started to pull her arm from its socket. Lief panicked and utter fear filled his mind. That was when Lief learned the miracle of suspended time.

The magnitude of the situation caused a sensory overload that blew a fuse in Lief's mind, freezing his perceived reality. Everything in motion stopped moving, except for the creative space between Lief's ears. Lief imagined what might happen if he couldn't get her arm out of the door. And he pictured all of the immediate and future pain that she would endure as a result. He looked forward in time and saw Sarah going through school having only one arm and feeling less than her peers. In his vision, schoolmates made fun of her, causing her to come home and cry everyday. He looked further into the future and saw her struggling with loneliness during college, being one of the only girls who had not yet experienced a romantic relationship. Then he imagined the guilt he'd have, blaming himself for the accident because he overlooked the danger of where they stood. She might have developed a resentment towards him, because he didn't prevent it.

All things considered, he knew he could not let any of those things happen. With time still frozen, he summoned the greatest power he could harness at that moment, the power of denial, a component in the law of attraction, the part where one shed's all thoughts of things undesirable to make room for the desirable. With the force of a neutron bomb, he sent shock waves of doubt across the horizon of time, obliterating all that hadn't happened yet. Before the inevitable nightmare of the next moment returned, he filled the empty space with a more positive plausible plan of action.

He knew that pulling her arm out of the door was going to hurt her, but much less than the alternative, so he established that it wasn't the time to be ginger with her. In that stillness of time, Lief calculated the exact movements and force needed to save her arm. The timeless moment ended and he executed his plan. With one swift movement while grasping Sarah tight, he twisted his entire upper-body back, freed Sarah from the elevator, and fell into the fat lady behind him. Baby Sarah released a blood curdling scream and the large lady behind them walloped like an upset sea lion as they all fell backwards. Lief leaped forward and out of the elevator before he knew the condition Sarah's arm.

BING! The sound of the elevator arriving at his floor startled Lief and brought him back into his present moment, standing there next to Sarah. The elevator door opened, but Lief paused, contemplating whether or not they should step into it. A large fifty-something Samoan lady, wearing a tropical patterned Moo Moo, scoffed, then asked Lief if they were getting in. Still hesitant, Lief did not answer. Instead, he grabbed Sarah's arm, the one that had almost been lost on that infamous elevator ride all those years prior, then guided her away. As they raced to the stairs in an attempt to beat the elevator up to the next floor, Sarah didn't understand what was going through her father's mind.

"Uh, dad. Why didn't we take the elevator after waiting all that time?"

"You do want to keep both your arms, don't you?"

His response was absurd to her, but she let it be and didn't ask for an explanation. The two beat the slow moving elevator to the Lido deck and were able to get in the growing dining line much sooner than anyone on the elevator.

—— ——

Lief had tortured himself by remaining gluten-free on a previous cruise, but he had no such notions on his current one. The portions in the formal dining room were small, but he could order as many dishes as he wanted, giving him the opportunity to sample everything. That evening he started with the escargot, followed by a caesar salad with braised Chilean sea bass for an entree. Still not satisfied, he ordered and additional entree of fillet mignon, and the infamous chocolate melting cake à la mode for dessert.

On their last cruise they had learned to ask for a table by themselves in order to avoid the chance of being seated with an elderly couple from Galveston that might make chit chat by discussing the various crops that do well in the maritime tropical climate of southern Texas. Or worse, they'd want to talk politics. Sarah needed work on her social skills, but Lief believed those kinds of conversations would only set her back in life.

After dinner, they headed back to their room. Lief gave Sarah what was to be her only instructions during that cruise.

"Sarah, you have run of the ship. Make new friends. Come back to the room whenever you want, except I want you here every evening at six so we can get to dinner on time. Mkay? Oh yeah, do whatever else you want, but don't lose your key again."

Sarah agreed to all terms before running down the stairs to her teenager club. Lief grabbed a towel and walked across the ship to the jacuzzi on the Serenity Deck, a twenty-one or older section at the aft of the ship. It was full of drunk college women on spring break, all wearing dental floss bikinis.

Surrounded by several beautiful and nearly naked women, Lief thought of Kay. He remembered that cell phone use for calls or internet while at sea was unaffordable. A break from the digital world would have been great for Lief, but it meant he wouldn't be able to talk to her for a few days. Even though it was a short disconnection, the thought didn't settle with him well. He knew the discomfort was separation anxiety and not a healthy component in a relationship. Lief accepted his predicament, knowing it would help him from falling into the co-dependency trap.

Lief did, however, need to find something to divert his constant thoughts of Kay so he thumbed through the ship's event schedule. The 8:30 karaoke in the Avant Gard Lounge did the trick. He sang a couple of songs, but spent most of his time pondering the possible correlation between obesity and incredible singing. *Throat Fat?* It didn't take long for Lief to get his fill of what would prove to be embarrassing memories for many the following day. One moment he wished he could have wiped from his memory was Ms. Moo Moo's edition of "I Touch Myself."

— ⁓

The next four days were a repeat of the first, sans karaoke. Also, the ship made two stops, one at the California island of Catalina and one at Ensenada, Mexico. Sarah and Lief briefly got off the ship at each stop. In Catalina, they visited a museum where they learned that the island was an alien hotspot. During their stop in Mexico, Sarah bought a fake silver bracelet and Lief bought a pack of Chicle gum, just to get a pesky street vending kid off his back.

One evening Sarah returned to their room wearing her father's green cap with a name tag on it that read "Moose".

"Moose, huh?"

"Yup, that's the name they gave me."

"I like it."

Truth be told, it warmed the cockles of his heart.

When they awoke on the day of debarkation, they could see the shore approaching in the distance. The sky-scrappers were visible through all of the L.A. smog. Lief made an unusual observation. *Those emission laws are actually working. Huh?* Lief and Sarah bid farewell to the twenty-four hour pizza and ice cream buffet, teen club, and the Serenity Deck jacuzzi, then exited the ship. Their four-day cruise was the perfect amount of time. If it had been any longer Lief would have missed Kay too much. He had become affected by her. But most important, the goal and reason for the cruise had been met. Sarah found comfort in her own skin while socializing with other kids her age. That helped Lief feel accomplished when they started their drive back home.

CHAPTER 6

HOMELAND

Red skies stretched across the horizon the morning as Lief and Sarah drove home from L.A. The weather reminded Lief of the saying "red skies at morning sailors take warning". It was a handy forecasting phrase that Lief had heard in military weather school in his early twenties. He took warning.

Ever since Lief's worked as a weatherman for the Navy, he no longer saw bunnies in the clouds. Instead, his appreciation for the sky's beauty was transformed into something akin to a psychoanalysis of a schizophrenic. Nonetheless, the weather guessing process became a reflex for him, and he was certain that inclement weather was on its way. According to his best guess, there would be heavy rain showers and gusty winds within the hour.

So called "bad weather" was good weather as far as Lief was concerned, because for him the more unstable it was, the better. To him it meant something was happening, it was engaging, exciting, and it provided something clear skies could not- uncertainty. He once had the honor of experiencing one of the most forceful weather phenomena possible when a tornado formed just fifteen feet from him, unleashing utter chaos. He scratched his head ever since, wondering how he survived when the tornado destroyed the town around him. The more quizzical aspect of the occasion was that he had never felt more alive.

Waiting for the weather to hit, Lief chatted at Sarah hoping she would chat back. Lief shared some useless trivia with her. He was full of little tidbits of facts, or things he chose to believe were facts. He was also known to embellish somewhat as well to make things more interesting.

"Kiddo, you want to know something cool?"

"No"

"So, I-5, Interstate 5, the road we are now on is part of the Pan-American Highway, the longest road in the world. It stretches all the way from the top of Alaska and all the way down to the Cape of Good Hope at the tip of South America. That's from the Arctic Circle and almost all the way down to Antartica. Is there an Antarctic Circle? Yeah, there's got to be, it stretches all the way down close to the Antarctic Circle. That's pretty cool huh?"

"Sure"

"Doesn't that make our drive more interesting? We are on the longest road in the world!"

Sarah may have found it fascinating like her father, but downplayed it, like Lief would have done at her age. She was him, a teenage girl version, a mini Lief. Because of that, Lief knew that getting through her teens was going to be an uphill battle. Her early adulthood wouldn't be a cake walk either. The fact that she had the disposition of an alcoholic who hadn't drank yet stood to make matters worse.

Sarah looked off the highway, into the hundreds of diagonal rows of almond trees. Aligned like stripes, they created an optical illusion as they drove past. They became one singular row remaining in the same place, the way a film becomes one moving picture after its thousands of individual pictures moved in front of the lens.

"Kay! Shoot, I forgot to call her."

"Shoot? What's this, you normally swear."

"What the fuck are you talking about, now zip. You're always talking useless facts about the road, yelling at other drivers. It gets old. Seriously, my gosh, now zip it, I'm calling Kay. I don't need any of your yip-yap in the background."

Sarah smiled as he auto-dialed Kay on the hands-free, using his hand.

"Sweetheart! You're back! I thought you'd call earlier. I started to think you sank somewhere in the Pacific."

"No, we didn't sink. It's good to hear your voice. I missed you. Oh- Just to let you know, you're on speaker. So don't get into your murderous plots or your other criminal activities. Ok?"

"Oh yeah, Sure. Hey Sarah! How are you?"

"Good"

"That's good. Did you have fun? Did you keep your father out of trouble?"

"Yeah"

"Trouble, please. Yeah, I got a little wild at the trivia competitions. I really hit the coffee before doing too much karaoke. So, how have you been?"

"Ha, Whatever. I've been good. I missed you, but I managed. Guess what?"

"What?"

"I talked to my mom the other day and I made plans to go visit her on the Jersey Shore this summer."

"Cool! How long do you plan on being there? Wait- Oh my gosh, I can't believe that I forgot to mention that I may be going on a little road trip of my own- Well with Bigfoot."

"How cool. You'll have to tell me more about that. As far as my trip, I think I'll be gone a couple weeks, maybe a little less. It depends on what kind of deals I find with the flights. Oh no! Babe, I have an important call that I've been waiting for coming in. It's my shrink, she wants to schedule me in. Can I call you back as soon as I can?"

"Of course, get your call. Talk to you soon."

Lief didn't get to his call in time which was fine by him. His thoughts returned to Kay and the timing of her trip and the loose plans around the timing of his trip. With the two so close to each other it appeared that providence was brewing something.

Sarah asked her dad to put on the Pixies, one of Lief's favorite bands.

That was a pleasant surprise for him. It reminded him of when she first developed an appreciation for sci-fi, allowing them to watch a slew of Lief's favorite movies together. She had begun to shed the one-size fits all childhood skin when she starting developing an appreciation for many of the finer creative accomplishments. It was a show of true promise as far as Lief was concerned.

There was nothing but clear skies all the way home.

"Well, it's a crapshoot."

"What's a crapshoot?"

"The weather is a crapshoot."

"Oh"

Lief was just glad he didn't tell Sarah his weather forecast. He may have lost some credibility, but Sarah had been well aware for years that he was often full of shit.

———

The sun set hours before they pulled up in their driveway. Esther the Cat was waiting for them in their parking spot, as if she knew that they would be returning right then. Lief once read about animal telepathy in a book on ESP which described scientific experiments that monitored an animal's ability to know when their owner was coming home. It proved that many animals went to the entrance of their house the second that its owner had the intention of returning home. It was those sorts of observations made the universe that much more interesting to Lief. They were all pieces placed in the grand puzzle of existence.

Lief grabbed a handful of luggage, walked past the cat without giving her any props for her show of psychic abilities, grabbed the large stack of mail from the box, and walked into the house, immediately feeling a sense of comfort from the familiar smell of his little Cotati home. As he sorted through the mail he read one of the senders aloud. It absorbed so much of his attention that he didn't notice that he was stopped in the middle of the blood stain he left on the carpet.

"Huh? Genetech Laboratories. That's the- No way!"

It was the results of his paternity test. He threw the rest of the mail aside, then used special care to open the envelope without causing any unnecessary damage. It contained pages of medical jargon and charts that made zero sense to him. He found a summation on the last page, where he scanned for a conclusive sentence that would end his twenty-one year old mystery. Thinking that he may have found it, Lief read it aloud.

"The alleged father is not excluded as the biological father of the tested child- What? Fuck this cryptic, double negative bullshit and tell me if I'm her fucking dad!"

He gave himself a second to cool down in order to regain some focus before he gave the letter another shot.

"Ok. Not excluded- What the fuck? How about you're the father or you're not the father? -Based on the testing results obtained from analyses of the DNA loci- Loci? Common, you're killing me. Blah blah, -DNA loci listed, the probability of paternity is 99.9998%. Hmm, well, that sounds pretty conclusive."

Sarah, who had collapsed on the couch the second she got in the house, listened to her father read the letter.

"What's that?"

"It's a letter that says you have an older sister."

"Cool"

Lief set the letter down on the coffee table and took a seat. He was awestruck and beside himself. Like with the call from the police, his life had once again taken a permanent turn. He was happy, but it was much more than that, it was much more than he could ever understand.

For the most part, he was uncertain about how to move forward. He didn't know if he should he call her, what to say, and how she would react if he did. He decided that thinking too far ahead was only going to cause him needless anxiety. Regardless, he couldn't resist going down that road.

For the previous month or so, a small voice inside him had been telling him that she was his daughter. Because of that, his heart had begun to make plans without giving the logical component of his brain a chance to catch up. The fact that he made plans to see her, even before he read the letter with the conclusive DNA results, served as more of a road sign on a path his heart had already embarked. Next, he needed her permission to visit her on his road trip, the trip that was manifested with her in mind.

Early the next morning, Lief called his new oldest daughter who lived in Rapid City, South Dakota. As the phone rang, he found himself in uncharted territories. It was tricky business because it was hard for him to gauge how she would react.

The call was routed to voicemail. Lief wanted to hang up, but instead he left a message.

"Good morning, or afternoon for you actually. Ah… the results are in and I am your biological father. I thought it might be appropriate that I call instead of texting. You can at least hear my voice this way. I don't want to overstep my bounds here, but I am trying to figure out what's best, as far as moving forward with things, considering the circumstances. Please let me know what you think is best. In the meanwhile, I thought I would mention that I'm going on tour with my band soon and I will be out your way. I could schedule a stop in your town along the way to meet, if you want. I dunno, I guess just let me know how you feel about, well a meet. Take your time, think it over. I'm happy with whatever you decide. Ok, well I hope you are having a good day. Talk to you soon."

For the next half-hour he beat himself up for leaving the voicemail, thinking that he may have alienated her by suggesting a visit. Then he'd tell himself that it was reasonable. The more time that passed after leaving the message, the more he went back and forth on his feelings about the call.

Sarah was due back to her mother's home that morning. While Lief drove her there, he tried to get a better read on her thoughts around having an older sister out there. He went a subtle route by asking Sarah how she felt, knowing she had an older sister, but got nowhere so he took a more direct approach.

"Kiddo, I think it's pretty exciting that we know about Leslie. What do you think?"

"I dunno"

"I dunno? That's it? She's your sister. Not only that, she has a baby, and that baby makes you an aunt and me a grandpa. Holy fuck, I'm a granpa. Not like a regular grandpa cause I didn't raise her, but technically, whatever. Anyways, most people would be happy to get this kind of news. Do you want to meet her."

"Maybe"

"Ok, well, I'll try to make that happen."

"Cool"

He wanted more than just "cool" from Sarah. He knew pressing her too hard wouldn't go anywhere though. Lief suspected that she always had more that she wanted to say, but just didn't know how. Having an older sister had to be more than just cool to her. It was possible that she was having a hard time forming absolute thoughts around it, just like her father.

A tritone sounded from Lief's phone, informing him that a text had come in. He fumbled about to find his phone while driving, picked it up, and read it. He was disappointed that it wasn't Leslie, but he was happy to see that it was Kay. It Read: "Hey Baby, Call when you can. I can't wait to see you xoxoxo:)"

"Hi! BAck i cant wait to see you neither. Talking Sadie to her Moms. Call you on the way back. XXXOOO.» Reading his own text, he saw a typo that he couldn't live with because he thought it may lower Kay's opinion of him. "Shit Im driving auto correct fucked up my test. Neither". "Fuck, that was supposed to be either not neither"

Kay didn't let him know that that she didn't care about his typo, but only to avoid texting him back while he was driving so he could keep his eye's on the road.

Lief arrived at Brena's house to drop Sarah off. He had previously decided to work on more loving communication skills while dropping off and picking her up.

"Kiddo, I had a good time with you. Call me if you need anything, I'll be around ok?"

"Ok"

Lief even gave her a big hug and forced himself to tell her he loved her. Her mumbled response was unintelligible.

Lief called Kay on his way back home.

"Hi sweetheart! When do I get to see you today?"

"Just as soon as I can get to you. So, I meet with my shrink at 2. Afterwards?"

"Ok, just don't talk to him too much and get free as soon you can. You know- That's actually perfect, I should just be finishing a set with Bigfoot beforehand. I can come to your home afterwards, around 4:30-5?"

"I'll see you then."

Lief had a hard time containing his excitement. He visualized the exact moment that he would see her.

Lief recalled a line Shakespeare borrowed from Marlowe, *"If you don't love them when you first see them then you never loved them at all"*. Although he didn't remember the exact quote, he knew they had someone like Kay in mind. Their sparks had been a fire hazard ever since they first met in dreamland. It was as if they had finally met their match. Lief was done with the same old unremarkable dating life because he felt all the women he met came in two or three versions of the same with a mixture of interchangeable parts. Kay was different and nothing about her was interchangeable with anyone he had ever met before. She was smarter than him, she was adventurous, she was beautiful, she saw Lief for who he was, and most important she was the funniest girl Lief had ever met.

In the early evening, they met all giddy, like shy, awkward kids. They decided their time would be well served by going to see a new Sci-fi movie, Transcendence, staring Johnny Depp. Lief saw a trailer for the movie and thought it was interesting, but guessed the movie would fall flat because Depp had been gradually loosing his star power for years.

Lief wasn't there for the movie, he was there for Kay. They could have done anything and he would have loved it. He suspected it was important for him to fill the boyfriend role and partake in the common dating activities.

When they got there, Lief was happy to discover only one other person in the theater. He was an elderly man who was sitting several rows up, and on the other side of the theater.

The movie started off well, then went down the tubes as Lief expected. That was when the two love birds made things interesting in the back of the theater. Kay started massaging the top of Lief's leg which led to her rubbing the inside of his thigh before her hand moved up his inseam, closer and closer to his promised land. Then it happened. She unfastened his giant belt buckle, the one with a giant «L» on it, unzipped his fly, and mad the movie worth the price of admission. Lief checked to see if the old man noticed any of their quicker movements or rustling around. He seemed unaware of what the two were doing in the back of the theater, so Lief thought he and Kay could take it a step further. He unbuttoned and unzipped her pants. She stood up and pulled them and her panties off, right there in the theater. Then, with an angelic voice she whispered into his ear.

"Reverse cowgirl?"

"My thoughts exactly"

They did their best to keep the noise down, but as Kay approached climax, she couldn't hold back. At first she tried to mute her moaning with her hand over her mouth, but as they approached climax, she let go and started screaming.

"Oh fuck, oh fuck. Fuck-fuck-fuck-fuck, oh fuck, oh fuck... FUCKKKKK!"

Lief, again looked over at the old man, who no doubt had noticed them at that point. He was gone, which meant that they needed to split too, and fast. There was no post-sex talk as Kay dressed faster than a fireman, summoned to a four alarm fire. They ran out of the emergency exit just as fast.

Back at Kay's they laid still in her bed. Kay's head rested on his chest and was hypnotized by the beat of his heart. Neither one said a word to each other, telepathic or otherwise. There were no words or thoughts that could describe where they were and what they felt.

— —

Over the following week, Sarah's outlook on life continued to improve and Kay and Lief's relationship bloomed evermore. One day while Lief was driving home from the town of Sebastopol all the cars were moving slow as per usual, but something was different. Lief had been driving behind a slow and rickety VW Westfalia for what must have been ten minutes. The VW had been driving ten miles under the speed limit the entire time. *What's going on,* he thought. *How long have I been behind this douchewad?* Lief remembered that he needed to honk at, speed around, and flip off the driver so he did, but he wondered why it took him so long to come to his senses. Lief pondered the oddity of the circumstance before a few moments passed and he figured it all out. *It's her!*

Lief called Kay.

"Hello Sweetheart."

"Hey Babe, how are you?"

"Good, What's going on?"

Kay sensed something was up.

"Nothing, Well actually, I just had to tell you something."

"Yes?»

"Hmm, well, Bigfoot and I are playing in Petaluma later. Weren't you and your friend going to be down there this afternoon?"

"Oh yeah. We were going to do coffee and a meeting. I can ask her if she'll drop me off where you're playing then I could get a ride with you afterwards."

"That actually works perfect. We'll be at the same spot on Petaluma Blvd."

"It's a plan then. Was that all?"

"Was what all?"

"You sounded like you had something else to tell me."

"Yeah, kinda."

"Well?"

Lief took a deep breath and sighed.

"Ok, I'm driving behind this slow hippy-fuckhead and it took me, like, a while to get mad at him."

"Oh my God. You're such a weirdo. So? You got mad while driving? That's so unlike you. And... You felt you needed to tell me this?"

Lief sighed again. That time Kay grew concerned that something bad had happened.

"Yes, I mean, yeah, I always get mad at cars, but this time it took me a while because my mind was elsewhere."

"Your mind was elsewhere. Hmm."

"Err, Here goes. I think I'm affected by you."

Relieved that something bad didn't happen, Kay contemplated what he could have meant. *Affected?* His strange phrase began to make sense to her and her heart fluttered.

"Affected?"

"Yeah, I mean, it just occurred to me that I've been thinking about you quite a bit and it's changing the way I do things and now I realize that you... Well- You affect me is all."

"Ok? This isn't a bad thing is it?"

"Umm, It's terrible."

That time Kay heard what he said, but knew what he meant. And it wasn't much of a surprise to her because she was already aware that they were in love. It was nice, however, for her to hear Lief tell her, in his own strange way.

"You affect me too."

"Geez, I miss you."

"Me too. I look forward to seeing you play this afternoon."

Lief could hear her smiling which, in turn, affected him all the more.

Bigfoot and Lief met in the center of Petaluma, amongst the large grey stone brick buildings from the 1800's. Bigfoot had good news for Lief.

"Dude, it's official, I can do the trip for sure. I got three weeks, maybe four off from work. I can leave as early as June."

"No way! Awesome! Let's leave as soon as possible then."

Overwhelmed with excitement about the trip, they delayed their set and sat on the nearby park bench to work through some initial details of the epic journey to be. During their chat, Lief told Bigfoot that he would commit to getting a cinema camera for sure. Bigfoot's excitement grew. Lief found it the perfect time to bring up his desire to route the trip through Rapid City, South Dakota. Once Bigfoot was onboard with including Rapid City Lief explained why he wanted to go through the town to begin with. Bigfoot was shocked.

"Dude, are you serious?"

"Yeah, it's- Well, I'm very serious."

"What the fuck? Ok, let me get this straight. You knocked someone up when you were- Hold on, let me do the math. You knocked this lady up when you were like 16-17 and then never knew about it until now?"

"No, not exactly. I knew she was pregnant and then had a kid, and I was initially told she was mine. That was before she told me that the kid wasn't mine, but only after I asked for a paternity test. I even found out this other guy was on the birth certificate. So I assumed he was the dad too. I mean, why wouldn't I? It turns out she was raised thinking he was her biological father too."

"Wait- I don't get this. How did you find out, or think to find out?"

"I dunno, it's kinda weird. It just never settled right with me. After I got sober I decided to look into it. Oh yeah, and that's not the weirdest thing. She has a baby daughter."

"What? What? You're a grandparent? Hahaha! Oh man. Dude, you are not going to hear the end of this. It's like that dude on the Povich talk show, Lief, you ARE the father."

"Whatever"

"So, what does Kay think about all of this?"

"I just got the test results back. I haven't had the chance to tell her. I kinda don't know how to approach her about it."

"Good luck with that man. What about the trip? Had you mentioned anything about the possibility, our loose plans?"

"Sort of. I was going to wait until it was more cement to tell her more though. I guess I'll tell her when I see her in a bit. She's going to come by and watch us play."

"K dude. Let's get started then. We can plan more of the trip later."

Forty-minutes into a set, Gas Station Rose, the blooming street band that was about to take on several large city's throughout the U.S., were about to wrap things up. They had been shown much gratitude and received many tips that day, but Lief was a little bummed that Kay had't shown.

"What do you think? One more?"

"Yeah, let's do one more."

As they started to play, Kay walked up and dropped a five-dollar bill into the case. Lief cut into the song to thank her.

"Hey baby! Thank you. This is our last one, it's for you. Could you get a video of us on my phone?"

"What, from over here?"

"Perfect! Ok, this is our version of Such Great Heights, you know the one from the UPS commercial."

Kay knew the song, but recalled it being a techno-ish song, so she was interested in hearing how they were going to pull it off with luggage and a guitar. She was surprised to hear them start in with a blue grass rhythm.

Kay was filled with butterflies while she filmed the two. She was on top of the world- That was until an unsettling text popped up on Lief's phone. The message was from someone named Leslie and it read, "I would love it if we met up when you are in town. Let me know when you think you'll be in my area.» Kay's heart dropped because, as she saw it, it could mean only one thing. It meant Lief was not the person she thought he was and more important- It meant he wasn't in love with her as much she was with him. For the first time, she allowed fear to guide her feelings with Lief. He noticed she stopped filming in the middle of the song. She looked disappointed before faking a smile then she looked away. Lief didn't know what was going on with her, but, for an unknown reason, his stomach dropped, taking his breath with it.

After finishing the song, they packed up in record time. They had been getting faster at breaking down the gear every time they played, but that time Lief packed quicker than usual so he could find out what was going on with Kay. He handed Bigfoot all the money in the case as they had arranged. Bigfoot was appreciative.

"Are you sure man? I'd be happy to split it with you."

"Naw, it's fine. You're going to need the money for the trip. Like I said, I've got a bit coming in."

Lief then turned to Kay, noticing how glum she was.

"Ready to go babe?"

She nodded as her mouth formed a smile, but her eyes were a hundred miles away.

"What's wrong?"

Her response was as disingenuous as her smile.

"Nothing"

Bigfoot approached the two.

"Hey, any chance you can give me a lift to my house?"

"Yeah. No problem."

Lief turned back to Kay, still puzzled, but thought it best to dig deeper into her obvious despondence later. Until then, he was going to pretend everything was ok too.

"He just lives a couple mile away. We could all go together. That way we can tell you about the busking tour we're going to do."

"Tour, huh? sounds interesting."

Kay's cause for sadness grew when she found out what Leslie meant by "when you are in town". Bigfoot sensed a growing thickness in the air inside the Tin Can. He knew Lief remembered how to get to his home, but Bigfoot needed an excuse to break the silence.

"You remember where I live, right?"

"Leslie Way, right?"

Kay perked up when she heard the name of the street.

"Yup, 3602. So Lief, you going to fill her in about the road trip?"

Kay turned to Lief.

"Yes, tell me about your road trip?"

"Yeah, well, I kinda mentioned it to you earlier on the phone, before you had to run. It wasn't for sure, but Bigfoot and I just worked it out. We're going to take the show on the road, probably circle the entire western U.S. Oh yeah- And we're going to film it too. We'll get the other buskers we run into along the way too."

"Wow, sounds fun. Are you going to see friends along the way? You mentioned your friends and family were scattered across the country."

"Yeah, I hope. It'll be a good opportunity to anyways, especially if they let us crash. We're just starting to plan though."

Lief helped Bigfoot in with his gear when they got to his house. Kay waited in the car suspecting that Lief was about to give her a smoke and mirrors version of his true intentions with the, so called, rode trip when he got back to the car. He hadn't even sat down before Kay started prodding him.

"You were about to tell me about your trip."

"Wow. Who's suddenly the eager beaver?"

Kay did not respond. Instead, she looked at him, tight lipped, like a mother expecting an explanation from a child who had just done something wrong. It became clear to Lief that she wasn't happy about the idea of his trip, or maybe something more.

"Alright? So, I've kinda been putting this together, at least in thought, for a while now. I plan on buying a real cinema camera, like a real one, the kind you'd film a movie theater movie with, so Bigfoot and I can do a loop around some of the U.S. to busk and also film others street performing as well. We're thinking about going as far east as Austin, maybe New Orleans. That's amazing isn't it?"

Kay sat quizzical, trying to formulate another, more strategic question, hoping to corner him into a response that would reveal more than he intended. She tilted her head, giving the indication that she was about to speak, but she refrained once more to give herself time to remove any heightened emotions indicative of her intentions.

"Huh. When are you guys planning on going?"

"We are going the beginning of June. We figured we'd go for about three weeks."

"Huh…"

"Huh? That's all you got? Just huh? Ok, what's bugging you sweetheart? I can tell something's wrong."

Lief continued to press her, trying to find out the cause of her unusual behavior. For some reason, the usual tethering of their minds was blocked.

"You do realize, I'll be leaving for New Jersey for over a week, probably the same time you'll be getting back, right?"

"Really? Oh shit, that's right."

Lief, a consummate problem solver, began to think of a solution.

"Well hang on. Let me think about this."

He racked his brain for something that could work. He began to tap his forehead, which meant he was close to a good idea. Kay squeezed in a few more thoughts before he had a chance to speak.

"I think I'd have a hard time going that long without seeing you, I kind of like you, you know?"

"Awww, sweetheart you know I feel the same. Just so you know, nothing is ever set in stone. I can talk to Bigfoot. It's really all kind of tentative actually."

"Really?"

"Yeah. So here's what I'm thinking. I can see what Bigfoot thinks about postponing the trip a little- Wait a minute… What if we made the trip like a coast to coast thing and timed it so I could visit you out in Jersey? Maybe around the same time you get there, so I could be back in California around the same time? What do think? I mean, do you think your family would mind if I crashed there a day or two?"

"Yeah, I suppose they'd like to meet you. You think Bigfoot would be ok with that?"

"I bet he would. Why not? I think he'd like to see the whole country. If I went to see you in Jersey, he'd get to go to New York like he's always wanted to."

"You'd really do that?"

"Yeah, totally. Do you remember when I told you that I'm affected by you?"

She outwardly acknowledged, but questioned his sincerity. He was taken aback at the lack of a response.

— —

As previously planned, Kay stayed at Lief's home that night. They sat up in his bed for a while. Kay remained distant the entire time. She kept her communication to a minimum, that was until she prepared to say something after a troubling sigh. Lief knew she was about to disclose, at least, something behind the reason for her sadness. His stomach again sank. Kay continued.

"Maybe we should slow things down until you get back."

"What? Really? This doesn't add up. Is this part of what seemed to be bugging you earlier?"

"Nothing was bugging me, I just know how it goes on the road."

"Kay, this makes no sense. I mean everything we have been communicating is contrary to this. I know this isn't how we feel."

Kay got down to the brass tax.

"Don't you think that you'll meet other ladies on the road?"

"Babe, I meet lot's of people on the road, but I don't fuck them, especially when we are, you know, affected like we are. Seriously? Think about it, I'll be on my way to see you, you're the only person that entirely consumes my attention, so nothing's going to happen."

"You promise?"

She asked him this with puppy dog eyes. Lief had never seen her so expressive. Although he wanted to console her worries, he could only think about how much he loved her.

"Lief, you hold my heart in your hands and if you hook up with anyone else, it'll fucking kill me."

"Baby, I can't tell how nice it feels to know that you are this concerned about me, but you have to know how outlandish this is. You know how I feel about you. Please, it has to be something else. What's gotten into you?"

Kay moved as if to speak, then bit her lip.

"Kay, Please, spit it out. What is it?"

"Who's Leslie?"

"Oh geeze, I get it now. You saw the text?"

"Well you asked me to hold your phone. So, you're planning on visiting her on your trip?"

"Yes, she's actually the biggest reason for my trip. I was trying to find an excuse to be in her area in South Dakota."

"What?"

"Kay, Leslie is my twenty-one year old daughter. Remember the remote possibility that I mentioned, the one about me possibly having another daughter? The one that grew up thinking someone else was her father because his name was on the birth certificate? Ah, let's see, the one with the certifiably crazy mother? Ring any bells?"

"Yeah, but you said you didn't know if she was yours."

Her jealous look began to fade.

"I got the genetics test back. She is my daughter. I just found out when I got back from the cruise. It was late when I opened the letter and we've been so busy, I just hadn't had a chance to tell you yet, at least time to tell you in detail, including the plans to see her and how all of this played into my loose planning of the trip. I was actually just going to tell you about her and my plans to see her. I was waiting to find out what was wrong with you first."

Kay didn't know how to respond. Her jealousy turned into relief followed by confusion. Matters of the heart were as difficult for her to decipher as they were for Lief.

"Oh yeah. This is weird. Ready for something really crazy?"

"Sure, there's not much I can think of that would surprise me more than I already am."

"She's a mother of a newborn, which, biologically makes me a grandparent. A fucking grandparent. What do you think about that? You're dating a granpa."

"Wow! I- I don't know? I'm happy for you? It's kind of big. A little too big to, to understand all of my thoughts right now. A grandpa? Now- No, that is pretty weird. You're just a little too young for that."

"Yeah. I know, I know, fair enough, the grandpa thing is too weird, but it is what it is. Ew, I hate that saying. Anyways, when the genetics test came back I had a lot of thinking to do. I decided it was the next right thing to do, to see her. It's what my heart told me to do before I knew for sure, on paper for sure. It's weird- I know. Anyways, She just got back to me. I had been waiting to see how she felt about me going out there."

"Wait- You mentioned this trip to me before you ever knew that she was your daughter, right? You couldn't have been planning to see her then."

"Yeah, that's what I meant about my heart urging me before I knew. Ok, let me put it this way. You know how we kind of know each others thoughts sometimes?"

"Yeah..."

"So, open your mind to the idea of what's behind all of that. Ok. Now, I didn't know for sure, but I had been sort of receiving- That's the best way I can put it, I was receiving this feeling that she was mine. Then my feelings began looking for a way to see her. It was like I was beside myself watching the trip fall into place."

"I can see how that would happen. Is Bigfoot cool with you guys going all the way up there?"

"Yeah, he didn't care. We're playing music on the road and filming a fucking movie. Who would care much about taking it though Rapid City? Besides, he gets it."

"Alright. Wait- How are you even going to be able to afford all of this, not working for so long?"

"Let me back up for just a second. I forgot to mention that years ago, Bigfoot and I briefly, and I mean briefly, talked about setting up some gigs on the road, so I knew that this trip, whatever you want to call it, was there. The thing that brought all of it back up for me, was my contact with Leslie which led to the test. She was the catalyst, and no, I didn't tell Bigfoot that. I didn't need to because, like I said, we talked about something remotely similar before. It's just that now everything seems so aligned for me because of her, you know? As far as affording the trip, I have a bit of money saved up and I'll have some coming in, due to me being a disabled vet and all. And, this is very therapeutic for me. Yeah, I'll barely be scraping by, but I know it's the right thing to do."

"Huh, it does all seem to fit together, especially now with you talking about visiting me too."

Kay began to sound excited herself, although she was holding back so she could ease her way back from her initial anger, to appear more level headed. Lief knew what she was doing and found it endearing.

"Baby, I can't wait to see you there and meet your family. This is it, I know with every fiber of my being that this is currently my correct path. I have no way of knowing exactly what's going to happen out there. The cool thing about knowing what the right thing to do is that, it doesn't matter so much what the result is."

Kay leaned into Lief and gave him a tight bear hug. The kiss that followed would have inspired Klempt. Lief was in the moment to the fullest, but he did not want to let the excitement rock him too far into some sort of mania. Instead, he held her while thanking the universe for making life so interesting and fulfilling. *Thank you for bringing me my love.*

Kay responded aloud.

"It brought my love to me too."

CHAPTER 7

-GEAR: ✔

One step at a time preparations for the trip fell into place. Pushing back the trip ended up working out better for everyone. It meant that Bigfoot had two more weeks to save money and Lief had enough time to take Sarah to her last two scheduled counseling appointments. During that time, Kay was able to sell her mom on having Lief stay with them a few days on the shore. It became apparent that the entity who controlled all of the levers and knobs of existence, the one that made gravity pull, the one who made light stretch, and the one that transmitted risky ideas everywhere, was the same one that was in complete support of the epic journey to be.

Lief spent the next month educating himself on everything he would need to film, in his mind, a full length feature movie that would be worthy of, at least, a film festival entry. All of the equipment that he'd need to get, would be contingent on the camera he purchased. That made the camera the first priority. All he knew was that the local electronics store's 1080p high definition camera was not going to cut it for the big screen. He was dreaming much bigger, but after doing a days worth of research for the right camera, he found himself buried in technical jargon and endless possibilities. Lief turned to the advice of a trusted musician/ filmmaker friend of his from Pittsburgh, PA, a man strangely named Oreo.

Oreo was the genius son of a black father who was a cryptologist for the CIA. His white mother was a professor of music theory. Most reasonable humans would be correct in assuming that his parents did not give him the name Oreo. It was a name given to him by a racist schoolyard bully, who was trying to insult him. In a move that baffled the bully, Oreo embraced the name, then insisted everyone else refer to him by it as well. Lief believed Oreo chose the name for his own entertainment purposes. People had a hard time knowing how to react to a mulatto man who introduced himself as Oreo. During any given introduction, people would pause when they heard his name, then they'd fumble before addressing him thereafter. Oreo always followed any introduction with a mischievous smile that concealed something akin to an inside joke. He was all about entertainment, which is what led to Lief and Oreo becoming friends to begin with.

Years back, Oreo discovered a youtube video of Lief playing an original folk song called «The Ballad of El Guapo and the Invisible swordsman.» Lief wrote the song about a nonexistent prequel to the comedy "Three Amigos" which starred a few of the greatest comedic minds of all time: Steve Martin, Chevy Chase, and Martin Short. Lief, however, did eventually go on to write screenplay to accompany the song. Oreo was ecstatic to discover that there was another person out there who appreciated the movie as much as he did. Oreo was midway through a documentary about the intriguing cult culture left in the wake of "Three Amigos". Oreo's documentary included all sorts of background information on the making of the movie. The grand finale for the documentary was a filming of a "Three Amigos" themed concert that Oreo had put together. It was a modern rock tribute to the score from the original film, along with a few extra surprises. One of those surprises was Lief's performance of his song "The Ballad of El Guapo and the Invisible Swordsman." They remained friends ever since they met at the show.

Needless to say, Oreo had a lot more experience with film-making and film-making equipment. Oreo was happy to offer Lief technical consultation on his audio/visual needs. He suggested Lief go with the

Black Magic Cinema Camera. It was a rather groundbreaking camera that consumed a large amount of data in each shoot. Oreo explained that the biggest benefit of the camera was the amount of clarity one could get out of a small, zoomed in section of the original frame. That created a million more options in the editing process. The camera cost a lot less that many other cinema cameras of its caliber, but it would still set Lief back three-thousand dollars.

Lief trusted Oreo's expertise and ordered the Black Magic Camera along with a list of just about everything else that Oreo recommended. It was a long list that included a brand new beefy computer, an expensive Hollywood standard editing program, tons of external storage, a slew of audio components, several lenses, tripods, a camera bag, all kinds of cables and cords, a transfer dock, a camera rig with a matte box, a counter weight for the rig, extra back-up batteries, and a partridge and a pear tree. Lief had never imagined how much tech went into making a film, let alone the cost.

Lief became versed in film equipment by the time all of his purchases were made. He had larger things in mind with all the film gear though. He was thinking about future projects, making the purchase all the more sensible. All along the purchasing process, Lief kept thinking of the second screenplay that he wrote and how it would be a perfect film project to follow with all the new film gear. He had a good felling that he may never return to the mundane employment of others. The more Lief committed his money and his time to his new way of a life, the more free he felt from the constraints of his past nominal existence.

━ ⌒

As synchronicity would have it, Bigfoot and Lief's plotted course brought them through Pittsburgh around the same time Oreo had planned a grand opening party for his music Studio, Studio Oreo. Learning that Lief would be in his area, Oreo postponed his party by an entire week, just so that Lief and Bigfoot could attend. Lief was honored by his gesture, so he made the time of the party the half way point of the trip. That meant that Lief needed to do all of his planning around getting enough playing, filming, and traveling done prior to arriving at the studio party. That also meant that visiting Kay on the Jersey Shore would need to take place beforehand in order to avoid backtracking.

Looking at the first half of the planned trip, Lief and Bigfoot knew there was little time for additional sightseeing outside of the areas that they had planned to perform. After Pittsburgh, they could relax and move at whatever pace they pleased. Lief was an experienced traveler so he knew the degree of difficulty the first half of the trip would present, but he also knew he could pull it off. It remained uncertain how well Bigfoot would be able to handle the intensity of the trip though. Bigfoot had not been on the road much before. He hadn't even been to Los Angeles, one of the biggest cities in his own state of residence. Lief considered how that might affect the trip, but he put that unknown in a bag with one hundred other uncertain elements of the trip, trusting that events would continue to fall his way.

⁓

Video gear accumulated at Lief's home with ninety-nine percent being online orders because in store purchases proved to be twice as expensive. He tracked the transit of each piece as they shipped off. A camera rig, microphones, cables, lenses, storage cards, tripods, and even Lief's gigantic new fully loaded desktop Mac computer arrived at his home over the next week till there was just one missing piece. That was his Black Magic Cinema Camera that he began to affectionately refer to as The Black Mamba. It was supposed to arrive first which made Lief start to worry a lot.

The seller of Black Mamba listed it as being shipped from northern Washington, but Lief later found out that it was being sent from Southern Canada. The story was that the camera was hung up at customs because the shipper filled out the declaration form incorrectly. After Lief sent ten emails to the seller that fetched no response, it became clear that he had just been suckered by a scam artist in Canada, and for three-thousand dollars.

Lief didn't have the money to hire an international lawyer to sue the Canadian seller and he didn't have enough money to buy another camera. Even if he found one he could afford, it wouldn't arrive on time. In the end, Lief came to terms with the reality that there would either be no movie, or there would a miracle taking place. Continued worry wasn't going to do him any good so he did his best to let go of his fears around the situation.

The next time Kay visited Lief's home, he couldn't wait to show her his growing pile of film equipment. He wanted her to know how serious he was about making a real film and that it was not all just some pipe dream to him. More than anything, he wanted her to know that he had the gumption to follow his dreams. She let him know that she received his message loud and clear.

"Wow, baby how do you know what all of this stuff does?"

"Ha! Good question. Not a fucking clue. I'm hoping it'll all be intuitive enough for me to figure out though."

"Hey- What's that? Is that a caterpillar on your lip?"

"What, my stubble? I just forgot to shave the mustache area of my face today. Naw- I'm growing a mustache for the trip."

"Good luck with that. Not to change the subject, but would you mind fucking me real quick?"

Kay words were pure and spoken with the voice of an angel, a glorious porn angel.

The miracle that Lief hadn't expected to happen, happened the next day in the form of an email from the camera seller. In the email, he apologized for all of the delays and proved the camera was on its way by providing a tracking number that verified his sincerity. Not only did the seller lay Lief's fears to rest, he refunded Lief fifty-bucks for the delay. Lief's faith was restored in humanity. Lief tracked the camera all along its journey to his home so that he'd be ready with a small camera to film himself receiving the package. To Lief, buying all the gear was part of the journey and he wanted all of it on film.

It was a Saturday and the package was due at 2pm. Lief figured he had plenty of time to go for a short bike ride to his usual coffee shop to get his usual black coffee. It was the same coffee shop that he'd meet most of his dates at, but it was also the only coffee shop with hot baristas in the area. He questioned his behavior in continuing to view the attractive women at that shop because he knew his girlfriend was much prettier than anyone he'd see there. He came to two possible conclusions: one was that pretty girls were nicer because they were used to being treated nicer, and the second conclusion was that, after nearly thirty years of trying to perfect the art of the chase, he had become programed to position himself nearest to the most suitable game.

As fate would have it, when Lief arrived at the pretty girl coffee shop, he discovered that an all male crew was working that morning. Lief referred to that kind of scenario as a «sausage fest». Sans hotties, and only because he rode his bike all the way there, he went ahead and ordered a coffee. Before he had a chance to sit down, he saw that he had a voice mail after missing a call.

His laid back Saturday morning turned into one of sheer panic. The delivery company informed him that he missed the delivery of a package that required a signature. He also learned that his package would not be redelivered for three days due to the Memorial Day weekend. That was not going to work for him because he needed as much time as possible to learn how to operate the camera before the trip. In a hail Marry attempt, Lief called the delivery company and requested a redelivery, in exchange for a cold beverage and doughnuts for the driver.

The company got ahold of the driver, presented the offer, and a deal was struck. Lief bought the doughnuts on the way home. The driver arrived the exact second Lief returned home, so he didn't get to film the delivery, but he was able to exchange the junk food for a heavy package from Canada.

Lief used his smaller camera to capture the unveiling of the crown jewel of his filming arsenal. The filming could also provide proof for any legal action, in case the camera was not in there. With care he opened the large box with a kitchen knife. There were several components in the box that Lief had expected as part of the camera package. Lief described the function of each item as he unloaded, then placed them each of them on the kitchen table. Underneath the all of the peripheral items, he was left with one large box, large enough to house the camera. Opening the box, he found more styrofoam packing peanuts around another box that was glossy and black. By that point, he felt like he was playing with a Russian Matryoshka doll, but the camera was indeed cradled in the center. All he had left to do was make sure everything worked. That would prove to be a much, much more difficult task that he had assumed it would be, although educational nonetheless.

Everything needed for the trip had arrived, allowing Lief to direct all of his attention to Sarah and Kay before his departure. Sarah and Lief filled the daylight with quality time each day before he left, while Kay and Lief alternated stays at each other's home every night. In his time with Sarah, Lief saw that much of the pain she was suffering receded as she worked through her problems with her many therapists.

In his remaining days with Kay, they watched movies, drank too much coffee, and took long walks, but the majority of their time was spent in the bedroom where they became more acquainted in one week than most couples would in a year. Their level of connection in the bedroom was beyond measure. Several times during the act of making love to Kay, Lief felt that they had been transported to a surreal world that glowed neon. Those moments were a meeting of mind, body, and soul. As extraterrestrial and magnificent those encounters were, Lief suspected that the more spiritual aspects of their incredible sex may have been due to the sex swing and black lighting that they'd often use on their more adventurous evenings.

The day before leaving, Lief placed roof racks and a large aerodynamic travel box on top of the Tin Can. That evening he put his larger items that he would not need to access as often on top of the car. It was no easy task getting into that cargo box which was nearly eight feet off the ground. Next, he loaded the expensive gear in the cab, making sure to leave adequate space for Bigfoot's things. It was late when he finished packing, but he wasted no time getting into bed with Kay when he was done.

As Lief and Kay fell asleep, they looked forward into the coming days, knowing that they'd miss each other, but they were both also confident that their connection would grow stronger. On all the previous nights that they slept next to each other, they'd spoon for just a few minutes before getting too warm and separating. That last night was different. They held each other till morning, sharing the same body temperature, feelings, dreams, waking thoughts, and bad breath.

Lief left the room to brush his teeth and get dressed. He put on his American flag vest, a pair of red jeans, and his belt with its oversized, obnoxious belt buckle. Before he left, Lief returned to his love laying in his bed. With care he placed his hands on the sides of her beautiful face and kissed her plump smiling lips then he walked out of the room. Kay never took her eyes off of him as he departed. She heard the sound of the Tin Can starting up and driving away. When she could no longer hear the car in the distance, she spoke to herself aloud.

"I'll see you in Dirty Jersey."

Lief was already driving south on Highway 101 when he replied.

"See you there."

Bigfoot was waiting in his driveway with all of his baggage and luggage/drum gear when Lief arrived. Bigfoot was wearing the same American flag vest as him. It was a gift from Lief who was happy to see that Bigfoot liked it enough to wear it on the first day of the trip.

"Dude! Right on, you go the memo. Haha!"

"Fuck yeah I got the memo."

Bigfoot bid farewell to his nurturing parents before boarding the Tin Can. A ceremonious high five was shared and the two new filmmakers hit the road.

"Check it out, I have the camera outside of the rig right now so that we can film while we drive. That's if you feel so inclined. It's right behind me. Do you mind, at least, getting the Golden Gate when we get there?

"Totally. Good idea!"

Driving through San Francisco was not the quickest way to complete the first leg of the trip. Milage-wise, it may have been shorter, but traffic-wise, it put them back at least an hour. Lief had never filmed a real movie before, but there was no doubt that he knew how to tell a story. Their story was to begin with a misfit street band called Gas Station Rose driving the Tin Can over the foggy San Francisco bay by way of the Golden Gate Bridge, and then through the famous city with its unmistakable pointy skyline, obsolete trolley cars, victorians stacked like dominos, and its thousands of lost tourists driving around like idiots.

CHAPTER 8

CAR LEGS

Vanda, as identified by her employee name tag, proved to be one of a few good omens at the onset of their voyage. She was the drive through coffee barista at their first coffee stop, an hour into the trip. She expedited their order of two black coffees to the drive up window in no time flat. Lief and Bigfoot couldn't help but notice her bewitching gaze before and after collecting the payment. Then they noticed her firm breasts, nestled in her black lace bra, exposed through the crook of her loose v-neck shirt when she bent over further than necessary while handing them their coffees. Vanda didn't try to adjust her posture one bit when she saw where their eyes were pointing. Instead, she paused and looked at her chest to see how much she had revealed before she looked back up with an even more seductive look. Leaning back behind the drive through window frame, she rolled a lock of her hair around her index finger, before she asked the provocative paradoxical question that Lief would never be equipped to answer with accuracy.

"Is there anything else I can do for you?"

"No thank you. We're good."

Bigfoot wasn't quite as ready to drive away and leave Vanda in the rear view mirror forever. He interjected in an attempt to hang onto to their moment with Vanda for just a while longer.

"Yes, actually, could we get some unrefined sugar?"

"Of course, let me grab some for you."

Lief could see her adjusting her shirt once she turned around to get the sugar. Lief assumed she was covering up and he began to feel like a pervert for ogling. That was until she returned with her shirt pulled down further. She took twice as much time leaning out of her window, not to mention that she bent over further that time as well. It became apparent that she adjusted much more than her shirt. Lief and Bigfoot were frozen and rendered powerless when they saw the upper edges of her light brown aureolas, peaking out above the lace of her lowered bra. When Lief was able to break his eye's upward from her tractor beams, he saw that she was biting her lip. Seeing as how they weren't going to be moving in with her and that they had a movie to film, they tipped her well and got back on the road.

Even though the Tin Can and Vanda parted ways, the moment would remain as a mental picture forever etched in the forefront of Lief's mind, reminding him that the universe would always be mysterious and gracious when he went with it's flow. It also reminded him to always go to that same coffee shop when he was in the area.

Lief wasn't sure if Vanda's nip slip was a figment of his imagination or not. He consulted with Bigfoot for conformation.

"Bigfoot, did you just see what I saw?"

"Uh-huh"

When Lief turned to look at him, he couldn't help but notice an unmistakable pitched tent under the furry lining of Bigfoot's suit. Lief's face soured before he recoiled, turning his neck towards the road so quickly that he pinched a nerve in his neck.

"Ouch! Fuck that hurt."

"What happened?"

"Nothing, it's an- It's an old neck strain thing."

Loaded on coffee with San Francisco behind them, the road seemed like deja vu to Lief, who had recently driven to L.A. with Sarah. The next step was to find the perfect music to set the tone for their mammoth undertaking of a trip. Although Lief was eleven years Bigfoot's elder, the two respected each other's musical taste. There was not much space between them in that regard. If there was, they probably wouldn't have been friends.

They put in a War on Drugs CD after Bigfoot gave a small history of the band which included praise for Kurt Vile's guitar contributions. Their music was a knock off of the early eighties Don Henley, Dire Straits, and Bruce Springsteen's more lively rock songs. Lief was quick to appreciate the band, because he already loved the style. He had fond memories of listening to that genre back in the early eighties. He wondered how Bigfoot's appreciation for the sound might have differed from his due to Bigfoot having no real time exposure to its origin. All he knew was its reincarnation. It didn't matter. It was the right music at the right time for them at that moment.

They drove out of the East Bay area and into the rolling windmill hills infested with speed traps. Lief was confident that so long as he stayed around his cushion of ten miles over the speed limit, he wouldn't be getting any tickets due to his veterans license plates. He had a theory that the plates served as a sort of cloaking device. His rationale was that most cops are republicans as are most vets. So, while driving through liberal states like California, he believed he'd receive their sympathy with close calls. He wasn't going to push it either. He pressed forward at seventy-seven miles per hour.

Lief was going to be doing the majority of the driving on the trip because Bigfoot had a limited suspension on his drivers license, which meant he could only drive to and from work. They rationalized the trip being a form of work because they were gigging, albeit on the street, but they were filming a movie, which could make them money. The "limited" part of his license wasn't going to matter much once they left the state anyway, or so they hoped.

The issue with Bigfoot's driving privileges played an interesting and complicated role in his and Lief's friendship dynamic. A year and a half prior Bigfoot had borrowed Lief's car and totaled it after he passed out on heroine while driving. Much water had passed under that bridge and Lief had forgiven Bigfoot enough to get back to playing music with him. Because both of them had the disease of addiction/alcoholism their continued friendship was a result of Bigfoot's efforts to get and stay clean and sober and Lief's understanding. Lief was supportive of his recovery. He believed Bigfoot could stay sober just as he had, but Lief had no doubt that their friendship would only last as long as they both remained drug and alcohol free.

After making a pitstop in Bakersfield, about and hour outside of L.A., the two discussed travel logistics in an effort to make their money go further. Lief had enough for his portion of gas, food, possible lodging, and then a couple thousand for emergencies and any other gear that may be needed if something essential broke. Although Lief did not have much accessible money, it was more than he had ever had during any previous road trip. Bigfoot's budget was much tighter. Lief had already agreed to pay for two thirds of the gas in order to make the trip feasible for Bigfoot. Splitting the cost for a room or any other unexpected cost impacted Bigfoot's wallet much more than Lief's. It was for that reason Lief had promised they would employ every money saving trick that he had learned in his many travels. He explained several tricks for low cost traveling.

"What is it that you spend the most money on day to day? Gas and food, maybe caffeine right?"

"Yeah, probably"

"Ok, so not much we can do about the gas, except just parking the car and walking to wherever we want to go in the cities. As far as food goes, we can always get cheap bulk items and even free samples at any Costco that we go by, and they are everywhere, not to mention gas is also cheapest there. As far as caffeine, well, that'll be free. I brought us more than enough loose leaf tea and travel brewing containers. Those are in the bag behind you. I also took the liberty of stocking up on as much bulk dry snacky-snack type stuff too, also in the bag. Pretty good so far, huh?"

Lief looked proud when he paused to soak in praise from Bigfoot, but he didn't get much more than an unenthusiastic response.

"Sounds pretty good. Did you have more?"

"Yes, yes I do. So, we are traveling and we are under a slightly different set of circumstances, like we'll be needing to find a place to sleep every night, right?"

Lief paused, but it was obvious that Bigfoot wanted Lief to speed things up.

"Ok. Yes, and?"

"Hold your horses, I'm getting to that. Ok, as we previously planned, we have the five or six planned stops, where we know we are going to stay for free with my family and friends. We have camp gear and we spotted a few feasible national parks along the way. Then, as a last resort, we figured we could always rearrange things in here and try to sleep in the car-"

"Yes, yes, and yes. Is that it?"

"No, no, and no. It is not. When I was married to Cat I was entitled to the her employee room rate at the Marriott. Believe it or not, it was only about forty a night to stay."

"Yeah, but you don't still get that, right? You guys got divorced like five years ago."

"Correct young Padoan, but you still have much to learn. They provided me with a document, the room rate form, several years ago when I was still married. All I'd have to do was make a reservation with the employee code and then show them the room rate form that expired 90 days after it was issued."

"Again, that was five years ago."

"What I realized a couple of years ago is that because they sent it to me in an email, in an editable, strange kind of PDF format, I could simply just type in a new date. Then a two-fifty night rate in a luxurious suite becomes forty."

Leif smugly raised his eyebrows and smiled, utterly impressed with his ingenuity.

"No way! Wait. What if they check with her?"

"Then we're fucked. It's only happened once, in Pittsburgh. That sucked. They called her to double check, and she got all mad, I got embarrassed, and the hotel then gave me the option to pay the full amount or leave. I left and stayed in a crappy hotel and was eaten by bed bugs. We'll do fine though. Remember, we have the car as a last resort."

"Oh, Ok. I'm down."

"Shit! There is one more thing. Unfortunately, I just realized that the forms I have on me are out of date, and only checked for the more expensive, "Friends & Family". I put it on my list to doctor that one up, but I now realize that I forgot. After I got busted trying to use an outdated spouse rate in Pittsburgh she was pissed, but still several months later she gave me a form that I actually qualified for, the "Freinds" rate. That's the one I found."

"Dude, you're killing me. Do we get the discount or not?"

"Chillll. Short story long, it turned out that the discount was only half off, still really fucking expensive. So what I've done since then, is I still made the reservation under the "spouse rate". They've never noticed at the counter, so I've still only had to pay the forty. Cool, huh?"

"If you can edit the form why don't you just fix it so we don't have to take the chance."

"Good question. The answer is…"

Bigfoot took a deep breath and sighed.

"The answer is that I don't have the program to do it. It's on my desktop at home."

Bigfoot had no reaction. He was done with the tutorial. He leaned his head against the window and pretended to sleep.

The pair arrived in Los Angeles, where the first order of business was to visit Lief's grandmother. It was a rare treat that he'd have the chance to see her twice in the same year.

The plan was to visit his grandma briefly before meeting up with Greta, a high school classmate of Lief's that lived in greater L.A. area. Greta's house was a potential place to stay the night for free. Lief's grandmother's house was out of the question because she never had house guests stay the night. If Greta's place didn't work out the plan was to use Lief's travel skills and stay at the Marriott. Although they'd get an amazing rate, they didn't want to use that option too often, especially that early in their trip considering the risk.

Greta was beyond beautiful, at least in her youth. Lief could never place what it was that made her stand out as much as she did in his mind. He had always been attracted to Latin women, but never had yearned for a woman for that fact alone. Her hourglass figure was a ten, and she had a pleasant disposition. Her happiness was plain to see because her persistent smile rested nicely just beneath her high cheek bones and right between two painfully cute dimples.

When Lief was in school with Greta, he had to keep his thoughts about her to himself because she was his buddy's girl. He was left to admire from afar, but the taboo nature of his thoughts towards her enhanced the attraction.

Before setting out on the first leg of the journey to LA, Lief had to double check his motives with her. He asked himself why he conversed with her prior to the trip, knowing he risked making decisions that could affect his relationship with Kay. It occurred to him that his digital mingling may have been a result of a subconscious desire to conquer a regret he had in not revealing his attraction to her during his unambitious youth. Maybe if he learned, in person, that she was attracted to him as well, he could lay the fantasy to rest. Still, he knew it was a dangerous game.

Tracing his steps back to their most recent acquaintance, he remembered that it was Greta who had initiated contact after finding him on Facebook. That was only a day or two before he ran into Kay at the park. Those things in mind, he could have ended the negative judgment he was having of of himself, but still it felt like it was either a trap or a test. But his conflict continued to confuse him to no end. It proved to be great fodder for self searching, self searching that would be necessary for him to have a long lasting relationship with Kay. He needed to see how Kay, the incredible new variable, changed his previous ways.

At last, Lief remembered that he was never privy to the big picture which also meant that he had no way to control it. His best results came from following his feelings on most decisions, but that also meant he had to maintain his contact with them. He also learned, though often forgot, that any perceived problem he'd encounter was fear driven. An awkward statement from someone he heard speaking at an AA meeting years before entered his mind. In between his ears, in a spirited and hopped up southern holy roller voice, Lief heard *"Jesus, take this one."* Although Lief cringed, he casted semantics aside because he got the gist. Still, he doubted Jesus would help him not fuck Greta. He employed the help of the creator of all creation, the ever expanding universe and everything in it, including Jesus. Lief felt covered.

CHAPTER 9

GANGLAND

Exit seventeen led the Tin Can off of Interstate 5, just past the heart of Los Angeles and into Bellflower. Bigfoot was in a world he had never seen before. He grew nervous looking at the razor tinsel topped concrete walls adorned in gang graffiti. To Lief, the grit of L.A. was a familiar briar patch that held a certain charm, but not enough charm to ever live there again.

Eleven minutes later they pulled into Bellflower Grandma's driveway. She heard them pull up and she went out front to greet them. She smiled and waived her hands in excitement as she approached the car. Inside, Bellflower Grandma offered them the quintessential grandmotherly offerings of cookies and milk. Lief didn't feel great about having to tell her that he was gluten and lactose-free, but he also needed to keep his diet in tact while he traveled. All of his clothes were tight enough as they were. Declining his grandmother's thoughtfulness was one of those asshole maneuvers that Lief was infamous for.

Lief showed Bigfoot his grandmother's upright piano in her living room.

"Dude, this is the first instrument I ever played."

"That's cool."

Understandably, Bigfoot wasn't interested in the piano or visiting Lief's Grandma. He was biding his time until they could leave. He grew frustrated when Lief suddenly ran out of the house to grab the camera from the car because it signaled that their stay would be extended for whatever Lief had in mind.

Lief's grandma was the person who introduced him to playing music and therefore useful in explaining his love for music. In that sense, she was one of the several reasons that Lief was filming the movie to begin with. He showed her the camera.

"This is what we'll be using to film musicians playing out on the street around the entire country, starting right here in L.A."

"Lief, that sure looks like a fancy camera you got there."

"Thanks. We're actually going to Venice beach today to film street musicians down there. They are always interesting musicians down there."

"Well, you're right about that. There are lots of interesting people down there."

"Hey grandma, would you mind playing us a quick tune so I can try to figure out how well the sound is picked up on this?"

"Oh, I guess I can try to play you something. Don't laugh though. It's been a while since I've played for anyone."

The two agreed not to laugh as she thumbed through the sheet music stowed in the piano bench.

"This should work. This is modern music for me."

She started in with a Barry Manilow tune from the 70's. While she played, Lief was transported to another time in his youth when his grandmother had played the same song for him. The familiar smell of the furniture, the sight of the antique television next to the piano, and the weathered ameba shaped patterns in the golden shag carpet reinforced his memory. He was again the happy child in wonderment witnessing the magic delivered by the hands of his grandmother and her musical wizardry. He sang aloud to the chorus of "I Can't Smile Without You".

Lief hadn't been at Grandma's long before he received a text from Greta, letting him know where he could meet her.

"Grandma, I'm sorry, but I gotta run. We have to meet my friend and see if we're able to stay at her home tonight."

Goodbyes where exchanged all around.

"Nice to meet you, Bigfoot. And Lief, come here, give your grandma a hug. I love you. Thanks for stopping by to visit this old lady."

She finished saying her goodbyes then handed each of them forty dollars and told them to get something nice from her. As Lief suspected, his pleas for her to take the money back got him nowhere. His grandma then added one last thing before they parted.

"I almost forgot- Are you two planning on going through the Blue Ridge or Smokey Mountains? I can't remember which is which, they may be the same."

"I'm not sure. Where are they?"

"I think they are on the east side of Tennessee, around the Carolinas. I don't quite remember. I'm sure you two brought a map and could find them if you are close. Anyway, your uncle Gary went through them recently and told me all about them. He couldn't stop talking about how beautiful that they were. He said they were not to be missed if you are ever in that area."

"That sounds pretty hard to pass up Gramma. I know we'll be close, so I'll do my best to hit them."

After a few more hugs and goodbyes they drove away, waiving until they were out of the driveway and half way down the street. Lief, again, wondered if that would be his final goodbye with her. Lief also wondered if his thinking on the matter was morbid or outside the norm.

—◦ ◦—

Upon further review, the text Lief received from Greta mentioned that she did not have much time to visit which ruled out a possible stay at her place. It was looking like they were going to have to pay for a stay at the Marriott. That also meant that they were going to be testing the discount experiment on day one of the trip. If they failed, meaning if Lief's ex was called, they would not be able to use his counterfeit discount form for the remainder of the trip.

They found a nearby Marriott in the downtown L.A. area and Greta agreed to meet them there. That was when Lief realized that if he was caught using a fake form Greta would be showing up to the scene of a possible crime and that would be embarrassing. Another aspect and dilemma presented was that Greta was a cop. Things could get sticky.

Lief's nerves were tense when he approached the twenty-something attendant at the hotel's front desk. It had been decided that it would be best if Lief checked in alone. He was wearing a gold ascot tucked into his American flag vest and had no shirt on underneath it. To throw in an additional distraction, he carried his fancy camera in with him. He hoped it would make the person checking him in wonder more about who he was and what he was doing there, rather than reviewing the discount form.

After the scripted hospitable greeting, the attendant looked Lief up and down. For all she was concerned he was the real deal, and possibly a celebrity. Not only did his slew of distractions make the young lady so nervous that she paid no attention to the form, but he distracted her from the fact that a celebrity wouldn't need a discount to begin with.

Lief secured the deal with a swipe of his credit card for his forty-dollar night stay that included breakfast, access to the jacuzzi, and the fitness center. They even gave him an upgrade on his room to meet his suspected celebrity standards.

Lief went to a door at the other end of the hotel and waived for Bigfoot who ran across the parking lot with a few of their bags.

"Did it work?"

"Yup"

They were amazed at the sheer size of the place, never-mind the full kitchen and lavish decor. Greta texted from the front desk before they had a chance to settle into the room. Lief asked her to meet them at the room because he wanted to avoid any unnecessary questions at the front. Lief was quick to check his appearance and fix his hair before Greta reached the room. He was taken aback when he saw her because she wasn't the smoking hot Latina woman that he knew in his youth, she was the enhanced, mature version. She had the same beautiful smile with dimples, but her body had entirely settled into perfection. Lief found himself nervous and unworthy to greet her, but forced words, trying to sound casual.

"Greta! So good to see you! Wow, you look great!"

She didn't shy away from expressing her thoughts about Lief's looks either.

"Hey there, long time no see. Fancy room! You look good too. I mean- You look really good."

Bigfoot was introduced. She was cordial and didn't react to his unfashionable furry exterior as every other person on the planet had when meeting him for the first time. She was focused on Lief, rambling as if she were nervous as well. Lief continued to look her up and down, studying her alluring figure as she spoke. She was an anomaly to Lief because she defied all of mid age's entropy, fat from salted caramel mocha's, and mainstream motherly fashion. While she continued to speak, he stole a peak at her upgraded breasts. He put forth a consorted effort to keep his inappropriate thoughts to himself. *Hot fucking Damn! Boob job. That's it.* His effort to not make an ass out of himself crumbled when he next spoke.

"Oh my gosh Greta, You're a GILF!"

He froze, realizing the negative implications of what he had just said. For a moment he was saved because she didn't get what he said. She didn't stop trying to figure out what he meant though, placing each letter next to the other in her mind. It wasn't adding up. Lief had dug himself into a hole. Because Greta's great looks were not accompanied by much of any discernible deductive reasoning skills, it was clear he needed to incriminate himself by explaining what he meant.

"You know, GILF, G-I-L-F"

"G-I-L-F... Huh? G-I-L-F? I don't get it.

Bigfoot, embarrassed for Lief, rubbed his brow, lowered his head, and pivoted away from the conversation at hand. Lief tried to brake it down for her.

"You know, like MILF, but for a grandmother."

"MILF? What's a MILF?"

"Ah- It's not important. I mean it's something people say when a mother is attractive. That's all."

Lief prayed that he could leave it at that without any further explanation, but that was not the case."

"Got it, thank you… But, the way you said it, it was like an acronym."

Lief froze and turned red in the face. Bigfoot internally cringed as if he observed someone smacking their finger with a hammer. He interjected because he could no longer bear the discomfort.

"MILF, mother I'd like to fuck, but with a G for grandmother, turning it into grandmother I'd like to fuck."

"Yes, but it's not that I want to fuck you- Shit! I mean when I say it, It's not like I'm saying I want to fuck you. It's just a saying, like I said."

Greta finally understood, and noticed his embarrassment by the growing flushness of his cheeks. In order to avoid the eminent awkwardness that would follow throughout the rest of their visit she let him off the hook.

"Oh yeah, Okay. Yeah, thank you, I guess? Wait- Aren't you a recent grandparent too?"

"Yeah, that's right. So weird."

"That makes you a GILF then too, right? We are the first two grandparents the class of '93 produced."

Lief seized the opportunity to move past the exchange and suggested that they move on.

"So, what do you guys think about going to Venice Beach? Maybe getting a snack on the way there?"

Without any objections, they did exactly that.

When they arrived at the beach they were shocked at the twenty-dollar fee for parking. On top of that, they had to circle the parking lot for twenty minutes before they found a spot. At least it was close to the beach path.

L.A. was the largest defiance of nature that Lief could think of, but its microcosm called Venice Beach, with its run of the mill freaks, athlete freaks, homeless freaks, and every freak in-between, sent its strangeness soaring. It was the perfect place to film their first street music set for the movie.

Lief and Bigfoot lugged their band gear on two luggage carts. Greta helped out, carrying some film gear as well. They walked along the walkway above the beach, searching for the perfect spot to set up. The cool ocean breeze fanned the heat rising from the sand. Large silicone and scantily clad breasts rested on top of hundreds of sunbathing women across the beach. Meat-heads scavenged like crabs in the sand for the slightest signaled interest from the equally superficial ladies. Above the beach, roller skaters and beach cruising bicyclists weaved between the slower moving looky-loos such as Lief and Bigfoot. The pungent aroma of weed billowed out of the medical marijuana dispensaries along the windy walkway. Holding his breath to the best of his ability, Lief observed the various forms of recreational activities. Pickup basketball players oscillated between hoops in the chained linked courts. Behind them were sets of still rings that looked like pendulums in their A-frames. Then there was the outdoor Muscle Beach Gym, where iron was pumped by the body builders, juxtaposed by the lanky skaters, that skated snake lines between the bowls and vert ramps at the adjacent skate park.

Venice Beach was laid out the way Lief had always seen it depicted in the movies, all except for there being absolutely no street musicians. There was not a single one out that day. Without other musicians to film, they set up to film themselves in an open area next to the skate park, between several palms that encircled a flat plain of crab grass. Greta used her cell phone to film them unloading their luggage carts, opening the cases, placing mic stands, and stretching chords every which way between all of the equipment. All of the looky-loos momentarily diverted their attention from the oiled tits, asses, and steroid bumps on the beach. They narrowed their focus towards the two man band, then straight past them and onto the giant cinema camera that said "Yeah, that's right. They're that good."

Towering cumulous clouds moved in on the beach, bringing with them an ominous shadow of death. They swallowed the sky and blotched out the sun. Cobalt lumps of mammatus formed on the belly of the darkest clouds. Lief knew the beautiful shapes were a sign of mother natures's deception because a rage lurked above in the large clouds that had grown into thunderclouds. Although something felt wrong, he continued preparing for their set, knowing it would be a short one.

A crowd gathered around their patch of grass. Lief pressed record on the camera and ran behind the mic in front of his luggage amp. Bigfoot sat at the throne of his luggage drum kit, swirling his sticks and waiting for his queue. Lief addressed the crowd.

"We're Gas Station Rose and we have a few songs for you. This first one is a song about how you never really die, if you believe in Star Wars. Ready? One, two-"

The two started in with an original song called Old Ben. The drums set into the motion of a train carrying the distorted rhythm of the electric guitar pumping like steam from the engine. Then Lief used his words.

"Old Ben I know why you weren't afraid, to go away, cause you never went away- You're here to stay- That's very tricky of you Old Ben.
You could have cut him in two- Couldn't you? But
you did what you had to do- Old Ben.
Gone, but not for long- You reappeared, illuminated- Arrested
our fears. Now your strength can not be broken.
Old Ben please show us the way, cause we
barely escaped the dark yesterday.
It's closing in. We're running thin.
Please help us. You're our only hope- Old Ben.
Gone, but not for long. You reappeared, illuminated- Arrested our
fears. Now your strength can not be broken. Now your strength
can not be broken. Now your strength can not be broken!
Old Ben, I know why you weren't afraid...
Not afraid...
Old Ben, I know why you weren't afraid...
Not afraid...

Old Ben, I know why you weren't afraid…
Not afraid…

Three minutes after starting, the small crowd became a large crowd. They showed their appreciation with hoots, hollers, whistling, and clapping. Never before had the band received such a resounding response. Lief knew the song and execution were good, but inside he knew that most of the enthusiasm was due to the large camera pointing at them. It told those walking by that the musicians were worthy of praise. Lief learned an important lesson about the sizzle of the spotlight. He always knew that a large number of the population needed to be told which performers to appreciate, and that when they were pointed in the right, or wrong direction they'd appreciate the act. It that case the direction of the camera was more useful that what it filmed. Although the quality of the songs and their performance took a back seat to the ballyhoo, the attention felt nice and he'd take it till sundown.

Lief set his guitar down to double check on the camera. When he looked at the screen display face, he was frozen with terror.

"Memory card full! WHAT? That's four-hundred and eighty Gigs! It can't be full! Fuck! Fuck! FUCK!"

Just then, lightning came crashing down onto the beach behind them, no more than four-hundred feet away from them. Waves of screams rippled from the spot of impact.

"They're hit! It hit them!"

"Move! Move! Move! RUN!"

"Someone call 911!"

Everyone on the beach ran for cover. Greta called emergency services, giving the dispatcher her credentials with hopes of expediting a response. The on site life guards rushed to the scene on ATV's, while nearby paramedics followed. Bigfoot blurted out an inappropriate comment that couldn't have been timed any worse.

"I hope they believed in Star Wars."

"Dude. That's wrong. That's the craziest shit I've ever seen. Let's get! Just pack up! Get out of here and find some cover quick. This is all fucking fucked! Fuck!"

They haphazardly piled everything on the luggage carts and found cover in a nearby Taqueria at the top of the beach. They were lucky to get a seat at the soon to be filled restaurant before other beach dwellers were turned away at the door. Most of the employees at the taqueria huddled at the front window of the restaurant, trying to get a peek at the commotion. Needless to say, it took a while to order food. They all ordered various taco plates once the server came around.

Lief was quiet and stuck in his head about what had just transpired. He was just as thrown off about the lightning strike as he was about the film storage situation. Both situations competed for his attention, not allowing him to form solid thoughts on either.

"What the fuck just happen? Seriously? I can't believe those people were hit and I can't believe we're out of storage- Already!"

Greta disapproved Lief's comments.

"Lief, How in the hell can you even be thinking about your film at this point?"

"It's kind of like thinking of how we were hungry, then went to get something to eat. Well, while also trying not to get struck by lightning ourselves. I dunno, I guess I'm confused."

Bigfoot interjected.

"We're all understandably wound up at this point. Let's just eat these lightly salted fresh tortilla chips and be grateful that Mexican people invented taco's and brought them to California."

Greta was quick to set Bigfoot straight.

"Excuse me. Taco's and Mexican's were here before- You know what, that's just- Whatever, hand me the salsa please."

The tacos arrived and all was quiet outside of the soccer game blaring from the flatscreen at the bar. Lief returned to his thoughts about the camera storage, the considerable investment that he had in all of the equipment, and how his failure stood to ruin his credibility. Then Lief took a broader look at the situation, running through the ramifications of everything at play. It was then that he saw his worries were inconsequential compared to the real reason he was on the road. He was going to see Leslie and nothing else mattered. His seeing her, no matter how the visit played out, would bring him something that money, social status, and a successful movie never could. Meeting Leslie just might help heal the gaping hole in his heart.

Greta took notice of Lief's distance and tried to get more of his attention. Pretending to get a better line of site on the soccer game above the bar, she leaned over in front of him, exposing more and more of her amazing breasts. It was the second time that day that he was blessed with an exclusive viewing of that often shrouded female art form, some of God's best handiwork in his opinion. They were a kryptonite for him and had steered him to danger many times. The boob situation grew deadly when she turned from the tv to eye-fuck Lief. Bigfoot saw what was going on and made small talk.

"These tacos are hitting the spot."

The other two did not respond, nor did they notice that Bigfoot was still there. He slapped some cash on the table and joined the gawking crowd in front of the restaurant.

As soon as Bigfoot left, Greta placed her hand on Lief's knee, making it clear that she would give him what he longed for in his youth. He fought his thoughts, but his better judgement was wedged deep between her breasts and was suffocating. He thought of Kay and how she worried about the women he would meet on the road and there he was, day one, fucked. Greta kept at him.

"You know, I actually don't have to go home too early tonight. I mean how often do you meet an old friend? Hey- I know! What are your plans later? I only live about twenty-minutes away."

"Well, I do have to figure out what to do about this memory problem or else, or else I'm fucked."

"Fucked huh? Yeah, I can see how that's important, would it be helpful if you used the internet at my house? You know, to research and whatnot?"

The thought ruminated in Lief's head for a moment. He knew he'd be screwed for sure if he went there. She was looking better with each second that passed. He imagined how she would feel. His heart raced as did his thoughts. *I've never done a cop before.* Then Lief thought about the last embrace he had with Kay. Not a second later, he felt the cosmic chain linking him to Kay, even with Greta's hand running circles on Lief's thigh.

Lief had a lot of opportunities throughout his life to have amazing sex with beautiful women all over the world. His sexual history was a large part of his identity. He knew he was as close as one could get to being a sex addict, if he hadn't already crossed that line. With his love still in mind, he imagined her luscious lips, her spellbinding gaze, and that amazing place between her legs that was all for him if he just recognized, for once in his life, that it was his turn to keep the girl instead of throwing her away out of fear of loosing her at some later point.

Lief recalled the Zen philosophy that the cup is already broken, the idea that it had a beginning, a middle, and an inevitable end. The trick was to understand its transitory nature, and appreciate it the same, in totality, in every stage of its life cycle. Kay was no cup, but he saw that he was on the verge of jumping from the beginning of her to the beginning of someone else in order to deny an uneventful middle and dreaded end. He saw that, for years, he had been attempting to live in a relationship's perpetual beginning phase by breaking it before it got old, before he'd look for the next. A thought, one he never heard before, blew like a blow horn in the busy chatter of his mind. *The cup is too good to break!* Lief repeated the thought out loud.

"The cup is too good to break."

Greta tilted her head, perplexed at his strange words.

"Haha! What? No one is asking you to break the cup- Weirdo."

"Sorry, I was lost in a thought."

"Funny man. Let's get going. You can just follow me there."

Lief looked at Greta's tits again, then spoke to them.

"Yeah, you know, they have internet at the hotel too, and I need to skype with Kay later."

"Kay? Who's Kay?"

"Kay's my girlfriend that I told you about when we were messaging on Facebook. Remember I said her and I had just started dating? You know a while back?"

Lief knew Greta remembered, but was hoping he could use a little side action. Lief found himself more resolute than ever. Greta backtracked and turned on a dime.

"Oh, yeah, I wasn't sure if you were still together. That's nice. Yeah. You know, I should get going. I just realized there is probably going to be some traffic."

"You're right. Traffic is a bitch down here. It was nice to see you."

Lief reviewed the check.

"Can we split this into thirds?"

He had never asked a woman pay for anything. In his mind, he was sticking it to her. She hadn't done anything wrong, but he almost did. Greta forked over her share, they stood and shared a cordial hug before she split quicker than OJ fleeing a murder scene. Lief sat back down to soak in the satisfaction and gratitude he was experiencing. He recognized that he could have never walked through such dangerous grounds remaining unscathed on his own volition. He passed a one night stand for the ages and walked right through a one way door into a new frontier where he had one less unmanageable shortcoming.

The next morning Lief awoke with some serious morning wood and a possible solution for the storage problem.

"Bigfoot! Dude! We can commandeer a Mac at a Best Buy and transfer the data to the four terabyte drive, then wipe the card to free up more room!"

"Cool, I'm going to sleep some more first."

"Sorry. I woke up a little manic after dreaming about how to salvage this movie."

Bigfoot yawned while trying to respond. He was tired, but the yawning stuck out in Lief's mind as a disinterest.

"Ok, that's great. So are we going to stop at Best Buy after every hour of filming?"

"I thought of that, and no. We can film the majority of the shots in Pro Res, using much less storage, and then do the money shots in RAW format. That said, we'll need a couple stops to transfer data."

"Yeah, That should actually work."

Bigfoot knew that his desire to sleep would never match Lief's enthusiasm, so he rolled out of bed.

"Wow! You're up early. Must be the free breakfast."

Bigfoot gave him the bird.

The breakfast selection was much larger than either of them guessed. There were five chaffing dishes filled with everything that one could possibly order from any Denny's diner. There were waffle machines, eggs, bacon and sausage, breakfast cereals, various toast and bagels, and an assortment of yogurt. There were four different types of fruit juices. The breakfast alone would have cost the same as their night's stay. Lief did not pass up the opportunity to point it all out to Bigfoot.

"Our stay has been well worth the low cost, wouldn't you say?"

"Uh, yeah. I can get used to this."

Lief scoured through the feast, finding an adequate amount of gluten free dishes. Bigfoot found Bigfoot food as well.

They ate like truckers then rushed to the freeway in the direction of Best Buy which was only five miles away. Then they sat in forty-five minutes of traffic before reaching their exit.

The Best Buy security were perplexed as Lief entered the store with his arms full of electronics that he carried to the Mac section at the back of the store, bypassing the returns desk. Lief found an appropriate Macbook to "demo".

Bigfoot's demeanor made it clear that he was put-off by Lief's urgency to create more space on the storage card. To Bigfoot, Lief was hogging their road time. Lief inquired into Bigfoot's discontent.

"Dude, are you alright?"

"Not really. I didn't think we'd be taking so much time doing this in L.A. I mean it's not like we are even seeing the cool stuff down here. You know, I just don't want to spend my time in an electronics store."

"Really? Seriously? We're filming a movie. I've spent a pretty penny on this. If we don't do this the movie is finished. We can't film anything without doing this. I thought you'd understand. Look, I can do this on my own. It should only take a half-hour or so. Why don't you take off? Take the car even. Go check out the area."

"Dude, we're in Compton. I'll get shot. I'll just get my board and skate around the lot. It's cool. Call me when you're ready to go."

Lief understood his point of view. Bigfoot had never seen L.A. and he probably wanted to do the whole tourist thing. Lief had overlooked that aspect when they planned the trip. He also knew that things never went as planned on the road, but the unexpected events had a way of working themselves out, often in the most interesting ways. Bigfoot didn't understand that yet, but he was getting his first lesson on the matter.

The interchange between the two was revealing for Lief. He saw a side of Bigfoot that he hadn't seen before. He learned just how much of an entitled, unhappy child Bigfoot was. Lief just hoped he wouldn't have to pacify him the rest of the trip.

Lief brushed off Bigfoot's attitude and proceeded to work on his possible filming solution. He ran the memory card through its dock that was connected to the computer, which pumped the data out of the full card, and into the external hard drive that was connected to the other end of the computer. He got everything set just before a sales associate approached. The sales guy inquired about all the wires and equipment strewn across the table. Lief explained that if that particular computer could preform what he needed to do, that he was going to buy it. He went further to explain that the only way he could know that it worked, was to try it there. The sales person gave him all the time and room he needed. Lief started the transfer and the progress bar showed that the process would take fifteen-minutes.

Lief walked around the area looking at all the computer gadgets. When he returned to the computer, he rechecked the progress bar, thinking there would be a minute or two left and that he'd be able to pack up and leave. That was not the case. For whatever reason the process extended itself and the progress bar indicated that the transfer was going to take two and a half hours. Lief's head dropped because he knew that he was going to have to buy the computer to run the data transfer process in the car while they drove. It turned out he wasn't lying to the salesperson about buying the computer after all. Lief walked out of the store with a brand new Mac Book and nearly half of his budget wiped away.

CHAPTER 10

EAST

Setting out to find the rest of America, there was a feeling of optimism in the air. After breaking free from more Los Angeles traffic, they took a left turn and drove east. It was strange for Lief to think that they'd be headed in the same direction for a week.

They drove through the dessert on their way to Lake Havasu, Arizona. Stopping in Lake Havasu was a slight departure from a more direct route that they could have used to cut through the rest of the southwest. But it was a necessary stop for Lief because he'd never forgive himself for being so close to Havasu without visiting the Garcia's, his surrogate family from his youth.

After Bigfoot's sour disposition in L.A., Lief realized that he might have caught flack for visiting family rather than staying at a more noteworthy place in Arizona if they had not agreed on it before the trip. The fact that Lief had to consider Bigfoot's mood on the matter on the second day of the trip was not a good sign.

Casting all negative thinking aside, Lief gave Bigfoot the background on how he became family with the Garcia's. He explained that him and Raul Garcia were best friends ever since they met in Sunday school when there were eight. He explained how Raul and him were the most rambunctious of all the other Sunday school kids. Their mischief was not limited to, but included pulling the fire alarm during church on several occasions, blocking walkways with pianos, turning a fire extinguisher into a pipe to smoke pot, making inappropriate sounds on the Church's PA system, and becoming too aquatinted with the young ladies in the congregation. The last transgression got Lief kicked out of the church when he was a teenager.

Lief's behavior also didn't go well with his own family who sent him off to juvenile hall whenever he acted out. That was always after beating him pretty good. Fortunate for Lief, Ricardo and Juanita, Raul's parent's, where more tolerant than Lief's family and they took him in after one of his worse beatings. The Garcia's treated him much better that his own family ever had, and that they loved him as one of their own.

Twenty-five years prior the entire Garcia family, including Lief, took a trip to Lake Havasu all the way from Sacramento. Ricardo and Juanita were prospecting for a retirement property which they found and moved to several years later.

The data transfer was working like a charm in the car. The full memory card's dock and external hard drive were both plugged into a power converter that was plugged into the cigarette charger.

"Dude- Why don't cars just have plugs, like the regular kind with the two- You know, things? Why the cigarette lighter plug? I mean it's in a hundred percent of the cars, but most people don't even smoke."

"I dunno. Why do you care?"

"It just doesn't make any sense is all."

Lief further explored the thought about how a cigarette lighter in a car must have originated as a luxury feature, maybe an upgrade for the savvy and sophisticated smoker. His thoughts drifted into the possible history of the car cigarette lighter, because his obsessive mind couldn't let it go. Most of the time his OCD was a curse, but every once in a while it uncovered a few amazing discoveries, deeper meaning, and awareness of underlying patterns in the world. Lief also felt it better to be stuck in a thought than to be running between a thousand of them. It was one or the other with him.

Eventually, Lief's demanding curiosity led him to Google for an answer to the mystery on his phone. He found a good explanation, then read his findings out loud.

"Cigarette lighter receptacles in an automobiles were originally created to light cigarettes, but became the standard DC powers supply for automotive portable accessories... blah, blah, blah, ...disadvantaged due to it's relative size and carries a low current... Well that's pretty fucking stupid."

"Lief, do you mind just keeping your eye's on the road? I'll drive if you want."

"Sure, let's switch at the next gas station."

Bigfoot made it clear he needed to use the restroom when he ripped a nostril searing fart.

"Wheew-eee! That's off the tip off the ol' log."

"Gross!"

Lief rolled down all four windows and opened the sunroof.

"Dude, could't you wait? I told you I'm stopping at the next gas station."

"Ha! You said gas station."

"There's something seriously wrong with you."

"Speaking of that, I've always wondered what the meaning is behind the band name. What was the inspiration behind Gas Station Rose?"

"It wasn't a reference to farts."

"Really?"

"Yeah, Really. Ok, I'll tell you if you don't blow up the car again."

"I'll do my best, but we are going to be in this car a long time."

"Whatever. So, I was living in Reno with this stripper for two years. We really got along too, even though she was a stripper. It wasn't a problem because we trusted each other. Anyways, one time I bought one of those trashy fake roses at a gas station- You know, the silk ones?"

"Yeah?"

"It was a joke, and she appreciated it cause we had the same humor. For the rest of our relationship I'd always get her those. Well, every once in a while when I'd stop for gas."

"Huh, so I finally know the mystery behind our band name. I feel so much more complete."

"That's not all actually. So, I got to thinking that some people out there got them as a real romantic sentiment, not as a romantic joke. I thought about that, and I realized that it was just as thoughtful and sweet as any other romantic gesture actually. Trashy, but still from the heart. Like- Sweetheart, this is for you. While I was filling her up today, I thought of you, so I picked this up. I told Josie, the stripper-"

"Wait- don't tell me that was her stripper name."

"No. It was Tessa or Tess. Shit- You know, I don't remember. Anyways, I told her that I thought it would make a good band name and she totally agreed. One day I looked up Gas Station Rose to see if it was already taken by another band and the first thing that came up was about crack pipes. It turns out crackheads go into gas stations to buy those roses, maybe it's the miniature kind, but they'd get them along with Brillo pads to make pipes. They'd use the glass part from the bottom of the rose or something. So I said- Perfect! That's going to be my next band name."

"Ah man, that's cool. That's what you call a double entendre. But, I always pictured it was like a lady named Rose who worked at an old style gas station."

"That works too. That would make it a triple entendre."

— ⁓

A new situation presented itself when they pulled into a Chevron. Lief found pump #11. Lief twisted the key to turn the car off, but stopped himself in the act quickly when he came to his senses.

"Oh shit! I have to keep the car running. If I stop it it'll kill the power to the data transfer and there's an hour left for the process. I'd have to start all over!"

In that scenario, it was possible that a new file would be created alongside the old file, taking up twice as much space in the hard drive. The gas was going to have to be pumped with the car running. Lief figured if big rigs could do it so could he. Lief stayed on the look out for gas station attendants. He also made a mental note to time the data transfers according to the fuel range in the future. Bigfoot relieved his bowels, they got hot water for tea, checked their emails, and then got back onto the road.

Lief initiated a conversation from the left field.

"So, I was thinking about keeping politics out of the film. It seems like we have a great opportunity to rise above the programed rhetoric. What do you think?"

Bigfoot pointed to his closed mouth then tried to mumble a response, because for some reason he couldn't open his mouth.

"So, you can't talk right now?"

Bigfoot confirmed with a nod.

"Because?"

Bigfoot, again, pointed to his mouth and mumbled.

"Ok, hmm. Well then, I had a couple thoughts about dining throughout the day, and please, you don't need to say anything. I'll just kind of run them all by you and I'll just assume you agree if you don't have anything to say about it. I was thinking that you could pick up the tab for our next two meals today."

Bigfoot shook his head in opposition and mumbled before Lief return to his shenanigans.

"Yeah? Wow, you really like that idea? Great! Also I thought maybe you can get us coffee, say, for the rest of the week?"

Bigfoot shrugged him off.

"Wow! That's great man. You're a good friend. I'm going to put some music on. You like Maroon Five right? Oh shit! I just thought of a new name for them- Monistat Five. Ha! What do you think? Oh, whatever, I'll just put some fresh Monistat Five on."

That time Bigfoot nearly convulsed while mumbling. He slapped Lief's hand away from the control knob on the dash board. Bigfoot swallowed whatever was in his mouth and yelled.

"No fucking way man!"

Leif burst into laughter.

"What the hell did you have in your mouth?"

"It's my medicine to block my receptors."

"Your receptors?"

"Yeah, so that I won't crave, you know, any drugs. Alright, so I won't crave heroine. The further I get away from using it, the easier it is not to pick up. I'm tapering off the pills too, but I have to let them kind of absorb under my tongue for about five minutes. The funny thing is that whenever I take them at home, my brother pulls the same shit you just did."

"I have to tell you, I'm a little surprised so many people are using heroine these days. It's like they never heard what happened in the 60's and 70's. I was always too scared to touch it. I knew I'd be hooked the first time I tried it. It's basically like the most addictive drug ever. And man- I have done just about everything, but not heroine. Oh yeah, and the whole needle thing- Fuck that! I'd never touch a needle for anything. Freaks the shit out of me."

"Have you ever used Vicodin?"

"Yeah, I got hella addicted too, especially once I learned how well it went with beer."

"It's an opiate, just like heroine, just a smaller dose. When Oxys came out, it was like the trumped up version of Vicodin. Doctors were giving it to everyone so everyone had that in their medicine cabinets. It was so powerful, people kept going back for more until the doctors cut them off. Then they'd go find another doctor and complain about a new ailment of some kind and get a new prescription. Kids would take it from their parents cabinets and became addicted too. They were the ones that found out that they could easily crush and snort it. People even figured out how to smoke it."

"Snort it? Smoke it?"

"Yeah, there was some big legal thing about that too. I mean everyone knew it was super addictive, but when the FDA found out it was basically tailored as a street drug by the pharmaceutical company, it really put the breaks down. There was this big epidemic on the streets and the company was seriously fined. They had to remanufacture it as- What do they call it? Tamper resistant? Yeah, that's it- Tamper resistant. They cracked down on it in all sorts of ways and then even the doctors stopped prescribing it as much because it had become a liability. Now you got the supply lower on the street, but people still needed their fix. They turned to heroine which was even better. It flooded the streets and that's what happened to me."

Bigfoot's explanation was all syntax with no semantics. It was as if he was repeating verbiage from a drug counselor. Lief could see that he had no solid connection to the dangers it posed him. Lief was already suspect of Bigfoot's recovery plan. He thought it was what was considered by many recovered addicts, the easier softer way. He came to believe it would fail until he hit a sufficient bottom, that or found a miserable death. Lief had observed the later of the two scenarios to be the most common outcome.

"Hey, do you mind if we listen to the radio for a bit?"

"Totally. That'd be nice. I actually had forgotten that there were still radio stations. It's been so long since I listened."

The radio background noise screeched and hissed between chipper traditional Mexican music before Bigfoot zeroed into an english speaking station that was in the middle of a commercial break. It turned out to be a news station. Bigfoot almost moved passed it, but he stopped when heard the announcer say something about Venice Beach. Their ears perked up to listen to what was a news report about the lightning strike on the prior day, the one that happened right after the camera ran out of memory. Lief's anxiety spiked as he fumbled words around, trying to form a quick response.

"Dude! There! There! That's- That's the- The fucking strike man. Keep it there! That's the one! We were there!"

The report went on to explain that there was one fatality and another thirteen left injured, seven of them hospitalized. There was a father and daughter among the injured. The father had been teaching his daughter how to surf when one of two bolts hit the water near them, knocking them both unconscious. The daughter came to first and found her father floating. Her quick response saved her father's life.

As the reporter continued to provide more details of the story, Lief's mind connected to the stark reality that it could have been him and Bigfoot that were hit. He thought of how strange it was that they were there and he wondered if there was any sort of deeper meaning to it all. He then found himself experiencing it all through the eyes of the reported daughter. He felt her urgency to jump into action after seeing her father in the water, to do whatever she could to save her father not knowing if he was alive. Lief felt her confusion, denial, and anger after she dragged him onto the beach. He intuitively knew she felt no sadness in that moment. Sadness would come later, when all hope was lost. Lief found himself back in his living room, having just received the call from the police about Sarah. He was struck with clarity while witnessing the fragility of life. But that time, from a different angle, he was able to see much, much more. Lief realized that life's fragility was the essence of existence that gave way to its sweetness. He saw that it was life's uncertainty that was the root of sensation, and in that, Lief may have found the true strength of all creation.

Lief solidified his thoughts with something more tangible. He thought of the violin. He knew that the finest sounding violins were a result of the quality of the wood, the precise shape of its arches, and most important and more to the point, its looseness and fragility that remained. Violins are not fastened with the strength of nails or screws, instead they're assembled with the smallest amount of glue to allow a warmer reverberation that could better carry sounds of sadness, triumph, and serenity. Lief saw how life, like the violin, would not be as rich if it were made unbreakable. Rather, it was life's uncertainty that provided the richest tones in the music worth living for.

Thoughts of the lightning strike pained him by reminding him of Sarah's suicide attempt, but after the opportunity for more introspection he moved closer to accepting its totality. Bigfoot also found a deepness to the lightning experience which he expressed at the end of the news report.

"Cool shit man."

He resumed a search for a more lively station with actual music.

While fuzzy white noise continued between stations, Lief thought of a song and began to hum it before quietly singing the words.

"...mmm mm mm heard you laughing. mm mmm that I heard you-"

At that moment Bigfoot tuned into a radio station that was playing the exact song that Lief was already singing on cue, word for word.

Mouth agape, Bigfoot was beside himself.

"What the fuck dude?"

"I dunno. Sometimes that just happens. Actually, it happens a lot lately. I'll think of someone and they'll call right then or I decide I need a coffee and then, right there, where I'm driving, there's a coffee shop. It always happens then I'll notice that it's 11:11 or 1:11. And that's, that's the weird thing. Actually, the other day I thought I haven't seen bees around in a while- You know, wondering if there was still a bee problem. And then, just then, a swarm of them flew at me from around the corner. Weird shit, huh?"

Bigfoot looked at him almost as if he didn't know him anymore.

"Very..."

"Come to think of it, I actually haven't told anyone this before, but I think Kay and I kinda speak to each other..."

"You speak to each other, and?"

"Yeah, sorry. Well, I think we speak to each other, sort of telepathically. I mean, just sometimes. I guess I kinda don't think it's a good idea to tell too many people about that. You know, cause they'll think I'm schizophrenic or something.

"No, I buy it man. What do you think it is we do when we play? When we're playing all synced up- It's definitely telepathy. Bands have to, especially the good ones. I think while playing we reach this higher consciousness where we are past verbal language. We get in this creative space and we just know. Like I know know when you're going to wrap up a song early, even without you tipping the neck of your guitar. I'll be looking down, but I'll know where you're going with things.

"Cool. Yeah, you're right. Weird. Look- 111 miles to go to Lake Havasu. Yeah, that's a little weird too. Kinda auspicious. That's one of my favorite words by the way."

CHAPTER 11

THE BRIDGE

The two travelers reached Havasu and stopped at Love's gas station to refill and stretch their legs while Lief tried to get ahold of Raul. Bigfoot made a keen observation on the way out of the air conditioned Tin Can.

"Lake Havasu is fucking hot."

Lief agreed.

"Fucking A"

They continued the fuck banter into the station store.

"How's your fucking day going Lief?"

"Fair to fucking midland. It's fucking fair to midland."

It was Lief's turn to get gas. While he was standing in the long line to pay, he studied the cashier, a wiry and wrinkled sixty something year old caucasian man who was an obvious smoker due to his hack and smoke tarnished fingers. Because the line was long, Lief created a possible back story for Gill, a fitting, but imagined name. Making up stories about people was the second phase of people watching for Lief.

According to Lief's imagination, Gill used to work as a bartender at a dive bar in a town with a cooler climate, maybe St. Louis, but he decided to escape the humidity of the Mississippi and move to drier climate to help ease the discomfort of his tuberculosis. He hated leaving his home behind, even though the neighborhood had fallen into hard times. Knowing he would never return, he robbed the corner crack dealer at gunpoint. His name was Snowball. Gill, then fled with the loot in his piss yellow piece of shit Yugo. He drove to the Mississippi, had one last look at his beloved river, and then threw his sawed-off musket into the old swimming hole he used in his youth. Then he drove his shitty Yugoslavian manufactured car towards the Greyhound station. It backfired along the way before breaking down a few blocks short of the station. He bought a ticket for Death Valley, but did not reach his destination because on a stop he found Lake Havasu to be perfect. The bus driver informed him that he could not give him a refund for the unused portion of his ticket much to Gill's chagrin. A sixty-three year time span brought him from birth to Havasu where he stood in a cloud of dust, holding all of his Earthly possessions, most of which were in a green US Navy seabag. He had a carton of unfiltered Pal Mall's, a few shirts, an eight-ball, seventy-three dollars in his wallet, some lint in his pocket, and memories of his sweet Mississippi in mind. When the dust cleared, Gill saw a newfangled gas station with a sign in the window that read: WE'RE HIRING.

Lief had been too caught up in his imagination that he forgot that he was in the "real" world. Lief flinched when Gill tried to get his attention.

"Young man, how can I help you?"

"I'd like some fucking gas please. Number Three."

He replayed what he had just said to Gill, who had no knowledge of his friendly fuck banter with Bigfoot. Gill gave Lief some serious stink eye, then swiped his card through the reader.

"Go ahead and filler' the fuck up."

Gill was a quick study.

"Ha! Will fucking do, thank you sir."

Lief smiled on the way out.

Lief called Raul while he filled the tank. The two had been communicating over Facebook for a while, but it had been ages since they heard each other's voice. Lief was calling because he had been unable to reach Raul for a few days. Lief wasn't worried though because

Raul knew what day he'd be arriving. Raul didn't pick up so Lief left him a voicemail.

When Bigfoot returned to the car, Lief suggested they find an air conditioned coffee shop to wait in until they heard from Raul. Lief was surprised to find no resistance from Bigfoot.

— —

They chatted it up at a Starbucks near, what looked like, the center of town. Bigfoot was back to his typical, non-irritated self though Lief began to wonder who the real Bigfoot was. In California he always got along with Bigfoot, but they only saw each other for a couple hours a week, if that. It was possible that Bigfoot was a dick during the rest of his week. Due to their prolonged close proximity on the trip, Lief was certain he would get to know Bigfoot more than he'd ever care to, long before the trip's end.

Bigfoot wanted to know more about the Garcia's. It was possible his interest was more of an attempt to get to know Lief better.

"So Lief, you said you guys met in church?"

"Yup"

"Wait- You were a mormon when you were a kid, right?"

"That's right"

"I always forget that. It's so fucking weird, I just can't see it. Is he still Mormon?"

"Yeah. Him and his family are pretty devout."

Lief explained that Raul and him found different paths as they grew up. Lief had been disfellowshipped from the church when he was sixteen. Raul continued on in the church and even served a mission to help recruit for the Mormons when he was nineteen. Although Lief had found another calling for himself in life, he was proud of his friend's religious accomplishments.

As soon as Bigfoot and Lief finished their drinks, Raul returned Lief's call.

"Lief! Man, it's good to hear your voice."

"You too. It's been too long."

"I'm stoked you're in town. Sorry I didn't catch your call earlier, Maria's in labor right now."

"Wait- What? You mean like right now, right now?"

"Yeah, she's right here. Maria, say hi, it's Lief. She's just pushing right now- What baby, not you Lief- Ok, she says hi."

"Hi Maria. Raul, hey man I'll leave you be. I was just letting you know I'm here. Maybe you can call me later when you have a chance."

"Oh yeah, no problem. Look, I've arranged for you to stay with my parents tonight, they're really looking forward to seeing you. I'll text you their number. Cool?"

"Yeah, but only when you have a chance."

"I'll text it right away. Oh, I almost forgot, I pulled a permit for you to play at the stage at the base of the bridge. If anyone bothers you, the police, whoever, just give them my name."

"No way! But, wait- How'd you do all of that?"

"I'm the city clerk. Just park in the lot on the west side of the bridge. You can go there whenever you want. I'll get over there in an hour or so."

"Thanks Raul. That's so cool. Congrats on the addition to your family. See you soon."

They saw ten signs leading them to the bridge that was two miles away. It made sense to Lief that the otherwise modest town would want everyone to see the landmark. At one point the town must have spent all their money on purchasing the bridge, along with shipping it over. Considering how the town was set up, it would be impossible for anyone, including Bigfoot, to visit Lake Havasu without admiring the magnificent relic and appreciating of the painstaking task of relocating the famous bridge to the small desert city. Bigfoot proved him wrong.

"Wow, cool bridge. It looks Medieval. Why would such a small town build such a nice bridge, in the middle of the dessert?"

"You're fucking with me right?"

"No. I can see how it may bring a few tourists here, but it's not like it's the Golden Gate."

"No. You're right, it's not like the Golden Gate, but it is Medieval and nearly a thousand years older that the Golden Gate Bridge."

"Dude, the U.S. has only been around a couple hundred years. We couldn't have settled this area until, what, a hundred years ago, max."

"Haha! Oh my gosh. Dude you really don't know."

Bigfoot grew impatient again.

"Know what?"

"This is the famous London Bridge. You know, from London, shipped over here brick by brick. The one the song is about. "London Bridge is falling down, falling down, falling… Nothing? Really? You don't know the song? How did you graduate preschool without memorizing it."

"I didn't go to preschool."

"Hmm. Ok, well, that explains things. This is a famous old bridge. You know what- It, it doesn't matter. I think this is where we park."

When they parked, the outside temperature gage on the dash read 111°.

There was a long, long, long staircase that led to the walkway and stage just under the bridge. It was on the long, long, long staircase that they transported their heavy cases of equipment without the assistance of their luggage carts. That would have been a difficult task in non-inferno temperatures. Half way down the stairs, Lief understood why Raul was always posting pictures on Facebook of the daily temperature reading.

They set down the first load of gear on the stage which was located directly underneath the bridge, near the edge of the lake. They looked up from the stage, and tracked the same details of the bridge as their eyes rolled up the old grey stone behind the stage, then followed its arch to the first gigantic leg comprised of even larger stone bricks that ran into the water beneath.

A historical and geographic connection came full circle for Lief when it occurred to him that when he was twenty he had walked over the Thames in London on the bridge that replaced the London Bridge. The memory was significant to Lief for some reason, even though he didn't know why. Later he'd realize his feelings were those of gratitude for having the opportunity to travel and see the world in a way that could't be experienced in a travel book or documentary.

Bigfoot howled under the bridge to hear his voice echo.

"Oh my God Lief, the acoustics are amazing here!"

"Damn fucking straight, they are"

Lief's words echoed all the way to the ears of a family with small children who were walking towards them along the walkway.

After one more trip up and then back down the long, long, long stairway in the 111° Arizona desert heat, they again broke their time record for setting up to play. Raul arrived right as they finished. He was a hefty and jovial Mexican of average height. Most times he'd dress in a post-punk-esque manner, but that day he was sporting the hipster casual look with his top-siders, pants pegged to his calves, tucked t-shirt, and a beaning wore on the back half of his head.

"Raul! Good to see you man! By the way, this is Bigfoot."

"Nice to meet you Bigfoot. That isn't you're real name is it? And, wow! It must be warm underneath all of that fur."

"Ha. I'm not the one wearing a beanie. And no, it's not on my birth certificate. People just call me that."

Raul raised his eyebrows as an involuntary response to Bigfoot's abrasiveness, but responded like a true gentleman while pivoting to Lief.

"Touché. Lief, long time no see. What the? Love the ascot man. Nice touch. Alright, I saw the pictures of the luggage on Facebook. They are too cool!"

Lief had almost forgot about his ornate neckwear. He had bought several ascot's to wear along with his American flag vest and bright, tight britches, all of which he referred to as his "high performance" clothes designed to improve his performances.

"Oh, thank you. Did Maria have the baby yet?"

"Not yet, I'm only able to stay for a few, then I've got to get back over there."

"Do you know if it's a boy or a girl yet?"

"Oh yeah, It's another boy, Jesus. We decided to go with a more unique name this time. I think he'll hatch in about an hour and a half by my best estimate."

"Great name! Don't let us hold you up."

"No, no, seriously. This isn't exactly my first rodeo."

"True. Oh- Hey, so we're playing all around the US and filming it, but we are also trying to film other street musicians. Do you ever see them around here? Are there any?"

"Not a lot, but there is one guy that plays a saxophone. The times I've seen him, he plays right on that bench over there. He's a certifiable nut though. He's always saying inappropriate things to people, offending tourists. You'd be better off not running into him."

"Ok then. Thanks."

Lief readied to play.

"Bigfoot, you set?"

"Yup, ready when you are."

"K, Raul we'll bust a few out while you're still here. Thanks again for making arrangements for us to play under the bridge here."

"Not a problem"

"Hey, you know, since you're here, would you mind panning the camera across the stage while we play? You could leave it on the tripod. It's all set up and will rotate smoothly."

"You got it man."

A few curious tourists perched on the benches in front of the stage.

"We're Gas Station Rose and we have a few songs for you."

Lief hit the distortion pedal an began grinding out the rhythm to what could only be described as an angry gypsy song called "Claustrophobic Kamikaze". Bigfoot followed with a beat that could never be categorized in the annals of drum patterns.

"Alcoholic, drug addict, OCD, ADD
Sex feign, porn feign, just about feign
Road rage'n, masturbating
Gone because I don't like waiting
Claustrophobic Kamikaze
Xenophobic, not a Nazi
Paranoid, just plain annoyed
I heard the news today, Oh boy
Codependent, unrepentant

Where the hell's my disinfectant
Hypochondriac, pyromaniac
Got third degree from that match
War mongering, carpet bombing
Shove your protest song up your ass
HEY!!..."

The few people that had gathered, looked to each other with deep concern, scratched their head's, and then walked away in fast fashion. Raul clinched his teeth and grinned. Lief took note that the song might have been inappropriate for that particular venue. He followed with "Love on the Holodeck", a song about having sex in outer space. It didn't bring the crowd back.

The sweat pumping out of ever pour on Lief's face was causing his sunglasses to slip down his nose. He had to lean his head back while finishing the song to keep them from falling off. He misplaced a few chords in the process. Bigfoot shook his head at Leif, displaying more of his piss poor attitude.

Lief could care less that the audience left, or that he wasn't giving his best performance. Lief was well aware of the magic of editing. Even in the blistering heat, Lief was one-hundred percent in the moment. He wasn't in an office or stuck in traffic and he wasn't working for the man. He was underneath the London Bridge playing his music on his own terms. He was traveling and filming a movie while wearing in high performance clothes. He was living a dream.

When Lief and his strange friend arrived at Ricardo and Juanita's home they were greeted with air conditioning, hugs, and authentic Mexican food. Not only had it been too long since Lief visited the Garcia's, it seemed like a lifetime since he had eaten real Conchinita Pibil. Bigfoot and Lief practically inhaled the slow roasted pork that was soaked in that God sent savory orange marinade. Each chunk was so tender that they had to carefully balance each fork-load so that the meat wouldn't fall apart before they could get a bite. Lief was reminded that he was a gringo when he observed the Garcia's eating with ease by scooping the Conchinita in their tortillas. He followed suit.

During the meal, Lief and Bigfoot thanked them for their generosity. After that, the conversation was sparse, but much of the essential catch up was accomplished.

Bigfoot hit the sack in the room Juanita had made up for him while Lief stayed up to talk to with his surrogate parents. They all reminisced about the times that Lief stayed with them all those years back. Lief did the majority of the talking.

Ricardo had the demeanor of a stone. He didn't speak much, but when he did, his delivery was gruff. His coarseness was only a cover for how loving he was. It was an effective way to get people to listen to him. Lief didn't know it, but he modeled much of his tone towards Sarah after Ricardo. Lief took notice that, either Ricardo softened over the years, or he was having a hard time containing his happiness in seeing Lief, because he broke form and cracked a smile a couple of times while talking.

"Remember coming down here with us when we looked for property, I dunno, twenty-five and a half some odd years ago, right?"

"Of course I do. That was a fun trip."

"Yeah, all but you're terrible gas all the way down, that got old quick."

Juanita chuckled. Lief confessed although he was embarrassed.

"Oh yeah. Sorry bout that."

Ricardo noticed Lief's embarrassment and changed the subject.

"What's this I hear about you being a grandfather and having a twenty-one year old daughter, Grandpa?"

"Yes, I do have a nearly twenty-two year old daughter. Her name is Leslie and she has a baby girl. And yes, that makes me a grandpa. I just found out for certain after ordering a DNA test several months back. So, I figured the next step was to go out to see her."

Juanita was less talkative than usual. She looked as if she was enjoying seeing Ricardo talk as much as he was. She was just as loving as Ricardo, but she never tried to hide one bit of it. When Ricardo finished speaking for a moment, she jumped in to pick Lief's brain on the matter as well.

"How do you feel about all of it?"

"I'm excited and, at the same time, a little confused. Also, I'm starting to feel a little old."

"The biggest joy in our lives is our grandchildren. It's a real blessing Lief, I'm happy you have the chance to get to be a part of their lives now."

"Thank you. Me too, but I'm not sure that's what she wants at this point. It's just a meet. I figure it'll be a good start to let her know about half her heritage and my family's medical history, and you know, stuff like that."

Ricardo yawned and then stood up to share a few last thoughts before heading to bed.

"That's a good start. Lief, you'll figure it out, you've always done that. In the mean time, don't be such a stranger. We miss hearing from you, Ok?"

Juanita echoed Ricardo's sentiments before they retired to their room. Lief went to bed that night with much contentment having visiting with his two loving quasi-parents.

— ~

The next morning Lief and Bigfoot prepared for the road once again. The sun was blistering at 9 a.m. though its starburst, neon orange rays were a spectacular sight. Next to the car parked in the driveway, the two Californians stretched out with a few yoga poses to limber up before their long drive that laid ahead.

Across the street, a bald old man wearing pajamas smoked a cigar on his way to get his newspaper on the sidewalk. When he bent over to pick it up, he caught a glimpse of the peculiarities in the opposing driveway. It must have looked like ballet or synchronized swimming to him. Due to the odd sight, he failed to look down at the paper while bending over and he lost his balance, falling face first into the cement.

His wife had also been observing the strange activities from behind the screen of the front door until she saw her husband hit the ground, then rushed to his aid. Although her attention was focused on helping her husband and his bleeding forehead, she couldn't take her eye's off of Lief and Bigfoot, causing her to trip over her husband and fall to the ground as well. Lief nudged Bigfoot.

"Hey man, let's get out of here. I think we're weirding out the neighborhood."

CHAPTER 12

CRATERLAND!!!

Havasu, with all of it's charming hellfire and brimstone, had to be left behind by the two sweat-soaked travelers. They had a mission to complete, but before heading further east a coffee and snack stop was in order. They stopped at a grocery store called Food City. Lief chuckled after reading the name of the store. At that point the heat was twisting Lief's perception to the point that he thought things were funny when they were not. It was an appropriate name for a grocery store, but he had to make something of it.

"Bigfoot! We made it! After toiling through all of our hardships on the yellow brick road, we've finally reached the Food City."

"Ha. I don't get it."

"Let me guess, you've never seen Wizard of Oz?"

"Wizard of what- Oz? What, is it a heavy metal event or something?"

"Oh my gosh dude! It's a movie. You're being honest, you've never seen it?"

"No. What's the big deal?"

"Nothing. It's just one of the biggest movies ever made. Actually, come to think- you kind of remind me of the lion character in it."

They got their snacks, Lief found his coffee, and they were off.

They drove east through the rolling ochre, umber, and siena desert that was adorned with Saguaro cacti and Joshua trees. The sparse vegetation praised the same purple heavens that the distant mesas protruded towards, only to fall flat like upside down anvils. Desert scenery was always easy for Lief to accept. It was beautiful and simple. It also brought Lief pleasant memories of the Road Runner and Wile E Coyote cartoons that he'd watch as a child. Admiring all that was around him, Lief let his mind drift into dreamscape that truckers called "white line fever". Upon first hearing the condition, Lief thought it implied cocaine use, but was assured it was just a pleasant meditative theta state of mind that long drives often produced.

The exact name for Lief's unusual mindset was not important, but it's contents would forever fascinate him. His thoughts wandered into a steel warehouse sized vault that opened with his approach. Inside, the air was cool and comfortable. In the vault, there were scattered cardboard file boxes, some stacked two or three high. Each box he'd open had a surprise. Some contained unsorted feelings, some had groundbreaking ideas, and a few held undiscovered and missed opportunities. Several more where filled with joy or fear, but the majority were no more than good and bad memories. Although he opened scores of boxes, there were too many of them to explore in one visit.

Most of the boxes were banged up and covered in dust, except for one stack of boxes that were crisp and new. They called out to Lief, attracting his attention. He opened one and discovered that it contained only gratifying moments with Kay that had not happened yet. In one of the moments, they cruised through turquoise topical seas. In another that was further down the road, they walked hand in hand between cedars in the snow in goose-down coats. His favorite memory to be was of them having late night sex in Tin Can that was parked between a fleet of taco trucks. A guilty smile spread across Lief's face as he focused in on the smaller details. *I wonder what the story was- Is to be here.*

Although Lief wanted to explore the scene more, something else beckoned his attention and grew increasingly more annoying.

"Lief. Hello. Are you in there? Dude, what the fuck? Can I have some of your po-ta-to chips?"

Lief was pissed at Bigfoot for yanking him out of his life vault. There were so many more files that Lief wanted to explore, especially the ones with Kay.

"Yes. You can have some po-ta-to chips. Why ask me like that?"

"Seriously? I asked you like three times."

"Really?"

They were somewhere between Flagstaff and Winslow. As fate would have it, Bigfoot again turned on the radio, and again, his timing was impeccable. After turning the dial through staticky white noise and accordion laced Mexican polka music, a strong signal came through that was carrying the voice of a manic spokesperson. It sounded like the infomercial legend Billy Mays giving a play-by-play of a monster truck event. The announcer's excitement made whatever he was talking about sound like the most important discovery since sliced aliens in Roswell.

"METEOR CRATER- Come visit- METEOR CRATER- Meteor Crater is the biggest crater ever. It was caused by a giant asteroid fifty-thousand years ago- METEOR CRATER. Nearly one mile in diameter and five-hundred and fifty feet deep- METEOR CRATER- It's the biggest CRATER on the planet Earth- METEOR CRATER- Visit METEOR CRATER, It's just a few miles south of Interstate 40, Seventeen miles west of Winslow, on METEOR CRATER Road. Come see METEOR CRATER..."

Crazy Mays, another name Lief invented, continued the crazed message ad infinitum. while Lief and Bigfoot turned toward each other, and nodded. They had just passed Meteor Crater Rd. before they heard the message. It seemed as though the power of the broadcast seized all manual controls in the Tin Can, because like the Death Star pulling in the Millennial Falcon, the Tin Can found itself automatically turning around before floating to the parking lot of the crater's visitors center.

"Bigfoot! This crater, this METEOR CRATER has to be in the film!"

Bigfoot agreed whole heartedly.

"Oh yeah"

Lief mimicked Crazy Mays.

"METEOR CRATER- It's the biggest fucking CRATER on the planet Earth. METEOR CRATER- Visit METEOR CRATER."

"Hahahaha!"

They were hoping they'd be able to see the crater from the parking lot so they didn't have to drag the equipment far. That was not the case. Logic soon pointed to fact that whoever owned the park wouldn't make any money that way. It was fenced off and the ticketing agent told them it was only viewable after paying forty dollars for a tour. The two mulled it over.

"I dunno Bigfoot, that coked up announcer on the radio sure made it sound worth it."

"Yeah, but forty bucks?"

They decided that the money would be be better spent on a hotel. That didn't mean that they were going to surrender either. Lief had a brief thought that stopped him dead in his tracks.

Like typewriter bars striking a blank sheet of paper, Lief nervously tapped each of his fingers against their respective thumbs in rapid succession. It was a typical anxious tic for him that indicated he was trying to recall a thought. The thought was there and it was great, but then just like his other greatest thoughts, it was lost.

"Oh shit. Never mind."

Returning to the Tin Can, defeat at Meteor Crater appeared imminent. Before turning the keys in the ignition, Lief paused once more, attempting one last ditch effort to summon his idea. That time there was a buzzing between his ears. He looked in the direction where the original thought came to him. Then, like a brick falling on his head, one of the best ideas that he ever had returned.

"WE CAN USE THE CAMERA TO GET IN!"

"What do you mean? Like ask them if we can film it?"

"Yes! We offer to film it as part of our documentary called Amazing U.S. Parks or something official sounding. They'll see our huge camera and then we hand them release forms so we look even more legit and they'll totally let us!"

"You really think so Lief?"

"I'm positive!"

Lief changed his clothes to fit the part of a documentary reporter, though a slightly more eccentric version. He put on a tan collared shirt accompanied by a golden ascot. He asked Bigfoot if he wouldn't mind holding the camera to play the part of the camera man. Bigfoot agreed, but Lief detected reluctance and resentment on Bigfoot's part. If there was one thing that Lief learned about Bigfoot on the trip to that point, it was that Bigfoot had an unhealthy sense of entitlement, the same sort that a snotty suckled only child has, although Bigfoot had a brother. Lief figured that his mother may have breast feed him too long.

The two approached the ticket agent looking like a professional Hollywood film crew, ready to do a routine segment. After a brief explanation, the ticketing agent put Lief on the phone with the manager of the facility. Lief explained to the manager that they had planned to include the crater in their, to be, nationally televised documentary called "Amazing U.S. Parks", but that someone on their team dropped the ball and failed to communicate the visit.

The manager didn't care that their visit was unscheduled. To her it was the exact kind of publicity that the park had been looking for. She was so excited that she rushed downstairs to meet them.

"Thanks for allowing us in without prior notice. We had a little miscommunication with our- hmph- previous intern, if you catch my drift. We made it, nonetheless. Yay! We're here!"

"We're certainly glad you did. This is great! I would have one request though. We need to make sure that your viewers know that this is a private park and not a national or state park. Would you make that clear somewhere in your program?"

"Of course. I'll start the introduction to the segment with that. Before we can include you in our feature documentary it's required that we get a signature on this release form. It's standard procedure and just let's our production company that we got your permission to film."

"Not a problem. I'm very familiar with those. We've had lot's of filming done here."

The sizzle of the camera accompanied by a little smoke and mirrors got the two inside for free. Not only did the two get full access to the crater and all other parts of the facility, they were assigned their own personal tour guide who took them all throughout the meteor museum.

Their guide's name was Ernesto. He was a forty-something Mexican-American with a flare for presentation. He explained that the crater had been used in an assortment of sci-fi type films. Ernesto also explained that the area was used to train the first astronauts going to the moon so they could get used to walking around a moon-like terrain in their spacesuits.

While the history of the crater was fascinating, Bigfoot indicated that the camera was getting heavy. Lief asked Ernesto if they could jump to the crater part of the tour because they were on a tight schedule. Ernesto obliged and guided them up a long hallway filled with all sorts of other historical pieces associated with the crater as well. It was apparent that he was having a difficult time walking past each of them without explaining their historical relevance. Bigfoot and Lief were there for one reason and one reason only. They wanted their dose of METEOR CRATER and Crazy Mays made no mention of a bunch of required chit-chat to see it. They were already sold on its magnificence.

At last, they breached all gates blocking view of the crater when they walked through the doors at the end of the long museum hallway. From the doors they would still have to walk across a large cement deck to see the crater. Outside the wind was ferocious. Ernesto had to hold his hat to keep it from blowing away. Lief knew that the wind would eliminate any sort of sound quality, but it presented a great opportunity for him to dub in the audio of the exciting and comical METEOR CRATER commercial.

Ernesto walked in front of the two to tell them more about the crater as they approached. Bigfoot lowered the camera to send a clear signal to their overzealous tour guide that anything he said wouldn't end up on film, then they walked past Ernesto towards the railing at the edge of the deck. The far rim came into sight first and looked like a run of the mill mountain range, but as they walked closer, the peak of the range curved towards them. The closer they walked to the edge of the deck, the more they could see the rim take on more of a circular shape, like the top of a deep terra cotta bowl. When they reached the railing the entire crater laid in front of them in all of her red rocky roundish splendor.

Lief imagined them presenting the crater as a sort of a crescendo in the film that they could accompany with a blazing rendition of "Battle Hymn of the Republic". To Lief, it wasn't the crater itself that made it noteworthy. The crater was nowhere near as cool as the guy on the radio made it sound, that would have been impossible. And it wasn't worth the forty that they were supposed to pay to see it. The real value of the footage was the way that they got in for free because of the large camera. That was the story worth telling. It added a good dose of levity to the otherwise dry content of the film. Any further usage of the camera's clout to get them any otherwise restricted or exclusive footage would be hilarious. Lief knew it could serve as a comedic timing that would remind the viewer of their discovery at the METEOR FUCKING CRATER.

Bigfoot panned across the crater's entirety. Ernesto walked in front of the camera to talk about the usage of the crater in other films. The wind was so strong, Ernesto had to yell to be heard. As he spoke, a gust folded a flap on the matte box in front of the lens. Bigfoot continued to shoot, unaware of the camera obstruction, making it obvious to Ernesto that the two had no idea what they were doing. He laid off of the professionalism, guessing that film wasn't going anywhere. Lief saw that Ernesto was on to them. It was time to make their exit.

Lief grabbed the camera from Bigfoot.

"Well, thank you so much Ernesto. We loved your presentation. We are really behind on our schedule and need to get back on the road.":

"You are most welcome. Say, surely you two must be hungry. Before you rush off why don't you join me for some tacos at my apartment next door?"

Again, They both thanked him graciously for the tour and the taco offer, but explained that they really were in a crunch for time.

Bigfoot and Lief double timed it through the long hallway towards the exit. Ernesto kept pace with them on the way out, stopping them before they could get out the door. He leveled with them.

"Hey, look guys. I think it's great, your whole project and I hope you make something of it. If you're not in too big of a hurry I got some beer in the fridge too. You can relax some before getting back out there, It's a while to the nearest town."

Bigfoot was first to respond.

"Really? Thanks man, I'd love a drink."

Lief pieced together Ernesto's ulterior motives to get the two to stay when he recalled what he earlier assumed was an accidental pat on the ass, realizing it was no accident at all.

"Bigfoot, we really do have to run. Ah- Ernesto. Thanks. Thanks again. Have a nice day."

In the parking lot, Lief changed into clothes more befitting of the desert. Bigfoot did not, but he did give props to Lief for a plan that came together.

"Dude. Lief, you totally called it! That was awesome!"

"Totally. But, hmm… Did you get a weird vibe from Ernesto?"

"Do you mean because he was homo for you?"

"Yeah, that."

"Dude, it's the ascot. It looks cool and all, but it makes you look like Freddie Mercury, combined with your mustache and tight pants."

"Duly noted."

On their way back to Interstate 40, the street band spotted a stage-like red rock formation. It looked like mars and was too perfect to pass up filming a quick song or two for the film. The wind was still heavy and would ruin the sound of their performance, but they filmed, nonetheless, shitty sound and all. The wind blew their hair and fur to the side as the two rocked on the red mars terrain. It would not be the most notable footage in the movie, but it was good enough for a book cover.

CHAPTER 13

AUSTIN CITY LIMITED

(without an ascot)

Estimating, their arrival time in Austin Texas proved difficult. Lief's sister Kirsten would be waiting to let them into her home where the'd be able to stay the following evening. She and her husband Ron were on the go so it was important for Lief to give her as much advance notice as possible. The straight driving time with gas station stops accounted for was fourteen and a half-hours, but if they lost momentum and stopped for the night, Austin would be a full day away. Trying to plan around getting a hotel was a conundrum of its own. If they reserved a hotel along the way and didn't end up tired by the time they got there, they'd want to keep driving, but wouldn't be able to without a cancelation fee.

After much careful consideration, they decided to make the unsafe choice of driving straight through the night. Lief called Kirsten to let her know that they'd be there by morning. The plan was for them to take turns sleeping while the other drove. Their strategy would not only get them there sooner, if it went well, they'd be able to try the same trick down the road on the trip, sparing them the trouble of making additional sleeping arrangements.

Lief wasn't close with most of his family, but he looked forward to seeing his big sister. She was two years older than Lief and was his first buddy in life. Kirsten was the other artist in the family. Even though they grew up to have much different personalities, he suspected she was a large part of why he picked his particular family. Lief's idea that people selected which family they'd have in life was just a theory, although he had a hunch he'd find sufficient evidence to back it up sooner or later.

Lief looked over at Bigfoot who had been quiet for some time. It looked like he was experiencing white line fever himself before he snapped out of it and pulled a bottle of pills out of his pocket. He slipped one under his tongue. Lief remembered that Bigfoot would not be able to speak while the pill dissolved so he, again, took advantage of the opportunity to mess with him.

"Bigfoot, I didn't know how to bring this up, but there have been a lot of guys around the music scene in Sonoma County that have told me that you've been recruiting for a boy band."

Bigfoot mumbled then flipped Lief the bird.

"Someone told me the band name even. What was that? Oh yeah, I remember, Back Alley Boys. Yeah, that's it. Anyways, how's that going? I mean, I don't mean to pry. If that's something you're keeping close to your chest, say nothing. I'll totally understand."

Bigfoot pointed to his mouth, mumbled some more, and shook his head. Five-minutes went by before the pill dissolved under his tongue, at which point he was quick to respond.

"Dude, that's going to get old real quick."

The highway stretched for what seemed like an eternity, while all along the way Lief was thinking of Kay. He was missing her terribly and couldn't wait to see her in New Jersey. He could feel her heart beating from two-thousand miles away, although it seemed she was sitting beside him. He felt her breath on his neck causing the nerve endings throughout his entire body to tingle. In physiological terms, he knew that the sensations he was experiencing were the result of chemicals being released in his body when he thought of his love. Beyond the physical mechanics, he knew that something less tangible was happening, something more spiritual in nature, something that didn't need to be fully understood or explained.

"I'm going to ask her to marry me."

Lief was taken aback by the words that sprang from his mouth. Bigfoot was also surprised.

"What? Dude- Really?"

"Yeah... Yes, I know I should. I'm going to get her a ring and then ask her in Jersey."

"Wow! That's, that's- Wow! That's quite the leap man. You have bigger balls than me."

"Really? I dunno, we've never really compared our ball size before, but that's mighty generous of you to assume that mine are superior to yours. Yeah, you're probably right though."

"Dude, what's wrong with you?"

Bigfoot chuckled at Lief's offbeat dry humor.

Five hours into their drive after their stop at the crater, Lief noticed that their highway had woven itself into the old Route 66. It reminded him of an old song that was a cover of an even older song. Lief downloaded it. Depeche Mode's version of "Route 66" was playing within the minute. Lief was flooded with high school memories, though Bigfoot had no basis for understanding for the genre. His knowledge of the era and it's mod movement was limited and there had not been any good knockoffs of the sound since then. Needless to say, he did not get his kicks as Lief did.

Onward into the night the two bid farewell to the old highway and headed south on 84 towards Lubbock. They alternated driving, roughly, every two hours, but the drive proved treacherous as the morning approached. That particular highway changed its speed limit every time they'd near a new town because it became the main thoroughfare. Whenever Lief slowed the car to adjust to the new required speed or turned into a curve in the road while Bigfoot slept, Bigfoot would feel the slight change in motion and jump up and freak out, then gripe at Lief for his unsafe driving. It was due to his post traumatic stress disorder resulting from his careless, drug induced accident that destroyed Lief's previous car, Tin Can #1.

Each time Lief got an earful, he relived the anger he had towards

Bigfoot for crashing his car while on drugs. Lief also knew to let it slide to keep the peace, but he suspected that his patience would not last long. The small seed of a suspicion that was planted in LA., the thought that they may not finish the trip together, had begun to sprout.

Whenever it was Bigfoot's turn to drive, Lief not only got a break from driving, he had a chance to get some rest, and a much needed break from something he started to refer to as Bigfoot bitching, or the abbreviated version, "BB".

Five-minutes after Lief fell asleep, Bigfoot burst in a manic fit.

"Oh shit! Oh shit, oh shit, oh shit!"

Leif jumped to attention and saw the flash of red and blue lights from a highway patrol car behind them as Bigfoot was pulled over.

"Dude, I'm fucked. I only have my provisional license. He's going to take me to jail."

"Just stay calm. Everything will be fine."

Lief sounded sympathetic and he might have been at first, but when he got to thinking about it, he kind of liked how things were unfolding. Bigfoot getting arrested may have been a godsend. It may have been a long awaited karma catching up. Redemption was being delivered to Lief. Bigfoot, the constant complainer and trumped up driving critic, was the one getting the ticket for speeding. Lief relished in his thoughts, *Poetic Justice.*

Being the bigger man, with larger testicles, Lief offered a comforting thought to help ease Bigfoot's anxiety while the officer approached the drivers side of the Tin Can.

"I wouldn't worry. The car has veterans plates. They dig that shit out here."

The officer performed the usual routine, asking for a license and the registration before he returned to his patrol car for a call to dispatch. The officer kept an eye on Bigfoot during the long call. Lief wondered what kind of deals Bigfoot was making with his maker before the officer returned to Bigfoot's window.

"Where's the owner of the car?"

Bigfoot, scared shitless, couldn't answer so Lief spoke up.

"I am officer."

"Can I see your identification please?"

Instead of handing over his drivers license, the more accepted form of identification, Lief gave him his Veterans ID card. The officer studied it then handed it back.

"Ok, well Mr. Bray, I clocked you going fifty-seven in a thirty-five mile per hour zone. I'm going to give you a break and give you five over the limit. If this is agreeable by you, I'd like your John Hancock right here, meaning that you'll agree to pay this here amount within ninety days. By the way, Mr. Wainwright, thank you for your service."

Bigfoot obliged, but remained shaken up when he inched back onto the road. He was also amazed at the officers leniency.

"Dude, how did you know he would be so cool?"

"I'm telling you, they love the military in these red states."

The morning had broken by the time they pulled into Kirsten's driveway. Lief was fortunate that the long stretch between Bigfoot's ticket and Austin was absent of any further "B.B." Kirsten and Lief had always gotten along well while growing up, but they had not seen each other in five years and they had only spoken on a few occasions during that time. Lief had little contact with the rest of his family as well. His lack of communication wasn't limited to just family, it was too much work for him to maintain relationships with most. To him, family shenanigans and friend's needs were liabilities, and considering Bigfoot, he was on the mark. Still, something seemed different as he approached his sister's door. He realized he missed her. It wasn't much, but it was enough to set a change of heart in motion. He wondered if that would be the way it would feel when he'd see more of his family along the way. It may have been the first steps of an unknowingly welcome mending process.

When they all met at the door, Kirsten and Lief hugged, although it wasn't their usual thing. In a business-like manner she greeted Bigfoot with a handshake.

"It's Bigfoot, is it?"

"Yeah, that's what they call me."

"Well, Bigfoot it's nice to meet you. So, Lief, Bigfoot, I've made you some breakfast. It's not much, it's a scramble with some veggies. I hope that works for you. I'm sorry to greet and run, but the office needs me. If you don't mind, I'll show you around real quick. I have some beds made up and set some towels out. Your timing worked out well, cause the girls are with their Dad in Utah, so you get their rooms. Beats the couch and air mattress."

"Aw, thanks Kirsten. Breakfast smells great. And sorry if we held you up. We got here as quick as we could. Actually, I'm just going to eat and crash."

"Yeah, you both have to be worn out. Get some sleep. Ron and I will be back around 6 and maybe we can all go grab dinner. Oh, yes here's a key. Just lock up if you head out. I suspect you'll be checking out the downtown area. It's close, by the way."

"Cool, for sure. We're going to film some of the musicians down there, and we'll set up and play a few too."

Their exchange was succinct. Kirsten left, Bigfoot and Lief ate, showered, and then tried to get some sleep while thoughts of musical adventures in Austin entertained them both.

After only four hours sleep, they drove to the downtown area of Austin to scout around for a good place film. It struck Lief odd that there were no musicians out playing that day. The last time Lief had visited Austin, twenty years earlier, there were buskers lined up and down the streets all throughout the entire middle of the city.

The lack of people to film turned out to be a great opportunity for Lief to address some troublesome audio issues. On day one of the trip Lief discovered that the camera was only recording sound at half the volume as it should have. He hoped that he could adjust the problem in sound editing, but he'd rest much easier knowing that he had a fix for it while he was filming. He had overcome the memory dilemma, it was time to straighten out the sound. They were half way across the country, meaning they had collected nearly one quarter of the planned footage. That meant that there was a good chance that one quarter of the sound for the movie was fucked.

Lief's desire to record a movie, the kind that another person would sit through, was not high on Bigfoot's priority list. It was for that reason that Bigfoot, again, began to gripe when Lief said he needed to go to an audio store to buy something to somehow amplify the sound going into the camera. Lief called Bigfoot out.

"Dude, we are filming a movie right?"

"Yeah, but it feels like that's all we're doing."

"Ok, that would be true if the camera was actually working. What is it? I mean, we planned to film street musicians and our adventure in doing so. We planned all of this in detail. You agreed to all of it. We have stuck to the plan 100% and so far we have no usable sound. We never discussed making a silent film. That's kind of a big deal, no? If I don't fix this, there is NO movie. Furthermore, I have A LOT of money in this. Let's see- To the tune of ten grand."

"Yeah, well maybe you can drop me off somewhere to skate while you figure it all out."

"I would be happy to."

Lief located a guitar/ audio center and dropped Bigfoot off in a large parking near it. The lot had a plenty of contoured cement, sloped retaining walls, and drainage curves that were all ideal for skateboarding. It even met Bigfoot's lofty standards.

While Bigfoot skated, Lief studied the audio equipment section of the screeching lead guitar laden music store. He discovered that there was no full-proof fix for the sound. There were a few possibilities, but those could turn into costly mistakes. He'd never know until he was recording in real time. All the equipment he was looking at was packed into elaborate boxes that he'd have to buy to open. The sales associate had no idea which direction to point him in either, because he had no experience with sound equipment for film. Lief had to search the web for advice. There was not much there. The only clear solution Lief found was a condenser mic that did it's own separate recording.

Recording separately on a self contained condenser microphone was how the professionals filmed, but the pros also had sound editors that knew how to properly line the sound up with the corresponding scenes. That would have been a mess for Lief who hadn't even learned how to operate the high tech editing software. Lining up separately recorded sound would require the use of a slate board with each scene written on it. That meant each scene would have to be planned and prepared to a large extent. They were running and gunning and had no time to plan scenes. The condenser mic was out and Lief was at square one.

After bugging a sound specialist at the store with, what had to be, one-hundred questions, Lief discovered an almost certain fix with a miniature recording sound board, one that he could fix to the outside of the camera rig. It was overkill because it was a mini sound studio, capable of recording several tracks on it's own, but it did have the capability to amplify sound coming into the camera. The only drawback was the cost. After some quick calculations, Lief figured out that getting the mini sound studio would be cheaper than taking a chance on something else. Lief winced while dropping another two-hundred and fifty, then walked out of the store.

— ~

Lief splayed all of his equipment across a table in a nearby coffee shop. He underestimated how much gear he had accumulated and had to move to a larger table. There was still a remote chance that his attempted fix would fail. He handed its fate over to the hands of the universe. He was ready to accept the worst possible outcome, while, at the same time he imagined a positive result. *Here goes nothing. No- Here goes everything.* He turned it all on, adjusted a few knobs for a medium sound level, hit record for thirty-seconds, and then played it back. Lief yelled aloud in the crowded coffee shop.

"Fuck yeah! Oops, sorry. My camera works, it made me happy."

It increased the sound enough to carry on with confidence. The sound issue was no longer an issue.

Although Lief was happy about finding his sound solution, he was mum on the matter when he picked Bigfoot up around the corner.

"How did it go?"

"I think I got it. I bought a sound board to amplify it. I just have to find a way to attach it to the rig, maybe Velcro."

"Are you saying the we need to go to another store? Dude. I'm tired of waiting around. Can't we just get to the center of town and film a quick set."

"Bigfoot, I can't- Alright. You know what? Yeah, let's go downtown. When we get there I think we should do our own thing for a while."

Bigfoot and his skate board were dropped off downtown. Lief found a shaded spot to park and make the last remaining adjustments with the new sound gear. When he was done, he took sometime to walk around downtown Austin.

Lief was distressed. He found himself in a pickle about how to handle Bigfoot. Lief's body was in pain, he was tired, depressed, and grumpy all at the same time. He may have been experiencing his current funk for a while, but hadn't had a chance to let his feelings catch up. Now that they made themselves known, all he had to do was decipher them.

Giving his mind a moment to sort through things, Lief gathered that, along with his current funk, he was experiencing poor health. He tried to zero in on what could be the cause of his fatigue, odd aches and pains, and upset stomach. *Could it be that I'm hungry? Could it be that simple? Yeah, I'm hungry. Wow, that was easy.* Lief thought it was strange that he didn't notice his hunger earlier. His desire to make a better film trumped his physical maintenance.

He found a sandwich shop nearby. Lief disregarded his gluten intolerance and made a b-line for the shop, got an Italian sub, and then found a bench under a tree. His mouth dripped saliva with his first bite. His body was back on track in no time at all. His stomach stopped grumbling and his aches and pains subsided. The clarity of his thoughts improved so much that he could see the forest through the trees. His mind became so clear that he even grew close to discovering the reason that he felt like he had been swimming upstream ever since the trip started. Lief's neck and shoulder muscles had been painful and cramped since day one. He had been sinking, and if the remaining three quarters of the trip carried on the same way as the first quarter, Lief would need to seek the comfort of a straight jacket.

The root of his distress came into full focus. He had been in uninterrupted proximity with a crazy making energy vampire ever since he picked Bigfoot up in Petaluma. There was no longer a shadow of a doubt; Bigfoot and Lief would part ways soon.

While imagining the scenario in which Bigfoot was no longer in the car, Lief's body began to repair itself. The very thought felt like a massage that smoothed any remaining tension away. Lief heard birds chirping around him. The breeze that blew by him cooled his sweaty neck. As it passed, it tugged the last of Lief's anxiety away with it. He relaxed.

An unintentional smile formed on his face. Then his phone rang and it was Kay. She couldn't have picked a better time to call. That was probably why she did.

"Hey sweetheart, I was just thinking about you. How are you?"

"I'm good, I guess my ears where burning. Where are you?"

"I'm outside of a sandwich shop on a park bench."

"No, I mean on the planet."

"Oh, Yeah. I'm in downtown Austin. I'm actually looking right at the state capitol right now. Where are you at?"

"I'm still home. I'm getting ready to fly to the shore though. I leave tomorrow morning."

"Are you excited?"

"Yeah, I can't wait to see my mom and my brother, not his wife so much though. But I'm mostly thinking about you and hoping everything is ok though. I miss you like I can't tell you."

"Aww, baby, I miss you too, but why can't you tell me?"

"No- I mean I miss you like I can't ever remember missing someone so much."

"Ohhh, Got it. Me too, seriously. You know what I figured out though?"

"No. What?"

"Right now, while I'm sitting here in Austin, I'm as far from you, distance wise, that I'll be for the rest of the trip."

"Really? How do you figure? I mean you're still headed east right?"

"True, but you're switching coasts in the morning. I'm in the middle of the country, so every mile I go east from here will be towards you."

"Wow! You're right. I guess I'm geographically challenged or something."

"No. It's just counter intuitive, which makes it noteworthy."

"So baby, how are you doing?"

"Ha! Well, ugh… I've been really stressed. This trip, this movie is really taking a toll on me. It's funny, I was just kind of going through all of it in my head, sitting here on this park bench, looking at the capital."

"Oh no! I had a feeling that something was wrong. Why are you looking at the capitol?"

"I don't know. I guess I sat down in the first place I found and it's right here in front of me. It's all domey and it sticks out. Why did you think something was wrong?"

"Partially because I haven't heard from you in a while. And then it's weird- I kind of can feel your anxiety. I know it's weird to say, but I don't exactly know how else to explain it."

"No, I get it. I can feel this same kind of connection to you. When I was in L.A., I really felt like you were there with me. The thought of you helped me get through the whole lightning strike and after. Oh shit, I forgot to tell you about the lightning, some other time though. It's not important."

"Lightning? As long as you're ok, I guess. How come you're so stressed?"

"Well, I'm trying to get this movie done, right? You know, and I finally just figured out how to fix a sound problem I was having. It was at, like, half volume until today. While I'm going through all of this film stuff- Oh my gosh it's a fucking learning process. Anyway, Bigfoot has been giving me shit because I'm not playing tour guide I guess."

"That's fucked up."

"Yeah, right? So, I think he's been drug sick off and on and using or something. He's sooo sensitive. He's freaking out about my driving. Every time I switch a lane he's loosing his shit. I just can't stand to sit next to him."

"Aw baby, what are you going to do?"

"I think I just figured that out before you called. What I'm going to do is try to not let him get to me as much as possible, for just a while, now that I've identified him for the pussy asshat that he really is. I'm just not going to invest too much into his bullshit."

"Ok, but that that will only work for a while. You have a long way to go."

"Exactly! That is why after I get him to New York, where he has a hotel reservation, I'm going to dump his ass the next time he starts up. I'll take him to an airport or something. It'll actually be cheaper for him to fly home at that point."

"What about your movie? How will you finish it?"

"I think I have a fix for that too. We planned on giving the whole thing a fictitious ending, where we both get killed off, like in Easier Rider. You seen that?"

"Yeah, that's funny. Your idea, not the movie."

"Haha! Yeah, so, we'll get killed off, just not like getting shot, the way they died in that movie. Instead we'll die in a much more elaborate way. I was thinking that he'll get eaten by a bear and then later, I'll be attacked and swallowed by a shark, but then I'll burst through his stomach. I'll be dead from injuries too though. You see, very dramatic."

"Oh my God. Sheez, I'd expect nothing less from you. Baby- Oh shit, I gotta go. I have to meet my sponsor in five-minutes. I'm late. Hugs and kisses. I'll call you soon. I love you!"

"Ok, yeah you better get. X O, X O, X O. Love you too!"

Later, Lief met up with Bigfoot who shared the sad news that street performing had been outlawed in Austin, aka Live Music Capitol of the World, a city known for it's contributions and commitment to music. Austin City Limits, South by Southwest, and the Urban Music Festival were a couple huge regular shows that Lief could name off of the top of his head. He knew there were a hand full of many other notable music festivals as well. Lief had clear memories of how the sounds of the many street band's music mixed together with the other street music when he walked downtown. For Lief, that was the largest part of Austin's identity. It was the reason why he had loved the city so much. And it was the reason that he couldn't wait to return. He thought about the nonsensicalness of it. *What the fuck?*

The free flowing music had become governed and regulated by law. Lief could only think of how the Galactic Empire had first taken control of the beating heart of the nation in D.C. before its dark sided grasp clutched the throats of smaller local governments across the nation. To that, Lief's thoughts could no longer be contained in the confines of his mind.

"This is a fucking travesty! Let's set up and play right here."

"Right here? Dude, we're in front of a Whole Foods."

"Yeah. So? I don't like Austin anymore. I say fuck it. The quicker we film this and get the fuck out, the better."

"What about dinner with your sister?"

"Ah, I'll call her. You saw how busy she was. It'll work out better for her."

"Whatever you say man, your family, not mine. Let's Play."

The beautiful skyscraper skyline of downtown Austin was the perfect backdrop to the musical production that Lief and Bigfoot set for film. Pedestrians tipped well after witnessing and listening to the almost forgotten art of busking in the neglected streets of oppression. They played a half-hour, packed up before the fuzz could issue a citation for disturbance of the peace, and then hit the road for Louisiana, hoping that street music in the Big Easy was still alive and well.

CHAPTER 14

CHICORYLAND PART ONE

Rain poured as Gas Station Rose entered La Grange along Highway 71. Lief only knew of the town by way of ZZ Top's song by the same name. He hadn't had enough time to download and play more than a handful of the band's unique synth laced, blues fused, rock songs, before they dropped into the middle of Kenny Rodger's hometown of Houston. Before they could see what condition their condition was in, they were corralled in and out of the polluted city and into a slew of towns that Lief had only heard mention of through the sloshy vocals of Lucinda Williams as they headed into Louisiana. They didn't have time to stop in any of those charming, smaller towns that she sang about. From her descriptions, there was nothing but heartbreaks and hangovers to be found in any of them anyway.

The plan was to get to Baton Rouge to stay with Lief's paternal grandparents, Gran and Nana, as they preferred to be called. The Tin Can had many miles of road to cover and they didn't want to be inconsiderate by getting there too late in the evening.

Gran and Nana were a couple years short of being centenarians. Old age had taken its toll on their bodies, leaving them with a laundry list of health problems, but their minds were as sharp as tungsten needles. They were smart to begin with, but they maintained their cognitive capabilities with music study, constant reading, and an intolerance for reality television. Both of them had earned doctorates and were the heads of the academic, white collar fraction of Lief's family. Gran had a PhD in physics and Nana had a doctorate in music as an organist, to be specific. Lief didn't know them well and could count on his fingers the amount of times he had seen them. Lief's father, aka Senior, had a falling out with them when he left home at nineteen to join the Navy.

Forming new relationship's wasn't easy for Lief, but he knew that getting to know all of his family better wouldn't hurt. At least each of his grandparents were one quarter of his maker. While most people had a more heart felt relationship with family, Lief's connection with much of them was more of a biological tie. Though unfamiliar with them, he could get some insight into his genetic predispositions. Lief saw it possible that they all might find good reason to stay in contact after his visit.

The stormy weather along the way was welcome though the tension between Lief and Bigfoot was reaching a tipping point. It became obvious that Bigfoot copped a fix in Austin and was starting to come down. Lief's desire to boot Bigfoot grew, but he knew he had to exercise whatever kind of restraint that he could muster until New York. That was where an "I don't give a fuck" attitude served Lief well because he knew the "B.B." would likely continue. The pretending not to give a fuck turned into not giving a fuck. At times he forgot Bigfoot was there. It wasn't until much later in the drive that Lief attempted to speak with him.

"I can't wait to get some Chicory Coffee in N'awlins. Everyone's been telling me to get the chicory kind of coffee when I visit. Funny thing is, I've been there at least twenty times and I've never had it or heard of it until we were getting ready for this trip."

Bigfoot did not respond, nor did Lief think he would. He just looked out his window as if he were not wanting to face Lief. Lief blew it off and continued to look at the highway signs as he continued to drive along I-10.

"Lake Charles, huh, I heard about that in a Lucinda Williams song. Actually a lot of these towns we've been passing sound a little familiar."

Bigfoot, again, had no response. At that point, Lief was talking out-loud to himself before he started singing the Lucinda Williams song "Joy".

Bigfoot's stare was transfixed on the sheets of rain pouring down. Pretending there was no problem, Lief tried to engage Bigfoot. It took a while, but Bigfoot admitted he wasn't feeling well. Lief asked him if he needed him to stop for anything to help with his condition. Bigfoot declined the offer.

Knowing it couldn't make the mood any worse, Lief asked Bigfoot if he wouldn't mind filming some of the scenery outside so they could use it for background, in-between shots that they could add narration to when they spliced the film together. Bigfoot obliged, then went the extra mile and started to talk. In fact, he didn't just talk, he opened up more than Lief had ever witnessed. Needless to say, Lief was surprised. Bigfoot spoke as if he were dictating notes to himself about his brief catalog of events that led up to him going on their road trip. Lief interjected.

"Dude, This is great. What about I ask you questions leading to the specific things you've been talking about, you know like an interview?"

A bolt of lightning flashed with a roar of thunder, almost as if to put an exclamation mark on Lief's idea.

"Ok. Yeah, let's. And then I could interview you on what led up to you going on this trip. That's actually a good idea."

They gave it a good college try even though it was strange to be asking about things that they already knew at the answers to.

Lief asked basic soft ball questions, but Bigfoot surprised Lief when he veered away from small answers and gave revealing responses, some of which included too much information. He addressed the biggest elephant in the room when he opened up about his take on addiction and the events surrounding his car accident that destroyed Tin Can #1. Bigfoot gave explicit details about buying heroin in the Tenderloin district of San Francisco after he had given Lief a ride to The San Francisco airport for a flight to New York. He explained that it was not his intention to buy drugs when he drove through the city. Lief did not believe the part about Bigfoot's intention, but it was a step in the right direction for him. Lief knew that addicts were among the most skilled as deniers of their own truths.

Thoughts about denial, led Lief deep into his own mind while Bigfoot spoke. Lief subscribed to the philosophy that all people manifested their own reality, which made him question the value of one's individual perception compared to other's. His pondering led to several uncomfortable questions. *If this is my reality, are other people a figment of my imagination? If not, how do we coexist in the same plain of existence? If our realities overlap in the same plain of existence, who is the one living denial?*

Hyper-focused on the thought and in way too deep, Lief's fear grew although his blood pressure seemed to drop. A cold sweat broke across his forehead and neck. The threads of life's delicate fabric were pulled and began to unravel. He became weak, then slumped into the wheel, and grew nauseous. It was like a bad trip on LSD and it may have been a flashback.

His fear told him to go no further. He suspected that the fragility of his own reality laid insignificant around the corner. He felt as though he was one breath away from disappearing into nothingness. But the dangling carrot, the hope that there was more to existence, something more solid, told him to defy fear, to continue the thought further. He closed his eyes and activated a thought wiping atomic bomb from the center of his mind. At the same time, a massive gust of wind blew the car halfway into the other lane. Lief's head whipped back, leaving him sitting upright in his seat with beads of sweat rolling down his face.

"Lief, are you ok? You look really pale."

"Oh. Yea- Yeah. It's just that sometimes I hold my breath and forget that I'm holding my breath and, whew- I think I just did that. I'm fine."

"Oookaay. Do you mind re-asking me the last question so that I can be more to the point?"

"Yeah, of course. Just remember, we're going to chop this all up when we edit it anyways. If it turns out there is anything that you don't want to be included, you'll just let me know and I won't include it. It is for this very reason that I haven't asked you for a release form yet. This way you'll have veto power. You see?"

Bigfoot saw the logic and suggested they just move on to the next question.

— —

It was near midnight when they arrived at Nan and Gran's home in Baton Rouge. Lief's Grandparents, in their ripe old age, went to bed around 4 p.m., so showing up that late was not cool. As far as Lief knew, old people always went to bed early unless they had one of those home shopping network conditions, and they did not.

Nana heard them pull into the driveway and had the door open before they got to it. Nana invited them in, but there was no welcoming greeting. It was all business.

"You made it. You're late. Come on in and I'll show you to a couple of beds in one of our back rooms."

She slowly led them down a long hallway that had two lifetimes worth of pictures hanging on the walls. Most of them were black and white, but there were a few that were in sepia from the turn of the century, the prior century. The house smelled musty and it was evident that much of the household chores were difficult for them to keep up with. The condition of the home was not beyond a good day of house cleaning though.

When they arrived at the room, Lief asked if there was anything that they could help out with around the home while they were there. Nana was quick to answer.

"Yes, actually. Gran and I can use a hand with some of the gardening in the raised boxes out front. It's been raining quite a bit, so the weeds should come out fairly easy."

"For Sure. I'll get that taken care of first thing in the morning."

"You know, come to think of it, there are also a few things we may need moved around in the back too. I can show you them tomorrow, It's too dark out there now."

"Perfect, we'll help you with as much as we can. By the way, we figured we'd get back on the road around 10. I'll be sure to get up early enough to get those things done though."

—— ——

The next morning, the rain was coming down harder than the day before. It looked like the gardening would have to wait for clearer weather, but they would be gone by then. Lief and Bigfoot readied themselves for the day and were greeted by the grandparents in the kitchen. A mangy grey cat, resembling Bill the Cat from "Bloom County" comics, peered above a nearby sofa to investigate the strangers in the house. Nan and Gran had been up and at it for a while and had made eggs and coffee. Lief showed gratitude for their hospitality, Bigfoot did not.

"Thank you. That's not Chicory coffee is it? Everyone keeps telling me that I have to try it down here."

"Chicory? Oh Chicory. No, this is just regular coffee. I think they have Chicory in New Orleans for the tourists, probably at that Cafe Du Monde, I think it's called. Gran, do you remember what they call that establishment with the chicory coffee?"

He stared through to window and off into the distance, as if he didn't hear her, then offered a delayed response.

"What? Chicory? You know where it is, you already told them."

Lief wished he didn't ask.

"Well, I'll look for it there. It's too bad it's raining so much. I'm afraid we'll be gone before it stops. I was really hoping to help you weed the garden."

Nana wasn't letting him off the hook.

"It's easier to weed in the rain. The soil is soft, they come right out."

Gran nodded his head and grunted, agreeing with Nana. It was apparent that she did most of the talking in their home.

"That makes sense, I'll get right to it then."

Lief changed into grungier clothes that were suitable for wading through the mud, wishing he had brought his wetsuit. Bigfoot sat and ate breakfast which was just fine with Lief because he'd rather be spared the complaining than have assistance. The weather reminded him of his time living in Mississippi on the Gulf Coast when he attended weather school. The humidity left him soaked everyday, with or without precipitation.

The weeds came right out of the soil just as Nana said they would although he doubted that her or Gran ever tried to garden in the rain. After removing every weed he could find, along with several plants that were supposed to have remained in the box, he signaled for Bigfoot through the kitchen window. He was too wet to go in and needed Bigfoot to get him a change of clothes from his bag. Lief stripped down in the driveway and put on the dry clothes, once again, presenting an unusual sight for the neighbors. He changed as fast as he could to avoid drenching in the new clothes, then found Nana when he got back into the house.

"All done. Do you mind if I throw these in your dryer for a little while before we get back on the road?"

"Sure, it's right over here. Thank you for getting those weeds done. Gran's back hasn't been doing well as of late."

They walked by her electric organ along the way to the laundry area. Upon seeing the organ, Lief realized that he was presented the perfect opportunity to get another musician on film for the movie and presented the idea.

"Nana, any chance I could film you playing a song for our movie? I see you've kept your organ. The movie's about musicians you know. What do you think?"

"Oh my. It's been so long since I've played that thing. Why don't you let me think about that for a little while. I'm out of practice. Let me think if there's even a song that I could pull off."

Lief knew she'd agree. He was going to be waiting for his clothes to dry anyway. He quite liked the back story that the addition of his family's musical talents brought to the film, giving way to Lief's predisposition for his own musical appreciation.

As Lief suspected, she called him in to film, but only after giving a lengthy disclaimer to cover any results that might occur outside of a true perfectionist's impossible standards. It was obvious that she relished the opportunity. Lief set up and did quick sound check before she spread the sheet music on the music rack, straightened her posture, and then took a purposeful pause to give honor to the notes that would follow. Nana played a reverent tune that sounded like a funeral song. She pulled plugs above the keys, played two levels of keyboards, and pressed pedals with her feet. Lief had never seen so much multi-tasking with a single instrument.

There was a sense of eloquence as the final note sustained, regardless of the sound of Lief's shoes thumping in the dryer behind her. Lief considered how valuable the section of film was, knowing that he captured a piece of her life's work. He also knew that, as with his grandma in Los Angeles, his film of her might be the last footage of her life. His emotions took notice of life's magical, transitory nature.

Not waisting any time after filming, Bigfoot and Lief said their goodbye's. Gran shook hands and Nana sort of hugged Lief before they left. Into the monsoon they drove, towards a not so far away land called New Orleans, but only after they stopped at the Waffle House near the entrance of the eastbound I-10.

◆ ～

The closer Lief got to the Big Easy, the more his embarrassing memories from prior visits surfaced. He used to go there on the weekends when he was enlisted and stationed forty-five minutes away in Biloxi, Mississippi, while studying to be a weather man for the navy. Because his schooling was tough, he felt entitled to the weekend festivities in New Orleans. Back then, New Orleans was off limits to his Air Force compadres, so they'd refer to it by it's code name, downtown Boloxi before they would all go over there to party. Needless to say, Lief was intoxicated throughout all previous visits.

The city came into view from the freeway. It may have looked like any other metropolis to Bigfoot, but Lief knew the details of its haunted patina on its brick and rod iron streets underneath its huddled skyscrapers. It was Bigfoot's first visit. His knowledge of New Orleans was based on tales told by drug addicts that had lived there. Lief suspected that Bigfoot would be looking for a fix there, which may have been the cause of his sudden upward mood swing.

The towering downtown Sheraton hotel stood out to Lief, and brought back vague recollections of an off duty stripper, Red Stripe lager, "Caribbean Queen" by Billy Ocean, and two trips to the downstairs sundry for an assortment of refills. Then he spotted the Audubon Aquarium along the river front. He remembered the time that his he and his shipmate C.J. snuck in through a maintenance entrance. Although he was drunk at the time, his recollection of the penguin habitat was crystal clear. Through its glass tank wall he stood in a stupor watching groups of penguins flying underneath the water in schools, back and forth, one end to the other. He thought it strange that he couldn't remember one other thing about the aquarium though. Lief's thoughts drifted to ground zero of his New Orleans regrets that laid in the middle of the French Quarter, on a street appropriately named named Bourbon.

They had made reservations at Marriott Courtyard Hotel that was located five blocks from Canal Street. That's where the French Quarter begins and most common sense ends. When checking into their hotel, the concierge found a discrepancy with the discount form, a discrepancy that went unnoticed 97% of the time. The concierge explained that his form was checked as a discount for friends and family and not did not qualify for the, 80% off discount for employees and their spouses. Lief threw him a bullshit story, hoping he'd let him keep the larger discount.

"Oh yeah, I see that. Shoot. Looks like she checked the wrong box before printing it. Blasted- She won't be at work for two more days either."

"That's unfortunate. The good news is, I can get you in at one-eighty a night, the friends and family rate."

"Hmm, I had budgeted, for the spouse rate. I just stayed in Los Angeles with the same form for the spouse rate. You can call and confirm that with them. I mean you can see we have the same last name."

"No, sorry."

"Ok, give me a second."

Lief stepped away from the counter and consulted with Bigfoot.

The two could not afford to pay the one-hundred and eighty dollars plus another thirty for parking. They agreed that New Orleans was not the place to try and sleep in the back of the Tin Can, but two-hundred and ten dollars wasn't going to fly either. Lief searched his phone for other Marriotts in the area. At the same time, the parking attendant was asking for Lief's keys to the Tin can, which was blocking several other cars from getting through the driveway. The internet was moving at a snails pace and the line of cars grew and backed up into the street. A list of hotels came through on his phone just as a car began to honk at the valet who, again, asked Lief for his keys. Lief turned into a pressure cooker full of anxiety. Lief barked at the valet.

"Give me a second! I'll be right over."

Several more cars began to honk.

"I'm sorry sir, I need to move your car now."

"Bigfoot! I found one! Let's try this one. There's a Springhill Suites near here, it's owned by the Marriott too. The form should work there."

Lief told the frustrated valet to fuck off, then peeled out of the lot. They put the new address into GPS and followed the prompts.

"In three-hundred feet make a left turn."

"Oh shit! I left the form in there with the dude. He can call my ex now. Shit!"

"You have more of them, right?"

"Yeah, but man, if that dude calls her I'm fucked. But yeah, we can use another one. The good thing is that I found another spot, and close. Actually, it looked really close. I hope the directions got it right."

The GPS continued with the next prompt while Bigfoot pressured Lief with more questions.

"Turn left in seven-hundred feet."

"What if they notice the same thing? This is getting a little nerve racking for me."

Lief did not respond.

"Lief! Dude, what are we going to do?"

"That's it!"

"What's it?"

"We need to distract them. When we used the form in L.A. I was in full regalia with my American flag vest and ascot. Oh, and I was carrying the camera! That's right! The concierge was a lady, a young one, who probably thought I was a rock star or something. It's time to reenlist the ascot. We need to bring the camera in with us too. And most importantly, we need a female concierge."

"It's worth a shot."

Lief pulled over to change into his high performance cloths. He took another look at the directions on his phone.

"The GPS says it's .1 mile away. I hope it's right. It feels like we're going in a circle."

"It's just the one way streets around here. We'll find it."

Lief followed the directions further, making one more left turn before it said they had arrived. They were smack-dab back at the same parking lot where they started.

"Fuck! I told you this piece of shit was leading us the wrong way!"

"Wait- What's the name of the hotel?"

"Springhill"

Bigfoot pointed to a sign on the other side of the parking lot that read "Springhill Suites".

"Dude this is it. They share the same parking lot."

The parking valet, the one that Lief had just told to fuck off two-minutes prior, approached Lief's window. He did a double take at Lief, seeing him wearing a different set of clothes. It was possible that the valet thought Lief was a someone else, but there was no mistake that it was the same Bigfoot.

"Keys please"

"Changed my mind. Hey sorry about that before. I'm having a rough day. All that honking really set me off."

Lief handed him a ten dollar tip.

"It's not a problem. Here's your tag."

Lief and Bigfoot walked into the lobby of the Springhill Suites that shared a wall with the previous hotel. Lief carried in the camera with full rig, while Bigfoot carried a guitar case. Low and behold, it was a young woman at the counter. She had already locked eye's on the pair and was twisting her hair. Lief knew he had it in the bag. *Butter.*

"Hi, I recently made a reservation to stay the night."

She smiled at Lief as he handed her his i.d., credit card, and his room rate form.

"What brings you to the area?"

"We are doing a show later tonight."

"Exciting. Where are you playing? I'm looking for a show tonight."

"Bigfoot, what's the name of that club?"

"Ah, I dunno. It's ahh, It's in the car."

"It's on Bourbon, near St. Louis, next to some club called Razzoos"

To Lief's surprise, he remembered the name of a place from his prior visits. The boisterous front desk clerk began to bounce up and down with enthusiasm. Lief's perception of the world slowed to a roll and had become reduced to a hyper-focused narrow frame of her breasts. At the apex of each jump upwards, the momentum of her boobs continued towards the heavens, while her body returned to the Earth. The repetition would have set them free if she hadn't calmed down when she caught the attention of her superior. She let out a high pitched squeak.

"Ohh, I love that place. I'll look for you there. Wait- I thought that was a karaoke bar?"

"Yeah, it's next to the karaoke bar. I mapped the address earlier and for some reason Razzoos stuck. Road weary, what can you do? You'll find us. We're Gas Station Rose by the way. You can check us out online first if you like."

She paused and looked around to make sure the coast was clear, then leaned in closer to Lief to whisper.

"You know what? Let me do something here. I'm not supposed to do this, but we have an available suite on the fourteenth floor."

She handed Lief the small envelope containing the room key cards. Lief whispered back to her.

"Thank you."

"You're very welcome. I look forward to seeing you later."

The two kept their composure until getting into the elevator. Once inside, they turned into excited grade schoolers acting as if they had just discovered porn magazine.

"Dude! We pulled it off. Good one Lief."

"Yes we did. Did you notice she waived our parking fee too?"

"Really? Oh man, that's rad."

"This place is way better that the other one. We get a free breakfast here in the morning too. Forty bucks! I feel bad though because she's going to be looking for us tonight and we won't be there."

"Uh-oh, yeah. That's alright. We'll just leave early in the morning I guess."

The fourteenth floor wasn't only nice, it looked like the lobby to a modern museum. It had contemporary paintings that stretched down every wall in sight. The hallway was lit by lights hidden within the multi-layered ceiling. The room was even more impressive with it's deep red leather furniture, stretched exotic Brazilian hardwood desk, 60-inch flatscreen, full kitchen, and partitioned office. In the bathroom, dark polished marble covered every inch of the walls, counter tops, and the floor. The subtle light that rested on it's glossy surface highlighted the veins in the metamorphic rock. The lavish effect was enough to impress even the most adept geologist. Lief voiced an astute observation.

"It's funny. It was the back of the car or this. Score."

After settling into their luxurious room, they made some tea and came up with a game plan. They decided to do some recon in the french quarter for possible places to play. Along the way, they hoped to find some chicory coffee as well. Before leaving the room for the Quarter, Lief made a last minute decision to bring the Black Mamba out solo, without the cumbersome frame of the rig. That way he could conceal it in the camera bag. It wouldn't open any doors for them that way, but he'd be able to get some high quality footage if something jumped out at them, and knowing New Orleans, Lief knew something would.

Walking towards the quarter, they stumbled upon Harrah's Casino and decided to try their luck. Bigfoot had never gambled before, so he asked Lief where he would find his best odds. Lief explained that if he were good at either blackjack or craps that he'd have a good chance of making money there, but seeing as Bigfoot had never gambled before, he led him to the roulette table.

"This is easy man. Pick black or red and put your money on the one you decide. You'll have a 47/47 chance either way."

"47?"

"Yeah, well, around 47. It's actually 47.4. You see the two green spaces on the wheel? It can end up there too."

Bigfoot placed a twenty on black.

"Once you go black..."

The roulette operator was an elderly black woman who forced a smile after Bigfoot's awkward comment. She spun the wheel. The ball circled around and around the wheel as the look of excitement grew on Bigfoot's face. His eyes tracked every movement until he tensed up when the ball bounced between black, green, and red in the final moments before resting on black.

"Awesome! I just doubled my money. That's more than I have ever made in an hours worth of work."

"Good job. My turn to make some money."

Lief slipped across the aisle to the nearest penny slot and feed it a twenty.

"The only way to make money on these is in the bonus round, so bet low until you feel that it may hit, then up your bet."

Lief did just that, and in the third bet, he upped it to the max bet. He hit the bonus.

"Ok, now I'm going to teach you the most important part of winning money in the casino."

"Yeah, what's that?"

"Leaving- Quickly"

Lief cashed his slot winnings ticket and they walked out to find Canal Street on the next corner.

"Bigfoot, welcome to the French Quarter."

"The infamous French Quarter, so cool."

"That's right it's not just famous, it's In-famous."

Bigfoot looked at Lief, confused at his take on the word infamous.

"You know, the line from the Three Amigos. Please tell me you've seen it."

"Yeah, I saw it. It's just been a while. Whatever, it's hot as balls."

"Ahh, ok. To change the subject, I should warn you to watch your shit out here. Seriously, this is one of the biggest con, theft, pick-pocket zones on the planet."

Bigfoot took his advice and crossed his own camera bag over his chest, instead of letting it loosely dangle on his shoulder.

They observed a lone run of the mill guitarist playing on the street who they passed up to look into a large event causing a stir just a few blocks up the street. The event turned out to be a large production film being made that day. Several streets around Jackson Square were being used as sets and were blocked off for shooting. Leading to the areas of filming, there were large cables taped down, running all over the place from several power generators. There were at least five matching big rigs parked off to the side of the road that were all involved in the production in some way or another as well.

A short stair case led to an open door on the side of one of the truck trailers. Inside of the doorway, a guy sat in a chair, reading from a magazine.

"Excuse me, what are you guys filming here?"

"Pitch Perfect 2"

"No Way! Are you looking for any extras?"

"I think they have that all figured out, but you can ask the guy up there with a clipboard. We're just the camera trailer."

"Really? Any chance I can take a peek at your film gear? I'm filming a little movie of my own, all the way cross country, about street musicians. It'd be cool to see what the professionals use."

"Sure, come on up."

"Cool! Oh, is there any chance I can capture some of this on my stripped down Black Magic?"

"Black Magic huh? I've been reading about those. Sure."

Lief put the prime lens on his camera and began filming. They ascended a set of mobile stairs into the trailer where they found themselves face to face with a case holding the biggest camera lens that Lief had ever seen in his life.

"That's the Panavision PCZ and it's younger brother, the Primo goes there, but it's in use right now."

"That thing looks like a canon. I mean, not canon the lens, the one that shoots actual cannonballs."

"Yeah, she's a biggin."

"Just out of curiosity, how much does something like that run?"

"Oh, you know, I'm not sure what they went for. You can't really buy them anymore. They're only available for rent these days."

"Wow! Priceless!"

"No, I'm sure the rental company will come up with a price if we messed it up."

"Hey- This is a bit of an off subject, but do you know where I might be able to find Chicory coffee around here?"

"Never heard of it"

He brushed off another failed attempt at locating the coveted coffee before scanning the trailer with his Black Mamba Camera, then turned it on himself.

"Lief here, Bigfoot and I are on the set of Pitch Perfection 2 where we are visiting the camera trailer. Behind me here is the biggest lens known to mankind, the Panavision PCZ, I think. It's so big that it's priceless, you can only rent them. Cool, huh?"

Lief thanked the camera trailer guy and even got him to sign a release form, making it all legit. Bigfoot and Lief were so stoked about the footage they filmed that they forgot to look into being extras. They did, however, walk by the sets to take a peak at how large productions were done.

The set was too big for Lief to conceive. His own film was too big for him to conceive. The huge sets made his film's efforts seem so small. He couldn't help but think that his dreams of making films might have been an unsurmountable task. He sank into doubt, beating himself up, before remembering that discouraging thoughts were always just a phase of the artistic process. Casting his doubts aside, he doubled his efforts to find a cup of Chicory Coffee.

CHAPTER 15

CHICORYLAND PART TWO

Entering Jackson Square in the center of the French Quarter, Lief and Bigfoot spotted a zydeco street band playing in front of a large group of tourists. It presented a long awaited opportunity for them to film their first street band, so they made their way across the crowded square in a hurry to get a good shot.

The whole scene surrounding the music was perfect. A painter was set up with an easel panting the band as the crowd danced and clapped to the beat. In between songs, the band's washboard player picked up an extra vested washboard and slipped it onto the shoulders of a willing participant in the crowd. They jumped back into song while the new impromptu musician fumbled around, brushing up and down the metal board on his chest, mimicking the professional washboarder. Half way into the song, he found his rhythm and danced a funny jig in excitement.

Lief arrived with the camera after the song was already underway so he waited for the next song to start filming. In hindsight he wished he'd have jumped in and filmed it when he got there, because it was the band's last song. The crowd cheered and tossed fistfuls of cash into a banjo case that was opened for tips. And then the band was gone. All Lief could do was hope for an opportunity to film later in the day, but he wasn't holding his breath. They were over halfway across the country and hadn't filmed a single street band on their movie about America's street music.

His fears of failure hit a new low. He thought he was following his stream of life by taking on large, but not impossible project. To that point, it seemed as if he was swimming up stream. The task had begun to look impossible. Lief took a pause from his self inflicted ass-kicking when he received a call from Kay. Her call came when it was needed most and distracted him from the unintentional lie he was telling himself, the one that said he was making a crap film and failing at that.

Her call was brief and was just to let him know that she loved him and that she had arrived safe in New Jersey. However short the call, it turned out to be one of the more reveling calls he had ever received.

Kay sounded different. The difference wasn't in what she said as much as it was with how she said it. It was if there was something more like another layer that carried the warmth of her touch. Her cadence was hypnotizing and seized every bit of his attention before pulling him to the edge of something long forgotten. A large portion of his enduring restlessness receded. It wasn't until Lief grew as comfortable as could be, that the call revealed its true purpose. It was one more welcome check point in a string of deliberate circumstances that would all change his life forever, while at the same time, confirming that he was most certainly on course.

The extra layer in her voice activated a deep rooted desire that was planted in a dream from his childhood. Although it had been laying dormant in Lief's mind for the better part of his life, it was steering the ship without him ever knowing. It was of a broad thought that narrowed to the point of a pen, held by a female's silhouette, which wrote and spoke the words "We are each other's. Please find me with the light of your love". Those words and the feelings afterwards, had left him a boy with an obsession to fill a void that he couldn't understand.

The unspoken part of Kay's call made it clear as day that she was the voice of the alluring figure from his dream. The glass slipper fit when the light of his love for Kay had become bright enough to reveal the meaning and answer to the biggest mystery of his life, and both at the same time. She was the dream and at last they were each other's.

Lief knew his next move would need to be a leap of faith. But before the jump, he needed to put his money where his thoughts were and buy her a ring. He was going get that ring in the French Quarter.

"Bigfoot, You know what? I think I'm going to buy a ring for Kay here."

"Really? Cool."

"Yeah, this is the place to get it for sure. It's way better than in a strip mall somewhere. Anyways, I doubt you'd like to go with, so you want to just meet up in a bit?"

"Right on man. Sure, I guess I'll go look for that coffee. How bout' you just give me a holler when you're done?"

"Perfect! Talk to you soon. Wish me luck."

Lief found several jewelry shops and walked into a few, but none of them felt right, at least not for his wallet. He had seen many estate jewelry shops and decided to look in one to see if they might have something befitting Kay, something with a little of that charming New Orleans patina, but without the not so charming price tag. Kay knew he was on a shoestring budget which gave him some leeway. If she said yes, he knew he'd get her a bigger one later.

Between two fortune telling businesses, Lief found a jewelry shop that had both new and estate jewelry. As he looked through the display cases, Bigfoot called, bearing the unfortunate news that he was unable to find any chicory coffee. Lief gave him his coordinates so that he could join him then continued browse the unusual mixture of old and new jewelry. Each time Lief saw a price tag he could read, he'd worry that Kay might not say yes, and then he thought about how much money he'd be out if that were to be the case. The jewelry store clerk finished a transaction with another customer then greeted Lief.

"Hello my friend."

The slimy buddy-ness almost made Lief throw up in his mouth.

"Is there anything I can help you find?"

"Well, I'm looking for a wedding ring and I'm on a pretty tight budget so I'm possibly considering an estate ring."

"What kind of a budget are we talking about?"

Lief sighed.

"Geez, I can't really do any more than a grand, probably less."

"I see. You're probably not going to want any of estate jewels then. They are considerably more than many of the new ones we have within your price range."

The new information narrowed Lief's search. He was able to eliminate looking at half the store.

Bigfoot saw Lief through the window and joined him in the store.

"You find a ring yet?"

"Nope, still looking, but this one looks good."

"Dude! You should let me film this."

"Great idea!"

With the camera rolling, Lief asked the salesman how much the ring was.

"Let me pull than one out to give you a closer look."

Lief examined the ring. It was a roundish shaped diamond inset in a raised white gold band with smaller diamonds scattered around it. The large diamond had a brownish tint which would diminish its value in the eyes of the common bridezilla, but Kay was not the manic bride sort. It looked like the perfect starter ring for her. The salesman knew Lief was locked in on the ring so he came in for the close.

"It seems you may have found the right one, which I may add is a great choice. This is a certified three quarter carrot diamond which gives the appearance of a full carrot due to the way it is set in the white gold band. There is another eighth of a carrot in smaller diamonds encrusted in the band as well. This is considered a brown diamond and is an increasingly more popular style for those looking to avoid the typical pure clarity."

"And the cost?"

"Like I said, it's certified, meaning it will come with a GAI certificate containing a description of the stone and the appraised fair market value, which is $1500."

"Ouch!"

"Sticker shock, huh?"

"Like I said, I'm on a tight budget. I've put all of my resources into a movie that I am currently filming across the US, actually this has just become a part of it if you'd be willing to sign a release form. Come to think of it, if you did it would be a great form of advertising for you."

"A movie, like an in theater movie?"

"That's the goal."

"Sure. I'd sign it, I guess. Wait- There's not going to be any nudity in it is there? I could't if that's the case."

"Yeah, no nudity. Mostly just music and travel."

Bigfoot was on the spot with a fresh release form that the salesman signed with a smile. The salesman's distraction gave Lief time to look at the other rings without being bombarded by sales voodoo. But Lief had became transfixed on the tint of the brown diamond on the ring out of the case in front of him. Lief's anxiety was in high gear and was noticeable by the contraction of muscles in his jaw and temples. Lief remembered how creepy he looked when he'd become hyper focused as he was. He paused to speak to the camera and did his best Gollum impersonation.

"My precious"

The salesman feared Lief was going off course so he presented a him with an offer.

"I can do $1300."

Lief paused for a moment, knowing he couldn't even afford the lowered price. He prepared himself to walk, to assume, yet another failure that he'd chalk up as a sign that Kay would have said no anyway.

"You know, I appreciate your time, but I really have to stick to something under a grand."

Lief walked to the front door with every intention to leave, but the salesman stopped him.

"Hold on. I can see you really like it. Offer me a fair price."

"Ok, seriously, it would have to be around $900, I understand that's quite a bit less than your asking price- Ok. I can do this, if you can do a grand out the door. I'll take it."

Until that point, Lief had not given any indication that he was skilled in the art of sales, but the time had come for him to see how his sales kung-fu stood up to that of jewelry salesman. The salesman raised his brow as if to say touché, acknowledging that he stood in front of a worthy opponent. That was where the long pause started and the battle of the salesmen began, a battle where the first to talk lost. Lief had dropped all expression on his face and stood as motionless as a deadly alligator before a kill. The salesman sucked in his gut, held his breath, and stared straight into Lief's eyes. To Bigfoot, an uninitiated, the mental exchange may not have seemed like much, but to the trained eye lightning, lasers, bullets, and blades clashed between Lief and the clerk. The clerk took a breath and broke pose when he began to fidget with his hands as if he were countering fingers, pretending to make calculations. A bead of sweat rolled down his forehead. He then tried to draw Lief out with body language indicative that he was trying to formulate words, but needed assistance with what he wanted to say. That was a good trick, but Lief did not bite. He had already sized up his rival and knew he had won. He had stopped thinking about the sale and had diverted his attention to thoughts of lunch. The salesman took a large breath and conceded to the sale on Lief's terms.

"One thousand, out the door?"

"Yeah"

"Ok. Let's do this quick before my mom gets here."

Lief left the store, clutching his future in his hands. He put it all on the line with his purchase. If an emergency were to arise he'd have no money left to deal with it. He'd have a tight budget from there on in, but he knew it was worth the risk.

The two decided to split up and do their own things for a while before meeting up later in the day. Bigfoot said he wanted to get a nap at the hotel, but Lief knew Bigfoot wanted to get high and veg out. Lief stayed in the French Quarter to film its quintessential brick alleys, rod iron gates, advertised haunted houses, and hopefully a few street musicians. The more infamous and crazy New Orleans was not yet at hand. As with the Anne Rice vampires, the New Orleans faithful did not descend onto the cobblestone, bead, and vomit laden streets of the Quarter until the sun had set.

While walking around Lief noticed a PJ's coffee shop. He knew it was a chain shop because he passed one earlier. He thought it worth a try to see if they had any chicory coffee. Lief inquired inside with the purple haired twenty something barista gal.

"Hi, do you have chicory coffee here?"

"Chicory?"

"Yeah, you know the coffee that you can supposedly only get in New Orleans. The stuff that's supposed to be everywhere here, Chicory."

"No, we don't have it, I've never heard of it."

What the fuck? Regardless of their lack of Chicory, he ordered a plain old coffee so that he could use an outlet to charge his phone and formulate a strategy for proposing to Kay. The only scenarios he could imagine were more like calculations of sums on a pair of dice that he couldn't stop rolling. Each sum told a story of its own, but he was looking for the exact perfect one. He continued to play through each scenario he could think up, because no matter what was to happen next, his life was guaranteed to be be different. And to Lief different was exciting in itself.

He needed to share the news with someone besides Bigfoot. He knew he'd tell Sarah and his mom sooner or later, but he wanted to confide with a peer. It wasn't until then, that Lief made a depressing discovery at a conscious level. He realized he had no one to call. He went through all the contacts in his phone, then looked at his Facebook "friends" list, but in the end, he knew no one had any basis to care that he was going to ask Kay to marry him. His phone was full of people that he went to great lengths to lose contact with.

Failing to come up with any friends, Lief went ahead and called Sarah who picked up on his first attempt at reaching her.

"Sarah, It's your father. How are you?"

"Good"

"What have you been up to?"

"Nothing"

"Wow! That's great, and super interesting."

"When are you coming back?"

"I'm not sure. Maybe three or four weeks. I miss you though."

"Cool"

"Ok- Well, I have something exciting to tell you."

"Are you going to tell me that you bought me a pony again?"

"Of course I did. That goes without saying, but guess what else?"

"What?"

"I bought an engagement ring for Kay. I'm going to ask her to marry me. Cool, huh?"

"Yeah"

"Sarah, seriously, calm down. Don't get too excited yet. She hasn't even said yes yet, but if she does, she'll be your stepmom and she'll get to tell you what to do, like take out the garbage and brush your teeth and clean your room. What do you think about that?"

"She'll probably say no."

"Alright, you're ignorant. Ok, I gotta run kiddo. Take care. I'll call you soon."

"Bye"

Lief could tell she was happy to hear from him and he was happy to talk to her. He missed her, but he realized that he was not worried about her well being anymore. That was a timely realization because, on the emotional front, Lief had too much on his plate. He had yet to meet Leslie and the uncertainty involved in how that might go was enough without the attached movie and marriage proposal.

All of the heart-centric stimulus at play was enough to overwhelm the emotionally mature, let alone one such as Lief, who was well behind the curve in that area. His emotional development had been arrested when he crossed the invisible line of alcoholism in his early twenties. After that, and into his thirties, whenever he was faced with a challenging situation in life, including success, he drank his way through it instead of feeling it and then making the necessary adjustments. It was not a winning game plan because a person can't avoid life forever. When he stopped drinking he had some catching up to do and he needed a new plan to deal with life. He borrowed AA's plan which was tailored for a guy like him. The plan was simple, but no matter how simple, Lief needed a constant reminder of it. It asked him to trust that things would work out the way that they were supposed to. It also required that he try to be a good person, using his feelings and a few rules of thumb as a guide.

Lief had been letting the "be a good person" part of the plan slip for longer than he could remember. Somewhere in the vicinity of a few years, Lief had been lying to himself about his feelings, rendering them useless and allowing him to become a raging asshole. When things got too overwhelming, good or bad, he'd usually remember to get to an AA meeting. Nine times out of ten, in any given meeting, Lief would remember that everything was happening the way it was intended. He was in need of that reminder more than ever. He looked online and found an AA meeting taking place that evening, and just ten blocks from him.

⌐ ⌐

That night, Lief was the first to arrive at his A.A. meeting. There was rainbow flags attached to the building and reminded him of the businesses with gay owners in San Francisco in the Castro district. An attractive fake blonde woman arrived and was friendly with Lief as she opened up the building and prepared the room for the meeting. She did not strike him as a lesbian so he came to the conclusion that the rainbow flags were just a regional New Orleans kind of flag, not a gay pride thing. He had visited Cusco, Peru a few years prior where he learned that their flag was the same as the gay flag, just upside down.

The room filled with well dressed men and the meeting got underway. After the announcements and introductions, Lief looked down to double-check that he wasn't wearing his ascot. To his relief, he was not. When he looked back up, he caught the female secretary eye fucking him. As soon as he made eye contact with her, she spread her legs enough for him to see the black lace bands at the top of her fishnet stockings. Spreading further, the shadows between her legs receded. The room's lighting revealed that she wasn't wearing any panties. Lief saw everything, even the hoop piercing in her labia. She kept her legs spread until someone in the front row noticed the display and turned to see who was the intended recipient. Lief was caught red handed, looking up the pretty lady's skirt. She assumed a more modest position while Lief adjusted to hide his embarrassment. He didn't miss the irony in the fact that he was a straight man with an erection in a gay meeting.

Vagina aside, the meeting did the trick because he felt like less of an asshole afterwards. When the meeting was over, the group thanked him for visiting. He said good bye to all of them, including the female secretary, although she was walking the same direction as Lief. He knew that any further contact with her might put himself in a tempting and dangerous predicament. Still, he felt her sexual tractor beam, just as he did in Los Angeles with Greta. He adjusted his pace to fall behind, but the seductress adjusted her pace as well until they walked side by side. It became more awkward not to talk than to keep to himself. Lief initiated a conversation.

"Where are you headed?"

"I'm going to try to catch the last part of a Punk and Ska festival just up the way here. How bout' you?"

"Would that be called a skunk festival? Sorry, that was stupid, but I had to. Oh, and I'm just going to try and find my hotel."

"Really, where are you staying?"

"Near St. Peters and Julia."

"Wow, that's a ways. My car is parked near the festival. If you wouldn't mind checking it out with me real quick, I'd be happy to give you a ride back."

"That would be great. Geez, thank you."

Lief's favorite travel experiences had always been seeing the real heart of a city, far from the tourist traps, partaking in the music, meeting the pretty locals, and having sex with them. That was so much the case that

Lief believed that the only effective way to get a feel for a new area, was to have intercourse with a woman who lived there. It was for that reason that Lief knew he needed to run away from the situation he had gotten himself into. He certainly didn't need to get to know New Orleans any better.

He couldn't remember Big Easy's name, but all he could think about was her vaginal piercing, wondering how it would feel on his skin. He gave himself an objective moment and questioned his true motives for continuing to walk with her. *Yeah, she probably wants to have sex, but maybe the upskirt shot was unintentional. Maybe she's just being nice by offering me a ride. I am tired of walking.* His thinking about the matter was cut-off when she made her intentions clearer.

"Just in case you wondered, I'm not gay, I just like that meeting."

"Well, I'm not either. I didn't know what kind of meeting it was before I got there."

"Yeah that happens. You're pretty hot. I'm sure I wasn't the only one to notice."

"Ha! Thank you. That's nice of you."

It was crystal clear that she wanted to have sex with Lief. He was face to face with another test of his love and ability to be with Kay. He put his hand in his pocket and clutched the ring he bought for her. He was weak and Big Easy was kryptonite because he could use some attention, and she was his type. He could make it quick and no one would know. *I would know*, he thought. He thought of Kay's initial objection to his road trip. *She was right.*

He, again, was a conflicted man. A split second thought would be the difference between succumbing or running. The positive outcome of the interesting and experimental experience in L.A. showed him that he didn't always have to fuck up every relationship. The realization that he had a choice had been engrained in, at least, one of his neurological passageways, which meant he knew he could exercise it. Lief was one step away from exhausting his own will power to resist his old ways. Before putting his next foot down, he used a fraction of a second to call on the universe for the strength to just walk away. In stride, he put his foot down, pulled his phone out of his pocket, and told the pretty woman that he needed to make a phone call. He explained that he would try to catch up with her in a few minutes. He could see the disappointment on her face because she knew the unspoken engagement was off. Lief was sure she'd still find what she was looking for at her event if she only had a chance to sit down in front of someone and open up. They parted ways and he called Kay. She was not available, but he left her a loving voicemail, sparing all of the details.

He passed another test and persevered his primitive thinking. He decided he wasn't going to beat himself up too much for considering the opportunity for sex on the road. It was necessary for him to face and change all of his old habits at some point. Lief also knew that she was the one coming onto him and that he hadn't led her on one bit. The biggest take away for Lief was that the universe came to his aid again. It seemed everything happened exactly the way it was supposed to.

Lief made his way back to the hotel and Bigfoot was heading out of the hotel door when he arrived.

"Dude, I took a nap and then got restless. What do you think about filming tonight?"

"Hmm"

Going back out after his experience that evening would be pushing it for Lief, but he agreed. He felt like a gambler who couldn't resist taking the last of his cash to a seat at a black jack table near the exit of the casino. He needed to work on his impulse issues.

Back in the French Quarter they captured the New Orleans night life, although absent of any street music. There was so much humidity in the air that they needed to wipe the fogged-over camera lens every five minutes in order to get a clear shot. Either they were mistaken for part of the Pitch Perfection production or the camera was more powerful than they imagined because every drunk twenty-something out in the area approached them, wanting to be on film. Meat-heads thought walking in front of the camera, quoting rap lyrics while flexing would make it into the final cut. Lief was reminded of why he hated the club scene so much when he was in his twenties. He could never wrap his brain around how all of the posturing and grunting ever got anyone laid. While he was remembering the comedy of the club scene, a genius white boy began to hop around like a gorilla in front of the camera, contorting his hands and fingers as though he had cerebral palsy. He put his face inches from the lens saying something about "Westside" while in the south, and much closer to the east coast. That was when an inebriated twig figured, toe-headed girl with, what appeared to be floatation devices tucked under the skin on her chest, walked up to the poor handicapped boy, hooted, and then lifted her shirt, exposing her breast bags. She straddled his leg and began to convulse and then pulled the boy's face in-between her tits. Lief remembered that stupid came in all sexes and sizes.

"Lief, did you get that girl's tits?"

"I sure did. Too bad I promised the jewelry store guy that we wouldn't have any in the film. Something like that would have been funny to include."

"Something like that WOULD be funny to include."

"But wait… What are the chances that he'd even see the film? I'm thinking we could do something with this. What if we played the part about him saying he'd only agree to be in the film if there was no nudity in it, then we splice in that girl flashing her tits, then cut back into us saying that we would have no nudity, then flash back to more boobs. We can even find some raunchy porn from the internet to throw in there. We can do an entire montage out of it."

"Oh my God, Yes! Fuck yeah! We're doing it."

The next morning the free breakfast included in their reduced hotel rate of forty-bucks, had even more options than the hotel breakfast in Los Angeles. It was more like a casino buffet without the fake chef in the puffy white paper who cuts the not so prime rib. Even a drug sick Bigfoot couldn't complain. After breakfast they packed up and checked out of the hotel.

On their way out of town they stopped on Bourbon Street to get some footage of them busking. It was pointed out by many that it was against the law to play on Bourbon Street. It connected the dots as to why they couldn't find any musicians out there the night before. Either way, Lief was getting the sense that music just wasn't appreciated in the USA like it used to be. They played and filmed there anyway.

After a half-hour set Lief packed up the car while Bigfoot ran around the corner to take another emergency shit. Lief, again, beat the gear loading time record, even without Bigfoot's help. He had been waiting in the sticky heat for Bigfoot to return before he started coming up with conspiracy theories. *What the fuck can't he shoot up any quicker?* Just then Bigfoot walked around the corner with, what looked like, two iced coffees.

"Aww, how thoughtful. You shouldn't have, but hand me one quick. Thanks."

"Guess what?"

"What?"

"It's Chicory."

"The fuck you say?"

"The fuck I DO say."

At last, the two had their chicory coffee in hand as they drove north to Nashville. It tasted like regular coffee.

CHAPTER 16

MUSIC FUCKING CITY

Instead of taking their planned coastal I-10 route east through Biloxi, Mississippi they made a last minute decision to take a more northerly route out of New Orleans by way of I-59 towards their next planned stop in Nashville, Tennessee, aka Music City. Although Lief wanted to see the small Mississippi town he had lived in long before, Bigfoot had no desire to see a town he had no attachments to that would cause them to get to Nashville an hour later. Lief knew he would have to make compromises on the trip, and after being informed while in New Orleans that Biloxi was unrecognizable after Hurricane Katrina had demolished it in 2005, bypassing the small gulf coast city became one of those compromises.

Forty-five miles north of the Big Easy, they crossed the Pearl River into Mississippi where they pulled into a welcome center at the side of the interstate. They were hoping they had a public restroom. They both stretched when they got out of the car. That's when Bigfoot took notice a giant blue sign that they parked in front of.

"Welcome to Mississippi- the birthplace of American music. Huh? Lief, did you see this? American music was born here."

"What? No way. How?"

"I dunno, but that sounds pretty significant."

"Yeah, for sure. I like American music."

"Yeah. It's good."

"Right here? Right here? You don't say?"

At that point in their trip, pulling out the music and film equipment had become more of a burden than an opportunity so they had become selective about where and when they used it. The intense heat and humidity of the south added to the growing list of deterrents from using the heavy gear. They could have gone the rest of the day without filming due to the great footage from Bourbon St. Even though they were in a hurry to get to Nashville. The sole reason for their stop was to use the restrooms, and after seeing that they parked in the exact nine-by-sixteen foot spot where U.S. music was born, they knew they had to film another segment.

In the thick and steamy stickiness of the Mississippi air, they set up their instruments in front of the sign and positioned the camera low to capture both them and the words of historic relevance on the sign. Halfway through recording their first song in the location, a security guard with no apparent appreciation for music, approached and shut them down. Lief tried to reason with the stubborn guard, explaining that they just needed to film one song there that was to be part of a documentary about music. The guard didn't budge. He didn't care why they were there. He didn't want them there making noise and he demanded that they leave.

Knowing he would get nowhere talking to the guard, Lief set his guitar down in its stand and let the guard know that he'd leave as soon as he had a chance to use the bathroom. He had no intention on giving up that easy though. Lief knew it was time to enlist the power of the camera, but with someone who had more of an appreciation for music and more authority than the guard. Lief took the camera with him to the restroom that was located inside the welcome center.

Lief and Bigfoot used the restroom inside of the cool climate-controlled building while the guard stood at the Tin Can waiting for them pack and leave. Outside the restroom, but still inside the welcome center, they looked around at all the historical plaques, photo's, and mounted displays of state history, the majority of which were related to music. There was a small office in the corner of the building that was sectioned off by a large wrap around desk. Lief dinged the service bell at the desk. The cheerfulness of the heavyset red-haired office worker in her fifties preceded her to the counter to assist them.

"Welcome! My name is Grace. How ya'll doing today and how can I help ya'll on this fine morning?"

"Good morning Grace. My name is Lief Wainwright and my furry friend here is Bigfoot and we're-"

"Sweet heavenly molasses, I don't mean to cut you off Mr. Wainwright, but I have to say, Mr. Bigfoot, I absolutely adore the suit. That is outstanding sir- Sorry about that, go ahead."

"It is one of a kind isn't it? Anyway, Bigfoot and I are part of a production that is filming a movie about American Music and its roots. We're out of San Francisco, but we'll be doing our southern U.S. shoots out here over the next week-"

"Do what?"

"What? Filming? Ah… We'll be filming in the area, and just this morning we discovered your wonderful welcome center, well, really more of a museum here, and we hoped that we could include your center in our film. You know, just a quick shoot, get some of the displays in the film, maybe some of the grounds surrounding the center here, like that sign out there."

"Well butter my butt and call me a biscuit! You mean, that you'd like to film little ol' us?"

"If we could. Maybe you'd like to tell us a little bit about the place so we can include that as well."

"Oh my! Haha! I can't believe it. I'd love to. What do you want to know sweetheart?"

"I see lots of music history in here, maybe you can tell us about how this is the birthplace of American music. Also, would you mind signing one of these? It's just a legal permission slip."

Grace agreed and then jumped into a well rehearsed music history lesson. She said that, although, many of the roots for blues music came from Africa with the black slaves that were sent to the south, the music itself developed in America, right in Mississippi, as the countries first unique form of music in the late 1800's. Grace went on further to explain that the blues were the sweet sounds of the soul's resilience that could only be brought to light in darkness and that songs were often a form of prayer that were best understood during times of great suffering. Lief listened to her speak, but was brought to thoughts of his own darkest hours, times when his desire to continue living wasn't as strong. He remembered how all his observations during those times that followed took on new meaning and were enhanced, almost as if he had new levels of comprehension. Lief tried to imagine what the black people in the south endured back then, but the depths of that pain were well beyond his rationale. All he had was his personal worst to use for a frame of reference. She continued to speak about the evolution of the blues, from the delta to Chicago, but Lief could only pretend to listen. He had become stuck in thoughts of love for music and how grateful he was that it had always been there for him.

Bigfoot caught Lief's attention and pointed to the sign outside, where their music gear was still set up. Lief thanked Grace and pivoted to his desire to film a song in front of the large sign. Grace not only permitted them to do so, she sent one of her assistants to film their performance for their next monthly office meeting. Bigfoot, Lief, and the assistant, toting a large lensed camera, walked to the sign, right past the music Nazi guard. The guard was confused as to what he should do and remained in the vicinity while Lief harnessed his guitar and Bigfoot took the thrown of his kit. As soon as they started playing, the guard walked away with a bruised ego, but without creating any further confrontation.

Lief and Bigfoot were just outside of Nashville, in the town of Franklin, when they stopped for dinner at a Waffle House they spotted from the freeway. It was just after 10 p.m. and they were long overdue for food. Their meal was hearty and it weighed them down after their full day of driving and filming. Downtown Nashville looked to be thirty-minutes away from them and they had yet to make sleeping arrangements for the night. The Waffle House was surrounded by hotels that were looking more comfortable by the minute. It became inevitable, Nashville would have to wait until the morning.

They found another Marriott less than a quarter mile from the Waffle House and they made an online reservation even though they both were still nervous about the questionable legality of the counterfeit discount form. Lief had a sneaking suspicion that the gig was near up after the close call the day before.

The spacious lobby of the hotel was so empty and quiet that the sound of a cricket cricketing in the corner filled the entire area. It was an bad omen that there wasn't anyone at the front desk. Lief was forced to ring the bell for service. The loud echoing ring felt like an alarm on a car that they were trying rob. The front desk clerk would have all of the time needed to see the illegitimacy of the discount form without the distractions of a full line of impatient guests. There was a good chance he'd see all of the discrepancies and call Lief's ex to question her.

A young and sharp dressed black gentleman emerged, yawning as he walked to the concierge desk. He performed the check-in process as though he was sleepwalking, operating on shear muscle memory. They may have been able to get the discount without ever even showing the form. Still, it felt like a close call.

Regardless of how easy it was to get into the hotel, the following morning Lief went to a nearby copy center to doctor the room rate form in an attempt to lower his stress rate with future check-ins. There, he literally cut and pasted information from different parts of several forms and created a bullet-proof, unquestionable counterfeit. He made enough copies to get them through their trip, then several more for each month of the year.

━ ～

Making their way to Nashville, they saw the prominent Batman building smack-dab in the center of the city's unmistakable skyline. Closer, at the edge of the downtown area, they saw the gargantuan and curvy Music City Convention Center. It served as a nice greeting that preceded the happy sounds of live music that could be heard pouring out of the smaller music venues in the heart of the city. It was, after all, those sounds from the collective of brick and mortar dives and more reputable saloons that erected the towers of steel around them.

Amongst the surface venues they found the most relevant of them all, the Ryman Auditorium. Lief shouldered the Tin Can in a no parking zone in front of the sacred tabernacle. Sure that Bigfoot had never heard of the building, Lief explained its historical relevance.

"Dude, this is the birthplace of Bluegrass."

"I thought that town we went through in Mississippi was."

"Nope, that was the birthplace of Blues."

"No, I'm positive that the visitor center lady said bluegrass."

"She did, but it was in reference to the evolution of blues. Blue, Blue-grass. Get it? They just added to the word. Anyways, she was exaggerating the influence of her area. Bluegrass was more influenced by the mountain music around here, in the Appalachian's. It gained recognition here at the Ryman though."

"That's cool."

"Yeah, but there is a ton of other stuff that happened here. This used to be the Grand Ole Opry and where Johnny cash did his show. Wait! You know what?"

"What?"

"This is were Elvis Presley introduced June Carter to Johnny. That's pretty historical in itself."

"Wow! Yeah, you're right."

"So anyway, I gotta run out real quick and touch it. Can you wait here with the car so we don't get ticketed."

"Sure"

Lief ran up the short flight of stairs leading to the large white front doors. He touched one of the doors, and then brushed the glossy surface with his hand before touching the porous red brick surrounding the door. It was clear to Lief that the building was adorned by god because he could feel a warm aura of accomplishment surrounding it. He could even feel the vibration of music in the air. Never had Lief heard something of the spiritual realm present itself so clear in the physical world and its sound seemed to grow louder. The sound grew so loud that it drowned out all of the bustling bar music. Something about the sound started to upset Lief's stomach. Lief grew confused at the contradictory circumstances. That was until he turned his head and followed the sound to the Bridgestone Arena, just a block away. The large concert hall used outdoor speakers to air each performance onto the streets surrounding the arena. On that day, they transmitted a form of regurgitated rock mixed with perverted pop that was being referred to as country music by some.

The wretched sound pollution forced them out of the city center. They found their exodus a great opportunity to visit Third Man Records on the south side of the skyscrapers, on the outskirts of town, far from the sicking sound waves. Third Man was the reason that Bigfoot had wanted to go to Nashville in the first place. The studio was owned by Jack White from the alt-rock duo, White Stripes.

Third Man Records was a big attraction for musicians for a number of reasons. The biggest of which was its one of a kind antique recording booth. Anyone could play, record, and immediately produce an actual record. They even provided a three-quarter sized Martin guitar for musicians to use in the tiny booth. Neil Young, widely known as the biggest sound snob around, had once recorded an entire album using the old booth. Because the recording booth used technology from a century prior, it provided the exact same sound as a record would've back then, with all of its graininess and sound levels. But of the most importance, the finished product was pure. It had no effects whatsoever, outside of the natural occurring reverb in the coffin sized booth. That reverb was the same sound that has entertained the first humans on Earth when they'd yell into caves to hear their voices echo.

The studio was easy to find, but the parking situation around it and throughout the entire downtown area presented itself as the Achilles heel of Nashville. They couldn't find any free places to park and the cost of the few available paid parking spots was astronomical. Lief later learned that the lack of viable parking options kept the locals from going downtown ever since the meters were installed. As a result, all the tourists who paid out the ass for parking to mingle with the locals, mingled with other tourists.

After waisting ten dollars on parking ten blocks away, the duo reached the studio and the holy grail within. Bigfoot went in first to play his newest song. Lief filmed from the outside of the booth. The girth of the camera caught the attention of an attractive brunette employee there in the shop. She looked like a rockabilly/ 40's pin up girl mix, with her tucked bumper bangs and retro victory rolls in her hair. She offered Lief a brief rundown of the booth and the studio's history. While filming, Lief couldn't help but think of how amazing the footage was going to be.

It was Lief's turn in the booth and Bigfoot's turn on the camera. Just before entering the booth, a bolt of creative lightning struck Lief in the brain, implanting the perfect idea. He decided to record a song he wrote for Kay followed by his marriage proposal. He had been working on a song for her called "Slippery Slope." The second part of the plan would be to locate a record player once he got to New Jersey, but that was down the road.

Lief squeezed into the tight booth, placed a specialized coin that he had purchased from the front desk into a coin tray, slid it in, and then waited for a red light to let him know when to start playing. Through a clear glass display, he saw the internal mechanisms begin to move. A blank record was plopped onto the turning table and an arm with a needle folded onto it to write Lief's song. The red light lit and Lief got to work. The small Gibson guitar sounded great and the recording went well enough. Lief made a few small mistakes, but they were as genuine as the old time sound of the recording.

Bigfoot and Lief bought some memorabilia from the studio before coming up with a genius plan to grab their luggage gear, ten blocks away, walk back ten blocks, and then record themselves playing their best songs in front of the studio. Forty-five minutes later they returned with their gear and a, never to be paid, parking ticket. By filming themselves from the side of the studio, they were able to capture the studio and the city skyline behind them. A small group of people gathered around to watch them play, fascinated with the suitcase setup. Several of those that gathered were attendees of the NAMM music conference that had just wrapped up an hour prior at the convention center.

One of the spectators, a short stubby and balding man with the swagger of a successful business man, approached Lief when the two finished playing. He handed him a high quality business card embossed with a gold font. Lief ran his fingers across the top as if he were reading brail.

"I like what I heard, solid gold! Do you have any music on-line? Cause I like the whole suitcase music thing you got going on."

"Wow! Thank you, we do. It's under Gas Station Rose. There's about six original songs up there."

"Yes! More suitcase music. Tell me, are you two from the area?"

"No, we are from the bay area in California. We're on the road filming a movie about street musicians. We're playing and, obviously, filming ourselves in as many cities as we can."

"That's Great! I love it, the suite case band from California. Do me a favor, you have my card, why don't you give me a call when you get back home. I have a few ideas I'd like to run by you."

"Yeah, totally. Thanks!"

"Keep up the good work and enjoy the rest of your trip. More suite case music!"

Bigfoot approached Lief after the mysterious man walked away.

"Who was that?"

"I dunno, Bruce something or other. It's on the card."

Lief handed Bigfoot the card.

"Huh? Never heard of him."

Lief took a few pictures of the orange and cumulous laden troposphere that highlighted the Nashville skyline while Bigfoot waited for him in the drivers seat of the Tin Can. There was plenty more to see in Nashville, but the two got what they came for and it was time to move on. Lief got in the car, but promised himself a return trip to the music city. They set a course for Washington D.C.

CHAPTER 17

BLUE RIDGES TO THE BELTWAY

Sarah called Lief three hours into his drive to Washington D.C. Just moments before her call, Lief was thinking about how, four years prior, he and Sarah had visited the capital of the nation together. He had become accustomed to those kind of coincidences, so he did not make a point to mention it to her.

"Hey kiddo what's up?"

"Hi"

In typical Sarah format, she kept it short. The fact that she called, alone, was a significant sign that she loved her dad.

"Did your mom make you call?"

"No"

"Wow! Well there's a first. Cool. How are you?"

"Good"

"No way! Whoah, now hold on, don't get all manic on me, just slow down and breath, just calmly tell me what's going on. So you're good?"

"Yeah"

"Hey! Guess what?"

"What?"

"I'm on my way to D.C. Cool huh?"

"Yeah"

"Don't you wish you were going too?"

"No"

"You mean that you don't want to walk five miles between twenty Smithsonian's, through 118˚ temperatures?"

"Nope"

"Anything good going on? You having fun with your mom?"

"Just school"

"Alright. Did you call cause you missed me?"

"No"

"That's nice, I miss you too. So, I wasn't sure how soon I'd be back a couple of days ago, but I'm pretty sure I'll be back in three weeks now. I'll finally be done filming this movie. I'm going to see Kay on the Jersey Shore and then I'm headed back west towards home. I'll be seeing your sister soon too. Do you think that you'd like to meet her?"

"Sure"

"K kiddo. Well I'm going to be famous when I get back from this movie and then I'll buy you a limo, alright."

"Cool"

"Alright kiddo, I miss you. I'm glad you called. I'm going to get back to driving, mmm'kay?"

"Mmm'kay"

Lief was moved by Sarah's call. It reminded him of how grateful he was for having her in his life when, at one point, the story could have played out much differently. Lief took comfort in the thought that she was adjusting and finding happiness again. For the next several hours he continued those thoughts, along with his surrounding thoughts about her temperament before and after her attempted suicide. His heavy contemplation brewed into something else, something that would prove to make everything in his life make more sense.

Lief zeroed in on a central theme to his experience. It was poignant, but profound. He thought it was possible that he experienced the trauma with Sarah to understand that kind of pain and in the only way possible. It had to hit him in the center of the heart and, considering the size of his, it had to be a really good shot. But, its message was too big for him to understand at that point. He remembered a meaningful phrase, *We learn by teaching.* That's when he knew it was paramount that his thoughts and feelings should be documented in order to refine and then share them. He also suspected there was something in them that would start a healing process for other pains that he had been avoiding. Because Bigfoot was still sleeping, Lief knew he could get away with a small amount of note taking, possibly a short treatment for a screenplay while he was driving. Lief pulled out his phone and started taking notes, then began fleshing out the concept that he'd later turn into an outline.

He wanted to write something that could help other parents navigate a painful situation such as his own with Sarah. The meat and potatoes of the story would revolve around the true strength of unconditional love and that, no matter what, it could never be lost, not even to death if it came to that.

Lief scanned the highway's terrain as far as he could, looking for turns, possible junk, and wayward pedestrians before looking back down towards what he was writing on his phone. He kept his head at an angle which gave him a partial view of the road while he tapped out words like a stenographer, typing just enough to write the gist of the idea. More and more details flooded in though, faster than he could tap out with his two thumbs. Bigfoot continued to sleep, so Lief continued to write as much as possible before the beast awoke. His anticipated three or four minutes of note taking turned into an hour of writing a detailed outline and parts of a loose script. He even went as far as to add some camera direction. In doing so, he broke a cardinal rule of first draft screenwriting.

To a good degree, the first act mirrored his experience, starting just prior to his call from the police, then it described the terror that ensued. The second act began with the miracle outcome and the joys of watching his child and her emotional wounds go through a successful healing process. Midway through the second act, the heart of the story surfaced, revealing a far deeper meaning, one that held secrets even from him, the writer, steering itself into an exploration into the bonds of love and the unfathomable power of denial. It illustrated the strengths of the family of origin verses those that are chosen to be family. It explained how the denial of the worst possible outcome, paired with faith born of desperation, may just have allowed his daughter to remain in his same plain of existence.

The more he wrote, the more he learned about how far love could take someone, about how it changes shapes, and how it connected people that hadn't yet met. By the time he put his phone down, Lief found himself knee deep and halfway through his next project. Bigfoot was none the wiser.

Lief calculated the total driving time and distance of their travels to that point in the trip. He figured it to be a hefty thirty-six hours, with a distance of 3,200 miles. The thought took some steam out of his drive ahead. The timelessness he had been gifted while experiencing white line fever was gone and each mile thickened. Driving became more of a chore than ever. He felt like a dehydrated and sunburnt wanderer in the dessert in search of the respite of an oasis while vultures circled above.

Lief had been driving through Tennessee for quite a while before he started to lose his patience for the abundance of slow drivers around him. He reverted to his California commute mode, flipping off everyone who would not comply with his desired flow. Bigfoot was not happy about Lief's disposition, but also declined to drive in his stead. Lief was convinced that the drivers around him were conspiring to upset him and that Bigfoot was in on it too. After another thirty-minutes of his pissiness, something unexpected happened. Lief opened up to the tiniest possibility that he was the one being an asshole. He doubted it though. Just in case, he looked up an AA meeting, remembering that he always walked out of any given meeting in a better mood. He found a meeting ten miles from where he was and in the direction they were already going. And much to Bigfoot's chagrin, they attended that meeting.

At the meeting, Lief introduced himself as a visitor from the California wine country. Many chuckled at the ironic quip. Bigfoot spent the entire meeting in the adjacent snack room eating cookies and drinking coffee. Lief listened to stories of incomprehensible demoralization, desperation, hopelessness, discoveries, opportunities, hope, and paths to true freedom. It was exactly what he needed to hear at that exact moment.

While leaving the meeting, Ric, a man in his thirties with a thick Tennessean accent struck up a conversation with Bigfoot. Near the end of their exchange, he handed Bigfoot a copy of a Jason Isabel cd. Ric suggested that the two give it a listen, guessing by their appearance and demeanor, that they might appreciate it. He explained that Isabel was from the area. The act was serendipitous because, Lief was familiar with him and had seen him play in Napa, California as an opening act for Ryan Adams. That particular concert was, by far, the best and most special concert that Lief had ever attended.

Before they parted ways, Ric imparted a few more synchronistic words for the travelers. He knew they where headed east and urged them to drive through the town of Asheville, North Carolina, a town located along the Blue Ridge Mountains. He said the area was not to be missed. Taken aback, Lief recanted the words, *Not to be missed,* the exact words his Bellflower grandmother used to describe the mountain range. The message was not missed. In fact, at that moment, the message became a glaring highway sign from the universe, cemented into the ground on the side of the road. Then, just short of driving them there himself, Ric even drew out a map and gave them directions.

They thanked him and drove away as the sun had begun to set. Bigfoot looked over the handwritten map.

"You know Lief, this spot in the Blue Ridge mountains extends our drive only twenty to thirty-minutes.'

"True. And not to be missed he said. That's what my grandma said too. I don't mind going a little out of the way. I think we ought to take that route and stop there for the night. Nashville to Asheville."

"Sounds good to me."

It grew dark as Lief drove along I-40, past Knoxville, and into the Appalachian mountains. Bigfoot curled up against the window to sleep. Whenever Lief had to slow down or change lanes, Bigfoot would snap upright, thinking the car was going to crash. And each time Bigfoot woke, he criticized Lief's driving. Lief understood all too well that each of Bigfoot's over the top reactions to the car's movement were a direct result stemming from the time he crashed Lief's Tin Can #1 while he was high on heroin. Lief grew more resentful with each of Bigfoot's outbursts until his anger brought him back to the morning he got the news about his beloved car.

After waking up at his girlfriend's apartment in Brooklyn, he looked at his phone and saw the horrible Facebook message from Bigfoot. It read "I totaled your car. I'm very sorry. I'm going to take care of it." Lief was shocked as he ran through the immediate consequences of Bigfoot's actions. First, he knew that the insurance would not pay for any repairs on the car because the title had just been listed as salvaged after a recent accident and repair. That meant his car was gone, it meant that his job was gone, it meant that Sarah no longer had a way to get to Santa Rosa for school, and it meant that his dating life was over. He didn't have enough time to paint the full picture of his impending doom when another message flashed across his phone. It was from the airline that he was scheduled to use that day. It notified him that his flight out of New York was canceled due to a superstorm that was due to pass through the area. A quick call, wherein he learned that all three airports near him were closed, proved to make matters worse. Lief was due in Pittsburgh that night to meet Oreo and perform in his Amigo's concert/ movie.

Either of the revelations could have turned his world upside down on it's own, without the help of the other. But due to getting both articles of bad news at the same time, he had to imagine that the universe may have been conspiring to get his attention. He was able to approach each situation with more caution than he was used to using in other moments of distress. His suspicions proved accurate when observed what happened when he allowed himself to be calm. The world around him fixed itself in front of his eyes. He caught the last train to Pittsburgh, made the show, and met Oreo. Lief found out the shitty details of the crash while sitting in comfort on the train. He also learned that, through an impossible fluke, his car would be covered due to the insurance company taking too long to file his salvaged title. He was even able to reserve a rental car home from the airport, and the insurance paid for him to keep it until he purchased Tin Can #2. Lief loved that train ride so much that he used it again to get between Pittsburgh and New York on another occasion. Taking the train became one of his favorite modes of travel.

Lief felt better after running the entire story of the crash through his head, but he chose to remain upset at Bigfoot and his bitching throughout the rest of the evening. He knew that he only had to put up with him till New York, that or if it got too bad he knew he could just push him off of a Blue Ridge in the area.

Lief grew too tired to keep driving and pulled into a rest stop for the night. He hadn't noticed any road signs for a while and had no idea how close to Asheville they were. He reclined the seat as much as possible and fell into a sleep of sorts.

The morning light revealed something that Lief was unaware of when he parked the night before. The beauty that surrounded him was beyond his comprehension. Transcending all logical baseis of comprehension, he experienced a feeling of safety and love, as if his creator had given him a rare moment of refuge. He unknowingly had made it to the Blue Ridge Mountains. Lief got out of the car and was blown away by the beauty he saw at every angle as he turned to try to take it all in. A cool palette of colors splayed in front of him with the green of the pines closest to him, followed by the shades blue and purple ridges that scraped the shreds of cumulous clouds that nearly formed a ceiling above them. With the depth of the landscape, each layer grew softer by the mist. A shiver went down his spine when that same mountain mist seemed to reach out and touch his face, bringing him into a magical realm. *Am I in a Vortex?*

The magnificence grew in all of the space around him until Lief felt a little remorse knowing that he would never be able to adequately describe the majesty surrounding him. He suspected that the camera wouldn't either. His memory would fade and the image would dull. He needed to share the moment with someone that he could talk about it with later, to relive the beauty, even if only a fraction of it. Bigfoot would wake soon and would also witness its splendor, but Lief knew he'd never speak with him again after the trip.

The rest stop bathrooms there were no different than any other on the road. Pools of piss covered the floor and phone numbers for the lonely decorated the the tile walls. Lief had become used to the lack of aesthetics in the restrooms. He was grateful that he had a proper place to put all of the recycled coffee. On that occasion, he knew his urinal was in the middle of one of the most spectacular spectacles on God's green and blue Earth. Those mountains promised to keep him in good spirits for the rest of the day, regardless of Bigfoot or the cars around him.

Bigfoot was still asleep when Lief drove away for the rest stop. As synchronicity would have it, the first song that played out of the thousands of randomly shuffled songs in Lief's phone was the Fleet Foxes hauntingly angelic "Blue Ridge Mountains". Bigfoot awoke to the music. He seemed disturbed until he saw the mountains around him.

"Bigfoot, could you use Black Mamba to capture the mountains? We made it here, and they all were right."

"Oh yeah. Dude, they were totally right. I'm glad they directed us here too. This is- This is amazing."

"Yup. Not to be missed."

For the first time in a while, there was peace in the Tin Can from point A to B. It was needed too, because Lief saw that the path to New York was tolerable.

Much uncertainty still laid ahead for Lief. How would his daughter Leslie receive him? Would Kay say yes? Would her family accept him? Was he going to be able to assemble anything worth viewing from the footage he had? He knew he had to treat those concerns with the same logic he employed towards his sobriety, one day, or in that case, situation at a time.

＊ ＊

That afternoon they arrived at their prearranged hotel, just outside the beltway around Washington D.C. It was unclear which state they where in because they saw two separate signs within a mile of each other, one welcoming them to Virginia and and one welcoming them to Maryland. It didn't matter. They weren't going to be in the area long. They scheduled two nights at the hotel with one full day to play and film in the capital city.

After another free breakfast at a discounted hotel, the two headed to the political heart of the country. Then, after relieving their bowels in the restroom, they went to Washington D.C.

It was a quick drive to the center of D.C. where the two parked across the lawn from the Washington Monument. The dickish obelisk was to be the backdrop for the short set that they would film. The monument seemed to disappear in the background, blending into the sky due to the amount of sunlight that was out in force that day. Lief adjusted the camera's iris several times to no avail. After five minutes of adjustments, he gave up, hoping that the trumped up color editing software he had would make it reappear.

They hadn't yet finished setting up when the secret service rolled up on them to shut them down. It was something about the lack of a permit. Leif tried to curry favor with the agent by letting him know that he was a military veteran and they were just paying a quick tribute to the nation through song. The secret service agent was not swayed, but he did tell them that they could use the adjacent corner, which fell under another, less present agency's jurisdiction.

Lief thanked him and the band lugged their gear across the street. It was no easy task, due to all of the many cords that needed to be unplugged and replugged. The stands needed to be loosened, collapsed, and then re-tightened and when they got there, all of the sound levels needed to be readjusted. But, on that day, they shattered all previous take down and set up records. They accomplished both of the setup and teardown processes within seven minutes, which included running across the street. They squeezed out two songs before they were shut down again, that time by the District Police. Bigfoot didn't hide his anger.

"How the hell does that bucket guy get away with it down here?"

"He must have a permit."

Lief was ok with taking a break from playing music that day because there were so many National monuments to film. He also had hopes of getting lost in a few Smithsonian museums. They moved the car close to the capital building and made their way to the Library of Congress which they learned had just closed. Suspecting that other attractions would be closing, they ran through the botanical gardens and into the Native American Smithsonian. There, they learned that all of the Smithsonian's would be closing within a half hour.

Because Lief had been there previously with Sarah, he knew what was worth seeing and what they could afford to miss. He led Bigfoot to the American History Museum where they ran through to look for the original C3PO from the first "Start Wars". The robot was no longer being displayed there, but while searching for it they found a Thomas Edison showcase that displayed several noteworthy projects that he had been involved with. Lief told Bigfoot that it was sad that they made no mention of Tesla's contributions.

"It's funny how history can just seem to scratch a person out. Tesla was the man. Did you know that he used to work for Edison and designed many inventions that Edison got credit for, while Edison was off electrocuting elephants?"

"Electrocuting elephants?"

"Yeah, as a display of how superior his electrical power was, but Tesla, man Tesla, he had real visions. They would come to him like a real object that you and I see right in front of our faces. That was one in-tune individual. Oh, also his alternating current ultimately whooped Edison's direct current."

"Do you think that's where the band got its name? You know- ACDC?"

"Yeah, I mean no, not really"

Walking around a little more, they found the American flag that inspired Francis Scott Key to write the National Anthem. They also found Julia Childs kitchen, but it wasn't until on the way out that Lief and Bigfoot found the real gem of the Museum, the origin of motion picture display.

There they saw how it was a bet about a horse's gait that led to the first film. The story was that one gentleman believed that there was one brief moment that a horse had all of its the feet off of the ground at the same time while running. To prove his hypothesis, he got a high speed camera and took about a hundred quick shots of a horse running along a track. When he displayed slides of the photos in order and in a quick rotation, he not only won his bet, but also invented the motion picture. Lief joked about it.

"The moral of this story is that betting can lead to magical things that change the world forever. I'm all for hitting the next casino we come across."

"Where do you think that may be?"

"I dunno, probably in Pennsylvania, with the Amish."

"Funny. Do you think they have wooden slot machines."

"Good one Bigfoot."

With ten-minutes left, before all Smithsonian Museums closed for the day, they made a mad dash for the National Air and Space Museum, where they ran from one end to the next to see as much as they could before they closed.

"Bigfoot- Dude, It's a shame we couldn't have seen more. There is some cool shit in a bunch of these museums.

"Yeah, it's cool. Museums aren't really my thing."

"Alright. Well, we have to see some of the outside monuments that don't close, like the big ass Lincoln sitting in the giant chair, and the Vietnam wall with all of the names on it."

"Ok, I've wanted to see Lincoln. What about the White House?"

"Yeah, we can see that too it's just on the other side of Washington's monument there.

When they finished up with all the outdoor monuments that they wanted to see, Bigfoot took a pit stop in a port-a-potty. It took him longer than usual to conduct his business and when he came out, he seemed different. His face was blank and his eyes were glazed. He was a shell of a person, walking like a zombie on their way back to the Tin Can.

"Are you alright Bigfoot? You've seemed a little faded for a little while now."

"Yeah. I'm fine. Why?"

"Why? Really? I, ahh just told you why."

"Yeah, I guess you did. Oh shit!"

"What?"

"I gotta take a shit. Real bad. Where's a bathroom?"

"You just used one no more than five minutes ago."

"Dude! I don't need to explain anything to you. I've been backed up for a week, I gotta go. Fuck! Where's a toilet? I gotta go NOW!

Bigfoot dashed across the street for a Starbucks that was closing. He got in the side door that was propped open by a mop bucket, where he was met by an employee mopping the floor. She told him they had closed and asked him to leave. Instead of rationally asking her to make an exception, which is what Lief thought he would do, Bigfoot yelled at her.

"Look lady, It's an emergency and I just need to use the bathroom real quick or I'm going to shit myself!"

The worker again refused. Bigfoot turned red in the face as a vein appeared on his forehead and then he let out a monstrous scream that surpassed the vocal capabilities of any other human. From behind, he may have been mistaken for a bear. He laid back into the worker with a growling voice.

"Lady, you're a horrible person! I hope you shit your pants, real soon. You- You bitch! Argh! Fucking Bitch."

Bigfoot took off down the street so fast that Lief had a hard time keeping up. Bigfoot ducked into a fine dining establishment, ran straight past the host at the front, then into the back to find a restroom. Lief waited out front for a half hour. When Bigfoot resurfaced he acted as if nothing had happened.

"Everything ok?"

"Yeah, fine. Which way did we park?"

Lief had never done heroin before, but he knew that it caused constipation and not diarrhea. Although confused, he decided Bigfoot's bowel moment patterns weren't worth trying to decipher. Any concerns towards Bigfoot at that point would be an investment that he didn't have the time for. They would be going separate ways for a few days the following morning when Bigfoot caught a train to New York out of Philadelphia so that Lief could drive due east to meet Kay on the Jersey Shore. Their plans were to meet back up in New York. After that point, Lief's conscious would be fine with kicking him out of the car if he needed to.

～　～

That evening, Lief found a way to distance himself by reviewing previous film while wearing headphones. That was when Lief regretfully discovered that all of the footage from Nashville had no sound. It was possible that either the mic or the sound board weren't turned on while filming. His heart sank, knowing that the film was a loss.

Lief was broken. He needed to put thoughts of the film on hold and focus on the more uplifting aspects of the trip. He connected to happier thoughts when he imagined meeting Leslie. He then turned his thoughts to Kay, hopping they would bring him more happiness. But when he turned his attention to her he grew anxious. At first he couldn't understand the disconnect, but then remembered that he still needed to locate a record player for his marriage proposal. He knew he couldn't show up without one. Locating a record player that night became his top priority.

He looked online and found several audio stores along the way, but Lief found no one willing to let him play the record. He did find a thrift store that would hold a record player for him. The only problem was that it was four hours from the shore. Lief resigned his search for the evening, planning to pick it back up in the morning.

As he laid in bed that night trying to fall asleep, Lief couldn't help his thoughts from going back to the failing film. The longer he circled thoughts of all that had gone wrong with the film, the more hopeless he became. He started comparing it to the worst flops he had ever seen. That's when he remembered a documentary that had been made about twenty years prior called "American Movie". It was an amateur project made by the main character, who discussed how badly he had wanted to make a film. It was shitty, as shitty as a movie could get, but like a train wreck, Lief couldn't take his eye's off of it. He ended up making a connection to the dopey dude and his even dopier sidekick. They became underdog's that were impossible not to root for. Ultimately, the sloppiness of the film became a side show to the endearing gumption and passion of the filmmaker's perseverance in moving past all of the obstacles, the nay sayers, the costs, and self doubt, in order make his film, no matter how bad it turned out. The guy became the hero of his film, all because he accomplished his life long goal by finishing his movie.

The recollection of the film gave Lief hope. He accepted that he may never be able to salvage his film, but he was going to finish it. He knew there was no way around it's sloppiness. It became his goal to embrace every shitty second of it, hoping that there would be viewers somewhere that could do the same.

Once again, things seemed to lay where they were intended for Lief. There was hope that the film could be salvaged, Sarah was safe back home, he was on his way to see Leslie, Bigfoot was going to New York by himself for a few days, and Lief was about to put all of his chips on the table with Kay. Lief took one last look at his phone before falling asleep. He saw all he needed to see. The large numerals on the screen displayed that the time was 11:11.

ACT III

CHAPTER 18

SHORELAND

Not a moment too soon, Lief and Bigfoot arrived at the train station in Philadelphia after a inconsequential three hour drive from D.C. The plan from the beginning of the trip was for Lief to spend four days with Kay, while Bigfoot spent that time in New York, high on heroin most likely. Bigfoot would take Amtrak to the Penn Station in downtown Manhattan while Lief made a right turn towards New Jersey. Lief was already despising the fact that he was going to have to pick Bigfoot up in New York after visiting with Kay. Bigfoot had grown suspicious of Lief's desires to split up for good so he kept his bitching to a minimum to ensure a ride back home after New York.

Bigfoot stepped out of the Tin Can and grabbed his bags. He was cordial, telling Lief that he looked forward to regrouping in four days before he bid him adieu. That morning Lief wore his feelings on his sleeve and did not wish Bigfoot a happy visit to New York because he didn't give two shits about Bigfoot's experience there and he certainly didn't wish to regroup with him. Instead, he drove off without a response. Through the rearview mirror, Lief could see Bigfoot shaking his head in disapproval.

— —

The Jersey Shore sat only three hours from Philadelphia, but without his record player it still felt like a thousand miles away. He wasn't going anywhere until he found one. Kay was waiting for him, so he called to let her know he'd be running late. Explaining the delay would prove tricky for him though. He had no way to describe how important it was for him to get the player before he got there. That was, without causing suspicion and, in turn, ruining the element of surprise with his marriage proposal at the end of the song. He needed to lie.

Kay's phone rang four times and Lief was relieved that he'd be able to leave a voicemail instead of lying to her in conversation, but she answered the phone at the last second, before the call could be redirected.

"Baby, where are you? You almost here?"

"Good morning sweetheart. I'm in Philly. I just dropped off the beast. I can already feel fresh air in the car."

"Yeah, I bet. I'm sorry, I can only imagine, but hey, you don't have to see him for four days."

"True. So, I am only a three hour drive from you, but I have to stop to do something first."

"What? No- You get here!"

"Sweetheart, you know I want to be there already, but it's important and shouldn't take too long. I made you something, in Nashville."

"Really? Made it, huh?"

"Ok, I was going to try to keep it a surprise, but it'll be tough to at this point. It's a record that I recorded at Third Man Studios. You know Jack White form the White Stripes?"

"Yeah"

"It's his studio. And they have this old fashion record, like actual record, recording set up and I used to it to record a song for you."

"Aw, how sweet of you. Is it my song?"

"Yes, it's your song, but guess what?"

"What?"

"Jack White sat in on the recording! Awesome right?"

"No way."

"Yeah way. And so I have the record, but no way to play it for you so I have to check out a few thrift stores here for a record player so I play it for you."

"Can't you just get one here?"

"No. Sweetheart, they're not that easy to find. I have my best chances getting one here. And I want to play it for you when I first see you. Ok?"

"Alright. You better hurry."

Lief was ok with his white lie because it was a worthy diversion. It didn't matter though, because Kay knew something was up. He got back on the internet and found four second-hand stores, confident that one would surely have what he needed. The whole process reminded him of his quest to build the suitcase/PA system. He called two of the stores and was told there were no record players at either. He then drove around the city looking for the other two.

Lief did his best to make sense of the many one-way streets, while trying to find either of the two remaining stores. The GPS wasn't helping much as it led him in circles around the city. As anxiety set in, his driving became erratic. Lief's breathing grew heavy and he started yelling at the cars around him. As per usual, he hadn't realized that he was having a panic attack until it was too late and there was no going back until it ran its course. To a person on the sidewalk, he must have looked and sounded like a complete nutcase, truth be told, he was one.

Without the sensibility to pull over and recollect himself, Lief created a whirlpool of insanity and steered the Tin Can into the its center where nothing but rage existed, rage and a large box van that blocked his view of any street signs. His aggression prevented him from backing away from the van, a more logical approach to getting better visibility of the street. The phone rang. It was Kay. He picked up the call but couldn't get the handsfree to work so he hung up and screamed at the top of his lungs. Unbeknownst to him, the phone did not hang up. To save Lief the embarrassment along with added stress, she hung up and called back. On his second attempt, he got the hands-free to work. Anxious to know what was troubling him, she spoke first.

"Lief, I just called and the phone hung up. Is everything ok?"

He did not immediately answer because he had focused all of his attention on an attempt to boomerang around the left side of the giant van. Lief had not known that he was no longer on a one way street. He crossed into an opposing traffic lane, where a transit bus was coming straight for him. He squeezed the steering wheel tight and prepared for impact. Kay asked for a response from Lief several times, but all she heard was a blaring horn accompanied by the gruesome screeching of tires, a loud boom, and the sounds of shattering glass and metal crunching, then silence.

"LIEF! Baby, what's happened? I heard loud noises. Are you ok? PLEASE ANSWER! YOU'RE FREAKING ME THE FUCK OUT. You got to tell me what's going on. Please! Please pick up…"

Lief did not respond. She tried not to imagine the worst, but she knew she lost him. She lowered the phone to her lap. Although the phone line remained connected, her comprehension had hung up. She sat blank, looking down at the grains of Jersey Shore sand that had dried between her toes.

A muffled rustling sound caught her attention and she turned around to see what it was. There was nothing. Then she heard a the faint sound of a human voice near her. That time she did not turn around because she knew it was him, visiting her to say goodbye before fading into the hereafter.

"Kay"

"Yes dear?"

"Kay, I can barely hear you."

"What?"

"You sound distant. Can you put the phone closer to your head."

She was confused. Kay rolled her eyes down to her phone, paused, and then pulled it up to her ear.

"Are you there?"

"Huh?"

"There you are. Much better. Sorry about that sweetheart. I couldn't get the hands free to work. What's up?"

Kay's face reanimated and she took in a large breath.

"What? What? Oh God, you're ok?

"Yeah, I'm fine."

"What the fuck? I heard that sound and thought you died. Fuck! THANK GOD! You scared the shit out of me! What was that noise? Did you get into an accident?"

"No, no, no. Just some dumbass bus driver was driving in the wrong lane, then he turned into a phone pole. Fucking asshole almost hit me."

"Baby. I-want-you-to-pull-over and talk to me, ok?"

"Yeah, no problem. Done. How are you?"

"You're pulled over?"

"Yup"

"Ok, good. I wanted to tell you that I found an antique store near here that has a record player. They said you could use it to play your song."

"No way! That's awesome!"

Sirens and lights swirled on a pair of emergency vehicles that sped past Lief to the scene of the bus crash just behind him. The sound was so loud that Kay had to pull the phone from her ear.

"What was that?"

"Uh- Wow, it looks like it's for the bus."

"Get your ass out here, all-right?"

A police car drove by and Lief could see another one driving towards the crash as well. The second police officer took a hard look at Lief as he drove past, then made a quick u-turn towards the Tin Can.

"No problem, babe. Hold on for one second."

Lief drove like lightning over the top of a hill, then made a hairpin turn down an alley where he parallel parked in front of large garbage bin so that he couldn't be seen from the street. The policeman burned rubber past the alleyway. Lief waited for a moment, looked for signs of the cop in his drivers side mirror, and then headed for I-676 east for the Jersey Shore.

"I'm on my way."

—◦— ◦—

There was a calmness on the road that coincided with Lief's cooler head. The interstate led him over a bridge out of the city. He regretted not visiting a few of the historically relevant landmarks in the city that was brought to prominence by Benjamin Franklin, Lief's favorite historical figure of all time. Lief promised himself to revisit Philadelphia to get a better feel for the place in which Franklin invented the United States of America.

Deities aside, Mr. Franklin was the only person who embodied what Lief believed to be the most perfect human. If Lief ever had the gumption to be of maximum service to mankind, he knew he'd have to do his best to follow the path that Benjamin Franklin had paved. Lief recognized that Franklin's creativity catapulted the world into a new, more enlightened era.

Continuing his thoughts of Franklin while he drove, Lief wondered why so many people were honking their horns on the road that day. All he wanted was a peaceful drive to Kay. But, the noises continued, so he looked around to see what was going on. *What the fuck?* Several cars sped past him on his right, one of them flipped him off. He looked in his rearview mirror and saw another car tailgating him. Lief checked his speedometer and saw that he was only going the speed limit while in the fast lane. Embarrassed and ashamed of himself, he moved over to the middle lane as soon as he had the chance. *Ironical,* he thought.

He had violated his own rules of the road in, what may have been, the only place on the planet where other people drove just like him. After forgiving himself, and amongst a new heard of cars, he rejoined the fast lane and rejoiced in the splendor of a land where people got it. It was a good sign. The toll system, however, with its different fees involved in getting on and off of the freeway, baffled him, as did the fact he couldn't pump his own gas. Lief could tolerate the strange ways though. He knew that the odd customs he encountered while traveling gave reason for story telling later.

Thirty minutes away from Kay, Lief grew more nervous by the mile. He imagined his proposal and how he'd film it. There were some gaps in his vision as he ran through it. He'd get only so far picturing how things could pan out, and then his vision fell apart. Then he'd have to reimagine the scenario all over again. Each attempt fell short, until against his will, he left it all up in the air for chance to sort out.

As far as logistics went, it made sense for Lief to contact the store to make a few arrangements beforehand. First and foremost, Lief thought that getting their permission to film might avoid any last minute surprises. He also wanted to get an idea of the shop's layout. His call turned out to be a good idea, because the owner was so excited to have a marriage proposal taking place at his store, that he put the record player into the center of a secluded section of the store and instructed the shop employees to show them every accommodation. The phone call was all he needed to iron out the wrinkles in his proposal. He envisioned the whole scenario all the way through, and to his satisfaction he was able to turn his thoughts to Kay.

Lief finally reached the Jersey shore after he crossed the mile long bridge that led to Beach Haven Crest. In town, the rows of faded victorian homes were crammed between preserved 1940's era amusement parks, all set on a half mile wide strip surrounded by the Atlantic Ocean. Lief summed up the overall surrounding esthetics with an odd thought, *salt water taffy*.

When he made his final turn onto the street where Kay's family was renting their beach house, his heart beat fast and pushing all of the natural love drugs throughout his entire vascular system. His anxiety began to fade away, only to be replaced by a tingling feeling throughout his body.

Two blocks away, he could see Kay standing in front of the beach rental. Her long light blue summer dress flowed in the wind and was juxtaposed by the tan sand of the shore behind her. From the distance he could see her smile. The sight was spotless. He reached the edge of the earth and found his love holding it in place for him.

Out of over two-thousand songs stored in Lief's iPhone, the song "I'm on Fire", a song by the New Jersey native Bruce Springsteen, shuffled itself into the speakers of the Tin Can, at the exact moment that Lief arrived. Lief ran to Kay to hug her. His enthusiasm surpassed his ability to slow when he reached her. Lief almost knocked her to the ground, but he grabbed her tight and let his momentum send them into a twirling hug. The movements were like a slow dance to the perfect song playing alongside the swooshing waves of the Atlantic.

Lief looked into the eyes of his sweetheart.

"I missed you."

"Baby, I've missed you so fucking much."

"This will be the furthest I hope I ever have to drive to see you again."

"Wait- Is that Bruce Springsteen? I love this song. Did you put that on for me?"

"No, it just came on by itself when I pulled up."

"Very auspicious"

"Hey, that's my word. Ok- I'm sorry to have to rush you off so quickly, but we have to get to that store with the record player."

"Really? Ok. Why not relax for a moment? You've been driving a while. You can meet the family. They should be back from the beach soon."

"I wish I could, but this is time sensitive. I called that store, Shredded Whatever, and made arrangements for us to use the record player there cause I wanted to make sure they'd be open and all of that."

"Funny. I think it's Unshredded Nostalgia, what a name."

"That's it. I hate to rush you, but we kinda have to get there real quick."

"Okaaay. Let's get going then."

Lief ushered her into the car, then sped through town towards the antique store. On the drive there Lief kept his conversation to a minimum, speaking when spoken to, and with one or two word responses. Kay could here the chatter in his brain but couldn't decipher any of it, and neither could Lief. When she observed how stiff he was sitting in his seat, she knew something was up. She believed that he had recorded her a song, but she knew there was something else that he wasn't telling her. Lief detected her suspicion and spoke up.

"Baby, I'm sorry to have rushed right off to the store after seeing you.

It's just that I'm so excited about playing you your song that I recorded with Jack White. It's a big deal."

"I understand, sort of? Really, whatever you want babe."

"How has the shore been? Are you still happy to see your family?"

"It's been good. Well, it's been a little weird due to Christine. Remember me mentioning her before? My brothers wife? She's being, well… her usual self, complaining, jealous, critical, you know, a bitch. It sucks because my mom's grieving the loss of her partner of twenty-years, my sorta stepdad George. I'm sure I told you about him."

"That's right, you told me about her when I was in Austin. I'm sorry sweetheart. Hmm, that's really selfish of her to be so dramatical considering what your mom is going through. I wonder what her problem is. How are things with her and your brother?"

"They get along. He notices the tension, but what can he do? He's just stuck in the middle, so he just stays quite. He's really a good guy. You're going to really get along with him."

"I think this is it. Unshredded Nostalgia. Haha! What the fuck? Is that even a real word?"

"I like it. Let's hear this song."

"Just a minute. Can you give me a hand with some of this. I am going to film this."

"Of course you are."

The shop had the typical coppery and dingy antique store smell, but its aesthetics were more pleasing than any other antique shop that Lief had seen before. All the items were showcased, opposed to being crammed next to each, or worse, stacked, waiting to be sold. There was a respect given to each piece as if they were associated with one particular memory.

Lief identified himself to the young woman working at the counter. Knowing what was about to take place, she grew excited, but she straightened her face to avoid causing suspicion. She called for the shop owner who let them know he'd be down soon.

While waiting for the owner, Lief found an antique record player with a blooming brass speaker sitting atop a mahogany marble top pedestal positioned in the center of the side room. The edges of the marble surface were plumb to the floorboards, bringing much satisfaction to Lief's OCD. He set up the camera in the corner of the room, adjusted the sound levels, and then framed the shot so that he could hit record the moment the store owner showed. Lief's nervousness and over-preparation stood out to Kay. She might have figured out Lief's plan if she hadn't turned her attention to the owner who joined them in the room. He greeted them with a thick lisp and an overwhelming enthusiasm. His level of excitement added to her growing suspicion.

"Here's the lovely couple. Hello and welcome. I'm Bernard. This is my store. I hope this is what you had in mind."

"Hi! I'm Lief and this is Kay. Thank you so much for allowing me to play this here. What an amazing shop! This is going to be perfect for the film."

Bernard was flattered. He was in his sixties and a little overweight, but well dressed in a tailored and pressed red checkered shirt with violet slacks. His rolled cuffs matched his pants.

"Thank you both. Happy to have you here. I hope you don't mind, but I'd like to have a listen too."

"Kay and I wouldn't have it any other way."

Lief placed the record on the player while Bernard walked into the corner of the room, smiling and clasping his hands at his chest. At that point, Kay knew something was up before the warm sounds of the old-timey record poured out of the brass cornucopia speaker.

You walked funny for me

I walked funny for you

You said…

Kay alternately eyed the record player and Lief as the song played. *There's no Jack White*, she thought. Lief played and sang the song for her several times before and the guitar and the lyrics finished the same way as another time he played the song for her, still without Jack White. She quizzically looked to Lief. He held a tight smile while the scratchy static sounds of the record continued in the background. Then it hit her. Her heart leaped. Lief's voice resurfaced on the record.

Kay Yvette Jelling, Will you marry me?

Lief presented her with the ring and stood waiting for her answer. She pulled her hands to her face to cover her dropped jaw. Kay was a master at disguising her feelings, but in that moment she was rendered defenseless and the camera caught all of it. Eternal moments went by without an answer until Lief asked her again.

"Well… Will you marry me?"

Her hands fell from her face, exposing the tears running down her cheeks. She grabbed Lief and pulled him in close to speak into his ear.

"Yes. Of course I will. I want to spend the rest of my life with you."

Lief breathed a sigh of relief.

"Phew. Oh man- I'm so glad you said yes. You scared me there for a second. So, let's do that, we'll spend the rest of our live's together. Let's see if this fits."

He put the ring on her finger and it fit perfect even though Lief had no idea of her size.

"Baby, You know me so well. You couldn't have picked me a better ring."

Bernard wiped a tear from the corner of his eye with a handkerchief.

Before leaving the shop, they perused the store for the perfect piece of nostalgia to remind them of the day. They both settled on a thick iron wire fruit basket in the shape of a leaf that was seasoned in heavy patina. Lief purchased the unshredded piece from Bernard, who then took a few pictures of the two in front of his store and promised to email the photos after he touched them up. They had known Bernard for all of twenty-minutes, but having been together during such a bonding experience, it felt as if they were parting with family when they said goodbye.

On the way back to the beach house, Kay was quiet. Nothing of any worth could be put into words to accompany the magnitude of what had transpired in the shop. But that didn't stop Lief from jabbering.

"Nostalgic, yes, or preserved, maintained, antiqued, wax, or even kick-ass, but definitely not unshredded."

Kay smiled and put her hand in his lap.

At Kay's request Lief agreed not to mention their engagement to her family right away. Lief saw the logic in that. After all, he was going to be the impromptu stranger, crashing their planned vacation at the shore.

Upon their return to the beach house, Lief was introduced to the family, first to Irene, her mother, followed by Ben, her brother, and then the infamous Christine, the bitch. His uncanny ability to read people allowed him to like all of them at first sight, with an exception to Christine.

That night they all sat down for a pasta and garlic bread dinner. Lief understood that remaining gluten-free in New Jersey would prove difficult. Kay had told him that in Jersey pizza was it's own food group. It was eaten so often that the New Jersey governor, Governor Christie, passed legislation that prohibited pizza boxes from being put into the regular recycle or garbage bins. There was a separate garbage bin just for just pizza boxes there.

Half way through the meal, Christine noticed the ring on Kay's finger and pointed to it with a surprised expression on her face which could only be interpreted as *Is that what I think it is?* Kay nodded and Christine's eyes widened in excitement. Christine nudged Ben, who was just as shocked when he made the connection. Irene looked at everyone wondering what was going on until Ben pointed to Kay's ring.

"Whaawt? Whaawt? Is that- Whaawt?"

Irene was born and raised in New Jersey and had the thickest Jersey accent that Lief had ever heard. All of the vowels she used in her words where elongated and followed by a "w" sound. That made "what", "whawt" and "Car", "Caawr" and so on.

Kay didn't know how to answer her gawking mother's incomplete question, so she just sat with a smirk on her face until Irene almost choked on her food, trying to complete a recognizable question.

"Owh- My- Gauwd! Seriously?"

"Yes mom"

Irene looked back and forth between Lief and Kay. Her demeanor was disapproving.

"I'm just shauwcked. Well congrats, I guess."

Irene was speechless for the rest of the meal. That would be the only time that Lief would ever witness such a silence from his mother-in-law to be. Later that evening, Irene admitted that she was concerned at how soon they got engaged after less than a year of knowing each other. It didn't take her long to warm up to Lief though.

Lief was assigned to the living room hide-a-bed couch that evening. While he was unfolding the tucked bed frame and mattress, Irene entered the room and took a seat on the opposing couch.

"I've slept on it before. It's not that uncomfortable."

"I wasn't worried. I'm grateful you're letting me stay here for a couple days."

Lief saw that Irene wanted to have a talk with him, so he put a cushion back on the couch and took a seat. She asked him, first, about his family and upbringing, then anything else that could shine a light on his character. Each time Lief spoke, he bled honesty and she siphoned the last drop. She'd verbalize simple, benign questions, but somehow procured damning responses each time. The more he tried to keep a response simple, the more Irene would adjust her posture in an ever so subtle manner as to magnify her look of intrigue, causing Lief to tell her everything. At her request, Lief shared beliefs that even he ad been unaware of till they came out his mouth.

To Lief, it felt like a one way conversation. In it's duration, Lief had disclosed that he was a sober alcoholic that was raised Mormon, a high school dropout, a biological grandfather at the age of thirty-eight, a maladjusted youth who fought too much, and a musician who was receiving disability pay. He also told her about his undesirable mental conditions, including his PTSD, OCD, hypomania, and depression. He sustained heavy regret with each admission although she appeared unfazed.

Irene got all she needed then wished him a goodnight. As Lief laid in bed that night, he enacted the conversation in his head. He cringed as he recalled all the dim-witted disclosures that he was sure would haunt him.

— —

In the morning everyone except Lief and Kay went to beach. To Lief's surprise and relief, Kay told Lief that her mom really liked him, even after the previous night's conversation. With those worries behind him he was, again, free to relish in the thoughts of being engaged to Kay. Then it occurred to him that they were alone and would be for a while. The thought led to Kay's bedroom for some long awaited intimacy. Each time they had sex was better than the last and their thoughts of marriage enhanced the experiences all the more.

Lief and Kay laid in ecstasy for only moments before initiating another round, but were interrupted by the family's quick return from the beach. They had taken seats circled around the adjacent living room to discuss plans for the day. Kay joined them, trying to act as nonchalant as possible. A few moments later, Lief joined the group as well. The conversation ceased after Lief and Kay took seats among them. Lief looked to Kay, *Are we busted?* Kay's thoughts answered, *Mm-hmm.* While looking to Kay, he noticed her disheveled, j.b.f. hairstyle. *Yeah, we're busted.* Then Lief heard another familiar voice in his mind. It said: *Don't worry. You just keep my daughter happy.* He looked up and saw Irene staring straight at him. Lief was shocked that Kay's mother could communicate in the same way. *Is this a family thing?* Ben's thoughts, then, entered the curious conversation, *Can we move on and have lunch?*

— —

Through the remainder of Lief's stay, Kay's family took him in as one of their own. Kay explained that his presence may have been a useful distraction from the usual family dynamic and may have helped Christine mellow out a few notches. They all played a lot of backgammon, spent time at the beach, cooked together, and relaxed in the comfortable climate.

On the last morning before Lief's departure, Kay and Lief had a chance to visit his half sister, June and her family at Ft. Dix army base, just an hour's drive away. June's husband served as an airplane mechanic there. By coincidence, Lief's stepbrother Chet was stationed on the base as well. June and Chet were on opposite sides of Lief's family and had never met although Lief had tried several times to initiate contact between the two. Lief believed that their lack of contact was due to their differences in religion, the same reason he suspected Chet was unable to meet with him and Kay that day.

Lief hadn't realized how much he missed his younger sister until he saw her standing in the driveway, holding her toddler. Kay and June liked each other right off the bat. Their immediate connection did not surprise Lief. He was grateful that he had the chance to catch up with his sister, but found it unfortunate that June's husband, Brent, was away at work during their visit. Lief was also happy that he had a chance to interact with his young niece, Amy. She reminded Lief so much of June when she was a child. He saw flashes of how close he and his younger sister were, even when she was a toddler. She was one of his best friends. But, like with the rest of his family, they spoke less frequent over the years. Lief dismissed their distance as, what he thought was, the common occurrence he called growing up and growing apart. Though something in that visit made Lief stop and think that growing apart wasn't always necessary. When his former bond with his sister came into full focus, he considered the nature of the separation. He searched his mind as well as his heart before a somber answer surfaced. It was his alcoholism that drove him away from all of the friends and family that he cherished. In that revelation, Lief was able to see, yet, another angle of his terrible disease. Years of visits and conversations were lost between June and him, as well as with many other loved ones that should have remained dear. He knew there was little he could do about the lost time, so he allowed himself to be happy for the opportunity he had to pick up the pieces.

Lief left June's home a fuller person than he was when he arrived. His growth and greater awareness of his ability to love strengthened his bond with Kay. On their drive back to the shore, they had the longest wordless conversation that they had ever had. Their non-verbal communication became so fluid that it became difficult to distinguish whose thoughts belonged to who. They learned it didn't matter.

Irene was standing in the driveway when they returned to the beach house. She rushed them out of the car, insisting that they take part in her plans to honor her dearly departed George. George was half caucasian and half Chinese. Although George had been raised in the states, his family were immigrants, and had instilled much of their Chinese culture in him. One time, he and Irene performed a Chinese ritual of lighting a Kongming lantern, aka Chinese lantern, while they shared a wonderful moment watching it float off over the Atlantic. In remembrance of him, Irene brought a couple Chinese lanterns to the shore to light and set sail in the exact spot that her and George had years prior.

The sun was setting when they all went out to the beach to light the flying lanterns. Irene had forgotten how to get them to work, so the first lantern was more or less a trial run. It's directions instructed them to expand the wire framed rice paper by hand until it the hot air from the lit candle underneath expanded the frame on it's own. After that, it was supposed float up and away.

Lighting the lantern proved to be a difficult task because the rice paper began to catch fire when it tilted on its side. They put out the fire and relit the lantern, making sure to keep it upright on their next attempt. As the hot air expanded the paper inside the wire frame the group grew with excitement.

Along the top of the beach sat a row of houses with an unobstructed view of the ocean. In a home close to where the lanterns were being released, a family sat on a second floor balcony watching with anticipation as well. The lantern expanded and rose. Irene sent her sentiments with the lantern.

"Geowrge, baby, we're sending this to you."

The lantern struggled to rise at first, taking a sharp dive, appearing as if it was going to crash into the sand, then it swooped upwards into the sky. Everyone, including the family on the porch, began to clap at the spectacular sight of the luminescent lantern pressing against the darkening blue sky.

A sea breeze caught the lighted wonder, sending it away from the sea. Exciting and expressive sounds were shared by all. Their excitement grew with each inch that it ascended, until the breeze picked up, causing the lantern to sink several feet. It went straight for the family on the porch.

Their expressed excitement turned into vulgar exclamations when the lantern headed towards the father, who while in the act of ducking, tipped his full beer bottle off of the railing, sending it smashing into the ground. The lantern then hit the straw window shading that covered the sliding glass door. The shading burst into flames and the family scattered. The mother and young daughter screamed and ran in the house while the flames blazed in front of the entire window, threatening to digest the overhang as well. The father yelled for a bucket of water.

Christine was the first to flee the beach. She was soon followed by Kay and then Lief. Irene and Ben remained on the beach, standing in utter shock with their mouths agape. The father on the flaming porch turned to look at them with panic and then scorn in his eyes until a pitcher of water was delivered, diverting his attention. That's when Irene and Ben made a break for it as well.

Back at the house everyone breathed heavy, trying to catch their breath. Hunched over and wide eyed, Kay stood straight up to speak.

"Oh- My- Gauwd! Do you think they know where we live?"

"Babe, you're changing. You- You're becoming… one of them."

"Whawt?"

"The accent- You- You spoke like them."

"Oh whatever. Come on. So I slip every once in a while. No, seriously though, do you think they'll find us?"

Ben explained that they ran outside of the other family's line of sight. Irene, still breathing heavy, looked up at the ceiling.

"Geowrge sweetheawrt, we certainly put on quite the show for you."

CHAPTER 19

LANDS EDGE

Opening his eyes, Lief saw a mystical light piercing trough several cracks in the closed horizontal blinds. Purple beams bursted through the, otherwise, pure rays of light, each one illuminating the dust particles floating in the air, transforming them into dancing stardust. The light spoke to Lief, beckoning him to join its source. Trancelike, he grabbed the camera with its rig and tripod, then walked barefoot onto the beach at the end of the street.

The beach was empty and presented him with the perfect opportunity to film the uninterrupted horizon. He set up the camera, placed it on the tripod, and began filming. It was then that it occurred to him that the filming process reduced his three dimensional world into the flatland of two dimensions, then stored it in the form of ones and zeros for further review. The idea that it was possible to subtract a dimension while still detailing every other association with his experience got him thinking. He wondered how many other dimensions could be layered on top of the the ones he was aware of. Then he tried to imagine what that could be like.

He panned the camera right to left on the tripod. Then he centered the low lit sun in the frame. As the nearby star peaked over the gradual curvature of the planet, it pulled the coast closer to it, exposing its magnitude. The sun's orange center bled into a spectacularly red rim.

Accents of green slivers, surrounded by golden rays, spiked outwards, and stretched across the calm ocean. Many of the colors reminded Lief of his favorite painting, The Song of the Lark, a painting of an optimistic young farm woman walking barefoot in front of a rising sun, much like the one that was rising in front of Lief. Seeing a sun as similar, helped him better understand his attraction to the alluring painting. Lief knew that the sand between his toes was as cool as the dirt beneath the bare feet of the young farmer. Lief felt that the mesmerizing sun rising behind her bestowed to her the same satisfying completeness that Lief was experiencing.

Then something unfamiliar occurred. It became clear to Lief that his feelings there on the beach were the same as those that he had when he first experienced the painting. They were so much the same, that their differences in time and place became indiscernible, causing the two moments to combine into the same time frame. The intrinsic message of the painting, overlapping the depth of Lief's moment in the sand opened a space that contained another plain of existence, one with a fourth dimension that extended across the universe. Lief entered. The visible aspects were pinholes of light and glowing globes that he shot past like an arrow towards its target, but without the resistance of air. Outside of that which could be seen, the fourth dimension was comprised of certainty, an undeniable truth that could have no opposition. It was like the inception of an idea that took shape to reach full form, never to fade. When the crystal clear understanding solidified, Lief knew that he was afforded a rare glimpse across the vail of time, long before his human existence.

He was transported into his former residence, a nebula of soft pink clouds that cradled his consciousness within it's walls of creation. *This was my home.* Resting there without effort as a part of the whole, Lief experienced the time before pain and excitement. There was no conflict of any sort, but there was no shell of identity either. He asked his true and complete self whether or not he regretted ever leaving there, to have never had that single thought, the one that propelled him across the universe into the star-gate of his birth. His answer came as fast as his question: *I'd do it again in a heartbeat.*

A seagull flying overhead took aim and shit square onto his shoulder. It snapped him back into the existence he was more familiar with, reminding him that he was, no doubt, a perfectly flawed human being standing there on the beach. The sun had become too bright to film any longer anyway. Lief went back to the beach house to clean himself and pack while carefully trying to not wake anyone. He gave Kay a gentle kiss on the forehead as she slept, loaded the Tin Can, and then shut the back hatch. The crashing sound of the doors closing alongside the starting engine woke everyone in the house. He drove north to New York to pick up Bigfoot.

After thirty-dollars in tolls, Lief arrived in New York at the address Bigfoot had given him, the wrong address on the opposite side of town, in the kind of neighborhood that one gets shot in the face for being a stranger. It was frustrating for Lief on many levels, but the worst part was he had to pee badly, and there were no businesses or public restrooms in sight. He was left with one option, to piss in a bush along the side of the street. He took care of his business there and no one paid any attention to him. He looked to his left and saw another guy doing the same at the end of the block.

After getting the correct address from Bigfoot, Lief met him at a Starbucks in lower Manhattan. Lief even found a parking spot. Bigfoot asked Lief he'd like to film a short set then explained that he had found the perfect park for busking around the corner from them. Lief was still mad at Bigfoot for giving him the wrong address, alongside just about everything else about Bigfoot, so he wasn't feeling much like playing music with him. Truth be told, both of them were tired of lugging the gear after day one, but it had come to the point that they had also lost their desire to play music at all. Regardless, Lief agreed to play and lugged the gear once more, knowing after that morning he was ok with the idea of hanging up his busking spurs for a while.

On the way into the park, a film student from one of big colleges in New York greeted them and asked if they'd sign a release form, explaining that his class was filming a movie in the park that day. They both signed individual forms while Lief took notice of the many elements of their production. The film crew were all in their early twenties. Each of them had an assigned duty, duties that they all seemed to understand. A couple of guys held boom mics, a handful held reflective things for lighting, and there was a clapper lady who clapped the slate. The slate signaled the camera guy who captured several actors acting while he rolled the large camera along tracks that were held in place by sand bags. Caterers catered food to the entire crew. The production was nowhere near the size of the set in New Orleans, but that time the irony was not wasted on Lief. Lief's contrasted incompetence was in his face. Lief, again, felt defeated. He saw how there was a place in Hollywood for each of the crew members in front of him, but there'd be no room for a guy who's film ambitions were shaping up to be nothing but pipe dreams.

Lief imagined how much his film equipment would fetch when he sold all of it after returning home. Although he knew it wouldn't matter at that point, he set up the camera and sound equipment to film his two man band play his songs that would only ever be heard by a few. Lief thought of how Bigfoot was lucky for not giving a shit. Bigfoot made a keen observation though.

"Dude, it's a film inside a film."

"Yeah... You're right. Maybe we'll tear a hole in the space time continuum."

"What?"

Lief started strumming the chords to the first song so that he didn't have to answer a question that he had no energy to answer.

Although the weary Gas Station Rose luggage band started out sluggish, they found their rhythm quicker than usual. They played with mere muscle memory, allowing them to focus on the crowd more than they had before. Eye contact with the passerby's transformed them into an audience that stayed put. A couple of kids paid them that ultimate compliment by dancing to the music. The creative energy had become cyclical. The growing crowd gave the two their appreciation which Leif and Bigfoot feed off of, then sent it right back, but with a little more.

A lone electric guitarist who was busking on the opposite corner of the park, turned up his amp and noodled out a lead on top of Lief's rhythm, making the duo a trio for a brief moment. The audience in front of Lief and Bigfoot took notice of the additional instrument in the distance. Many in the small crowd showed their enthusiasm for the addition by cheering with high pitched whistling, hooting, and hollering, while a few even banged their heads, pumping the two finger sign of the horns rock salute. The despair that Lief had been experiencing along his drive to get Bigfoot had transformed into a happiness in his soul that welled into near tears. He was reminded of how New York never failed to prove itself as a magical place for him.

The crowd grew into the largest and most excited gathering that they had ever amassed. Money rained into Lief's open guitar case and then actual rain began to pour into the case as well, forcing everyone to file themselves back into a more predictable existence.

Rushing back to the car with their carts full of gear, Bigfoot got sentimental with Lief.

"Dude, I know we've had some tension on the road, but I got to say. I'm glad to see you."

"Really, that's cool man. Thank you. You too."

Lief believed his lie was justified in that instance after such an epic session with the talented fur ball. It was obvious that Bigfoot was high, meaning that most of his excitement was his drugs speaking. Lief wasn't about to look a gift horse in the mouth by not running with Bigfoot's artificial happiness. He would take it for as long as he could.

It wasn't until ten minutes of driving in his typical and begrudged "big city mode", that it occurred to Lief that he wasn't driving though just any run of the mill large city. He was driving in New York City which was something he always wanted to do, regardless of its bumper to bumper traffic. Since he was a kid and after seeing hundreds of driving scenes on the big screen that depicted the stereotypical noisy drive through the Big Apple, Lief dreamed of doing the same. He learned there wasn't much to it. All he had to do was drive forward for a fraction of a second then apply the brakes, which he would then hold for a minute or two before repeating the process. It was more or less just like driving down the 5 in LA. The difference was that in New York City Lief drove happily amongst thousands of yellow checkered cabs, all yelling at each other while clogging the arteries of the city, beneath the most spectacular buildings in the entire country. Lief started to understand the mutual respect that New Yorkers held for each other. The name calling didn't ever commence until someone un-synched with the rhythm of the city upset the flow. Even then, the yelling seemed more like encouragement from someone who was rough around the edges, but still cared. It worked for Lief. He mimicked the stereotypical New York commuters.

"Hey, I'm driving here. Yo- Jerk-off, why don't you use your fucking blinker? What's the hold up? You a fucking tourist or somethin'?"

Bigfoot found it amusing and joined in.

"Yo- You fucking mooley!"

"Dude! You can't say that, you'll get us shot. Don't you know what that means?"

"I dunno, I heard Eddie Murphy say it once."

"Yeah, he's allowed to, he's black. It's racist or something."

"Oh shit!"

"Wait!"

"What?"

"We are, right now, exactly as far east as we will get on this trip. It's nothing but west from here."

"This is the farthest I have ever been from the shire."

"Wow! Look at Bigfoot, quoting Lord of the Rings. You have seen a decent movie."

"I've seen plenty of them, I just don't remember them like you do."

"It's the drugs man. It's the drugs."

"Fuck you. You're probably right though, but still fuck you, you fucking mooley."

Lief shook his head, perplexed at Bigfoot's stupidity.

"Dude-"

Bypassing further explanation, Lief drove slowly out of the city and onto the open road, leading to their next stop, Pittsburgh.

CHAPTER 20

WEST

Desensitized to the difficulties of driving long stretches on the road, the six hours from New York to Pittsburgh would prove to be a breeze. Lief thought of all they had accomplished that far with the filming, ground covered, and people visited all across the entire country along the way to Pittsburgh, Pennsylvania for Oreo's Studio O party. All the meticulous planning to get there at 6 p.m. on that day was about to come to fruition. Lief was sure they'd enjoy the party itself, but knew he'd enjoy another aspect of it even more. His looking forward to attending the party at the beginning of the trip had shifted into looking forward to it being over, when he'd no longer have a schedule to keep. Also, after leaving the studio party and Pittsburgh, he'd be on his way to do the one thing that set the trip, the movie, and even the engagement in motion, Lief would soon meet his grown up daughter.

Two-hundred miles from Pittsburgh, they drove through the beautiful Amish country, persevered in all of its colonial splendor. Due to the bad visibility, a result of the heavy thunderstorms that cropped up along their route, they didn't get to see as much of it as they would have liked. Fortunate for them though, they made an unplanned stop due to low fuel in an interesting town named Hershey. When Lief pulled into an unassuming little gas station store to pay for gas, he discovered hundreds of giant candy bars for sale. He wasn't able to make the connection on his own, but with some help from the attendant, Lief learned that the many chocolate bars with the big letters in all caps that spelled HERSHEY, which matched the large letters that spelled Hershey on the road sign that "Welcome to the Town of Hershey- The sweetest place on the planet", were actually made in that town. They seemed much bigger in their hometown though. He bought two one-pound chocolate bars, one for Leslie, and one for Sarah. Little did Lief know that driving through the sweetest town on earth would stand as an omen for, what would turn out to be, the sweetest day Lief would have the opportunity to experience with Bigfoot.

Arriving at the gates of Pittsburgh, the GPS lead them into the city and then straight through and out of the city. The directions indicated that they had to drive thirty-miles more to reach their destination. Oreo had not mentioned that the studio was on the other side of the city and past the Allegheny county lines. It was inconsequential outside of diminishing their chances off busking in the beautiful Market Square in downtown Pittsburgh the following morning.

Lief wasn't much for backtracking.

They arrived at the address they were given right on time. It was a one story brick house that didn't look anything like a recording studio. Lief had to call Oreo to double check that he was in the right location. Oreo confirmed that they were, then directed them down a long staircase leading to a basement of the house.

The basement studio was huge with a large area sectioned off by canvas sheets. There was a handful of people having some drinks and socializing around a makeshift kitchen in the corner of the space. They were a friendly bunch and welcomed Lief and Bigfoot. Lief inquired into Oreo's whereabouts and learned he was disposed elsewhere. There were no women there at that point, but Lief assured Bigfoot that women would arrive. Oreo had promised Lief that there would be plenty of "hotties" in attendance.

All those in attendance were locals and were either musicians or part of a film crew. Lief and Bigfoot were the only outsiders there. They kept to themselves for the most part and waited for Oreo to surface. Bigfoot grew impatient and became his usual unhappy self in short order.

"So, where's your friend?"

"Knowing Oreo, he is putting some finishing touches on something in the studio. He's a bit of a perfectionist."

Bigfoot grabbed a red plastic cup and filled it full of something at the bar. Lief understood that Bigfoot needed a buffer between his inner awkwardness and the awkwardness of the event. Lief contemplated what it must have been like to be Bigfoot. He recalled what it was like to have that huge void in his chest and how he'd try to fill it with booze or something heavier, all the while knowing that he wouldn't be able to stop until he passed out. It was a numbing process.

Finally, twenty-minutes after they arrived, Oreo surfaced from behind the canvas curtain that was concealing the guts of the studio. He was disheveled and had beads of sweat rolling down his forehead and cheeks.

"LIEF!!! Hey buddy, you made it!"

"Hey Oreo! Good to see you. Thanks again for the invite."

"You know it man. And I'm guessing you're Bigfoot."

Bigfoot paused, stared blank faced at Oreo, and then sarcastically responded.

"Ha. Funny. Good guess-"

Lief spoke over Bigfoot's condescending response.

"So Oreo, looks like you've been hard at work. You doing some finishing touches in there?

Before Oreo answered they all turned their attention to a rustling sound behind the curtain. The sound was followed by an attractive blond in her twenties who was sporting a just been fucked hairdo. Oreo raised his brow.

"Yeah, you could say that."

"Can we take a peak at the studio"

"In good time my friend. I've got something special planned and I'm just waiting for a few others to show before I can let anyone in there."

Oreo wasted no time and ran into the middle of the gathering, stood on a chair, and tapped a drum stick on the side of his beer to get everyone's attention. He addressed the party in his usual, high energy, boisterous, and polished fashion.

"Everyone Listen up! I want to thank you all for coming out, especially you Stevo, we always knew you were a fucking homo, no offense Lief.

Stevo smiled, but Lief looked around confused, wondering if there was a homosexual in the room that was also named Lief. Having been born and raised in the politically correct capital of the nation, Lief was naive to Oreo's brash humor.

"Hey, by the way, Freddy Mercury called and he wants his look back."

That time, Lief got the misguided attempt at a joke, then gave Oreo the bird.

"Ha! You know I love you guys. Alrighty, everyone please help yourself to any of the various appetizers on the counter and mucho thanks to those who contributed. Also, help your self to the self-serve bar over here, aka the fridge. As you all are aware, this is a celebration for the unveiling of Studio O, for which I have put together an exciting presentation that I will be conducting in an hour or so. So please, I know it's tempting, but I'm asking that no one take any sneak peaks behind the curtain. Alright- One last thing, I'd like to point out that we have a couple of special guests in attendance. I don't mean to say that ya'll ain't special, I just wanted to point out that we have two guests that came all the way out from nutty California. One I pointed out already and, Ladies- Shit, I mean lady- Where the fuck are all the ladies? Whatever, they're on their way. Never mind then, moot point. Alright, Lief and Bigfoot have come all the way out from California to attend the party. Can the both of you raise your hands please? The furry one is Bigfoot. Please give them a Pittsburgh welcome. By the way, these two are in the middle of making a film about street musicians."

Oreo pointed to Lief.

"You bring the camera in?"

Lief gave Oreo a thumbs up.

"Awesome! So if you get a chance, you should meet these two, they are cool as a couple of refrigerated mother-fucking kosher dill pickles. Alright, again, thank you all for coming out and party on folks."

By Oreo's standards, the greeting was short. He always put on a show no matter what was involved. He brought energy with him whenever he entered any room. Sometimes his enthusiasm was a little over the top and off, but, nonetheless, he always strived to entertain. Lief was certain he would go far, in some direction or another.

Lief avoided most of the mingling by keeping his camera in his face, filming bits and pieces of the party. Bigfoot got over his pissiness and had become quite the social butterfly after having three or fourteen drinks. A couple of women even showed up, which prompted Oreo to call everyone over to the studio curtain so that he could start the presentation.

"The time has come that you all have been patiently waiting for, the grand opening of Studio O. In just a moment I will lift a portion of the curtain at which point I would like everyone to, calmly, and one at a time, enter and fill in towards the screen at the front of the room. Please be careful entering, it's pitch black in there. It's dark for a reason, as you will soon see."

Oreo pulled up an edge of the curtain and ushered his guests through. The guests all stood in the pitch blackness for less than a minute before fog machines filled the area with dusty smelling fake fog. Then heavy metal blasted while laser machines moved images all around the walls and ceiling in the studio. The music faded and the studio fell silent, but just long enough to startle the group with the thundering loudness of Oreo's voice that echoed throughout the studio.

"This is Studio OOOOOOO! Please feast your eyes on the screen in front of you."

The screen lit up with amazing computer generated images of a cartoon band playing in-sync with the music that had faded back in. Everyone showed their enthusiasm with a thunderous ovation. Then the cartoon band stopped playing and Oreo appeared on screen. Through witty and comical dialog he explained the story behind the studio. It was only a couple minutes long and then the music came back on as did the lights.

The studio was revealed and it was stellar. Lief felt it was worth all the bravado. There were about fifteen various amplifiers, several guitars, bass guitars, boom mic stands, two fully loaded drum kits, stacks of old school outboard gear, and all the cords that could possibly be used, times five.

Oreo sat on the throne of one of the largest drum kits Lief had ever seen. It was an over the top double bass kit that was so stocked that he'd have to swivel in a near full circle to hit all the crash, splash, ride, high-hat, top hats, cymbals, snares, toms, cowbells, and any other noise making drum diddalidoo's that were attached. Another drummer, resembling Thor, took a seat at a slightly smaller kit set up facing Oreo. Guitarists plugged in bass guitars and just plain old guitars, then adjusted their various pedals and amps. Oreo held his drumsticks above his head, waiting for every one to get set, then, just as the last knob of an amp was adjusted and everything fell silent Oreo readdressed the group.

"Let's have a moment of silence to honor all those who are no longer able to rock. Whether it be due to choking on their own vomit, plane crashes, tour buss crashes, overdoses, or spontaneous combustion..."

Oreo paused for a moment, then decided to soup up his already elaborate pre-battle speech.

"Wait- Stevo. STEVO. Hey man, could you pour out just a bit of your drink, you know, like the way gang members do it, so we can fully honor them? Yeah, in the- That mop bucket over there. No, no, that's a turkey fryer. It's the blue, the one, with the wheels. It's right behind you man. The-one-behind-you- Come on! Seriously? You don't see it?"

Steve didn't seem to mind taking orders, even for such a novelty, and he did eventually spot the bucket.

"That's the one. Thank you. Yeah, just a little bit. So that was for the homies. Cool. You guys ready? Now let's jam!"

He began beating his drum to a bloody pulp as all of the other musicians commenced as well. The two drummers were competing in a dueling drum session, playing as loud as they could, as they snarled and contorted their faces at each other. Lief wasn't sure how the winner would be determined, outside of awarding the one that banged his head and twirled his sticks the most. Bigfoot, a drummer himself, couldn't figure it out either. The bass players and guitarists couldn't keep up with the speed of the drums in their drum competition, so they just played as loud as they could. Lief and Bigfoot stood aside and watched because there was no room for them or their style of music. Also, they had no ability or desire to try to play louder than the rest of the group.

Lief couldn't handle more than a couple of minutes of the loud noise. Lief saw that Bigfoot wasn't into the ruckus either. Because there had been no indication that they would be offered a place to crash, it became clear that it was a good time to hit the road and hope find a suitable rest stop somewhere on the way to Chicago. Lief snuck out without any goodbyes. Bigfoot snuck out with a refilled red cup. It smelled like straight vodka.

Lief was happy he got to see his friend and was honored that Oreo scheduled the party so he could attend, but he underestimated how run down he'd become on his way there. He also underestimated how little interest he would have for anything, outside of seeing Leslie on his westward way home. He was done with all the fan faire he had built around his sole desire to see his daughter.

Lief drove towards her through the remainder of Pennsylvania and on into Ohio. He was hoping to make it across most of Ohio that night, if not all the way into Indiana. He was tired and Bigfoot was drunk. The car was ripe with smells of booze, Bigfoot's body oder, and chalky fake fog. All was quiet in the car outside of the ringing in Lief's ears. The thought of music nauseated him, much like the accidental taste of mint the morning after getting wasted on peppermint schnapps.

They were routed along HWY-76 and then up to I-80 West, a freeway Lief often used in California. It seemed strange for him to be on a freeway that he was so familiar with, but on the wrong side of the country. They hadn't been on 80 long before they passed a sign that read "Akron 17 Miles HWY-8 South". Akron had been on Lief's list of places to visit at some point during his lifetime, although it hadn't yet made it to his bucket list. Many years prior, Lief had a profound spiritual experience in Columbus, Ohio, which was just an hour and a half-drive from Akron. Due to what had transpired in Columbus, along with the surrounding circumstances, Lief was led to suspect that Akron's proximity probably had something to do with it.

He had been sober for a year when he visited Columbus. As a result, he had been experiencing many benefits from his new way of life. Everywhere he went with his new sober lenses made each place seem meaningful and new, but never as meaningful as Ohio had become for him.

He had been in the state for business and was visiting several cities in its southern reaches. He had felt a welcoming flow of creativity throughout his entire visit, which came to a head in Columbus, the night before he was to catch a plane home. That night he had fallen asleep thinking about a vibrant red cardinal that he had seen perched on a pine branch earlier that day. When Lief first saw the bird, he was astonished at how handsome the bird was. He had a hard time taking his eyes off of it, that was due in part to the fact that he had never seen a cardinal before, and the other part was due to the notice the bird took of him. His dream was a continuance of that brief moment that the bird and him had shared looking at each other earlier that day, though in his dream the cardinal stared straight into his mind, causing a psychic connection that allowed Lief to experience the cardinal's consciousness as though it was tethered to his own. He shared its simple thoughts and desired its modest desires. He understood the movements it was capable of, he felt its hunger, and he even saw through its eyes that were focused on its next meal, a squirming grub on the ground beneath. Just as soon as the cardinal initiated its swoop downward for the grub, a hawk snuck up behind the small red bird, and snatched it up with its large claws. Lief felt the cardinal's panic and increased heart rate as it struggled to escape the tight grasp of the hawk. Just as soon as the cardinal resigned to the futility of its struggle and accepted its defeat, Lief felt the peace that washed over it.

It was something about the bird's serenity while facing its death that struck Lief to the core, awakening him. Not only did he wake, but he sprang upright in his bed, as if an icy bucket of water had just been poured over him. It was not fear that woke him, it was quite the opposite. There he sat, experiencing perfection for the fist time in his life. In that moment he was as content as content could be, knowing that everything was as it should be, should have been, and would continue to be, including his inevitable, future moment of physical death. That was the spiritual awakening he was promised when he subscribed to the twelve steps of recovery that helped keep him sober. He had reached the twelfth step with the assistance of a cardinal and Columbus, Ohio. His life was changed forever, because, even though he often sank back into a fearful existence, he knew there was another version of life that was worth living for.

The significance of his experience there had prompted him to do some online research of Ohio, to see if there were any other documented experiences such as his. The evidence he was looking for jumped off his screen. It was staggering and started with all of Ohio's trailblazers and their contributions to the world. The Wright Brothers, Thomas Edison, eight U.S. presidents, Neil Armstrong, and Steven Spielberg were just a few noteworthy people that sprung from the Buckeye State. Lief considered most of them to be inspired, awakened men. It was no wonder that even its state motto "With God all things are possible" reflected its air of discovery. Per capita, Ohio's plethora of patents was surpassed only by California.

The most compelling case of the creative influence that the state possessed, brought Lief full circle to where his line of thinking originated. Akron, Ohio was the birthplace of the twelve steps, the same twelve steps that he ascended right past a certain alcoholic death, then up to the doorway to his spiritual awakening. According to his logic, Akron must have been the epicenter of it all and, therefore, a good place to visit.

Lief was five miles from the Akron exit when he calculated the time it would take to stray from the planned route. It would have taken them ten-minutes of additional driving to reach it, but it would also take ten minutes to get back on track. As tired as Lief was, he was torn on whether the extra drive was worth it. He couldn't come to a decision on his own, so he consulted the inebriated Bigfoot.

"Bigfoot, you awake?"

Bigfoot jolted forward in his seat.

"What- What the fuck?"

"I wanted to know if you were up."

"Yeah. Why?"

"Akron is ten minutes south of us, slightly off route. Wanna check it out?"

"Fuck no."

Lief was off the hook for not visiting, even though he was so close to it.

— —

They had been driving for an hour and a half and had already gone through five toll booths. While approaching another one, a tan sedan sped to the rear of the Tin Can. Lief, who was not in the mood for any type of competition, moved into the middle lane to let the aggressive car pass. The sedan followed him into the same lane and tailgated him for a quarter mile until all the lanes split for the different pay booths. The sedan then moved into the lane of another toll booth.

When Lief slowed to pay the toll, Bigfoot jumped up in his seat again, alarmed at the changing speed. Lief got through the toll booth quicker than the sedan, then proceeded onto the interstate in the middle lane so that the sedan could pass without any perceived challenge.

The sedan raced out of the toll booth and went straight towards them. Instead of going around them in the fast lane, the car approached on their right, passed them, and then cut them off and slammed its brakes, causing Lief to hit his as well. Again, Bigfoot freaked out as if death was imminent.

"What the fuck man?"

"Dude, I don't know what this guy's problem is. He's been tailgating us for a mile."

"Well don't piss him off. You're going to get us killed!"

"NO. I'm not going to get us killed. Just calm down."

The last thing Lief could tolerate at that moment was Bigfoot being critical of his driving, especially considering matters were out of his control. Lief remained calm on the outside, regardless of how much he wanted to yell at the other driver and strangle Bigfoot. Lief swallowed all of his dignity and moved into the far right slow lane. His passive maneuver was not good enough for the unstable driver who then jetted in front of him and, again, slammed on his breaks.

"LIEF! Knock-It-The-Fuck-Off!"

"Knock what off? Are you watching this guy?"

"Dude, just let me out of the car!"

There it was. They had driven 3,777 miles and Lief was 3,363.5 miles past past the point that he should have tolerated Bigfoot. It was precisely that 3,777th mile that proved to be Lief's breaking point. Lief slammed on the brakes and veered onto the shoulder, making a screeching stop. Lief screamed at the top off his lungs, growling like a death metal singer.

"YOU WANT OUT? Then GET THE FUCK OUT! I did nothing wrong! I avoided that guy at all costs! I have no control over other's actions. If I did, I would've got you to quit your fucking bitching a long time ago."

"Oh, I'm bitching?"

"Yeah, you've done nothing but bitch, bitch, bitch since the beginning of this trip. You bitch for no fucking reason. I slow the car down, you bitch, I speed up, you bitch, I make a turn, you bitch, I stop for needed film equipment, you bitch. Bitch, bitch, bitch, bitch, bitch! You know, I'm actually glad you have post traumatic stress disorder from crashing my car, you whining piece of shit! Teach you a fucking lesson, you ungrateful fuck!"

"Dude, you're an asshole!"

"I'm an asshole? I'm an asshole? Alright. I'm an asshole, but I'll tell you one thing I'm not, that's a fucking pushover. You can take your mother's tit out of your mouth and get the-fuck-out. I've been waiting to dump your ass on the side of the road since Austin. But, I was nice and got you to New York. Now I'm fucking done. Here's my back up plan, you get the fuck out, fly home, and kick rocks. It'll save you money anyway."

"Yeah? No problem, happy to leave your fucking death trap. Take me to the next rest stop. I'll take it from there."

The car was silent for the next couple of miles until they reached a rest stop on the outskirts of Cleveland. Bigfoot had been texting his parents and had made arrangements to fly to San Francisco out of Cleveland. Lief already knew Bigfoot's parents would, once again, come to his aid. Lief had come to the conclusion that their bleeding hearts would surely be the death of Bigfoot. *Who needs improvements when you have co-dependents.*

They pulled into the rest stop. Bigfoot got out, unloaded a couple of his bags, and walked away without saying a word. He left his larger things in the Tin Can, assuming that Lief would drop them off for him in California. He was correct in his assumption, though Lief was tempted to unload them.

Lief needed to use the restroom, but didn't want to take the chance of being in the vicinity too long in case Bigfoot changed his mind. Bigfoot turned his back to the car and Lief peeled out of the rest stop and back onto the freeway. Lief turned off his phone. There was no going back.

Although, Lief had imagined kicking Bigfoot out of the car many times, he had never imagined that the relief would be as instantaneous as it was. The toxic personification of perdition that sucked the sanity out of Lief was three miles behind him. The new air that flowed into the Tin Can grew fresher with the distance. The thought of having the rest of the trip to himself soothed his soul.

Even though Lief was happy that Bigfoot was gone, he remembered he was still mad at the asshole that was driving the tan sedan. He began imagining ways that he could have stuck it to him, but then an obscure thought formed. *I used to believe that everything happened for a reason. Could this be the case here?* Deep down, Lief knew that everything went down the way it should have, but his self-justified anger received nothing from that kind of logic.

His hardened thoughts soon softened enough for him to see how fortunate he was that the asshole did what it did. Lief didn't get a clear look at the driver, if he had, he may have seen a road angel behind the wheel, maybe one that used to drive in demolition derbies.

Lief scrolled through memories of the trip, all the way to the beginning and, outside of the intoxicating events on the Jersey Shore, witnessing the beauty of the Blue Ridge Mountains, and the gratuitous display of the vaginal ring in New Orleans, the road rage incident was the best thing that could have happened on the trip to that point. It was the catalyst to Lief's true freedom on the road. Lief looked at his clock and it was 11:11, reminding him that he still was on the right path.

Lief found a rest stop twenty-miles up the road. By moving a couple of things around in the back of the car, he discovered that there was plenty of room for him to sleep in it with comfort, something he could not do if Bigfoot was still in the car. That knowledge changed things, because no longer did he have to pay for any lodging for the rest of the trip.

The next morning Lief was sluggish and disheveled. Regardless of his appearance, he put on a hat to cover his bed-head, put the camera together, and then turned it to himself to film a short narrative of his situation.

"Good morning. So, we hit a little bump in the road last night and Bigfoot has decided to go solo. We ahh... parted ways just um, geez, outside of Cleveland I guess. He had been preparing for this a while. We had been working a few of his songs into the set, you know, with him playing guitar and singing and what not. His frontman skills really improved, so I know he'll do great. For me, well for me, huh. I think I'm done pursuing music as a possible career. I think I'm going to focus on film. I have to say- Man, I'm tired. I'm just- I'm just road worn. This has been more stressful than I could have imagined and it has taken it's toll on me. Phew... and, and now, now I'm in the interesting position of filming the rest of this movie alone. Hmm. Ok, I should mention this- Bigfoot and I had decided that we were going end the film with us staging our deaths. You know, in the spirit of Easier Rider. Bigfoot was going to get eaten by a bear and I was going to be eaten by a shark, but I was going to fight my way out through the shark's belly. But the shark and I would both die from the wounds we sustained. I guess no one ever wins in that scenario. Anyways, I'm going to move forward and accomplish the most important part of this trip, the thing that sent me out to begin with. I am going to meet my twenty-one year old daughter for the first time. I'm really excited, but really nervous at the same time. I guess that's what bringing yourself into the unknown is all about. I wouldn't want to be in any other position right now. I guess that's all I got right now. Alright, ok"

He waved goodbye to the camera and ended the recording.

It was time for Lief to use the restroom, get some food, and hit the road alone. Everything Lief needed was right there. He discovered that all the rest stops along the way to Chicago were much more elaborate than the basic west coast rest stops. They all had a least a couple of fast food establishments built in, some of them even had full restaurants. It was a tradeoff considering the costly toll system.

Lief was propelled back onto the road with a renewed sense of adventure. All he needed was some energetic music to accompany his upbeat mood. Ryan Adam's "Chin Up, Cheer Up" did the trick.

ACT IV

CHAPTER 21

MIDWESTLAND

Enthusiastic and foul-smelling, Lief crossed the Indiana state line. His scent was reminiscent of a road-worn hippy he once met in the parking lot of a Grateful Dead show, who was selling Sierra Nevada beer and Dachshund puppies from a stolen grocery cart. Lief remembered him saying something like *"Get your icy cold puppies."* Since then, Lief knew to reevaluate his life whenever he found himself smelling that way, or selling puppies for that matter. It was time for a shower or a heavy dose of patchouli oil.

Lief called his old roommate, Jay, who resided in Valparasio, a town not more than an hour outside of Chicago. Lief was hoping to visit his shower and say hi to Jay as well. Fortunate for Lief, Jay was home that day, sparing him an unpleasant sponge bath in a rest stop, or worse, a funky gas station bathroom.

Lief let Jay know that he was three-quarters of his way through a trip that was to circle the states. He also explained that he was on his way to visit a long lost daughter of his. Jay knew Lief's urgency and understood his anxiety and uncertainty all too well, having had a similar discovery later in life himself. It was Jay's discovery that spurred his move from California to Indiana, in order to help raise her.

Before getting to Jay's, Lief called Kay to give her the newest Bigfoot update. She expressed her happiness about Lief being able to complete the trip without all of the negativity that Bigfoot brought. He promised to give her frequent updates. Then he called Sarah, but was only able to leave her a voice mail.

After the calls, Lief thought of how fortunate he was to know people who were located in most of the populated areas across the country. He met them all over a twenty-year span of traveling. Far away people were easier to avoid pissing off, so he didn't burn too many of those bridges, and he had plenty of time to repair many of the bridges he had burned. There were more of the latter following his drinking career, as it was with Jay.

When Lief arrived at Jay's home, it was in and out. Jay knew Lief was blazing a trail across the country so he assisted him like he was a crew member in a pitstop in the Indiana 500. Lief didn't even get the chance to meet Jay's new wife and newborn because the two had just laid down for a nap before Lief got there. They shook hands, Jay handed him a towel, showed him the shower, they shook hands again and Lief was off for Chicago.

—— ——

Chicago was one of Lief's favorite big city's in the U.S., if not the world. He had been there over twenty times. Lief loved the cities aesthetics, with its awe-inspiring architecture of the lofty skyscrapers, and the many wonderful statues spread throughout. He also loved its functionality. He could get anywhere without getting lost or having to ask for directions. Chicago's "L" train's ease of use was a big factor in the city's pain-free navigation. It made sense to Lief that Chicago ranked lower than most other cities in the U.S. for drunk driving incidences, while having the highest percentage of bars, per capita, somewhere to the tune of eighteen-hundred in total.

As Lief drove, he visited a memory of a stroll he once took underneath Chicago's mirrored bean sculpture, Cloud Gate, in Millennium Park. His reflection walked in front of Lake Michigan while he moved towards the bean's center where he could see himself, then, walking above the grid shaped lines on the cement beneath. All of the lines stretched according to the curvature of the mirrored surface. For a moment, Lief's reflection vanished when he stood under the dead center of the sculpture, producing an unsettling feeling. Then he walked to it's opposite side and saw his reflection in front of the Chicago skyline with the Hancock building standing out as the most striking giant in the distance. His memories, then walked to the street and down several blocks where he was greeted by a green lion on the steps of the Chicago Art Institute, his favorite museum in the world.

The biggest reason behind his love for that particular museum, was that it housed his favorite painting, Jules Brenton's, Song of the Lark, the same painting that came to Lief's mind on the Jersey Shore during his otherworldly experience on the previous morning. He had first seen the painting with his mother early in 97, after he graduated Navy bootcamp in the nearby town of Great Lakes, also affectionally called Great Mistakes.

Lief and his mother were drawn into the small painting that was located right around the corner from the more well known painting of the farm couple with a pitch fork, "American Gothic". The two laid their eyes on "Song of the Lark" for a timeless moment, observing the brilliance of the colors behind the grungy, but optimistic teenage farm girl holding a sickle. Lief wondered what she was looking at and what it was that made her so hopeful. Years later, Lief learned that Bill Murray, the beloved straight-faced, dry-witted, and genius comic, once said that the painting had convinced him not to commit suicide after he bombed his first audition. He said that the heartening girl in lowly circumstances inspired him to move forward, because the sun rising behind her reminded him that each new day brought new opportunities.

Lief had last visited the museum and the painting three years prior, while he was in Chicago for business. He had forgotten where the painting was located, and the museum was closing. He almost gave up his search, but found it, just in the nick of time before it closed. He was alone in the room and viewed it in another timeless moment, letting it pull him in once more. Although his mother was not there in person on that visit, he had imagined her there just the same.

Those thoughts faded as he drifted back into the heavy traffic outside the big city. His desire to meet Leslie was surpassing his desire to see the painting that was fresh in his mind. Also, when Lief was visiting Kirsten in Austin, she told him to be careful when he visited Chicago because of the out of control crime rate, including thousands of shootings and hundreds of murders that were going on there. He knew he'd have a hard time seeing Leslie if he were dead, so he gave the stop more thought.

The scales tipped in favor of him skipping the innards of Chicago. He settled for waiving hello to the skyscrapers that he was able to see from the freeway, ten-miles away. Even though Lief was on the outskirts of the city, the traffic he experienced there was the worst he had been stuck in throughout the entire journey, even surpassing the gridlock of L.A. and New York. It took him two hours to drive thirty-miles.

Still in the midst of the horrific Chicago traffic, a muddled thought entered Lief's mind. *Don't swerve.* The out of place thought occurred without any initiation on his part. He wrestled with the strangeness of it, speaking aloud.

"Don't swerve? What the fuck? Don't swerve. Why would I swerve. Why would I think that? I'm in fucking traffic going negative five-miles per hour."

It didn't take long for him to dismiss the strange thought.

After much delay, Lief broke free of the traffic and was back on the open road towards Wisconsin. Driving into the town of Lacrosse, he was in awe at the beauty surrounding him. The landscape was comprised of farmland with fields so green, that he had only seen their rival overseas in Ireland. Rusty weathervanes propped up near red barns that were outlined with white fascia. Lief took notice of a classic red farm house with white wrap-around porch. It looked like freshly glued paper model. Lief even saw a genuine scarecrow near the crops by the home. The whole scene was like looking at an illustration in a children's book, with its straight lines, basic angles, and large areas of solid colors. It was simple and perfect.

At first glance, even the sun appeared so one demential that it may have been drawn on paper. But when the sun dropped closer to the horizon its colors blasted out of it. Golden and orange rays splayed like a vector, setting behind all of the picturesque farmland. It's rays poured over the homes and then onto the weathervanes, turning them into silhouettes, until the light fell to the ground, casting shadows behind all of the structures and bails of hay. The shadows stretched further and further until the darkness filled in the blanks.

Taking advantage of one of the two times in a day that it was possible to look directly at the sun without hurting his eyes, he stared straight into it, admiring its brilliance, letting it sooth his body like a warm bath. For a moment, Lief thought he had died and gone to heaven. He pinched his arm to check that he was still among the living. He, indeed, felt his arm, but then wondered if his perception of the pinch would be any different if he were dead.

Having analyzed how his body felt, he noticed that he needed to take a leak. The urge grew strong and the next town was at least thirty-miles away. He'd be seen for sure if he pulled over to relieve himself because there was still remnants of light in the sky, even though the sun had already set. Then he remembered a scene from the movie "Dumb and Dumber", one in which Jim Carey's character, Lloyd, had to pee while driving. Taking his friend's advice, Lloyd pissed into empty beer bottles, allowing him to continue driving without interruption. The character did, however, hit a slight snag when he filled the bottle and needed to switch bottles midstream, spilling some.

Lief looked at his empty twenty-ounce paper coffee cup sitting in the cup holder. Considering he had drank less than ten ounces of coffee since he last relieved himself, Lief was certain he could pull it off without any spillage. He unbuttoned his fly, positioned everything just right, and began peeing into the cup. He felt unnatural doing something that before then had been confined to a bathroom or outside on a tree somewhere, but it was more comfortable than he imagined. The simple act altered Lief's former paradigm of pissing. It was a sweeping utopian change to the status quo. So long as he kept his eyes on the road and the cup aligned, he could be free of several unnecessary stops for the remainder of the trip, and all future trips for that matter.

Lief soon felt as if he was enjoying the same comforting sunbath he had before the sun set. But the sun had set. *Residual pocket of warm air*, he wondered before answering his own question. *Nope, that's warm piss all over my seat.* His cup was overflowing.

"I only drank ten ounces! I got room for twenty! What the fuck?"

There was no other option but to pull over. He took the next offramp and parked the car on the side of the road. It had become dark enough that he might have gone unnoticed. Lief striped naked and pulled out the hand sanitizing wipes to pat himself down, taking a gypsy shower right there, before changing into a different set of clothes. He spoke to himself when he got back into the Tin Can.

"That Dumb and Dumber sure are full of shit man."

Leaving Lacrosse, Lief crossed the Mississippi and drove another three hours along the base of Minnesota before pulling into a Walmart parking lot to sleep for the night. He saw that there were several R.V's in the lot doing the same, so he figured it was safe enough. Before falling asleep he tried to reach Leslie again. Having no success, he called Sarah and reached her voicemail that was full and couldn't store anymore messages.

——— ——

Lief awoke just after sunrise and entered the reopened Walmart to get snacks and coffee before returning to the road. Rapid City was seven hours away. Each mile he drove emphasized the importance of meeting his oldest daughter who he never knew. Lief had grown afraid that Leslie didn't want to see him because she had not returned any of his calls. Still, he couldn't do anything but move towards her, try to sort out his feelings on the way, and hope he'd hear from her before he got there.

Lief was sorry that he had missed out on Leslie's entire life. He had not been there for her first word, her first bike ride, her first day of school, her first lost tooth, her accomplishments, her laughter and sadness. Nor did he have the ability to try to offer her any kind of guidance. Those were all moments experienced by the man that she had believed to be her biological father. Lief knew that, regardless of his biological connection to Leslie, another man raised her, and that made him her father. There was no way to change that, so Lief had to believe that it went down the way it was supposed to.

Lief had suspected early on that Leslie was his daughter. Leslie's mother, Rachel, had bi-polar and schizophrenic disorders, and was not a stable person. Lief discovered those things too late as naive teenager. She told Lief that Leslie was not his daughter just as many times as she told him that she was. Due to Rachel's duplicity, the ability of knowing the truth was near impossible, or at least at the time. Lief was two-months into a year stretch of living in his Volkswagen bus when Leslie was born. When Rachel asked Lief for child support, Lief requested a DNA test to establish paternity. Knowing that Lief had the common sense to follow legal procedure, Rachel vanished with Leslie.

At that time, the internet wasn't anything more than a couple of websites with a few chat rooms and it was far from being able to locate someone's whereabouts. If Lief had the money for a private detective to find Rachel and Leslie, he wouldn't have been living in a bus, starving, and weighing in at an unsubstantial buck-twenty while standing six feet tall. Lief was at a loss for what to do when he turned to his mother who did some digging through public records. Ms. Wainwright discovered that someone was listed as the father, and it wasn't Lief. That last piece of evidence was enough for the logical side of Lief to know that Leslie was not his, but his subconscious still cast doubts.

Although he decided to not look into paternity matters further, a part of him never let his curiosity rest. For twenty-one years, that sliver of doubt ate at him, never allowing him to have the self-respect needed to love himself or anyone else until Sarah was born. It was unfortunate for Lief that the bulk of his guilt was buried so deep that he wasn't aware of it.

After Lief experienced his major spiritual awakening in Ohio in 2008, he did a lot of soul searching. He discovered the biggest root of his many character defects. That root was a result of making the wrong turn at the biggest crossroad in his life. He didn't follow his heart in regards to Leslie. In order to move forward, Lief knew he had to do the right thing by finding, and then contacting Rachel for conclusive answers. His hopes were that he would be doing more good than harm.

Lief had set forward to do just that, find Rachel and Leslie. He knew it would prove tricky, even with the internet's capability, because she used three different last names. But he got a hit on one of her last names in Florida, where he discovered another name change that he searched. It produced another hit in Minot, North Dakota. Rachel was listed in a local newspaper that gave Lief enough information to do some more digging until he found a plethora of information on her. Lief learned where she worked, he discovered that she was still married to the guy on Leslie's birth certificate and that Leslie had a younger sibling. He even saw a picture of Rachel who was unrecognizable to him due to her massive weight gain. The most significant piece of information he found was her phone number, which he called just as fast as he could write it down. Rachel picked up. Lief revisited the call in his mind.

"Hello"

"Hi, I'm trying to reach Rachel?"

"Who may I ask is calling?"

"This is Lief Wainwright."

"Lief who? Wainwright? Oh my God! Lief- Lief from Sacramento, Lief?"

"Yes Rachel, It's me."

"Oh my God. Well- Wow! How have you been?"

"Look, Rachel, I'm not sure if my contacting you is a good idea or not, because the last thing I want to do is upset anyone. I just want get some kind of confirmation about Leslie."

"Lief-"

"Wait just a minute before you answer. If she is mine, my only intention is to offer whatever I can, to make whatever I can right."

"Lief, she's yours."

"She is. Ok. She's my daughter. Thank you. But… what happened? We were going to get the paternity test and then I couldn't get ahold of you. I had no way to reach you. I saw that her father was listed as Chase or something, but still I wondered."

"Lief, I'm so sorry. It's hard to tell you everything about this over the phone, but- Oh god, Lief, I left because I thought you'd try to take her from me. I was so afraid. Chase was someone that I had started dating around the same time. He had joined the Air Force and was being deployed. We went with him."

"Wow. That makes sense. Remember, I'm not calling to judge you or cause any other kind of harm. What can I do? I know that so many years have gone by, and she must be, what, fourteen? fifteen?"

"She's fourteen, but will be fifteen soon. She's here now. Wait one second."

Rachel called out for Leslie. Lief could hear Rachel speaking to her.

"Leslie, honey, remember that time, years ago, when we talked about how you maybe having another father?"

Lief pleaded with Rachel as loud as he could, trying to get her to stop what she was about to do, but the phone was away from her head.

"RACHEL, PLEASE. Rachel, don't do this. This isn't a good idea!"

"Leslie, this is him, it's true."

After a short silent pause, Lief heard Leslie burst into tears.

"Do you want to speak with him."

Lief continued his attempts to get Rachel's attention.

"RACHEL"

"Yeah, I'm still here."

"Rachel, What did you do? I didn't call to do this. The last thing I wanted to do was upset her."

Needless to say, Leslie had not wanted to speak on the phone after receiving the biggest shock of her life, but Lief and Rachel continued to speak for a short time. Rachel proved that she was just as mentally deranged as before. Lief left his number and asked that Rachel only give it to Leslie when she was, if ever, ready to talk. Lief got that call in 2014. The rest was history.

Lief was two hours outside of Rapid City when his phone beeped in an unfamiliar tone. It was a facebook message from Leslie which read

"Are you still planning on coming out to visit? It's ok if you can't, I just hadn't heard from you in a while." He hadn't considered trying to reach her through facebook. Lief was ecstatic to learn she still wanted to meet, but he was confused about why she didn't get his messages. He tapped out a quick response: "Hey! I'm glad you messaged me. I'm two hours east of you and on my way. I left a couple of messages." Leslie had to remind Lief that she had informed him of her number change before he left on his trip.

Lief felt stupid that he had forgotten such an important piece of information. The near miss that would have, without a doubt, ended in complete tragedy and it would have been all Lief's fault. All he could do was apologize to her and let her know how much he was looking forward to meeting her.

The two made arrangements to meet at local steakhouse. Lief decided early on in the trip that he would not film any of his meet with Leslie. He didn't want to trivialize the special moment. When Lief arrived early at the restaurant, he did, however, film himself in the parking lot, giving a brief synopsis of what led to the, soon to be, moment of truth. He included his anxiousness and overwhelming excitement to meet Leslie, the all grown up baby that he had only seen a couple of times, over twenty years prior.

The hostess greeted Lief when he entered the lobby.

"Table for one?"

"No thank you. I'm meeting someone. Do you mind if I look around a bit to see if she is here yet?"

"Go right ahead."

Before he left the waiting area, Leslie entered the restaurant. She was beautiful and stood at about 5'7" with long brown hair. She had her mother's cheeks, but she had Lief's mouth and eyes. His thoughts and feelings were beyond words, although that didn't stop them from fumbling out of his mouth.

"Hi. Hello Leslie, I made it."

"Hello, so did I."

She smiled at her biological father. Lief smiled back.

Even though science confirmed he was Leslie's father, the mere act of standing in front of her, comparing their similarities and feeling her presence, assured him, without a sliver of a doubt, that she was his daughter. The muscles that had been clenching his shoulders and neck tight, relaxed and his anxiety faded. Never again would Lief receive such a wonderful gift so long in the making. He, again, knew that he was in the exact perfect place at the exact perfect time.

The hostess sat both of them as they warmed up with some basic chit chat like "How was your drive?", "How do you like living here?", "So, Mt. Rushmore is near here?", and "How have you been for the last twenty-one years?" It wasn't until they got to the table that they moved into the less superficial conversation.

"Are you curious about your family history on my side?"

"Yes, very!"

"Ok, well, the good news is we have very good genes and longevity on both sides of my family. I am not aware of any patterns of any sorts of illness with the family either."

"That's good to know. What about nationality? I always knew that I had Italian. I don't know if my mom brought that up every five seconds back when you knew her, but she doesn't shut up about it now, you'd think she was royalty."

"Yeah, she did. You know what? That reminds me of a joke. Wanna hear it?"

"Yes, of course."

"Cool. It's supposed to be about vegans, but this should work. K, here it goes- How do you know if someone is Italian?"

"I don't know. How?"

"They already told you."

"Hahaha! That's great and so true. So, yes, I have the Italian from my mom, but my friends always guessed that I may be Persian or some other form of middle eastern too. Clearly not the case as I look at you."

"You can tell I'm not Persian? Actually, I'm Scots-Irish. Well, I'm actually a bit of a European mutt."

"Wow, I finally know my heritage and it's only taken twenty-one years. I grew up thinking that Chase, my father, was my biological father.

I started to have my suspicions though because as I grew up, I noticed that we looked nothing alike. I'm kinda tall for a girl and he's short, you know."

"I have to say that, when I first saw you a moment ago, and as I look at you now, I see a strong resemblance between us. It's strange, it's like I'm looking at me, but in female form, we look more like each other than your, well, sister Sarah and I do."

"I was really nervous to meet you today. I guess I wasn't sure if you really wanted to."

"No way! I wanted to see you more than anything. I'm sorry I was trying to reach you on your old number. I started to think we weren't going to meet when I couldn't get ahold of you, but I kept heading for Rapid City, hoping that I'd still get the chance. Geez, I can be pretty obtuse sometimes."

"No, no, it's ok."

"Truth is, I set out on the trip to see you. When we spoke, after I got the test results back, and I told you that I was going to be near your area in July to play music, I had not yet planned the trip. For a while I had talked about doing a music trip, but it wasn't until I did some thinking, after getting the test results that I thought it would be a nice way for me to present a visit. I didn't want you to feel any kind of pressure to meet me, like me coming all the way out from California. I know it may not make a lot of sense, but I just figured that if it seemed casual, and not out of the way, that you'd be more willing to meet me, so I put together the trip after we spoke. Then I had the idea to get the camera and film the whole thing. Then I found out that Kay, my girlfriend that I told you about, was going to be in New Jersey. It all just kind of fell into place. But, it began as me just wanting to meet you though."

The server interjected to take their order. Leslie ordered a chicken sandwich and Lief ordered a steak salad, although food was a million miles from his mind. He just wanted to talk to Leslie. She resumed the conversation.

"Before your trip you mentioned that you had gluten-free bread in the oven. Are you, what's that called?"

"Celiac?"

"Yeah, that's it. Are you Celiac?"

"You know, I'm not sure. Someone suggested that I try to go without gluten. She said that it may be causing me health problems like depression and inflammation. I gave it a shot and started feeling much better after a couple of weeks. I lost weight, most likely water weight, and my head got a lot clearer. I just felt better overall."

"Really? Maybe that's what's going on with me."

"See, knowing more about your genetic makeup is already paying off."

The remainder of the meal was filled with conversation about things both of them had wanted talk about since the test results came back. Walking out of the restaurant, Lief asked Leslie if she wanted to talk more at a coffee shop. Leslie thought that was a good idea.

———   ———

After they talked for another hour at the Starbucks up the street, Leslie let Lief know that she had to get back to her newborn who was being watched by her mother-in-law. They both acknowledged that there was not enough time to cover all the ground that they wanted to. Lief suggested that their getting together that day should be considered more of an introduction, a to- be-continued.

Before they parted, Lief asked her to wait a moment so he could go to his car to get something for her. He came back with the giant chocolate bar, the one that he bought for her in Pennsylvania. It was melted and flopped over on it's side as he handed it to her.

"Ooops, I guess it's the thought that counts right?"

"It is. Thank you."

"Leslie, I'm happy to meet you, I can't tell you how much this means to me."

Leslie extended her hand, offering a parting handshake. It was further proof of how much genetics played a part in behavior because it was clear that they both shared the non-hugging gene.

"Nice to meet you too. I look forward to talking more to get more aquatinted."

"For sure. My sentiments exactly."

CHAPTER 22

BLACKLAND

After visiting Leslie in Rapid City Lief could not contain his happiness and other feelings that he had yet to identify. They brimmed over his comprehension and breached the dam of denial he had built to contain his guilt that he carried for not following his heart to Leslie sooner. Lief's preconceived stream of life, a stream that had not included him having a relationship with a twenty-one year old daughter, became a thrashing river that redirected him through an enhanced version of his prior life. It was the way his life would have felt like without the uncertainty about Leslie. Past the past, he rolled through rapids that led him into a pool of forgiveness.

The result of the overwhelming improvement, once again, placed Lief in uncharted territory. It would take him some time for him to catch up with the majority of his feelings.

To the best of his ability, Lief had done everything he set out to do on his trip and saw everything he had hoped to see and more. Compulsion was his only driving force as he drove out of Rapid City towards Mt. Rushmore. After everything that he had been through and already seen on his journey, he didn't feel as though he'd get much from seeing the gargantuan faces carved into stone, but it was so close that if he didn't go there, he knew he'd kick himself later.

Thirty-miles southwest of Rapid City, he entered the Black Hills where Mt. Rushmore resided. He had only known the area as described by the Beatles in their song "Rocky Raccoon". He reached the saloon town of Keystone that sat adjacent to Mt. Rushmore, and found thousands of Harley-Davidsons swarming the streets. The Sturges Motorcycle Rally was taking place in the area. Lief was the only person driving a car amongst the bikers and they all took notice, making wretched faces as they stared him down. Lief held a suspicion that the majority of bikers were probably decent, soft people underneath all the facade. He believed that most of them just wanted to belong to something, maybe because their parents didn't let them join the Boy Scouts when they were younger. But as adults in biker pacts, they all got to play the parts of ruthless criminals, each one more ruthless than the next, soaked in sweat, viagra, alcohol, and inferiority complexes.

Like most other bikers on the planet, the majority of those gathered in Keystone had ponytails and long beards. They dressed in black leather vests, black boots, dark sunglasses, and form fitting skull caps. Although Lief was in a mental autopilot mode of sorts, he entertained himself with the thought, *I missed the memo to dress up for Charlie Manson day.*

Then the unusual and unsettling thought, *Don't swerve,* reoccured. Lief followed the odd thought with a crazy, out-loud, conversation with himself.

"Don't swerve? Really? Ok, fucking weirdo. I'll make a note of that."

But, the outlandish thought continued until he reached the park entrance that was charging twelve-bucks to get in. Lief presented his disabled veterans national parks pass and got in for half price.

On the surface it was easy for Lief to make a quick determination that he made out like a bandit with his veterans disability benefits, considering the attack that resulted in the benefits hadn't left him physically disfigured. But that day, in his unique state of mind following his visit with Leslie, his thinking was different. On that day he dared enter the memory of the attack and winced in its painful recollection. He considered his subsequent temperament ever since. His resulting trauma had led to anxiety and anger. He had previously turned to alcohol for relief, which led to alcoholism. His alcoholism led to failed relationships.

His failed relationships led to more anger and anxiety that required more drinking. Memories of the hellish vicious cycle that became his life reminded him that he earned everyone of those veterans benefits. He was lucky to be alive.

Lief left the Tin Can to see the monument that was not visible from the parking lot. He walked up a short path and found the carved faces in stone. As he stood in front of the famous Mt. Rushmore, all Lief could think about was how small it looked in person. He was disappointed. His let down was akin to seeing a fast food meal looking so plump and juicy on the menu board, before seeing it come out on a plastic serving tray, smaller, drier, and unsavory.

Lief was tempted to drag his once beloved suitcase amp and guitar to the base of the monument to film himself playing a song or two with Mt. Rushmore in the background. But he just didn't have it in him. Lief wanted to go home. He had been too far away from Sarah for too long and Kay would be back in California on the following day. He missed his house, the cat, his bed, his regular AA meetings, and even Sonoma county, regardless of all its bad driving and self righteous bigots.

His plotted course was due west to Seattle, then down through Portland to Lake Shasta, onto Mendocino, and then home. It would take him at least three more days to get back. The three-day option would not allow any time for sightseeing either.

Lief had already seen those places not long before the trip. The only reason he had planned on going through those cities in the first place, was so Bigfoot could also see them. They wouldn't have looked bad on film either. Done with Bigfoot and done with music on the trip, Lief adjusted his course to a more direct southwest route across Wyoming and Utah, and then straight across Nevada and California, and all the way back to his home on west coast.

The new route took him straight through Salt Lake City, not far from where his father, aka, Senior lived in Eagle Mountain. The two had been at odds for the better part of two decades, ever since Lief left home when he was sixteen. Their beef covered a wide array of issues, from religion to a mutual distain between Lief and his stepmother. Although

Lief hadn't spoken with Senior for some time, he called him, letting him know that he'd be in his area around 3 a.m. and that he could use a place to stay the night. Lief wasn't sure how his call would be received, but, to his surprise, Senior expressed that it was nice to hear from Lief and that he would be happy to put him up for the night. Their short conversation was one more step forward and added to several other steps forward that Lief had taken with his family while he was on the road.

In the blink of an eye, Lief found himself in Wyoming and heading west. He filmed the sun setting over the amber fields of grain that God had shed his grace upon with fingers of light. It was simple and easy to appreciate because there was no riddle that could be made of it. Lief had enough of those that he was working on. The sun and sky, plus a big yellow field, and a little breeze all seemed like good things to film. In doing so, Lief learned that the camera storage card was almost full, so he kept it short with a quick sweep of the horizon.

Once again, the thought *Don't swerve,* entered his mind, drawing an end to the serenity of the previous moments. Lief grew frustrated at the thought, mostly because, in his best estimate, it was as close as he had ever been to certifiably crazy. He had another thought, then lightened up. *If you can't beat them join them.* He started singing like a lunatic.

"Don't swerve, don't swerve, don't swerve... drive long
enough you'll hear it too. Don't swerve, don't swerve,
don't swerve... Maybe you'll go coo coo."

It had been dark an hour before he made a stop for gas. The woman behind the cash register at the middle of nowhere station was sporting a great plains mullet and a Mellisa Etheridge t-shirt. She was affable, a little too affable, and more than eager to speak.

"Where ya from cowboy?"

"Sonoma County?"

"No shit really! Wait... Sonoma County, where is that?"

"California"

"Cool. I went to Arizona once. My family all lives in Arizona now."

"What a coincidence."

"Yeah, exactly. I've only been there twice though. My family all had cattle up north near- ah... Flagstaff I think it was. No- Now wait. It wasn't Flagstaff. Oh my God! You ever been to Flagstaff?"

Lief had already turned to face the door after giving every other social queue that he intended to leave. It was all to no avail because she continued to ramble about Route 66 and then her dogs, Davy and Crockett, and how they were named after a the third president of the USA. It seemed she was neglected of regular conversation and education in the middle of butt-fucking-Egypt.

Lief couldn't take anymore of the diarrhea spewing from her mouth. He turned his back to her and embraced the true asshole within him.

"Look lady, that's all very interesting. Wait- No, it's not. I'm going to drive to Utah now. I do hope you have a wonderful evening."

"Oh yeah? My partner is from Utah-"

Lief was halfway out the door before she said one last thing to him, something that stopped him dead in his tracks.

"Don't swerve"

His gut dropped and goosebumps covered his entire body, raising his hair before he turned back to her. Lady Mellisa Mullet no longer resembled her previous self, nor had her last words been spoken in her previous voice. She morphed into someone strikingly familiar, although Lief could not quite place how he knew her. A shiver ran down his spine.

Fear forced him to look away, but, in a last ditch attempt to convince himself he was still sane, he did a double take, and that time was relieved to see that it was still jabber-mouth starring blankly at him. He wrote off the implausible situation as delirium from his life-changing events that day, along with being on the road too long. White as a ghost, he walked to his car and drove away. As Lief merged back onto the interstate he racked his brain, trying to place who the clerk morphed into. He recognized her voice and could almost place it. He spun through the rolodex of faces in his mind until he found the exact match. It took him a while, but he recalled that she was his nurse from his unfortunate-fortunate visit to the hospital after his collapse.

"Beth M., The fucking nurse from Santa Rosa. Weird."

He couldn't shake the thought as he drove, but his obsessive confusion was diverted for a few seconds when he looked ahead and observed a semi-truck pull over and turn on it's hazard lights. After he passed the truck, his peripheral vision caught something large and round moving along side and in pace with the Tin Can. When he focused on the strange object that appeared to be following him, it was no longer there, that or it was just a figment of his increasingly questionable imagination. He thought it had resembled a large tire, but that would have been impossible. At that point there wasn't a vehicle in sight, outside of the truck that had pulled over a quarter mile back. He continued looking for the suspected tire, but there was nothing. He laughed and began talking to himself out loud.

"Haha! Seriously? I got hicks morphing into a woman I barely know. I got strange thoughts and tires following me. Is it something in my coffee?"

Then, in a flash, a fear of impending doom swooped in upon him from all angles of the thick black recesses of the night. As it squeezed the breath out of his chest, the phantom tire that proved to be no phantom at all, outpaced the car and made a square turn ten feet in front of him. His eyes opened wide while the linear aspects of time suspended and allowed him to consult, both logic and his heart, during a rare eternal moment. He had experienced the same timelessness once before when he pulled six-month old Sarah's arm out of the elevator door on the cruise ship all those years back. The meaningless thought, *Don't swerve,* returned, that time with all the depth of the deepest significance in the world. That time, the thought was crisp and it had a voice behind it. It was Sarah's.

Just as soon as Lief understood the meaning of the thought, time resumed and the mysterious tire was no more than three feet in from of him. To avoid the tire, Lief swerved to the right and drove off the raised highway, down a sharp slope flecked with large rock formations and boulders. The front end of the car hit a four-foot tall boulder, causing the great Tin Can to flip end over end, while twisting through the air like a graceful gymnast. In-between flips, it hit several other rock formations before dismounting upside-down. It smashed like an accordion into the face of another large boulder at the bottom of the steep slope.

Strapped in by his seatbelt, Lief sat inverted while his blood and life trickled onto the roof that had smashed against his head. His consciousness had been knocked out of the physical world. His eyes were closed, but he saw a great light that grew brighter until it was blinding. A voice within him asked if he was in the tunnel to the afterlife. Then, the driver of the semi-truck that Lief had just passed reached through an opening in the smashed windshield of the Tin Can, sliced Lief's seatbelt with a pocket knife, pulled him out, and laid him on the ground before calling 911. When the ambulance arrived, Lief was inches from death.

ACT V

CHAPTER 23

DEAD

The sleepy staff at the Memorial Hospital of Carbon County fired up the coffee pots in the break area of the emergency room after they received word that Lief was being transported there with severe injuries. The hospital sat in the otherwise sleepy Wyoming town of Rawlins. Being a small town, the majority of the repairs needed there were confined to injuries from minor car accidents, wayward tractors, and drunken brawls. Lief's visit promised to be, at least, good practice for the emergency deprived nurses and doctors.

When the E.M.T.'s arrived at the hospital with Lief, they made so much noise during their frenzy to the emergency surgery room that they woke Annie, that night's on call nurse. She poked her head out of her sleeping quarters to see what was causing all ruckus. Although she wasn't yet summoned, she knew she would be needed. Annie jumped into her scrubs and joined the ranks of the masked, puffy green people that formed a semi-circle around Lief, who had been placed on the spotlit center stage of the operating table. There were trays splayed with shinny pointy things in front of the beeping, blinking machines with screens. The surgical team hoped for signs of life, but their well wishes diminished when the EKG monitor displayed only the tiniest of blips. Those tiny upticks soon flattened, forcing them to use the defibrillator. Lief was jolted three different times, each round producing a spike in the line, but he had lost too much blood and its shallow flow wasn't enough to keep his heart pumping. The audio of the EKG fell monotone. Lief was pronounced dead at exactly 11:11 p.m. Annie, the newest nurse at the hospital, hid behind a dividing curtain to cry.

Annie was a gorgeous woman by anyone's standards. She could have been Marilyn Monroe's daughter with her blond hair, voluptuous curves, and magnetic personality. She looked quite similar to Kay in many ways. One of Annie's greatest qualities was her ability to fill any room with her presence the moment she entered. It was due to her giant heart that carried around such a big love for everyone. It was so big that she had to try to hide it from those around her, especially with her being fresh out of nursing school. She had just witnessed her first death and was crushed, but didn't want to be thought of as inexperienced and soft. Street credibility was just as important in their hospital as it was in gangland.

Annie was assigned the unfavorable task of carting Lief's lifeless body to the morgue in the lower level of the hospital. As she pushed the gurney towards the elevator, she observed how peaceful he appeared. She thought about how she could have used a man like Lief. Her odds of finding a suitor in Rawlins was good, but the goods there were odd. Lief, at least, was attractive in her opinion.

Waiting for the elevator to reach her floor, an unorthodox thought piqued her curiosity, prompting her to look both ways down the hallway to see if anyone was around. She was contemplating something that was risky by her standards. A clear coast and her compulsion ended her dilemma before she adjusted his hospital gown enough to sneak a peak at his manhood. She relished in the moment thinking how far back her last sexual encounter was. There it was, the full monty, starring right back at her. She was, in no way, a necrophiliac, but she was a little turned on nonetheless. She thought looking at porn was immoral so it had been a while since she had even seen a penis. Now that she was a medical professional, she could justifiably write off her curiosity as science.

The elevator door dinged and she readjusted his gown before the doors opened so that the security cameras on the elevator wouldn't capture her mischief. While she pushed the gurney onto the elevator, her hand slipped of it's rail and poked the side of Lief's arm. Although it was just incidental, she paused to rest her hand upon his arm, apologizing for the abrupt contact. She looked to him as if he would respond. She shook her head, laughing at her absurd late night/ early morning thinking. Annie had not yet finished criticizing herself when Lief opened his eyes and looked her in the face. Annie screamed, jumped back, slipped on the slick linoleum, and hit the floor. Suzy, another ER nurse, had been near and ran to her aide while Annie continued to scream.

"He's alive! He- He- He looked at me. He looked right at me."

"Annie it's ok. It's OK. Just calm down. This happens all the time. In my experience, it's a very common occurrence for a limb to move or then eyes to open. Come here and feel the muscle spasms in his arm."

Annie did just that and indeed felt his bicep twinge. Suzy began to gloat at her superior medical knowledge.

"You see, just some residual effect-"

Suzy stopped mid-sentence when Lief's eyes reopened a moment after Annie held his arm.

"DEAR JESUS! HE'S ALIVE! We need to get him back in there, STAT!"

He was rushed back into the trauma room and hooked back up to the heart monitor. That time Lief had a pulse, but it was faint as could be and he was not breathing on his own, so they hooked him up to life support and gave him a blood transfusion. Lief stabilized and was moved to his own room in the long term care unit of the hospital.

━ ⌒

Lief's consciousness had been moving through a bending tube of bright swirling, multi-colored light, with an even brighter opening at the end of it. He didn't know why he was there nor did he care. He was in no pain and felt no emotions outside of contentment. His only desire was to continue moving towards the end of the interesting light tunnel, because, with each inch he moved towards the opening, the more his contentment grew. It wasn't until he was resuscitated and then suspended by life support that he stopped moving forward. He was floating somewhere in the middle while the spectacular lights continued to dance around him. His consciousness could only identify his location as in-between.

His desire to keep moving made him aware he was stuck, and in turn, he experienced a discomfort that grew more the longer he wasn't moving. The dancing lights grew tiresome to Lief. He paused to consider that his situation was abnormal. He was in some strange tube of light, restless, irritable, and discontent. Lief's discomfort lead him to question why he was there to begin with. Retracing his steps, he remembered he was going somewhere and that he needed to keep going. Then, from an ubiquitous vantage point, he saw Kay carrying luggage through an airport, Leslie smiling while twirling with her baby girl, the mulleted lady cashier playing air guitar in an empty gas station in the middle of nowhere, and a troubled nurse leaning against wall outside of a hospital room where a familiar, but empty man laid on a hospital bed. Lief narrowed his focus onto the curious man. The longer he looked at the man, the more an urgency to finish something set into Lief. Then, in the blink of a mind's eye, he lost his omnipresent perspective and found himself back in the plane of his Earthly concerns, sitting in a chair, across from the body on the hospital bed. Perplexed, Lief looked around the room to suss out the situation before taking a closer look at the body on the bed.

"What? That's me. But wait- If that's me, who am I then? And what is up with all of these tubes? Oh shit... I swerved."

Lief's essence and body where separated, but not severed. In fact, both of them remained very close to each other. His Earthly awareness was contingent on the life support that put oxygen into his lungs and nutrients into his veins. The larger part of Lief's identity was the Spirit Lief who sat across the room in a chair, not visible to those in the physical dimension. He was, more or less, imitating life at that point with hopes of returning to his body as soon as possible. He didn't have to breath, but he still went through the motions. He didn't need to eat but he was hungry. He could float away but he wanted to feel his heart and all of its partitions for those he loved.

— —

A day went by and during that time, the hospital had contacted his mother, Ms. Wainwright, after locating Lief's medical records which contained his emergency contact information. Ms. Wainwright was devastated and made immediate arrangements to get to him with hopes of coercing him out of his coma. She shared the news with anyone that she thought may want to know, especially those that could offer support. Brena and Sarah made arrangements to see him and would be arriving the same time as Ms. Wainwright. Although she was aware of Kay and Leslie, she had no way to contact them, so they both remained in the dark as to his whereabouts and predicament. Lief's father had church business to attend to and could not make it out. He promised to pray for him though.

Spirit Lief felt terrible about all of the concern he caused his love ones. Lief was especially tortured at Kay's worries that grew with each failed attempt to contact him. All of the concerns for his wellbeing made him all the more determined to get back into his body as fast as he could.

In an attempt to resurrect his body, Lief laid within the space of his body on the hospital bed. Nothing happened. He just heard the constant beeping on the EKG and hideous breathing noises coming from the accordion-like ventilator.

"Fuck! What the fuck do I need to do to get the fuck out of here?"

Early coma protocol required an hourly monitoring of Lief for any signs of improvement. Annie volunteered to do all of Lief's monitoring while she was on duty. Most times that she entered his room, Spirit Lief would jump up and down, waiving his arms and screaming, and each time his actions in the sprit realm went unnoticed. It didn't take him long to readjust his strategy.

On one of Annie's visits to list his vitals, Spirit Lief sat motionless in his chair and observed her. There was something in the way she looked at him. It was as if her task was not routine, instead, her work appeared a labor love. Lief wasn't sure, but he suspected that Annie had a unique concern for him, as if he were dear to her. Although his heart belonged to Kay, Lief felt a nonconflicting connection to Annie that soothed him. It ran parallel to his love and understanding of Kay, and even enhanced it. On that particular visit, Annie seemed attuned to Lief's observation of her, because she began to speak to him in a caring way.

"How are we doing today Mr. Wainwright? Cat still got your tongue? It appears you're not ready to move on yet. I just want to let you know that I'm pulling for you. I hope you get better real soon."

Annie paused to look towards the door before whispering to him.

"Also please forgive me for, you know, the sneak peek."

Although Lief knew he wouldn't be heard, he replied anyway.

"Don't worry. I'm flattered."

As she spoke to Lief, she rubbed his arm in a consoling manner. As their flesh, once again, touched, the EKG went berserk. Lief's spirit was sucked back into his body. She turned away from Lief to see what was happening on the monitor. When she looked back, she saw him trying to remove his oxygen tube. Again, Annie jumped back then ran out of the room frantically and bumped right into the head of the intensive care unit, Dr. Stevens. Her momentum swung her face first into the wall and then flat to the floor.

"He's conscious! He's conscious! He's trying to remove his tube."

Dr. Stevens helped her up and the two sped into the room. Lief's oxygen tube was laying on the floor next to bed. Dr. Stevens called more help to the room through the intercom, while also demanding that a new breathing tube be brought. Lief's vitals dropped more each second that did not have oxygen. Both Spirit Lief and Lief grew blue in the face while gasping for air. When help arrived and a fresh tube was reinserted, the Liefs breathed and their faces' returned to their usual flesh tone.

With the problem resolved, Dr. Stevens scolded nurse Annie.

"I don't know what you think you saw, but he is certainly not conscious. How about the next time he involuntarily moves, you don't just go run out of the room screaming, alright?"

"Wait, I saw him deliberately grab it with his hand at the same time the EKG was going crazy. I know what I saw."

"Nurse, you're close to the end of your shift and you must be tired. How long have you been working here?"

"Doctor Stevens, I know I'm new, but that doesn't mean that I'm seeing things."

"Alright, thank you. Let's just leave this alone. Please finish your rounds and go home and get some sleep, ok?"

"Yes sir"

Physical Lief's levels evened out while the other Lief sat besides his spiritual self, making a slow connection between the dots of the events that had just transpired. *What was that? That was her! She did it somehow! I was here and then she talked to me and then I was there. No, that can't be. She talks to me every time she comes in here. She touched me- Is that it? That's it! I need her to do it again, but longer!*

Spirit Lief ran out of the room to catch Annie finishing her rounds. He found her down the hallway and reached out to grab her arms, but he passed right through her. He tried again and nothing happened.

"Come on! She touched before and it worked. Why isn't it working now? She has to touch my body. Fuck!"

Lief looked back down the hallway and saw his mother, Brena, and Sarah being escorted into his room. He returned to his chair to see them, even though he knew he couldn't interact with them. He was hoping one of them would touch him so that he would zoom back into his body again.

It destroyed Ms. Wainwright to see her son in such a condition. Brena tried to comfort Ms. Wainwright by rubbing her back. The thought of her grief drove a spike into Lief's heart. He did, however, find relief in his observations of Sarah though. She seemed peaceful looking at his body laying there. Ms. Wainwright leaned to kiss him on the forehead while Spirit Lief rubbed his hands together in anticipation of the reunion with his body. Much to Lief's dismay, nothing happened when she touched him. Next, Brena touched his arm and, again, nothing.

"Huh?"

Lief scratched his spirit head until Dr. Stevens entered the room to introduce himself to the group.

"Hello, I'm Dr. Stevens. I'm the presiding long care Doctor here. You must be his family."

"Yes. Hello, I'm his mother, Kathy Wainwright."

Awkwardly, not knowing how to respond, Brena just waived hello.

The doctor called the adults out of the room and into the hallway to speak with them privately. Sarah stayed and continued to look at her father's spiritless body. Spirit Lief was frustrated he couldn't tell Sarah how much he loved her and how much it meant to him that she came to visit. He looked at her bandaged wrist and fought back tears because the love he had for her, along with his unidentified feelings, were too overwhelming.

He sat, wondering how she felt, seeing him in that state. That was when she turned and looked at him in the chair. *Can she see me?*

"Yes, I can see you."

"You can see me?"

"Yup"

"Wait- How is this possible? No one else can."

"Yeah, but I'm your daughter."

In the hallway, Dr. Stevens explained to Ms. Wainwright that it was not possible to move Lief to a hospital closer to home due to his fragile state. He went on to explain that if his condition did not improve soon, they would have no medical basis to keep him on life support. Lief and Sarah turned their attention to the significant conversation in the hallway.

"I really hate to tell you this Ms. Wainwright, but he's barely hanging on. We've already declared him dead once. The best we can do at this point is hope for the best. Our standard protocol, with injuries as severe as his and possibly irreversible at that, is to remove life support after forty-eight hours if there is no improvement. And, unfortunately we haven't seen any improvements. We'll do what we can in the meanwhile."

Ms. Wainwright came back into the room, crying as she combed Lief's hair back with her fingers.

"Son, I'm here and I'm going to stay here until you pull out of this. You've always been a fighter. That's what you need to do now. I need you to use all the strength you have and wake up. Just wake up. We'll take care of the rest. Just wake up."

Brena and Sarah left and checked into their hotel room while Ms. Wainwright did just as she said she would. She stayed with her son, sitting across the room, praying that he would make it back. That meant Spirit Lief had to find somewhere else to sit.

Annie caught Lief's eye as she made her way out of the building, having just finished her shift. Lief knew he had to do something to get her to touch him once again. He couldn't stand seeing his mother continuing to suffer. Having no better plan, Lief followed Annie out of the building and into her car.

Lief sat in the passenger seat along side her and did everything he could to grab her attention while she started her car.

"Annie, I am going to keep talking to you until you hear me. Maybe something will get through at a subconscious level. I don't know, but I need you to go back into the hospital room and touch me, well more like grab me and hold on. I don't know how, but every time you do, I go back into my body. So please, plea-"

Lief was distracted by something strange happening when his arm moved through a magnified beam of sunlight bouncing off of the rear view mirror. The section of his arm that passed through the concentrated light appeared, however faint, in the physical realm, though Annie would have had to be staring straight at it to notice. Seizing the opportunity, Lief moved face to face with Annie, hoping that a beam of light would refract through him, allowing Annie to see him. Lief knew that if she saw him, he still wouldn't be able to talk to her, but she'd at least know who he was and maybe even go back to him in the hospital. If that didn't work, he considered the oddly humorous possibility of phantom charades.

Annie proceeded out of the parking lot, and accelerated onto the boulevard. Spirit Lief began to see a tube of light form around him. It was the same tunnel of light that he was in following his car accident.

Lief realized that the further Annie drove from the hospital and his own physical body, the more Lief moved out of his in-between state and into the other side of existence. Lief knew he couldn't go much further from his body if he wanted a fighting chance of being reunited with it.

"Common you fucking light, get the-"

Just then, a beam of light burst through Lief and straight into Annie's face. His face took form in front of her, and although she squinted due to the brightness, she saw his face.

"Mr. Wainwright?"

Her line of sight along with her mindfulness of the road were hindered by the bright light and Lief's illuminated face in front of her. She hadn't seen that a car had stopped in front of her and she smashed flat into the back of it. Lief departed the car a fraction of a second prior to the crash, avoiding his irreversible entrance to the afterlife through that twisting tubular tunnel of swirling lights. He cringed as he observed the impact from the side of the road, knowing it was his fault.

"Oh shit! Sorry Annie."

A confused and irked Annie stepped out of the car to assess the damage. The car she hit was a brand new BMW.

"Ha, great! What's next."

The driver of the luxury car got out to take care of the post accident exchanging of pertinent information. It was Dr. Stevens, who had just ended his shift as well.

A day passed and Lief showed no signs of improvement. Ms. Wainwright had remained by his side the entire time, outside of necessary restroom breaks. Annie had not returned because she had, involuntarily, taken time off due to the accident. Lief was concerned that he may have gotten her fired, but later he overheard other nurses in the hallway who joked about Annie's accident. That's when he learned that she would be returning in two days, one day past his scheduled unplugging.

The eve of Lief's certain demise was the longest night Ms. Wainwright had ever endured. At that point, Lief had accepted his fate and prepared for the next stage of his existence. He, at least, had seen something on the other side, so he knew there was something else out there. He wasn't certain, but he had a hunch that it was similar to the place he saw while looking into that spectacular rising sun on the Jersey Shore.

——— ———

It was near mid day when Dr. Stevens entered the room with a few nurses that were needed to conduct the procedure, using the sequence of steps to end life in the most ethical manner. It was explained to Ms. Wainwright that his breathing and feeding tubes would be removed. She was told he would pass in moments without the oxygen, or that, in the rare chance that he continued to breath on his own, he would pass within a few days without his food supply. Ms. Wainwright didn't need to hear how her son would pass. Any scenarios, besides his recovery, were gruesome thoughts for her. There was no possible consolation, no matter how the attempts were worded. Lief thought it would be much more ethical for them to skip all the superfluousness and put a pick ax to his head. Lief went through the motions of speaking to his mother, though his words would go unheard.

"Mom, don't worry. There's something I realized. There really is no death. The love you have for me can never be lost. I know this. It will be reflected wherever you shine your heart. That's when you'll feel it and know that I am there, included in it."

At that moment, Brena and Sarah joined them in the room. Sarah, again, turned to her father's spirit and smiled. Lief knew everything was perfect. Everything was just as it should be.

Dr. Stevens then addressed Ms. Wainwright.

"It's time Ms. Wainwright. Do you have any final words that you'd like to share with your son?"

She declined. As the procedure began, Nurse Annie entered the room in plain clothes. Things had not sat well with her following his mysterious showing in her car. And, although could not make sense of it all, Annie knew they had a significant connection and she wasn't going to let him slip with out her. Dr. Stevens was quick to chide Annie for her arrival.

"Nurse, I thought it was clear that you would not be working today."

"I'm not, I just had to be here for this. I hope it's ok. I just felt I needed to be here."

"Annie, I know you mean well, but this is a time for his family."

Ms. Wainwright could see some of her son's light in her and, although she couldn't explain why, she knew Annie needed to be there.

"Thank you Doctor, It's fine. Please let her stay."

They gathered around Lief's body on the bed as a nurse removed the IV from his arm. A small amount of blood dripped onto the bed sheets before the nurse could tape on the gauze. The sight only made it more difficult for Ms. Wainwright to conceive Lief's mortality. One of the other nurse's switched off the ventilator and prepared to remove his tubes, but she stepped back for a moment to allow Ms. Wainwright the space to kiss Lief on the forehead again. That time, she rubbed it in with her thumb.

By no coincidence the time was 11:11 a.m. when Lief's heart went flat on the monitor. Dr. Stevens hugged Ms. Wainwright who continued to weep. Annie smoothed her hand along Lief's arm and said goodbye. Again, in the exact moment of Annie's touch, the EKG jolted into a full-swing rhythm of up and down blips. Annie clasped his wrist that time. Dr. Stevens turned to Lief as he tried pulling at his not yet removed oxygen mask.

Ms. Wainwright's eyes lit up with optimism while the medical team scrambled to restart life support. Dr. Stevens wrestled with Lief to keep the oxygen mask in place. Lief's eyes rolled as he kept at his mask.

Annie knew Lief was trying to speak. She pleaded with the doctor to let him.

"Doctor, he's trying to say something. Please let him speak."

"Annie! Out now! You're not even supposed to be here."

"No!"

Annie put her elbow into Dr. Stevens' chest and, with all the strength she had, shoved him out of the way. He fell back, away from the table, giving Lief enough time to remove the breathing tube.

"Go ahead. Say what you have to say."

Lief looked around the room, then into the eyes of all of his loved ones surrounding him. Then he let his eyes rest on Annie. Calmness settled across his face before he spoke in the most serine, yet deliberate manner.

"Let me go. It's ok. Let go."

Annie hesitated, then obliged. Lief's heart, at last, rested.

A steady high pitched tone rang in the background of Lief's mind as he drifted through space and time until he reached a spot where he floated above a placid and glistening body of water. His reflection emerged from beneath, finding the surface of the water. He looked at his mirror image and smiled. The were no tubes connected to him, nor was there a hospital gown. He was stark naked. Lief smiled because, even in his transition to the afterlife, he found humor.

"Woo-hoo. I'm streaking."

Sparkling lights formed around Lief's reflection until it was gone. Memories surfaced on the plain of the water like a movie on a screen. The first was of Kay, on their serendipitous meeting at the park in Healdsburg. Her hair blew in front of her face while she was trying to hide her admiration of him. Then, Lief saw Kay standing with the Atlantic Ocean behind her. There, her face held back nothing. It expressed every bit of love she had for him. Kay's face lit up and morphed into Annie's face. The hospital room appeared behind her face while Annie clutched his arm. Next, the room's furniture rearranged behind Annie whose face then morphed into Nurse Beth. It was at that point that Lief realized that all three of them looked exactly alike. The rapid succession of their individual images where like separate frames of film becoming one in the light of his love. It became clear that their perceived differences were due to the associations he built around them. Without time and judgement, they were one and the same.

As Lief digested the truth, it warmed his being. He closed his eyes to shut out anything besides his appreciation that grew. He heard the vibrating Om of the universe. When he left his last remaining opinions behind, he could feel the magnitude of the magnificence around him until there was no separation between anything. One plus one equaled one. But the moment he separated himself from the whole, he reshaped as a unique conscious being. He reopened his eyes, fresh with the Akashic knowledge of the universe.

He was back above the reflecting water. That time the surface showed a beam of daylight breaking through an overcast sky. The light landed on a tombstone beneath it. In front of the stone was a congregation of his loved ones, all wearing black. Many of them shed tears. He did not see himself in the crowd and he began to put the pieces together. *This is my funeral.*

Observing the gathering from behind the stone, he could see beautiful flowers protruding around the edges. In front of the flowers, sat a propped picture frame. He wanted to move around it, to see which picture they chose, but he wasn't able to get the vantage point to do so.

The funeral faded from the surface of the water away and two female figures surfaced from it's depth, walking forward holding hands. It was Leslie and Sarah. They both smiled at him and he smiled back. They broke the plain of the water and grabbed Lief's hands, pulling him down into the water. The overwhelming light returned, swallowing all of them.

The light turned violet and white, forming a small circle above him. He, again, saw figures standing above, surrounding him, outside of the edges of the glaring light. Leif squinted and the light recessed enough for him to focus on one face above him. It was nurse Beth M. She was overwhelmed with emotions, trying to hold back the tears of joy that welled up in her eyes.

Leif regained full focus and looked around. He was in a familiar room with familiar smells and sounds, though he couldn't place anything. He was surrounded by a full medical team who began to clap when he took several deep breaths. Beth adjusted the pillow beneath his head. She sniffled, wiped her eyes, and regained her full professional composer before speaking to him.

"Welcome back Mr. Wainwright. You took a hard fall and you've been out for quite a while. I've been looking after you. You have no idea how much I've been pulling for you."

The rest of the medical staff left the room, leaving Leif in Beth's capable hands. Leif's confusion began to fade and he realized/ remembered he was in front of his love. One of her tears feel on his cheek while she was looking down at him. She apologized and wiped the tear with her thumb. He smiled before his eyes wandered off into the distance. Leif squinted and began to cry as well. Beth leaned in and hugged him like a mother hugging her child.

"Leif, I- I know you're probably confused right now, but do you remember anything? Anything at all?"

"Beth, right?"

"Well- What? Wow! How could you possibly know that? I forgot my name tag today."

"It all seemed so real."

"What seemed real?"

"The trip, you- I mean Kay... or was it Annie? Ugh... Yeah, I don't know. It's not making-"

"Aww honey, take it easy. You don't need to explain. You've been unconscious since you got here, after you hit your head at your home. You couldn't know me because you were unconscious. No matter what they said, I knew you were still in there though. Your confusion is pretty normal, at least for a while. It'll all come back eventually?"

"No, I do, I know you, but you were Kay, I met you here and then on the shore, you said yes."

"I said yes? It's alright. I'm just me, Beth, Nurse Beth."

Leif paused and then put his hands to his face to conceal the well of tears that began to overflow out of the corners of his eyes.

CHAPTER 24

LIFE ETERNAL

Heavy hearted, Leif and Beth strolled along a groomed green field that was surrounded by weeping willows and manicured shrubs. They held hands as they walked until Beth wrapped her arm around Leif, leaning her head onto his shoulder. He embraced her as well.

Leif was relaxed, but pensive. He was thinking about his inexplicable and heartfelt journey around the United States. His journey felt as real as the ground beneath his feet. The cool air that touched his face took him back to his morning he was in the midst of the Blue Ridge Mountains. Beth's arm around his shoulder felt like Kay's loving embrace. But, ever since he returned to the hospital in Santa Rosa, he had endured conflicting opinions and ridicule behind, what was deemed, just a figment of his imagination. He had been misunderstood by everyone, especially when he spoke about the connections he made with all of those he set out to see and those he met along the way. He had new and reinforced heart strings connected to them all. Lief knew that his recent experiences were not real in a practical sense, but if they didn't exist in another scope of understanding, he'd have no comprehension of his love for Beth. He would have had no way of walking with a heart full of acceptance and love instead of emptiness, considering everything.

Leif knew that he would never fully be able to explain, to anyone's satisfaction anyway, the magnitude of his otherworld experience to anyone. The few that Leif shared his story with, all felt he needed to move on from it and find more constructive thoughts. He understood that when most people had vivid or wild dreams, they'd discard them somewhere along the way on their commute to work. Leif's mom, his daughter, and even Beth believed that his story about his travels were a copping mechanism for depression, or that he was having trouble distinguishing fantasy from reality due to his head injury and loss of blood. Whatever the case, they felt sorry for him, but still, they all grew uncomfortable when he spoke about "The Dream", including his shrink.

Leif's understanding of the world was not the same, nor would it ever be. The extra, overlapping layer of existence that he referred to as the Heartland was, according to his heart, undoubtably real. Whether that place was located in another plane of existence or in a parallel universe didn't matter. It all came down to the simple fact that it was what he chose to believe, just as he chose to believe everything else that he had experienced since the day he was born.

In order to make peace with those around him, he quit talking about his past altogether. He was open to the possibility of writing a metaphorical memoir about it ten or twenty years down the road, though. Lief figured no one would put him in a padded room at that point.

Leif once read that anything worth anything could never be lost, but he never subscribed to that belief before visiting the Heartland. In the time that followed his journey, he understood what those words meant all too well. He even went as far as to add "Sometimes it just waits on the other side of the universe" at the end of the expression.

Beth led Leif into the rows of tombstones.

"Sweetheart, it's this way."

As he looked at the direction they were headed, Leif remembered seeing all of it before. It was the tombstone that he saw in the mirror surface of the lake as he traveled home. He could see the divots in the grass from the feet of those that stood there during the ceremony. He recognized the trees in the background, the sun shining down, and even the flowers, though they had wilted.

Leif walked around the glossy granite stone and, for the first time, faced the frame he had struggled to see before. It was a picture of Sarah that Leif took just after her Junior High graduation. She was wearing an elegant orange dress with ruffles, purchased just for the event.

Sarah was fourteen and beyond beautiful with her long blond hair that was flawlessly parted to the side and straightened. The photo captured her smile and true essence better than any others that had been taken of her. Her confidence radiated more than Leif had ever noticed before, even though her self-esteem and happiness had begun to fade around the time she became a teen.

While Leif thought back to the moment that the picture was taken, everything, all at once, fell into place. Leif knew that he would have no more new experiences with Sarah that could be captured and frozen in time on film. He also knew his memories of her would never be sufficient. He had already accepted those thoughts and had all the consolation that he would ever need. Because of his journey around the Heartland though, Leif learned it was impossible to lose the ones you love. His experience had left an open door into that place were all love resided. In that sense, Sarah's departure created nothing more than the same sort of empty nest any parent experiences when their child grows up, only to return for the occasional visit.

That knowledge satisfied Leif. His day there at the cemetery was a perfect day that never need be repeated. It was for that reason Leif never returned to her grave. To do so would have made no sense to him. Her body was returned to the earth, there was a stone with her name on it to prove she had been there, and at its base was a picture of a beautiful young woman, despite having only one arm.